# LORD OF THE FLIES

## CASEBOOK EDITION

CASEBOOK EDITION
TEXT, NOTES & CRITICISM

*William Golding's*

# LORD OF THE FLIES

EDITED BY

*James R. Baker*
*Arthur P. Ziegler, Jr.*

A PERIGEE BOOK

This is a work of fiction. Names, characters, places, and
incidents are either the product of the author's imagination or
are used fictitiously, and any resemblance to actual persons,
living or dead, business establishments, events or locales
is entirely coincidental.

A Perigee Book
Published by The Berkley Publishing Group
A division of Penguin Putnam Inc.
375 Hudson Street
New York, New York 10014

ISBN 0-399-50643-8

First Perigee edition: September 1988
Fourteen previous printings by G. P. Putnam's Sons

The Penguin Putnam Inc. World Wide Web site address is
http://www.penguinputnam.com

Printed in the United States of America

38   37   36   35   34   33   32

# Acknowledgments

————◆————

A casebook edition of any work of literature is necessarily the result of work and good will by numerous people. We are deeply indebted to the writers who contributed the original materials contained in this volume.

We also wish to thank the authors, editors, and publishers who so kindly granted permissions for use of the previously published materials collected in this volume. Full acknowledgment for their valuable aid is printed in the headnote for each of the articles as well as original sources of publication.

The editors gratefully acknowledge the special courtesies of William Golding, J. T. C. Golding, Frank Kermode, Donald R. Spangler, Bruce P. Woodford, A. C. Willers and James Keating. The Introduction to this book originally appeared in the *Arizona Quarterly*. It is reprinted here (revised) by permission of the editor, Albert F. Gegenheimer.

For her expert aid in preparing the manuscript, our thanks to Mrs. Paul V. Anderson, and our special gratitude to Miss Helen Davidson, who not only performed routine secretarial duties but offered advice and kept spirits buoyant with her penetrating wit.

J. R. B.
A. P. Z., Jr.

# Contents

# Contents

# Foreword

## ARTHUR P. ZIEGLER, JR.

It is most astonishing and lamentable that a book as widely read and frequently used in the classroom as William Golding's *Lord of the Flies* has received so little analytical attention from the critics. True, it has not been neglected; this volume attests to that. But despite the profusion of essays by a number of well-known and worthy critics, few close analyses of Golding's technique can be found among them, few explications of the workings of the novel will be discovered.

Indeed, despite a running controversy over the meaning of the novel, critical articles fall largely into a pattern of plot summary and applause for the arrangement of the novel's materials followed by observations on Golding's view of human nature, often embellished with the critic's response to that view.

There are exceptions—they will be found among the essays in this book—like Claire Rosenfield's psychological study of meaning, Carl Niemeyer's comparative study of the novel and its antipathetic predecessor *The Coral Island*, Donald R. Spangler's penetrating study of the function of Simon, and William Mueller's discussion of the use of the various hunts.

Further explorations are needed in many areas, however, among them a careful scrutiny of the opening descriptions of Ralph and Jack in Chapter One. It is useful, but perhaps not very subtle, to point out that the former is immediately declared the "fair boy," that he, like the angel Gabriel, sounds a horn that announces good news—that of survival—that Jack with his angular frame, black cloak and cap, and red hair is Lucifer-like.

More Biblical parallels must be developed—the paradisiacal setting, the symbolic nakedness or near nakedness of all the boys except Jack and his followers—but most especially needed is a study that explains items that do not comply with the original Biblical pattern but that perhaps serve as tip-offs to the theme and the ironies that Golding employs without fully delineating until the last page, for instance the "response" of the paradise to the boys—first from the heat, then a bird with an echoed "witch-like cry," then the entangling creepers (more like the Eden of Milton than Genesis)—together with the important information that Ralph, not Jack, has a snake-clasp belt, that Jack wears a golden badge. We have implications very early that Golding's view is not simple, traditionally Christian, or predictable in spite of the title, that it is a complex rebuttal to the ever-present faith in man's potential for regeneration and redemption. Here is a fruitful area of research: do all these elements of the novel, some seemingly inconsistent, even extraneous, operate in unified support of theme?

Symbolism is one of the most puzzling aspects of this book. The names of the four major characters are a perplexing illustration. Simon, the mystic of the group, has a name clearly linked with an Apostle of Christ, the one, strange to say, who denied Him three times. (Simon does deny the objective existence of the beast, but is this a parallel?) Jack also has such a name, since his first name is a nickname for John, the announcer of Christ, also a follower of Christ, and his last name is Merridew, an echo at least of Mary. Ralph's name, oddly enough, is unrelated to the New Testament and in fact is said to be akin to the Anglo-Saxon *Raedwulf*, "wolf-council." Piggy's nickname appears even more incongruous because it is Simon rather than Piggy who is slain as a substitute pig. The only instance in which a name seems incontestably appropriate is that of Roger, where etymology directs us to the Anglo-Saxon *Hrothgar*, "spear-fame." [1]

In *The Coral Island* the three protagonists are named Jack, Ralph, and Peterkin Gay. Golding claims that he changed the latter name to Simon to emphasize his priestly qualities[2]—implying some intention on his part to make at

---

[1] Golding's recorded interest in Anglo-Saxon makes it unlikely that he should be unaware of this etymology. See E. L. Epstein, "Notes on *Lord of the Flies*," below, p. 277.

least one name symbolic—while another critic insists that
Peterkin is altered not to Simon but to Piggy.[3] But that is
beside the point. The central question is, "To what extent
do the names function symbolically?" Do we just select
Simon and Roger and, because inconvenient, forget the
others? Or is there another more subtle solution?

We are also mystified by the relationship between *Lord
of the Flies* and *The Coral Island*. Before undertaking a
study of Golding's book, must one study Ballantyne's? To
what degree do details in the former depend upon the latter, and, more confusing, to what degree do both books con-
tain the same details because of similarity of setting?

No one has produced a full-scale synthesis of the symbols
of the novel either, nor has anyone prepared a fully adequate
study of characterization. Ralph himself is an enigma. Does
he represent the idealist and Piggy the pragmatist? Or the
reverse? Why are Piggy and Jack foes from the start, but
Ralph and Jack friends for a considerable length of time?
Is it important that Ralph disdains Piggy for so long? Why
does Ralph the leader have such difficulties controlling the
littluns even though they instantly recognize him as chief
rather than Jack? Why doesn't Ralph establish a closer bond
with Simon? Why does Golding have Ralph enjoy drawing
blood? As one examines the novel closely, he may find himself confronted with a highly ambiguous protagonist, and
for what purpose? Do these complications help or hinder the
operation of the novel? These are vital matters in evaluating
it.

One could add to this list of needed studies indefinitely:
a detailed look at the use of war and fighting (they are
important from the first page to the last), a discussion of
the relationship of nature descriptions and events, a look at
the historical predecessors of the mountain and how they
bear on the novel (Calvary, Sinai, Ararat, Olympus, to name
a few possibilities), the cause of the evil (Is it really
"original sin"?), and so on.

---

[2] Frank Kermode and William Golding, "The Meaning of It
All," *Books and Bookmen*, 5 (October 1959) p. 10. See below
in this volume p. 199. Note Golding's statement that the novel
was worked out "very carefully in every possible way."

[3] Carl Niemeyer, "The Coral Island Revisited," *College English*, 22 (January 1961), p. 242. See below in this volume, p.
219.

Yet in spite of the gaps in the criticism, some commendable studies have been undertaken, and we have tried to assemble the most useful of them in this book. Supplementing them are two interviews with Golding in which he discusses both his own conception of the novel and related matters.[4]

Through our arrangement of and notes to the articles, we have tried to reflect the intricate texture of the novel as illustrated by the critics and to point up areas of perplexity and disagreement. The bibliography at the close of the volume indicates possibilities for further reading and study.

---

[4] The reader, of course, will wish to weigh any artist's view in the light of the continuing critical dialogue surrounding the "intentional fallacy." Frank Kermode calls Golding's views in question in "The Novels of William Golding," *International Literary Annual*, p. 19. See p. 206 below.

# Introduction[1]

## JAMES R. BAKER

*Lord of the Flies* offers a variation upon the ever-popular tale of island adventure, and it holds all of the excitements common to that long tradition. Golding's castaways are faced with the usual struggle for survival, the terrors of isolation, and a desperate but finally successful effort to signal a passing ship which will return them to the world they have lost. This time, however, the story is told against the background of an atomic war. A plane carrying some English boys, aged six to twelve, from the center of conflict is shot down by the enemy and the youths are left without adult company on an unpopulated Pacific island. The environment in which they find themselves actually presents no serious challenge: the island is a paradise of flowers and fruit, fresh water flows from the mountain, and the climate is gentle. In spite of these unusual natural advantages, the children fail miserably and the adventure ends in a reversal of their (and the reader's) expectations. Within a short time the rule of reason is overthrown and the survivors regress to savagery.

During the first days on the island there is little forewarning of this eventual collapse of order. The boys are delighted with the prospect of some real fun before the adults come to fetch them. With innocent enthusiasm they recall the storybook romances they have read and now expect to enjoy in reality. Among these is *The Coral Island*, Robert Michael Ballantyne's heavily moralistic idyl of castaway boys, written in 1858 yet still, in our atomic age, a popular adolescent classic in England. In Ballantyne's tale everything comes off in exemplary style. For Ralph, Jack, and

[1] Copyright 1964 by James R. Baker.

Peterkin (his charming young imperialists), mastery of the natural environment is an elementary exercise in Anglo-Saxon ingenuity. The fierce pirates who invade the island are defeated by sheer moral force, and the tribe of cannibalistic savages is easily converted and reformed by the example of Christian conduct afforded them. *The Coral Island* is again mentioned by the naval officer who comes to rescue Golding's boys from the nightmare they have created, and so the adventure of these *enfants terribles* is ironically juxtaposed with the spectacular success of the Victorian darlings.[2] The effect is to hold before us two radically different pictures of human nature and society. Ballantyne, no less than Golding, is a fabulist[3] who asks us to believe that the evolution of affairs on his coral island models or reflects the adult world, a world in which men are unfailingly reasonable, cooperative, loving and lovable. We are hardly prepared to accept these optimistic exaggerations, though Ballantyne's story suggests essentially the same flattering image of civilized man found in so many familiar island fables. In choosing to parody and invert this image Golding posits a reality the tradition has generally denied.

The character of this reality is to be seen in the final episode of *Lord of the Flies.* When the cruiser appears offshore, the boy Ralph is the one remaining advocate of reason, but he has no more status than the wild pigs of the forest and is being hunted down for the kill. Shocked by their filth, their disorder, and the revelation that there have been real casualties, the officer (with appropriate fatherly indignation) expresses his disappointment in this "pack of British boys." There is no basis for his surprise, for life on the island has only imitated the larger tragedy in which the adults of the outside world attempted to govern themselves reasonably but ended in the same game of hunt and kill. Thus, according to Golding, the aim of the narrative is "to trace the defects of society back to the defects of human

---

[2] A longer discussion of Golding's use of Ballantyne appears in Carl Niemeyer's "The Coral Island Revisited." See pp. 217-223 in this volume.

[3] See John Peter's "The Fables of William Golding" on pp. 229-234 of this volume. A less simplistic view is offered by Ian Gregor and Mark Kinkead-Weekes in their Introduction to Faber's School Edition of *Lord of the Flies* reprinted on pp. 235-243 in this volume.

nature"; the moral illustrated is that "the shape of society must depend on the ethical nature of the individual and not on any political system however apparently logical or respectable." [4] And since the lost children are the inheritors of the same defects of nature which doomed their fathers, the tragedy on the island is bound to repeat the actual pattern of human history.

The central fact in that pattern is one which we, like the fatuous naval officer, are virtually incapable of perceiving: first, because it is one that constitutes an affront to our ego; second, because it controverts the carefully and elaborately rationalized record of history which sustains the ego of "rational" man. The fact is that regardless of the intelligence we possess—an intelligence which drives us in a tireless effort to impose an order upon our affairs—we are defeated with monotonous regularity by our own irrationality. "History," said Joyce's Dedalus, "is a nightmare from which I am trying to awake." [5] But we do not awake. Though we constantly make a heroic attempt to rise to a level ethically superior to nature, our own nature, again and again we suffer a fall—brought low by some outburst of madness because of the limiting defects inherent in our species.

If there is any literary precedent for the image of man contained in Golding's fable, it is obviously not to be found within the framework of a tradition that embraces *Robinson Crusoe* and *Swiss Family Robinson*[6] and includes also those island episodes in Conrad's novels in which the self-defeating skepticism of a Heyst or a Decoud serves only to illustrate the value of illusions.[7] All of these offer some version of the rationalist orthodoxy we so readily accept, even though the text may not be so boldly simple as Ballantyne's sermon for innocent Victorians. Quite removed from this tradition, which Golding invariably satirizes, is the directly

---

[4] Quoted by E. L. Epstein in his "Notes on *Lord of the Flies*." See below, p. 277.

[5] *Ulysses* (New York: The Modern Library, 1961), p. 34.

[6] See Golding's remarks on these novels and *Treasure Island* in his review called "Islands," *Spectator*, 204 (June 10, 1960), 844-46.

[7] Thus far, attempts to compare Golding and Conrad have been unsuccessful. See Golding's remarks on Conrad (and Richard Hughes's *High Wind in Jamaica*) in the interview by James Keating on p. 194 in this volume. See also William R. Mueller's essay, p. 251.

acknowledged influence of classical Greek literature. Within
this designation, though Golding's critics have ignored it,
is an obvious admiration for Euripides.[8] Among the plays
of Euripides it is *The Bacchae* that Golding, like Mamillius
of *The Brass Butterfly*, knows by heart. The tragedy is a
bitter allegory on the degeneration of society, and it contains the basic parable which informs so much of Golding's
work. Most of all, *Lord of the Flies*, for here the point of
view is similar to that of the aging Euripides after he was
driven into exile from Athens. Before his departure the
tragedian brought down upon himself the mockery and dis-
favor of a mediocre regime like the one which later condemned Socrates. *The Bacchae*, however, is more than an
expression of disillusionment with the failing democracy. Its
aim is precisely what Golding has declared to be his own:
"to trace the defects of society back to the defects of human
nature," and so account for the failure of reason and the
inevitable, blind ritual-hunt in which we seek to kill the
"beast" within our own being.

*The Bacchae* is based on a legend of Dionysus wherein
the god (a son of Zeus and the mortal Semele, daughter of
Cadmus) descends upon Thebes in great wrath, determined
to take revenge upon the young king, Pentheus, who has
denied him recognition and prohibited his worship. Dionysus wins as devotees the daughters of Cadmus and through
his power of enchantment decrees that Agave, mother of
Pentheus, shall lead the band in frenzied celebrations. Pentheus bluntly opposes the god and tries by every means to
preserve order against the rising tide of madness in his
kingdom. The folly of his proud resistance is shown in the
defeat of all that Pentheus represents: the bacchantes tram-
ple on his edicts and in wild marches through the land
wreck everything in their path. Thus prepared for his vengeance, Dionysus casts a spell over Pentheus. With his judgment weakened and his identity obscured in the dress of a
woman, the defeated prince sets out to spy upon the orgies.
In the excitement of their rituals the bacchantes live in illusion, and all that falls in their way undergoes a metamor-
phosis which brings it into accord with the natural images
of their worship. When Pentheus is seen he is taken for a

---

[8] On several occasions Golding has stated that he has read
deeply in Greek literature and history during the past twenty
years.

lion[9] and, led by Agave, the blind victims of the god tear him limb from limb. The final humiliation of those who deny the godhead is to render them conscious of their crimes and to cast them out from their homeland as guilt-stricken exiles and wanderers upon the earth.

For most modern readers the chief obstacle in the way of proper understanding of *The Bacchae*, and therefore Golding's use of it, is the popular notion that Dionysus is nothing more than a charming god of wine. This image descends from "the Alexandrines, and above all the Romans—with their tidy functionalism and their cheerful obtuseness in all matters of the spirit—who departmentalized Dionysus as 'jolly Bacchus' . . . with his riotous crew of nymphs and satyrs. As such he was taken over from the Romans by Renaissance painters and poets; and it was they in turn who shaped the image in which the modern world pictures him." In reality the god was more important and "much more dangerous": he was "the principle of animal life . . . the hunted and the hunter—the unrestrained potency which man envies in the beasts and seeks to assimilate." Thus the intention and chief effect of the bacchanal was "to liberate the instinctive life in man from the bondage imposed upon it by reason and social custom. . . ." In his play Euripides also suggests "a further effect, a merging of the individual consciousness in a group consciousness" so that the participant is "at one not only with the Master of Life but his fellow-worshipers . . . and with the life of the earth." [10] Dionysus was worshiped in various animal incarnations (snake, bull, lion, boar), whatever form was appropriate to place; and all of these were incarnations of the impulses he evoked in his worshipers. In *The Bacchae* a leader of the bacchanal summons him with the incantation, "O God, Beast, Mystery, come!" [11] Agave's attack upon the "lion" (her own son) conforms to the codes of Dionysic ritual: like other gods, this one is slain and devoured, his devotees sustained by his flesh and blood. The terrible error of the bacchantes is a punishment brought upon the

---

[9] In Ovid's *Metamorphoses* the bacchantes see Pentheus in the form of a boar.

[10] E. R. Dodds, *Euripides Bacchae*, Second Edition (Oxford: The Clarendon Press, 1960), p. xii and p. xx. Dodds also finds evidence that some Dionysian rites called for human sacrifice.

[11] From the verse translation by Gilbert Murray.

land by the lord of beasts: "To resist Dionysus is to repress the elemental in one's own nature; the punishment is the sudden collapse of the inward dykes when the elemental breaks through perforce and civilization vanishes." [12]

This same humiliation falls upon the innocents of *Lord of the Flies*. In their childish pride they attempt to impose an order or pattern upon the vital chaos of their own nature, and so they commit the error and "sin" of Pentheus, the "man of many sorrows." The penalties, as in the play, are bloodshed, guilt, utter defeat of reason. Finally, they stand before the officer, "a semicircle of little boys, their bodies streaked with colored clay, sharp sticks in their hands." [13] Facing that purblind commander (with his revolver and peaked cap), Ralph cries "for the end of innocence, the darkness of man's heart" (186-87); and the tribe of vicious hunters joins him in spontaneous choral lament. But even Ralph could not trace the arc of their descent, could not explain why it's no go, why things are as they are; for in the course of events he was at times among the hunters, one of them, and he grieves in part for the appalling ambiguities he has discovered in his own nature. He remembers those strange interims of blindness and despair when a "shutter" clicked down over his mind and left him at the mercy of his own dark heart. In Ralph's experience, then, the essence of the fable is spelled out: he suffers the dialectic we must all endure, and his failure to resolve it as we would wish demonstrates the limitations which have always plagued the species.

In the first hours on the island Ralph sports untroubled in the twilight of childhood and innocence, but after he sounds the conch he must confront the forces he has summoned to the granite platform beside the sunny lagoon. During that first assembly he seems to arbitrate with the grace of a young god (his natural bearing is dignified, princely) and, for the time being, a balance is maintained. The difficulties begin with the dream-revelation of the child distinguished by the birthmark. The boy tells of a snakelike monster prowling the woods by night, and at this moment the seed of fear is planted. Out of it will grow the mythic

---

[12] Dodds, p. xvi.

[13] *Lord of the Flies*, p. 185. All quotations are taken from the edition contained in this volume. Subsequent page references will appear in parentheses.

beast destined to become lord of the island. Rumors of his presence grow. There is a plague of haunting dreams—the first symptom of the irrational fear which is "mankind's essential illness."

In the chapter called "Beast from Water" the parliamentary debate becomes a blatant allegory in which each spokesman caricatures the position he defends. Piggy (the voice of reason) leads with the statement that "life is scientific," adds the usual utopian promises ("when the war's over they'll be traveling to Mars and back"), and his assurance that such things will come to pass if only we control the senseless conflicts that impede progress. He is met with laughter and jeers (the crude multitude), and at this juncture a littlun interrupts to declare that the beast (ubiquitous evil) comes out of the sea. Maurice interjects to voice the doubt which curses them all: "I don't believe in the beast of course. As Piggy says, life's scientific, but we don't know, do we? Not certainly . . ." (81). Then Simon (the inarticulate seer) rises to utter the truth in garbled, ineffective phrases: there *is* a beast, but "it's only us." As always, his saving words are misunderstood, and the prophet shrinks away in confusion. Amid speculation that he means some kind of ghost, there is a silent show of hands for ghosts as Piggy breaks in with angry rhetorical questions: "What are we? Humans? Or animals? Or savages?" (84). Taking his cue, Jack (savagery *in excelsis*) leaps to his feet and leads all but the "three blind mice" (Ralph, Piggy, Simon) into a mad jig of release down the darkening beach. The parliamentarians naïvely contrast their failure with the supposed efficiency of adults, and Ralph, in despair, asks for a sign from that ruined world.

In "Beast from Air" the sign, a dead man in a parachute, is sent down from the grownups, and the collapse foreshadowed in the allegorical parliament comes on with surprising speed. Ralph himself looks into the face of the enthroned tyrant on the mountain, and from that moment his young intelligence is crippled by fear. He confirms the reality of the beast and his confession of weakness insures Jack's spectacular rise to power. Yet the ease with which Jack establishes his Dionysian order is hardly unaccountable. In its very first appearance the black-caped choir, vaguely evil in its military *esprit*, emerged ominously from a mirage and marched down upon the minority forces as-

sembled on the platform. Except for Simon, pressed into
service and out of step with the common rhythm, the choir
is composed of servitors bound by the ritual and mystery
of group consciousness. They share in that communion, and
there is no real "conversion" or transfer of allegiance from
good to evil when the chorus, ostensibly Christian, becomes
the tribe of hunters. The lord they serve inhabits their own
being. If they turn with relief from the burdens of the platform, it is because they cannot transcend the limitations of
their own nature. Even the parliamentary pool of intelligence must fail in the attempt to explain all that manifests
itself in our turbulent hearts, and the assertion that life is
ordered, "scientific," often appears mere bravado. It em-
bodies the sin of pride and, inevitably, evokes in some form
the great god it has denied.

It is Simon who witnesses his coming and hears his words
of wrath. In the thick undergrowth of the forest the boy
discovers a refuge from the war of words. His shelter of
leaves is a place of contemplation, a sequestered temple,
scented and lighted by the white flowers of the night-
blooming candlenut tree, where, in secret, he meditates on
the lucid but somehow over-simple logic of Piggy and
Ralph and the venal emotion of Jack's challenges: There, in
the infernal glare of the afternoon sun, he sees the killing
of the sow by the hunters and the erection of the pig's
head on the sharpened stick. These acts signify not only the
release from the blood taboo but also obeisance to the mystery and god who has come to be lord of the island-world.
In the hours of one powerfully symbolic afternoon Simon
sees the perennial fall which is the central reality of our
history: the defeat of reason and the release of Dionysian
madness in souls wounded by fear.

Awed by the hideousness of the dripping head (an image
of the hunter's own nature) the apprentice bacchantes suddenly run away, but Simon's gaze is "held by that ancient,
inescapable recognition" (128)—an incarnation of the beast
or devil born again and again out of the human heart. Before he loses consciousness the epileptic visionary "hears"
the truth which is inaccessible to the illusion-bound rationalist and the unconscious or irrational man alike: " 'Fancy
thinking the Beast was something you could hunt and kill'
said the head. For a moment or two the forest and all the
other dimly appreciated places echoed with the parody of

laughter. 'You knew, didn't you? I'm part of you? Close, close, close! I'm the reason why it's no go? Why things are as they are?' " (133). When Simon recovers from this trauma of revelation he finds on the mountaintop that the "beast" is only a man. Like the pig itself, the dead man in the chute is fly-blown, corrupt, an obscene image of the evil that has triumphed in the adult world as well. Tenderly, the boy releases the lines so that the body can descend to earth, but the fallen man does not die. After Simon's death, when the truth is once more lost, the figure rises, moves over the terrified tribe on the beach, and finally out to sea —a tyrannous ghost (history itself) which haunts and curses every social order.

In his martyrdom Simon meets the fate of all saints. The truth he brings would set us free from the repetitious nightmare of history, but we are, by nature, incapable of receiving that truth. Demented by fears our intelligence cannot control, we are at once "heroic and sick" (96), ingenious and ingenuous at the same time. Inevitably we gather in tribal union to hunt the molesting "beast," and always the intolerable frustration of the hunt ends as it must: within the enchanted circle formed by the searchers, the beast materializes in the only form he can possibly assume, the very image of his creator; and once he is visible, projected (once the hunted has become the hunter), the circle closes in an agony of relief. Simon, call him prophet, seer or saint, is blessed and cursed by those intuitions which threaten the ritual of the tribe. In whatever culture the saint appears, he is doomed by his unique insights. There is a vital, if obvious, irony to be observed in the fact that the lost children of Golding's fable are of Christian heritage, but when they blindly kill their savior they re-enact an ancient tragedy, universal because it has its true source in the defects of the species.

The beast, too, is as old as his maker and has assumed many names, though of course his character must remain quite consistent. The particular beast who speaks to Simon is much like his namesake, Beelzebub. A prince of demons of Assyrian or Hebrew descent, but later appropriated by Christians, he is a lord of the flies, an idol for unclean beings. He is what all devils are: an embodiment of the lusts and cruelties which possess his worshipers and of peculiar power among the Philistines, the unenlightened, fearful

herd. He shares some kinship with Dionysus, for his powers
and effects are much the same. In *The Bacchae* Dionysus is
shown "as the source of ecstasies and disasters, as the enemy of intellect and the defense of man against his isolation, as a power that can make him feel like a god while
acting like a beast. . . ." As such, he is "a god whom all
can recognize." [14]

Nor is it difficult to recognize the island on which Golding's innocents are set down as a natural paradise, an uncorrupted Eden offering all the lush abundance of the
primal earth. But it is lost with the first rumors of the
"snake-thing," because he is the ancient, inescapable presence who insures a repetition of the fall. If this fall from
grace is indeed the "perennial myth" that Golding explores
in all his work, [15] it does not seem that he has found in
Genesis a metaphor capable of illuminating the full range
of his theme. In *The Bacchae* Golding the classicist found
another version of the fall of man, and it is clearly more
useful to him than its Biblical counterpart. For one thing,
it makes it possible to avoid the comparatively narrow moral
connotations most of us are inclined to read into the war-
fare between Satan (unqualifiedly evil) and God (unqualifiedly good). Satan is a fallen angel seeking vengeance on
the godhead, and we therefore think of him as an auton-
omous entity, a being in his own right and prince of his
own domain. Dionysus, on the other hand, is a son of God
(Zeus) and thus a manifestation or agent of the godhead
or mystery with whom man seeks communion, or, perverse
in his pride, denies at his own peril. To resist Dionysus is
to resist nature itself, and this attempt to transcend the laws
of creation brings down upon us the punishment of the god.
Further, the ritual-hunt of *The Bacchae* provides something
else not found in the Biblical account. The hunt on Golding's island emerges spontaneously out of childish play, but
it comes to serve as a key to psychology underlying human conflict and, of course, an effective symbol for the
bloody game we have played throughout our history. This

[14] R. P. Winnington-Ingram, *Euripides and Dionysus: An Interpretation of the Bacchae* (Cambridge, England: Cambridge
University Press, 1948), pp. 9-10.

[15] See Ian Gregor and Mark Kinkead-Weekes, "The Strange
Case of Mr. Golding and his Critics," *Twentieth Century*, 167
(February, 1960), 118.

is not to say that Biblical metaphor is unimportant in *Lord of the Flies*, or in the later works, but it forms only a part of the larger mythic frame in which Golding sees the nature and destiny of man.

Unfortunately, the critics have concentrated all too much on Golding's debt to Christian sources, with the result that he is popularly regarded as a rigid Christian moralist. Yet the fact is that he does not reject one orthodoxy only to fall into another. The emphasis of his critics has obscured Golding's fundamental realism and made it difficult to recognize that he satirizes the Christian as well as the rationalist point of view. In *Lord of the Flies*, for example, the much discussed last chapter offers none of the traditional comforts. A fable, by virtue of its far-reaching suggestions, touches upon a dimension that most fiction does not—the dimension of prophecy. With the appearance of the naval officer it is no longer possible to accept the evolution of the island society as an isolated failure. The events we have witnessed constitute a picture of realities which obtain in the world at large. There, too, a legendary beast has emerged from the dark wood, come from the sea, or fallen from the sky; and men have gathered for the communion of the hunt. In retrospect, the entire fable suggests a grim parallel with the prophecies of the Biblical Apocalypse. According to that vision the weary repetition of human failure is assured by the birth of new devils for each generation of men. The first demon, who fathers all the others, falls from the heavens; the second is summoned from the sea to make war upon the saints and overcome them; the third, emerging from the earth itself, induces man to make and worship an image of the beast. It also decrees that this image "should both speak and cause that as many as should not worship" the beast should be killed. Each devil in turn lords over the earth for an era, and then the long nightmare of history is broken by the second coming and the divine millennium. In *Lord of the Flies* (note some of the chapter titles) we see much the same sequence, but it occurs in a highly accelerated evolution. The parallel ends, however, with the irony of Golding's climactic revelation. The childish hope of rescue perishes as the beast-man comes to the shore, for he bears in his nature the bitter promise that things will remain as they are, and as they have been since his first appearance ages and ages ago.

The rebirth of evil is made certain by the fatal defects inherent in human nature, and the haunted island we occupy must always be a fortress on which enchanted hunters pursue the beast. There is no rescue. The making of history and the making of myth are finally the selfsame process— an old process in which the soul makes its own place, its own reality.

In spite of its rich and varied metaphor *Lord of the Flies* is not a bookish fable, and Golding has warned that he will concede little or nothing to *The Golden Bough*.[16] There are real dangers in ignoring this disclaimer. To do so obscures the contemporary relevance of his art and its experiential sources. During the period of World War II he observed first hand the expenditure of human ingenuity in the old ritual of war. As the illusions of his early rationalism and humanism fell away, new images emerged, and, as for Simon, a picture of "a human at once heroic and sick" formed in his mind. When the war ended, Golding was ready to write (as he had not been before), and it was natural to find in the traditions he knew the metaphors which could define the continuity of the soul's flaws. In one sense, the "fable" was already written. One had but to trace over the words upon the scroll [17] and so collaborate with history.

---

[16] See Golding's reply to Professor Kermode in "The Meaning of It All," p. 199 in this volume.

[17] In a letter to me (September, 1962) Professor Frank Kermode recalls Golding's remark to the effect that he was "tracing words already on the paper" during the writing of *Lord of the Flies*.

# LORD OF THE FLIES

a novel by

## WILLIAM GOLDING

# Contents

For my mother and father

# CHAPTER ONE

## The Sound of the Shell

The boy with fair hair lowered himself down the last few feet of rock and began to pick his way toward the lagoon. Though he had taken off his school sweater and trailed it now from one hand, his grey shirt stuck to him and his hair was plastered to his forehead. All round him the long scar smashed into the jungle was a bath of heat. He was clambering heavily among the creepers and broken trunks when a bird, a vision of red and yellow, flashed upwards with a witch-like cry; and this cry was echoed by another.

"Hi!" it said. "Wait a minute!"

The undergrowth at the side of the scar was shaken and a multitude of raindrops fell pattering.

"Wait a minute," the voice said. "I got caught up."

The fair boy stopped and jerked his stockings with an automatic gesture that made the jungle seem for a moment like the Home Counties.

The voice spoke again.

"I can't hardly move with all these creeper things."

The owner of the voice came backing out of the undergrowth so that twigs scratched on a greasy wind-breaker. The naked crooks of his knees were plump, caught and scratched by thorns. He bent down, removed the thorns carefully, and turned round. He was shorter than the fair boy and very fat. He came forward, searching out safe lodgments for his feet, and then looked up through thick spectacles.

"Where's the man with the megaphone?"

The fair boy shook his head.

"This is an island. At least I think it's an island. That's

5

a reef out in the sea. Perhaps there aren't any grownups anywhere."

The fat boy looked startled.

"There was that pilot. But he wasn't in the passenger cabin, he was up in front."

The fair boy was peering at the reef through screwed-up eyes.

"All them other kids," the fat boy went on. "Some of them must have got out. They must have, mustn't they?"

The fair boy began to pick his way as casually as possible toward the water. He tried to be offhand and not too obviously uninterested, but the fat boy hurried after him.

"Aren't there any grownups at all?"

"I don't think so."

The fair boy said this solemnly; but then the delight of a realized ambition overcame him. In the middle of the scar he stood on his head and grinned at the reversed fat boy.

"No grownups!"

The fat boy thought for a moment.

"That pilot."

The fair boy allowed his feet to come down and sat on the steamy earth.

"He must have flown off after he dropped us. He couldn't land here. Not in a plane with wheels."

"We was attacked!"

"He'll be back all right."

The fat boy shook his head.

"When we was coming down I looked through one of them windows. I saw the other part of the plane. There were flames coming out of it."

He looked up and down the scar.

"And this is what the cabin done."

The fair boy reached out and touched the jagged end of a trunk. For a moment he looked interested.

"What happened to it?" he asked. "Where's it got to now?"

"That storm dragged it out to sea. It wasn't half dangerous with all them tree trunks falling. There must have been some kids still in it."

He hesitated for a moment, then spoke again.

"What's your name?"

"Ralph."

The fat boy waited to be asked his name in turn but this proffer of acquaintance was not made; the fair boy called Ralph smiled vaguely, stood up, and began to make his way once more toward the lagoon. The fat boy hung steadily at his shoulder.

"I expect there's a lot more of us scattered about. You haven't seen any others, have you?"

Ralph shook his head and increased his speed. Then he tripped over a branch and came down with a crash.

The fat boy stood by him, breathing hard.

"My auntie told me not to run," he explained, "on account of my asthma."

"Ass-mar?"

"That's right. Can't catch me breath. I was the only boy in our school what had asthma," said the fat boy with a touch of pride. "And I've been wearing specs since I was three."

He took off his glasses and held them out to Ralph, blinking and smiling, and then started to wipe them against his grubby wind-breaker. An expression of pain and inward concentration altered the pale contours of his face. He smeared the sweat from his cheeks and quickly adjusted the spectacles on his nose.

"Them fruit."

He glanced round the scar.

"Them fruit," he said, "I expect—"

He put on his glasses, waded away from Ralph, and crouched down among the tangled foliage.

"I'll be out again in just a minute—"

Ralph disentangled himself cautiously and stole away through the branches. In a few seconds the fat boy's grunts were behind him and he was hurrying toward the screen that still lay between him and the lagoon. He climbed over a broken trunk and was out of the jungle.

The shore was fledged with palm trees. These stood or leaned or reclined against the light and their green feathers were a hundred feet up in the air. The ground beneath them was a bank covered with coarse grass, torn everywhere by the upheavals of fallen trees, scattered with decaying coconuts and palm saplings. Behind this was the darkness of the forest proper and the open space of the scar. Ralph stood, one hand against a grey trunk, and screwed up his eyes against the shimmering water. Out there, perhaps a mile away, the white surf flinked on a coral reef, and beyond that the open sea was dark blue. Within the irregular arc of coral the lagoon was still as a mountain lake—blue of all shades and shadowy green and purple. The beach between the palm terrace and the water was a thin stick, endless apparently, for to Ralph's left the perspectives of palm and beach and water drew to a point at infinity; and always, almost visible, was the heat.

He jumped down from the terrace. The sand was thick over his black shoes and the heat hit him. He became conscious of the weight of clothes, kicked his shoes off fiercely and ripped off each stocking with its elastic garter in a single movement. Then he leapt back on the terrace, pulled off his shirt, and stood there among the skull-like coconuts with green shadows from the palms and the forest sliding over his skin. He undid the snake-clasp of his belt, lugged off his shorts and pants, and stood there naked, looking at the dazzling beach and the water.

He was old enough, twelve years and a few months, to have lost the prominent tummy of childhood; and not yet old enough for adolescence to have made him awkward. You could see now that he might make a boxer, as far as width and heaviness of shoulders went, but there was a mildness about his mouth and eyes that proclaimed no devil. He patted the palm trunk softly, and, forced at last to believe in the reality of the island, laughed delightedly again and stood on his head. He turned neatly on to his feet, jumped down to the beach, knelt and swept a double armful of sand into a pile against his chest. Then he sat back and looked at the water with bright, excited eyes.

"Ralph—"

The fat boy lowered himself over the terrace and sat down carefully, using the edge as a seat.

"I'm sorry I been such a time. Them fruit—"

He wiped his glasses and adjusted them on his button nose. The frame had made a deep, pink "V" on the bridge. He looked critically at Ralph's golden body and then down at his own clothes. He laid a hand on the end of a zipper that extended down his chest.

"My auntie—"

Then he opened the zipper with decision and pulled the whole wind-breaker over his head.

"There!"

Ralph looked at him sidelong and said nothing.

"I expect we'll want to know all their names," said the fat boy, "and make a list. We ought to have a meeting."

Ralph did not take the hint so the fat boy was forced to continue.

"I don't care what they call me," he said confidentially, "so long as they don't call me what they used to call me at school."

Ralph was faintly interested.

"What was that?"

The fat boy glanced over his shoulder, then leaned toward Ralph.

He whispered.

"They used to call me 'Piggy.' "

Ralph shrieked with laughter. He jumped up.

"Piggy! Piggy!"

"Ralph—please!"

Piggy clasped his hands in apprehension.

"I said I didn't want—"

"Piggy! Piggy!"

Ralph danced out into the hot air of the beach and then returned as a fighter-plane, with wings swept back, and machine-gunned Piggy.

"Sche-aa-ow!"

He dived in the sand at Piggy's feet and lay there laughing.

"Piggy!"

Piggy grinned reluctantly, pleased despite himself at even this much recognition.

"So long as you don't tell the others—"

Ralph giggled into the sand. The expression of pain and concentration returned to Piggy's face.

"Half a sec'."

He hastened back into the forest. Ralph stood up and trotted along to the right.

Here the beach was interrupted abruptly by the square motif of the landscape; a great platform of pink granite thrust up uncompromisingly through forest and terrace and sand and lagoon to make a raised jetty four feet high. The top of this was covered with a thin layer of soil and coarse grass and shaded with young palm trees. There was not enough soil for them to grow to any height and when they reached perhaps twenty feet they fell and dried, forming a criss-cross pattern of trunks, very convenient to sit on. The palms that still stood made a green roof, covered on the underside with a quivering tangle of reflections from the lagoon. Ralph hauled himself onto this platform, noted the coolness and shade, shut one eye, and decided that the shadows on his body were really green. He picked his way to the seaward edge of the platform and stood looking down into the water. It was clear to the bottom and bright with the efflorescence of tropical weed and coral. A school of tiny, glittering fish flicked hither and thither. Ralph spoke to himself, sounding the bass strings of delight.

"Whizzoh!"

Beyond the platform there was more enchantment. Some act of God—a typhoon perhaps, or the storm that had accompanied his own arrival—had banked sand inside the lagoon so that there was a long, deep pool in the beach with a high ledge of pink granite at the further end. Ralph had been deceived before now by the specious appearance of depth in a beach pool and he approached this one preparing to be disappointed. But the island ran true to form and the incredible pool, which clearly was only invaded by the sea at high tide, was so deep at one end as to be dark green. Ralph inspected the whole thirty yards carefully and then plunged in. The water was warmer than his blood and he might have been swimming in a huge bath.

Piggy appeared again, sat on the rocky ledge, and watched Ralph's green and white body enviously.

"You can't half swim."

"Piggy."

Piggy took off his shoes and socks, ranged them carefully on the ledge, and tested the water with one toe.

"It's hot!"

"What did you expect?"

"I didn't expect nothing. My auntie—"

"Sucks to your auntie!"

Ralph did a surface dive and swam under water with his eyes open; the sandy edge of the pool loomed up like a hillside. He turned over, holding his nose, and a golden light danced and shattered just over his face. Piggy was looking determined and began to take off his shorts. Presently he was palely and fatly naked. He tiptoed down the sandy side of the pool, and sat there up to his neck in water smiling proudly at Ralph.

"Aren't you going to swim?"

Piggy shook his head.

"I can't swim. I wasn't allowed. My asthma—"

"Sucks to your ass-mar!"

Piggy bore this with a sort of humble patience.

"You can't half swim well."

Ralph paddled backwards down the slope, immersed his mouth and blew a jet of water into the air. Then he lifted his chin and spoke.

"I could swim when I was five. Daddy taught me. He's a commander in the Navy. When he gets leave he'll come and rescue us. What's your father?"

Piggy flushed suddenly.

"My dad's dead," he said quickly, "and my mum—"

He took off his glasses and looked vainly for something with which to clean them.

"I used to live with my auntie. She kept a candy store. I used to get ever so many candies. As many as I liked. When'll your dad rescue us?"

"Soon as he can."

Piggy rose dripping from the water and stood naked, cleaning his glasses with a sock. The only sound that reached them now through the heat of the morning was the long, grinding roar of the breakers on the reef.

"How does he know we're here?"

Ralph lolled in the water. Sleep enveloped him like the swathing mirages that were wrestling with the brilliance of the lagoon.

"How does he know we're here?"

Because, thought Ralph, because, because. The roar from the reef became very distant.

"They'd tell him at the airport."

Piggy shook his head, put on his flashing glasses and looked down at Ralph.

"Not them. Didn't you hear what the pilot said? About the atom bomb? They're all dead."

Ralph pulled himself out of the water, stood facing Piggy, and considered this unusual problem.

Piggy persisted.

"This an island, isn't it?"

"I climbed a rock," said Ralph slowly, "and I think this is an island."

"They're all dead," said Piggy, "an' this is an island. Nobody don't know we're here. Your dad don't know, nobody don't know—"

His lips quivered and the spectacles were dimmed with mist.

"We may stay here till we die."

With that word the heat seemed to increase till it became a threatening weight and the lagoon attacked them with a blinding effulgence.

"Get my clothes," muttered Ralph. "Along there."

He trotted through the sand, enduring the sun's enmity, crossed the platform and found his scattered clothes. To put on a grey shirt once more was strangely pleasing. Then he climbed the edge of the platform and sat in the green shade on a convenient trunk. Piggy hauled himself up, carrying most of his clothes under his arms. Then he sat carefully on a fallen trunk near the little cliff that fronted the lagoon; and the tangled reflections quivered over him.

Presently he spoke.

"We got to find the others. We got to do something."

Ralph said nothing. Here was a coral island. Protected from the sun, ignoring Piggy's ill-omened talk, he dreamed pleasantly.

Piggy insisted.

"How many of us are there?"

Ralph came forward and stood by Piggy.

"I don't know."

Here and there, little breezes crept over the polished waters beneath the haze of heat. When these breezes reached the platform the palm fronds would whisper, so that spots of blurred sunlight slid over their bodies or moved like bright, winged things in the shade.

Piggy looked up at Ralph. All the shadows on Ralph's face were reversed; green above, bright below from the lagoon. A blur of sunlight was crawling across his hair.

"We got to do something."

Ralph looked through him. Here at last was the imagined but never fully realized place leaping into real life. Ralph's lips parted in a delighted smile and Piggy, taking this smile to himself as a mark of recognition, laughed with pleasure.

"If it really is an island—"

"What's that?"

Ralph had stopped smiling and was pointing into the lagoon. Something creamy lay among the ferny weeds.

"A stone."

"No. A shell."

Suddenly Piggy was a-bubble with decorous excitement.

"S'right. It's a shell! I seen one like that before. On someone's back wall. A conch he called it. He used to blow it and then his mum would come. It's ever so valuable—"

Near to Ralph's elbow a palm sapling leaned out over the lagoon. Indeed, the weight was already pulling a lump from the poor soil and soon it would fall. He tore out the stem and began to poke about in the water, while the brilliant fish flicked away on this side and that. Piggy leaned dangerously.

"Careful! You'll break it—"

"Shut up."

Ralph spoke absently. The shell was interesting and pretty and a worthy plaything; but the vivid phantoms of his day-dream still interposed between him and Piggy, who in this context was an irrelevance. The palm sapling, bending, pushed the shell across the weeds. Ralph used one hand as a fulcrum and pressed down with the other till the shell rose, dripping, and Piggy could make a grab.

Now the shell was no longer a thing seen but not to be touched, Ralph too became excited. Piggy babbled:

"—a conch; ever so expensive. I bet if you wanted to buy one, you'd have to pay pounds and pounds and pounds —he had it on his garden wall, and my auntie—"

Ralph took the shell from Piggy and a little water ran down his arm. In color the shell was deep cream, touched here and there with fading pink. Between the point, worn away into a little hole, and the pink lips of the mouth, lay eighteen inches of shell with a slight spiral twist and covered with a delicate, embossed pattern. Ralph shook sand out of the deep tube.

"—mooed like a cow," he said. "He had some white stones too, an' a bird cage with a green parrot. He didn't blow the white stones, of course, an' he said—"

Piggy paused for breath and stroked the glistening thing that lay in Ralph's hands.

"Ralph!"

Ralph looked up.

"We can use this to call the others. Have a meeting. They'll come when they hear us—"

He beamed at Ralph.

"That was what you meant, didn't you? That's why you got the conch out of the water?"

Ralph pushed back his fair hair.

"How did your friend blow the conch?"

"He kind of spat," said Piggy. "My auntie wouldn't let me blow on account of my asthma. He said you blew from down here." Piggy laid a hand on his jutting abdomen. "You try, Ralph. You'll call the others."

Doubtfully, Ralph laid the small end of the shell against his mouth and blew. There came a rushing sound from its mouth but nothing more. Ralph wiped the salt water off his lips and tried again, but the shell remained silent.

"He kind of spat."

Ralph pursed his lips and squirted air into the shell, which emitted a low, farting noise. This amused both boys so much that Ralph went on squirting for some minutes, between bouts of laughter.

"He blew from down here."

Ralph grasped the idea and hit the shell with air from his diaphragm. Immediately the thing sounded. A deep, harsh note boomed under the palms, spread through the intricacies of the forest and echoed back from the pink granite of the mountain. Clouds of birds rose from the tree-tops, and something squealed and ran in the undergrowth.

Ralph took the shell away from his lips.

"Gosh!"

His ordinary voice sounded like a whisper after the harsh note of the conch. He laid the conch against his lips, took a deep breath and blew once more. The note boomed again: and then at his firmer pressure, the note, fluking up an octave, became a strident blare more penetrating than before. Piggy was shouting something, his face pleased, his glasses flashing. The birds cried, small animals scuttered. Ralph's breath failed; the note dropped the octave, became a low wubber, was a rush of air.

The conch was silent, a gleaming tusk; Ralph's face was dark with breathlessness and the air over the island was full of bird-clamor and echoes ringing.

"I bet you can hear that for miles."

Ralph found his breath and blew a series of short blasts.
Piggy exclaimed: "There's one!"

A child had appeared among the palms, about a hundred yards along the beach. He was a boy of perhaps six years, sturdy and fair, his clothes torn, his face covered with a sticky mess of fruit. His trousers had been lowered for an obvious purpose and had only been pulled back half-way. He jumped off the palm terrace into the sand and his trousers fell about his ankles; he stepped out. of them and trotted to the platform. Piggy helped him up. Meanwhile Ralph continued to blow till voices shouted in the forest. The small boy squatted in front of Ralph, looking up brightly and vertically. As he received the reassurance of something purposeful being done he began to look satisfied, and his only clean digit, a pink thumb, slid into his mouth.

Piggy leaned down to him.

"What's yer name?"

"Johnny."

Piggy muttered the name to himself and then shouted it to Ralph, who was not interested because he was still blowing. His face was dark with the violent pleasure of making this stupendous noise, and his heart was making the stretched shirt shake. The shouting in the forest was nearer.

Signs of life were visible now on the beach. The sand, trembling beneath the heat haze, concealed many figures in its miles of length; boys were making their way toward the platform through the hot, dumb sand. Three small children, no older than Johnny, appeared from startlingly close at hand where they had been gorging fruit in the forest. A dark little boy, not much younger than Piggy, parted a tangle of undergrowth, walked on to the platform, and smiled cheerfully at everybody. More and more of them came. Taking their cue from the innocent Johnny, they sat down on the fallen palm trunks and waited. Ralph continued to blow short, penetrating blasts. Piggy moved among the crowd, asking names and frowning to remember them. The children gave him the same simple obedience that they had given to the men with megaphones. Some were naked and carrying their clothes; others half-naked, or more or less dressed, in school uniforms, grey, blue, fawn, jacketed or jerseyed. There were badges, mot-

toes even, stripes of color in stockings and pullovers. Their
heads clustered above the trunks in the green shade; heads
brown, fair, black, chestnut, sandy, mouse-colored; heads
muttering, whispering, heads full of eyes that watched
Ralph and speculated. Something was being done.

The children who came along the beach, singly or in
twos, leapt into visibility when they crossed the line from
heat haze to nearer sand. Here, the eye was first attracted
to a black, bat-like creature that danced on the sand, and
only later perceived the body above it. The bat was the
child's shadow, shrunk by the vertical sun to a patch between the hurrying feet. Even while he blew, Ralph noticed the last pair of bodies that reached the platform above
a fluttering patch of black. The two boys, bullet-headed
and with hair like tow, flung themselves down and lay grinning and panting at Ralph like dogs. They were twins, and
the eye was shocked and incredulous at such cheery du-
plication. They breathed together, they grinned together,
they were chunky and vital. They raised wet lips at Ralph,
for they seemed provided with not quite enough skin, so
that their profiles were blurred and their mouths pulled
open. Piggy bent his flashing glasses to them and could be
heard between the blasts, repeating their names.

"Sam, Eric, Sam, Eric."

Then he got muddled; the twins shook their heads and
pointed at each other and the crowd laughed.

At last Ralph ceased to blow and sat there, the conch
trailing from one hand, his head bowed on his knees. As the
echoes died away so did the laughter, and there was silence.

Within the diamond haze of the beach something dark
was fumbling along. Ralph saw it first, and watched till the
intentness of his gaze drew all eyes that way. Then the creature stepped from mirage on to clear sand, and they saw
that the darkness was not all shadows but mostly clothing.
The creature was a party of boys, marching approximately
in step in two parallel lines and dressed in strangely eccen-
tric clothing. Shorts, shirts, and different garments they
carried in their hands; but each boy wore a square black
cap with a silver badge on it. Their bodies, from throat to
ankle, were hidden by black cloaks which bore a long silver
cross on the left breast and each neck was finished off with
a hambone frill. The heat of the tropics, the descent, the
search for food, and now this sweaty march along the blaz-

ing beach had given them the complexions of newly washed plums. The boy who controlled them was dressed in the same way though his cap badge was golden. When his party was about ten yards from the platform he shouted an order and they halted, gasping, sweating, swaying in the fierce light. The boy himself came forward, vaulted on to the platform with his cloak flying, and peered into what to him was almost complete darkness.

"Where's the man with the trumpet?"

Ralph, sensing his sun-blindness, answered him.

"There's no man with a trumpet. Only me."

The boy came close and peered down at Ralph, screwing up his face as he did so. What he saw of the fair-haired boy with the creamy shell on his knees did not seem to satisfy him. He turned quickly, his black cloak circling.

"Isn't there a ship, then?"

Inside the floating cloak he was tall, thin, and bony: and his hair was red beneath the black cap. His face was crumpled and freckled, and ugly without silliness. Out of this face stared two light blue eyes, frustrated now, and turning, or ready to turn, to anger.

"Isn't there a man here?"

Ralph spoke to his back.

"No. We're having a meeting. Come and join in."

The group of cloaked boys began to scatter from close line. The tall boy shouted at them.

"Choir! Stand still!"

Wearily obedient, the choir huddled into line and stood there swaying in the sun. None the less, some began to protest faintly.

"But, Merridew. Please, Merridew . . . can't we?"

Then one of the boys flopped on his face in the sand and the line broke up. They heaved the fallen boy to the platform and let him lie. Merridew, his eyes staring, made the best of a bad job.

"All right then. Sit down. Let him alone."

"But Merridew."

"He's always throwing a faint," said Merridew. "He did in Gib.; and Addis; and at matins over the precentor."

This last piece of shop brought sniggers from the choir, who perched like black birds on the criss-cross trunks and examined Ralph with interest. Piggy asked no names. He was intimidated by this uniformed superiority and the offhand authority in Merridew's voice. He shrank to the other side of Ralph and busied himself with his glasses.

Merridew turned to Ralph.

"Aren't there any grownups?"

"No."

Merridew sat down on a trunk and looked round the circle.

"Then we'll have to look after ourselves."

Secure on the other side of Ralph, Piggy spoke timidly.

"That's why Ralph made a meeting. So as we can decide what to do. We've heard names. That's Johnny. Those two —they're twins, Sam 'n Eric. Which is Eric—? You? No —you're Sam—"

"I'm Sam—"

" 'n I'm Eric."

"We'd better all have names," said Ralph, "so I'm Ralph."

"We got most names," said Piggy. "Got 'em just now."

"Kids' names," said Merridew. "Why should I be Jack? I'm Merridew."

Ralph turned to him quickly. This was the voice of one who knew his own mind.

"Then," went on Piggy, "that boy—I forget—"

"You're talking too much," said Jack Merridew. "Shut up, Fatty."

Laughter arose.

"He's not Fatty," cried Ralph, "his real name's Piggy!"

"Piggy!"

"Piggy!"

"Oh, Piggy!"

A storm of laughter arose and even the tiniest child joined in. For the moment the boys were a closed circuit of sympathy with Piggy outside: he went very pink, bowed his head and cleaned his glasses again.

Finally the laughter died away and the naming continued. There was Maurice, next in size among the choir boys to Jack, but broad and grinning all the time. There was a slight, furtive boy whom no one knew, who kept to himself with an inner intensity of avoidance and secrecy. He muttered that his name was Roger and was silent again. Bill, Robert, Harold, Henry; the choir boy who had fainted sat up against a palm trunk, smiled pallidly at Ralph and said that his name was Simon.

Jack spoke.

"We've got to decide about being rescued."

There was a buzz. One of the small boys, Henry, said that he wanted to go home.

"Shut up," said Ralph absently. He lifted the conch. "Seems to me we ought to have a chief to decide things."

"A chief! A chief!"

"I ought to be chief," said Jack with simple arrogance, "because I'm chapter chorister and head boy. I can sing C sharp."

Another buzz.

"Well then," said Jack, "I—"

He hesitated. The dark boy, Roger, stirred at last and spoke up.

"Let's have a vote."

"Yes!"

"Vote for chief!"

"Let's vote—"

This toy of voting was almost as pleasing as the conch. Jack started to protest but the clamor changed from the general wish for a chief to an election by acclaim of Ralph himself. None of the boys could have found good reason for this; what intelligence had been shown was traceable to Piggy while the most obvious leader was Jack. But there was a stillness about Ralph as he sat that marked him out: there was his size, and attractive appearance; and most obscurely, yet most powerfully, there was the conch. The being that had blown that, had sat waiting for them on the platform with the delicate thing balanced on his knees, was set apart.

"Him with the shell."

"Ralph! Ralph!"

"Let him be chief with the trumpet-thing."

Ralph raised a hand for silence.

"All right. Who wants Jack for chief?"

With dreary obedience the choir raised their hands.

"Who wants me?"

Every hand outside the choir except Piggy's was raised immediately. Then Piggy, too, raised his hand grudgingly into the air.

Ralph counted.

"I'm chief then."

The circle of boys broke into applause. Even the choir

applauded; and the freckles on Jack's face disappeared under a blush of mortification. He started up, then changed his mind and sat down again while the air rang. Ralph looked at him, eager to offer something.

"The choir belongs to you, of course."

"They could be the army—"

"Or hunters—"

"They could be—"

The suffusion drained away from Jack's face. Ralph waved again for silence.

"Jack's in charge of the choir. They can be—what do you want them to be?"

"Hunters."

Jack and Ralph smiled at each other with shy liking. The rest began to talk eagerly.

Jack stood up.

"All right, choir. Take off your togs."

As if released from class, the choir boys stood up, chattered, piled their black cloaks on the grass. Jack laid his on the trunk by Ralph. His grey shorts were sticking to him with sweat. Ralph glanced at them admiringly, and when Jack saw his glance he explained.

"I tried to get over that hill to see if there was water all round. But your shell called us."

Ralph smiled and held up the conch for silence.

"Listen, everybody. I've got to have time to think things out. I can't decide what to do straight off. If this isn't an island we might be rescued straight away. So we've got to decide if this is an island. Everybody must stay round here and wait and not go away. Three of us—if we take more we'd get all mixed, and lose each other—three of us will go on an expedition and find out. I'll go, and Jack, and, and. . . ."

He looked round the circle of eager faces. There was no lack of boys to choose from.

"And Simon."

The boys round Simon giggled, and he stood up, laughing a little. Now that the pallor of his faint was over, he was a skinny, vivid little boy, with a glance coming up from under a hut of straight hair that hung down, black and coarse.

He nodded at Ralph.

"I'll come."

"And I—"

Jack snatched from behind him a sizable sheath-knife and clouted it into a trunk. The buzz rose and died away.

Piggy stirred.

"I'll come."

Ralph turned to him.

"You're no good on a job like this."

"All the same—"

"We don't want you," said Jack, flatly. "Three's enough."

Piggy's glasses flashed.

"I was with him when he found the conch. I was with him before anyone else was."

Jack and the others paid no attention. There was a general dispersal. Ralph, Jack and Simon jumped off the platform and walked along the sand past the bathing pool. Piggy hung bumbling behind them.

"If Simon walks in the middle of us," said Ralph, "then we could talk over his head."

The three of them fell into step. This meant that every now and then Simon had to do a double shuffle to catch up with the others. Presently Ralph stopped and turned back to Piggy.

"Look."

Jack and Simon pretended to notice nothing. They walked on.

"You can't come."

Piggy's glasses were misted again—this time with humiliation.

"You told 'em. After what I said."

His face flushed, his mouth trembled.

"After I said I didn't want—"

"What on earth are you talking about?"

"About being called Piggy. I said I didn't care as long as they didn't call me Piggy; an' I said not to tell and then you went an' said straight out—"

Stillness descended on them. Ralph, looking with more understanding at Piggy, saw that he was hurt and crushed. He hovered between the two courses of apology or further insult.

"Better Piggy than Fatty," he said at last, with the directness of genuine leadership, "and anyway, I'm sorry if you feel like that. Now go back, Piggy, and take names. That's your job. So long."

He turned and raced after the other two. Piggy stood and the rose of indignation faded slowly from his cheeks. He went back to the platform.

The three boys walked briskly on the sand. The tide was low and there was a strip of weed-strewn beach that was almost as firm as a road. A kind of glamour was spread over them and the scene and they were conscious of the glamour and made happy by it. They turned to each other, laughing excitedly, talking, not listening. The air was bright. Ralph, faced by the task of translating all this into an explanation, stood on his head and fell over. When they had done laughing, Simon stroked Ralph's arm shyly; and they had to laugh again.

"Come on," said Jack presently, "we're explorers."

"We'll go to the end of the island," said Ralph, "and look round the corner."

"If it is an island—"

Now, toward the end of the afternoon, the mirages were settling a little. They found the end of the island, quite distinct, and not magicked out of shape or sense. There was a jumble of the usual squareness, with one great block sitting out in the lagoon. Sea birds were nesting there.

"Like icing," said Ralph, "on a pink cake."

"We shan't see round this corner," said Jack, "because there isn't one. Only a slow curve—and you can see, the rocks get worse—"

Ralph shaded his eyes and followed the jagged outline of the crags up toward the mountain. This part of the beach was nearer the mountain than any other that they had seen.

"We'll try climbing the mountain from here," he said. "I should think this is the easiest way. There's less of that jungly stuff; and more pink rock. Come on."

The three boys began to scramble up. Some unknown force had wrenched and shattered these cubes so that they lay askew, often piled diminishingly on each other. The most usual feature of the rock was a pink cliff surmounted by a skewed block; and that again surmounted, and that again, till the pinkness became a stack of balanced rock projecting through the looped fantasy of the forest creepers. Where the pink cliffs rose out of the ground there were often narrow tracks winding upwards. They could edge along them, deep in the plant world, their faces to the rock.

"What made this track?"

Jack paused, wiping the sweat from his face. Ralph stood by him, breathless.

"Men?"

Jack shook his head.

"Animals."

Ralph peered into the darkness under the trees. The forest minutely vibrated.

"Come on."

The difficulty was not the steep ascent round the shoulders of rock, but the occasional plunges through the undergrowth to get to the next path. Here the roots and stems of creepers were in such tangles that the boys had to thread through them like pliant needles. Their only guide, apart from the brown ground and occasional flashes of light through the foliage, was the tendency of slope: whether this hole, laced as it was with the cables of creeper, stood higher than that.

Somehow, they moved up.

Immured in these tangles, at perhaps their most difficult moment, Ralph turned with shining eyes to the others.

"Wacco."

"Wizard."

"Smashing."

The cause of their pleasure was not obvious. All three were hot, dirty and exhausted. Ralph was badly scratched. The creepers were as thick as their thighs and left little but tunnels for further penetration. Ralph shouted experimentally and they listened to the muted echoes.

"This is real exploring," said Jack. "I bet nobody's been here before."

"We ought to draw a map," said Ralph, "only we haven't any paper."

"We could make scratches on bark," said Simon, "and rub black stuff in."

Again came the solemn communion of shining eyes in the gloom.

"Wacco."

"Wizard."

There was no place for standing on one's head. This time Ralph expressed the intensity of his emotion by pretending to knock Simon down; and soon they were a happy, heaving pile in the under-dusk.

When they had fallen apart Ralph spoke first.

"Got to get on."

The pink granite of the next cliff was further back from the creepers and trees so that they could trot up the path. This again led into more open forest so that they had a glimpse of the spread sea. With openness came the sun; it dried the sweat that had soaked their clothes in the dark, damp heat. At last the way to the top looked like a scramble over pink rock, with no more plunging through darkness. The boys chose their way through defiles and over heaps of sharp stone.

"Look! Look!"

High over this end of the island, the shattered rocks lifted up their stacks and chimneys. This one, against which Jack leaned, moved with a grating sound when they pushed.

"Come on—"

But not "Come on" to the top. The assault on the summit must wait while the three boys accepted this challenge. The rock was as large as a small motor car.

"Heave!"

Sway back and forth, catch the rhythm.

"Heave!"

Increase the swing of the pendulum, increase, increase, come up and bear against that point of furthest balance—increase—increase—

"Heave!"

The great rock loitered, poised on one toe, decided not to return, moved through the air, fell, struck, turned over, leapt droning through the air and smashed a deep hole in the canopy of the forest. Echoes and birds flew, white and pink dust floated, the forest further down shook as with the passage of an enraged monster: and then the island was still.

"Wacco!"

"Like a bomb!"

"Whee-aa-oo!"

Not for five minutes could they drag themselves away from this triumph. But they left at last.

The way to the top was easy after that. As they reached the last stretch Ralph stopped.

"Golly!"

They were on the lip of a circular hollow in the side of the mountain. This was filled with a blue flower, a rock plant of some sort, and the overflow hung down the vent and spilled lavishly among the canopy of the forest. The air was thick with butterflies, lifting, fluttering, settling.

Beyond the hollow was the square top of the mountain and soon they were standing on it.

They had guessed before that this was an island: clambering among the pink rocks, with the sea on either side, and the crystal heights of air, they had known by some instinct that the sea lay on every side. But there seemed something more fitting in leaving the last word till they stood on the top, and could see a circular horizon of water.

Ralph turned to the others.

"This belongs to us."

It was roughly boat-shaped: humped near this end with behind them the jumbled descent to the shore. On either side rocks, cliffs, treetops and a steep slope: forward there, the length of the boat, a tamer descent, tree-clad, with hints of pink; and then the jungly flat of the island, dense green, but drawn at the end to a pink tail. There, where the island petered out in water, was another island; a rock, almost detached, standing like a fort, facing them across the green with one bold, pink bastion.

The boys surveyed all this, then looked out to sea. They were high up and the afternoon had advanced; the view was not robbed of sharpness by mirage.

"That's a reef. A coral reef. I've seen pictures like that."

The reef enclosed more than one side of the island, lying perhaps a mile out and parallel to what they now thought of as their beach. The coral was scribbled in the sea as though a giant had bent down to reproduce the shape of the island in a flowing chalk line but tired before he had finished. Inside was peacock water, rocks and weed showing as in an aquarium; outside was the dark blue of the sea. The tide was running so that long streaks of foam tailed away from the reef and for a moment they felt that the boat was moving steadily astern.

Jack pointed down.

"That's where we landed."

Beyond falls and cliffs there was a gash visible in the trees; there were the splintered trunks and then the drag, leaving only a fringe of palm between the scar and the sea. There, too, jutting into the lagoon, was the platform, with insect-like figures moving near it.

Ralph sketched a twining line from the bald spot on

which they stood down a slope, a gully, through flowers, round and down to the rock where the scar started.

"That's the quickest way back."

Eyes shining, mouths open, triumphant, they savored the right of domination. They were lifted up: were friends.

"There's no village smoke, and no boats," said Ralph wisely. "We'll make sure later; but I think it's uninhabited."

"We'll get food," cried Jack. "Hunt. Catch things . . . until they fetch us."

Simon looked at them both, saying nothing but nodding till his black hair flopped backwards and forwards: his face was glowing.

Ralph looked down the other way where there was no reef.

"Steeper," said Jack.

Ralph made a cupping gesture.

"That bit of forest down there . . . the mountain holds it up."

Every point of the mountain held up trees—flowers and trees. Now the forest stirred, roared, flailed. The nearer acres of rock flowers fluttered and for half a minute the breeze blew cool on their faces.

Ralph spread his arms.

"All ours."

They laughed and tumbled and shouted on the mountain.

"I'm hungry."

When Simon mentioned his hunger the others became aware of theirs.

"Come on," said Ralph. "We've found out what we wanted to know."

They scrambled down a rock slope, dropped among flowers and made their way under the trees. Here they paused and examined the bushes round them curiously.

Simon spoke first.

"Like candles. Candle bushes. Candle buds."

The bushes were dark evergreen and aromatic and the many buds were waxen green and folded up against the light. Jack slashed at one with his knife and the scent spilled over them.

"Candle buds."

"You couldn't light them," said Ralph. "They just look like candles."

"Green candles," said Jack contemptuously. "We can't eat them. Come on."

They were in the beginnings of the thick forest, plonking with weary feet on a track, when they heard the noises —squeakings—and the hard strike of hoofs on a path. As they pushed forward the squeaking increased till it became a frenzy. They found a piglet caught in a curtain of creepers, throwing itself at the elastic traces in all the madness of extreme terror. Its voice was thin, needle-sharp and insistent. The three boys rushed forward and Jack drew his knife again with a flourish. He raised his arm in the air. There came a pause, a hiatus, the pig continued to scream and the creepers to jerk, and the blade continued to flash at the end of a bony arm. The pause was only long enough for them to understand what an enormity the downward stroke would be. Then the piglet tore loose from the creepers and scurried into the undergrowth. They were left looking at each other and the place of terror. Jack's face was white under the freckles. He noticed that he still held the knife aloft and brought his arm down replacing the blade in the sheath. Then they all three laughed ashamedly and began to climb back to the track.

"I was choosing a place," said Jack. "I was just waiting for a moment to decide where to stab him."

"You should stick a pig," said Ralph fiercely. "They always talk about sticking a pig."

"You cut a pig's throat to let the blood out," said Jack, "otherwise you can't eat the meat."

"Why didn't you—?"

They knew very well why he hadn't: because of the enormity of the knife descending and cutting into living flesh; because of the unbearable blood.

"I was going to," said Jack. He was ahead of them and they could not see his face. "I was choosing a place. Next time—!"

He snatched his knife out of the sheath and slammed it into a tree trunk. Next time there would be no mercy. He looked round fiercely, daring them to contradict. Then they broke out into the sunlight and for a while they were busy finding and devouring food as they moved down the scar toward the platform and the meeting.

# CHAPTER TWO

## *Fire on the Mountain*

By the time Ralph finished blowing the conch the platform was crowded. There were differences between this meeting and the one held in the morning. The afternoon sun slanted in from the other side of the platform and most of the children, feeling too late the smart of sunburn, had put their clothes on. The choir, noticeably less of a group, had discarded their cloaks.

Ralph sat on a fallen trunk, his left side to the sun. On his right were most of the choir; on his left the larger boys who had not known each other before the evacuation; before him small children squatted in the grass.

Silence now. Ralph lifted the cream and pink shell to his knees and a sudden breeze scattered light over the platform. He was uncertain whether to stand up or remain sitting. He looked sideways to his left, toward the bathing pool. Piggy was sitting near but giving no help.

Ralph cleared his throat.

"Well then."

All at once he found he could talk fluently and explain what he had to say. He passed a hand through his fair hair and spoke.

"We're on an island. We've been on the mountain top and seen water all round. We saw no houses, no smoke, no footprints, no boats, no people. We're on an uninhabited island with no other people on it."

Jack broke in.

"All the same you need an army—for hunting. Hunting pigs—"

"Yes. There are pigs on the island."

All three of them tried to convey the sense of the pink live thing struggling in the creepers.

28

"We saw—"

"Squealing—"

"It broke away—"

"Before I could kill it—but—next time!"

Jack slammed his knife into a trunk and looked round challengingly.

The meeting settled down again.

"So you see," said Ralph, "we need hunters to get us meat. And another thing."

He lifted the shell on his knees and looked round the sun-slashed faces.

"There aren't any grownups. We shall have to look after ourselves."

The meeting hummed and was silent.

"And another thing. We can't have everybody talking at once. We'll have to have 'Hands up' like at school."

He held the conch before his face and glanced round the mouth.

"Then I'll give him the conch."

"Conch?"

"That's what this shell's called. I'll give the conch to the next person to speak. He can hold it when he's speaking."

"But—"

"Look—"

"And he won't be interrupted. Except by me."

Jack was on his feet.

"We'll have rules!" he cried excitedly. "Lots of rules! Then when anyone breaks 'em—"

"Whee-oh!"

"Wacco!"

"Bong!"

"Doink!"

Ralph felt the conch lifted from his lap. Then Piggy was standing cradling the great cream shell and the shouting died down. Jack, left on his feet, looked uncertainly at Ralph who smiled and patted the log. Jack sat down. Piggy took off his glasses and blinked at the assembly while he wiped them on his shirt.

"You're hindering Ralph. You're not letting him get to the most important thing."

He paused effectively.

"Who knows we're here? Eh?"

"They knew at the airport."

"The man with a trumpet-thing—"

"My dad."

Piggy put on his glasses.

"Nobody knows where we are," said Piggy. He was paler than before and breathless. "Perhaps they knew where we was going to; and perhaps not. But they don't know where we are 'cos we never got there." He gaped at them for a moment, then swayed and sat down. Ralph took the conch from his hands.

"That's what I was going to say," he went on, "when you all, all. . . ." He gazed at their intent faces. "The plane was shot down in flames. Nobody knows where we are. We may be here a long time."

The silence was so complete that they could hear the unevenness of Piggy's breathing. The sun slanted in and lay golden over half the platform. The breezes that on the lagoon had chased their tails like kittens were finding their way across the platform and into the forest. Ralph pushed back the tangle of fair hair that hung on his forehead.

"So we may be here a long time."

Nobody said anything. He grinned suddenly.

"But this is a good island. We—Jack, Simon and me— we climbed the mountain. It's wizard. There's food and drink, and—"

"Rocks—"

"Blue flowers—"

Piggy, partly recovered, pointed to the conch in Ralph's hands, and Jack and Simon fell silent. Ralph went on.

"While we're waiting we can have a good time on this island."

He gesticulated widely.

"It's like in a book."

At once there was a clamor.

"Treasure Island—"

"Swallows and Amazons—"

"Coral Island—"

Ralph waved the conch.

"This is our island. It's a good island. Until the grownups come to fetch us we'll have fun."

Jack held out his hand for the conch.

"There's pigs," he said. "There's food; and bathing water in that little stream along there—and everything. Didn't anyone find anything else?"

He handed the conch back to Ralph and sat down. Apparently no one had found anything.

The older boys first noticed the child when he resisted. There was a group of little boys urging him forward and he did not want to go. He was a shrimp of a boy, about six years old, and one side of his face was blotted out by a mulberry-colored birthmark. He stood now, warped out of the perpendicular by the fierce light of publicity, and he bored into the coarse grass with one toe. He was muttering and about to cry.

The other little boys, whispering but serious, pushed him toward Ralph.

"All right," said Ralph, "come on then."

The small boy looked round in panic.

"Speak up!"

The small boy held out his hands for the conch and the assembly shouted with laughter; at once he snatched back his hands and started to cry.

"Let him have the conch!" shouted Piggy. "Let him have it!"

At last Ralph induced him to hold the shell but by then the blow of laughter had taken away the child's voice. Piggy knelt by him, one hand on the great shell, listening and interpreting to the assembly.

"He wants to know what you're going to do about the snake-thing."

Ralph laughed, and the other boys laughed with him. The small boy twisted further into himself.

"Tell us about the snake-thing."

"Now he says it was a beastie."

"Beastie?"

"A snake-thing. Ever so big. He saw it."

"Where?"

"In the woods."

Either the wandering breezes or perhaps the decline of the sun allowed a little coolness to lie under the trees. The boys felt it and stirred restlessly.

"You couldn't have a beastie, a snake-thing, on an island this size," Ralph explained kindly. "You only get them in big countries, like Africa, or India."

Murmur; and the grave nodding of heads.

"He says the beastie came in the dark."

"Then he couldn't see it!"

Laughter and cheers.

"Did you hear that? Says he saw the thing in the dark—"

"He still says he saw the beastie. It came and went away again an' came back and wanted to eat him—"

"He was dreaming."

Laughing, Ralph looked for confirmation round the ring of faces. The older boys agreed; but here and there among the little ones was the doubt that required more than rational assurance.

"He must have had a nightmare. Stumbling about among all those creepers."

More grave nodding; they knew about nightmares.

"He says he saw the beastie, the snake-thing, and will it come back tonight?"

"But there isn't a beastie!"

"He says in the morning it turned into them things like ropes in the trees and hung in the branches. He says will it come back tonight?"

"But there isn't a beastie!"

There was no laughter at all now and more grave watching. Ralph pushed both hands through his hair and looked at the little boy in mixed amusement and exasperation.

Jack seized the conch.

"Ralph's right of course. There isn't a snake-thing. But if there was a snake we'd hunt it and kill it. We're going to hunt pigs to get meat for everybody. And we'll look for the snake too—"

"But there isn't a snake!"

"We'll make sure when we go hunting."

Ralph was annoyed and, for the moment, defeated. He felt himself facing something ungraspable. The eyes that looked so intently at him were without humor.

"But there isn't a beast!"

Something he had not known was there rose in him and compelled him to make the point, loudly and again.

"But I tell you there isn't a beast!"

The assembly was silent.

Ralph lifted the conch again and his good humor came back as he thought of what he had to say next.

"Now we come to the most important thing. I've been thinking. I was thinking while we were climbing the mountain." He flashed a conspiratorial grin at the other two.

"And on the beach just now. This is what I thought. We want to have fun. And we want to be rescued."

The passionate noise of agreement from the assembly hit him like a wave and he lost his thread. He thought again.

"We want to be rescued; and of course we shall be rescued."

Voices babbled. The simple statement, unbacked by any proof but the weight of Ralph's new authority, brought light and happiness. He had to wave the conch before he could make them hear him.

"My father's in the Navy. He said there aren't any unknown islands left. He says the Queen has a big room full of maps and all the islands in the world are drawn there. So the Queen's got a picture of this island."

Again came the sounds of cheerfulness and better heart.

"And sooner or later a ship will put in here. It might even be Daddy's ship. So you see, sooner or later, we shall be rescued."

He paused, with the point made. The assembly was lifted toward safety by his words. They liked and now respected him. Spontaneously they began to clap and presently the platform was loud with applause. Ralph flushed, looking sideways at Piggy's open admiration, and then the other way at Jack who was smirking and showing that he too knew how to clap.

Ralph waved the conch.

"Shut up! Wait! Listen!"

He went on in the silence, borne on his triumph.

"There's another thing. We can help them to find us. If a ship comes near the island they may not notice us. So we must make smoke on top of the mountain. We must make a fire."

"A fire! Make a fire!"

At once half the boys were on their feet. Jack clamored among them, the conch forgotten.

"Come on! Follow me!"

The space under the palm trees was full of noise and movement. Ralph was on his feet too, shouting for quiet, but no one heard him. All at once the crowd swayed toward the island and was gone—following Jack. Even the tiny children went and did their best among the leaves and broken branches. Ralph was left, holding the conch, with no one but Piggy.

Piggy's breathing was quite restored.

"Like kids!" he said scornfully. "Acting like a crowd of kids!"

Ralph looked at him doubtfully and laid the conch on the tree trunk.

"I bet it's gone tea-time," said Piggy. "What do they think they're going to do on that mountain?"

He caressed the shell respectfully, then stopped and looked up.

"Ralph! Hey! Where you going?"

Ralph was already clambering over the first smashed swathes of the scar. A long way ahead of him was crashing and laughter.

Piggy watched him in disgust.

"Like a crowd of kids—"

He sighed, bent, and laced up his shoes. The noise of the errant assembly faded up the mountain. Then, with the martyred expression of a parent who has to keep up with the senseless ebullience of the children, he picked up the conch, turned toward the forest, and began to pick his way over the tumbled scar.

Below the other side of the mountain top was a platform of forest. Once more Ralph found himself making the cupping gesture.

"Down there we could get as much wood as we want."

Jack nodded and pulled at his underlip. Starting perhaps a hundred feet below them on the steeper side of the mountain, the patch might have been designed expressly for fuel. Trees, forced by the damp heat, found too little soil for full growth, fell early and decayed: creepers cradled them, and new saplings searched a way up.

Jack turned to the choir, who stood ready. Their black caps of maintenance were slid over one ear like berets.

"We'll build a pile. Come on."

They found the likeliest path down and began tugging at the dead wood. And the small boys who had reached the top came sliding too till everyone but Piggy was busy. Most of the wood was so rotten that when they pulled it broke up into a shower of fragments and woodlice and decay; but some trunks came out in one piece. The twins, Sam 'n Eric, were the first to get a likely log but they could do nothing till Ralph, Jack, Simon, Roger and Maurice found room for a hand-hold. Then they inched the grotesque dead thing up the rock and toppled it over on top. Each party of boys added a quota, less or more, and the pile grew. At the return Ralph found himself alone on a limb with Jack and they grinned at each other, sharing this burden. Once more, amid the breeze, the shouting, the slanting sunlight on the high mountain, was shed that glamour, that strange invisible light of friendship, adventure, and content.

"Almost too heavy."

Jack grinned back.

"Not for the two of us."

Together, joined in effort by the burden, they staggered up the last steep of the mountain. Together, they chanted One! Two! Three! and crashed the log on to the great pile. Then they stepped back, laughing with triumphant pleasure, so that immediately Ralph had to stand on his head. Below them, boys were still laboring, though some of the small ones had lost interest and were searching this new forest for fruit. Now the twins, with unsuspected intelligence, came up the mountain with armfuls of dried leaves and dumped them against the pile. One by one, as they sensed that the pile was complete, the boys stopped going back for more and stood, with the pink, shattered top of the mountain around them. Breath came evenly by now, and sweat dried.

Ralph and Jack looked at each other while society paused about them. The shameful knowledge grew in them and they did not know how to begin confession.

Ralph spoke first, crimson in the face.

"Will you?"

He cleared his throat and went on.

"Will you light the fire?"

Now the absurd situation was open, Jack blushed too. He began to mutter vaguely.

"You rub two sticks. You rub—"

He glanced at Ralph, who blurted out the last confession of incompetence.

"Has anyone got any matches?"

"You make a bow and spin the arrow," said Roger. He rubbed his hands in mime. "Psss. Psss."

A little air was moving over the mountain. Piggy came

with it, in shorts and shirt, laboring cautiously out of the forest with the evening sunlight gleaming from his glasses. He held the conch under his arm.

Ralph shouted at him.

"Piggy! Have you got any matches?"

The other boys took up the cry till the mountain rang. Piggy shook his head and came to the pile.

"My! You've made a big heap, haven't you?"

Jack pointed suddenly.

"His specs—use them as burning glasses!"

Piggy was surrounded before he could back away.

"Here—let me go!" His voice rose to a shriek of terror as Jack snatched the glasses off his face. "Mind out! Give 'em back! I can hardly see! You'll break the conch!"

Ralph elbowed him to one side and knelt by the pile.

"Stand out of the light."

There was pushing and pulling and officious cries. Ralph moved the lenses back and forth, this way and that, till a glossy white image of the declining sun lay on a piece of rotten wood. Almost at once a thin trickle of smoke rose up and made him cough. Jack knelt too and blew gently, so that the smoke drifted away, thickening, and a tiny flame appeared. The flame, nearly invisible at first in that bright sunlight, enveloped a small twig, grew, was enriched with color and reached up to a branch which exploded with a sharp crack. The flame flapped higher and the boys broke into a cheer.

"My specs!" howled Piggy. "Give me my specs!"

Ralph stood away from the pile and put the glasses into Piggy's groping hands. His voice subsided to a mutter.

"Jus' blurs, that's all. Hardly see my hand—"

The boys were dancing. The pile was so rotten, and now so tinder-dry, that whole limbs yielded passionately to the yellow flames that poured upwards and shook a great beard of flame twenty feet in the air. For yards round the fire the heat was like a blow, and the breeze was a river of sparks. Trunks crumbled to white dust.

Ralph shouted.

"More wood! All of you get more wood!"

Life became a race with the fire and the boys scattered through the upper forest. To keep a clean flag of flame flying on the mountain was the immediate end and no one looked further. Even the smallest boys, unless fruit claimed them, brought little pieces of wood and threw them in. The air moved a little faster and became a light wind, so that leeward and windward side were clearly differentiated. On one side the air was cool, but on the other the fire thrust out a savage arm of heat that crinkled hair on the instant. Boys who felt the evening wind on their damp faces paused to enjoy the freshness of it and then found they were exhausted. They flung themselves down in the shadows that lay among the shattered rocks. The beard of flame diminished quickly; then the pile fell inwards with a soft, cindery sound, and sent a great tree of sparks upwards that leaned away and drifted downwind. The boys lay, panting like dogs.

Ralph raised his head off his forearms.

"That was no good."

Roger spat efficiently into the hot dust.

"What d'you mean?"

"There wasn't any smoke. Only flame."

Piggy had settled himself in a space between two rocks, and sat with the conch on his knees.

"We haven't made a fire," he said, "what's any use. We couldn't keep a fire like that going, not if we tried."

"A fat lot you tried," said Jack contemptuously. "You just sat."

"We used his specs," said Simon, smearing a black cheek with his forearm. "He helped that way."

"I got the conch," said Piggy indignantly. "You let me speak!"

"The conch doesn't count on top of the mountain," said Jack, "so you shut up."

"I got the conch in my hand."

"Put on green branches," said Maurice. "That's the best way to make smoke."

"I got the conch—"

Jack turned fiercely.

"You shut up!"

Piggy wilted. Ralph took the conch from him and looked round the circle of boys.

"We've got to have special people for looking after the fire. Any day there may be a ship out there"—he waved his arm at the taut wire of the horizon—"and if we have a signal going they'll come and take us off. And another thing. We ought to have more rules. Where the conch is, that's a meeting. The same up here as down there."

They assented. Piggy opened his mouth to speak, caught Jack's eye and shut it again. Jack held out his hands for the conch and stood up, holding the delicate thing carefully in his sooty hands.

"I agree with Ralph. We've got to have rules and obey them. After all, we're not savages. We're English, and the English are best at everything. So we've got to do the right things."

He turned to Ralph.

"Ralph, I'll split up the choir—my hunters, that is—into groups, and we'll be responsible for keeping the fire going—"

This generosity brought a spatter of applause from the boys, so that Jack grinned at them, then waved the conch for silence.

"We'll let the fire burn out now. Who would see smoke at night-time, anyway? And we can start the fire again whenever we like. Altos, you can keep the fire going this week, and trebles the next—"

The assembly assented gravely.

"And we'll be responsible for keeping a lookout too. If we see a ship out there"—they followed the direction of his bony arm with their eyes—"we'll put green branches on. Then there'll be more smoke."

They gazed intently at the dense blue of the horizon, as if a little silhouette might appear there at any moment.

The sun in the west was a drop of burning gold that slid nearer and nearer the sill of the world. All at once they were aware of the evening as the end of light and warmth.

Roger took the conch and looked round at them gloomily.

"I've been watching the sea. There hasn't been the trace of a ship. Perhaps we'll never be rescued."

A murmur rose and swept away. Ralph took back the conch.

"I said before we'll be rescued sometime. We've just got to wait, that's all."

Daring, indignant, Piggy took the conch.

"That's what I said! I said about our meetings and things and then you said shut up—"

His voice lifted into the whine of virtuous recrimination. They stirred and began to shout him down.

"You said you wanted a small fire and you been and built a pile like a hayrick. If I say anything," cried Piggy, with bitter realism, "you say shut up; but if Jack or Maurice or Simon—"

He paused in the tumult, standing, looking beyond them and down the unfriendly side of the mountain to the great patch where they had found dead wood. Then he laughed so strangely that they were hushed, looking at the flash of his spectacles in astonishment. They followed his gaze to find the sour joke.

"You got your small fire all right."

Smoke was rising here and there among the creepers that festooned the dead or dying trees. As they watched, a flash of fire appeared at the root of one wisp, and then the smoke thickened. Small flames stirred at the trunk of a tree and crawled away through leaves and brushwood, dividing and increasing. One patch touched a tree trunk and scrambled up like a bright squirrel. The smoke increased, sifted, rolled outwards. The squirrel leapt on the wings of the wind and clung to another standing tree, eating downwards. Beneath the dark canopy of leaves and smoke the fire laid hold on the forest and began to gnaw. Acres of black and yellow smoke rolled steadily toward the sea. At the sight of the flames and the irresistible course of the fire, the boys broke into shrill, excited cheering. The flames, as though they were a kind of wild life, crept as a jaguar creeps on its belly toward a line of birch-like saplings that fledged an outcrop of the pink rock. They flapped at the first of the trees, and the branches grew a brief foliage of fire. The heart of flame leapt nimbly across the gap between the trees and then went swinging and flaring along the whole row of them. Beneath the capering boys a quarter of a mile square of forest was savage with smoke and flame. The separate noises of the fire merged into a drum-roll that seemed to shake the mountain.

"You got your small fire all right."

Startled, Ralph realized that the boys were falling still and silent, feeling the beginnings of awe at the power set free below them. The knowledge and the awe made him savage.

"Oh, shut up!"

"I got the conch," said Piggy, in a hurt voice. "I got a right to speak."

They looked at him with eyes that lacked interest in what they saw, and cocked ears at the drum-roll of the fire. Piggy glanced nervously into hell and cradled the conch.

"We got to let that burn out now. And that was our fire-wood."

He licked his lips.

"There ain't nothing we can do. We ought to be more careful. I'm scared—"

Jack dragged his eyes away from the fire.

"You're always scared. Yah—Fatty!"

"I got the conch," said Piggy bleakly. He turned to Ralph. "I got the conch, ain't I Ralph?"

Unwillingly Ralph turned away from the splendid, awful sight.

"What's that?"

"The conch. I got a right to speak."

The twins giggled together.

"We wanted smoke—"

"Now look—!"

A pall stretched for miles away from the island. All the boys except Piggy started to giggle; presently they were shrieking with laughter.

Piggy lost his temper.

"I got the conch! Just you listen! The first thing we ought to have made was shelters down there by the beach. It wasn't half cold down there in the night. But the first time Ralph says 'fire' you goes howling and screaming up this here mountain. Like a pack of kids!"

By now they were listening to the tirade.

"How can you expect to be rescued if you don't put first things first and act proper?"

He took off his glasses and made as if to put down the conch; but the sudden motion toward it of most of the older boys changed his mind. He tucked the shell under his arm, and crouched back on a rock.

"Then when you get here you build a bonfire that isn't no use. Now you been and set the whole island on fire. Won't we look funny if the whole island burns up? Cooked fruit, that's what we'll have to eat, and roast pork. And that's nothing to laugh at! You said Ralph was chief and you don't give him time to think. Then when he says something you rush off, like, like—"

He paused for breath, and the fire growled at them.

"And that's not all. Them kids. The little 'uns. Who took any notice of 'em? Who knows how many we got?"

Ralph took a sudden step forward.

"I told you to. I told you to get a list of names!"

"How could I," cried Piggy indignantly, "all by myself? They waited for two minutes, then they fell in the sea; they went into the forest; they just scattered everywhere. How was I to know which was which?"

Ralph licked pale lips.

"Then you don't know how many of us there ought to be?"

"How could I with them little 'uns running round like insects? Then when you three came back, as soon as you said make a fire, they all ran away, and I never had a chance—"

"That's enough!" said Ralph sharply, and snatched back the conch. "If you didn't you didn't."

"—then you come up here an' pinch my specs—"

Jack turned on him.

"You shut up!"

"—and them little 'uns was wandering about down there where the fire is. How d'you know they aren't still there?"

Piggy stood up and pointed to the smoke and flames. A murmur rose among the boys and died away. Something strange was happening to Piggy, for he was gasping for breath.

"That little 'un—" gasped Piggy—"him with the mark on his face, I don't see him. Where is he now?"

The crowd was as silent as death.

"Him that talked about the snakes. He was down there—"

A tree exploded in the fire like a bomb. Tall swathes of creepers rose for a moment into view, agonized, and went down again. The little boys screamed at them.

"Snakes! Snakes! Look at the snakes!"

In the west, and unheeded, the sun lay only an inch or two above the sea. Their faces were lit redly from beneath. Piggy fell against a rock and clutched it with both hands.

"That little 'un that had a mark on his face—where is —he now? I tell you I don't see him."

The boys looked at each other fearfully, unbelieving.

"—where is he now?"

Ralph muttered the reply as if in shame.

"Perhaps he went back to the, the—"

Beneath them, on the unfriendly side of the mountain, the drum-roll continued.

# CHAPTER THREE

## *Huts on the Beach*

Jack was bent double. He was down like a sprinter, his nose only a few inches from the humid earth. The tree trunks and the creepers that festooned them lost themselves in a green dusk thirty feet above him, and all about was the undergrowth. There was only the faintest indication of a trail here; a cracked twig and what might be the impression of one side of a hoof. He lowered his chin and stared at the traces as though he would force them to speak to him. Then dog-like, uncomfortably on all fours yet unheeding his discomfort, he stole forward five yards and stopped. Here was loop of creeper with a tendril pendant from a node. The tendril was polished on the underside; pigs, passing through the loop, brushed it with their bristly hide.

Jack crouched with his face a few inches away from this clue, then stared forward into the semi-darkness of the undergrowth. His sandy hair, considerably longer than it had been when they dropped in, was lighter now; and his bare back was a mass of dark freckles and peeling sunburn. A sharpened stick about five feet long trailed from his right hand, and except for a pair of tattered shorts held up by his knife-belt he was naked. He closed his eyes, raised his head and breathed in gently with flared nostrils, assessing the current of warm air for information. The forest and he were very still.

At length he let out his breath in a long sigh and opened his eyes. They were bright blue, eyes that in this frustration seemed bolting and nearly mad. He passed his tongue across dry lips and scanned the uncommunicative forest. Then again he stole forward and cast this way and that over the ground.

The silence of the forest was more oppressive than the heat, and at this hour of the day there was not even the whine of insects. Only when Jack himself roused a gaudy bird from a primitive nest of sticks was the silence shattered and echoes set ringing by a harsh cry that seemed to come out of the abyss of ages. Jack himself shrank at this cry with a hiss of indrawn breath, and for a minute became less a hunter than a furtive thing, ape-like among the tangle of trees. Then the trail, the frustration, claimed him again and he searched the ground avidly. By the trunk of a vast tree that grew pale flowers on its grey bark he checked, closed his eyes, and once more drew in the warm air; and this time his breath came short, there was even a passing pallor in his face, and then the surge of blood again. He passed like a shadow under the darkness of the tree and crouched, looking down at the trodden ground at his feet.

The droppings were warm. They lay piled among turned earth. They were olive green, smooth, and they steamed a little. Jack lifted his head and stared at the inscrutable masses of creeper that lay across the trail. Then he raised his spear and sneaked forward. Beyond the creeper, the trail joined a pig-run that was wide enough and trodden enough to be a path. The ground was hardened by an accustomed tread and as Jack rose to his full height he heard something moving on it. He swung back his right arm and hurled the spear with all his strength. From the pig-run came the quick, hard patter of hoofs, a castanet sound, seductive, maddening—the promise of meat. He rushed out of the undergrowth and snatched up his spear. The pattering of pig's trotters died away in the distance.

Jack stood there, streaming with sweat, streaked with brown earth, stained by all the vicissitudes of a day's hunting. Swearing, he turned off the trail and pushed his way through until the forest opened a little and instead of bald trunks supporting a dark roof there were light grey trunks and crowns of feathery palm. Beyond these was the glitter of the sea and he could hear voices. Ralph was standing by a contraption of palm trunks and leaves, a rude shelter that faced the lagoon and seemed very near to falling down. He did not notice when Jack spoke.

"Got any water?"

Ralph looked up, frowning, from the complication of leaves. He did not notice Jack even when he saw him.

"I said have you got any water? I'm thirsty."

Ralph withdrew his attention from the shelter and realized Jack with a start.

"Oh, hullo. Water? There by the tree. Ought to be some left."

Jack took up a coconut shell that brimmed with fresh water from among a group that was arranged in the shade, and drank. The water splashed over his chin and neck and chest. He breathed noisily when he had finished.

"Needed that."

Simon spoke from inside the shelter.

"Up a bit."

Ralph turned to the shelter and lifted a branch with a whole tiling of leaves.

The leaves came apart and fluttered down. Simon's contrite face appeared in the hole.

"Sorry."

Ralph surveyed the wreck with distaste.

"Never get it done."

He flung himself down at Jack's feet. Simon remained, looking out of the hole in the shelter. Once down, Ralph explained.

"Been working for days now. And look!"

Two shelters were in position, but shaky. This one was a ruin.

"And they keep running off. You remember the meeting? How everyone was going to work hard until the shelters were finished?"

"Except me and my hunters—"

"Except the hunters. Well, the littluns are—"

He gesticulated, sought for a word.

"They're hopeless. The older ones aren't much better. D'you see? All day I've been working with Simon. No one else. They're off bathing, or eating, or playing."

Simon poked his head out carefully.

"You're chief. You tell 'em off."

Ralph lay flat and looked up at the palm trees and the sky.

"Meetings. Don't we love meetings? Every day. Twice a day. We talk." He got on one elbow. "I bet if I blew the conch this minute, they'd come running. Then we'd be, you know, very solemn, and someone would say we ought to build a jet, or a submarine, or a TV set. When the meeting was over they'd work for five minutes, then wander off or go hunting."

Jack flushed.

"We want meat."

"Well, we haven't got any yet. And we want shelters. Besides, the rest of your hunters came back hours ago. They've been swimming."

"I went on," said Jack. "I let them go. I had to go on. I—"

He tried to convey the compulsion to track down and kill that was swallowing him up.

"I went on. I thought, by myself—"

The madness came into his eyes again.

"I thought I might kill."

"But you didn't."

"I thought I might."

Some hidden passion vibrated in Ralph's voice.

"But you haven't yet."

His invitation might have passed as casual, were it not for the undertone.

"You wouldn't care to help with the shelters, I suppose?"

"We want meat—"

"And we don't get it."

Now the antagonism was audible.

"But I shall! Next time! I've got to get a barb on this spear! We wounded a pig and the spear fell out. If we could only make barbs—"

"We need shelters."

Suddenly Jack shouted in rage.

"Are you accusing—?"

"All I'm saying is we've worked dashed hard. That's all."

They were both red in the face and found looking at each other difficult. Ralph rolled on his stomach and began to play with the grass.

"If it rains like when we dropped in we'll need shelters all right. And then another thing. We need shelters because of the—"

He paused for a moment and they both pushed their anger away. Then he went on with the safe, changed subject.

"You've noticed, haven't you?"

Jack put down his spear and squatted.

"Noticed what?"

"Well. They're frightened."

He rolled over and peered into Jack's fierce, dirty face.

"I mean the way things are. They dream. You can hear 'em. Have you been awake at night?"

Jack shook his head.

"They talk and scream. The littluns. Even some of the others. As if—"

"As if it wasn't a good island."

Astonished at the interruption, they looked up at Simon's serious face.

"As if," said Simon, "the beastie, the beastie or the snake-thing, was real. Remember?"

The two older boys flinched when they heard the shameful syllable. Snakes were not mentioned now, were not mentionable.

"As if this wasn't a good island," said Ralph slowly. "Yes, that's right."

Jack sat up and stretched out his legs.

"They're batty."

"Crackers. Remember when we went exploring?"

They grinned at each other, remembering the glamour of the first day. Ralph went on.

"So we need shelters as a sort of—"

"Home."

"That's right."

Jack drew up his legs, clasped his knees, and frowned in an effort to attain clarity.

"All the same—in the forest. I mean when you're hunting, not when you're getting fruit, of course, but when you're on your own—"

He paused for a moment, not sure if Ralph would take him seriously.

"Go on."

"If you're hunting sometimes you catch yourself feeling as if—" He flushed suddenly. "There's nothing in it of course. Just a feeling. But you can feel as if you're not hunting, but—being hunted, as if something's behind you all the time in the jungle."

They were silent again: Simon intent, Ralph incredulous and faintly indignant. He sat up, rubbing one shoulder with a dirty hand.

"Well, I don't know."

Jack leapt to his feet and spoke very quickly.

"That's how you can feel in the forest. Of course there's nothing in it. Only—only—"

He took a few rapid steps toward the beach, then came back.

"Only I know how they feel. See? That's all."

"The best thing we can do is get ourselves rescued."

Jack had to think for a moment before he could remember what rescue was.

"Rescue? Yes, of course! All the same, I'd like to catch a pig first—" He snatched up his spear and dashed it into the ground. The opaque, mad look came into his eyes again. Ralph looked at him critically through his tangle of fair hair.

"So long as your hunters remember the fire—"

"You and your fire!"

The two boys trotted down the beach, and, turning at the water's edge, looked back at the pink mountain. The trickle of smoke sketched a chalky line up the solid blue of the sky, wavered high up and faded. Ralph frowned.

"I wonder how far off you could see that."

"Miles."

"We don't make enough smoke."

The bottom part of the trickle, as though conscious of their gaze, thickened to a creamy blur which crept up the feeble column.

"They've put on green branches," muttered Ralph. "I wonder!" He screwed up his eyes and swung round to search the horizon.

"Got it!"

Jack shouted so loudly that Ralph jumped.

"What? Where? Is it a ship?"

But Jack was pointing to the high declivities that led down from the mountain to the flatter part of the island.

"Of course! They'll lie up there—they must, when the sun's too hot—"

Ralph gazed bewildered at his rapt face.

"—they get up high. High up and in the shade, resting during the heat, like cows at home—"

"I thought you saw a ship!"

"We could steal up on one—paint our faces so they wouldn't see—perhaps surround them and then—"

Indignation took away Ralph's control.

"I was talking about smoke! Don't you want to be rescued? All you can talk about is pig, pig, pig!"

"But we want meat!"

"And I work all day with nothing but Simon and you come back and don't even notice the huts!"

"I was working too—"

"But you like it!" shouted Ralph. "You want to hunt! While I—"

They faced each other on the bright beach, astonished at the rub of feeling. Ralph looked away first, pretending interest in a group of littluns on the sand. From beyond the platform came the shouting of the hunters in the swimming pool. On the end of the platform Piggy was lying flat, looking down into the brilliant water.

"People don't help much."

He wanted to explain how people were never quite what you thought they were.

"Simon. He helps." He pointed at the shelters.

"All the rest rushed off. He's done as much as I have. Only—"

"Simon's always about."

Ralph started back to the shelters with Jack by his side.

"Do a bit for you," muttered Jack, "before I have a bathe."

"Don't bother."

But when they reached the shelters Simon was not to be seen. Ralph put his head in the hole, withdrew it, and turned to Jack.

"He's buzzed off."

"Got fed up," said Jack, "and gone for a bathe."

Ralph frowned.

"He's queer. He's funny."

Jack nodded, as much for the sake of agreeing as anything, and by tacit consent they left the shelter and went toward the bathing pool.

"And then," said Jack, "when I've had a bathe and something to eat, I'll just trek over to the other side of the mountain and see if I can see any traces. Coming?"

"But the sun's nearly set!"

"I might have time—"

They walked along, two continents of experience and feeling, unable to communicate.

"If I could only get a pig!"

"I'll come back and go on with the shelter."

They looked at each other, baffled, in love and hate. All the warm salt water of the bathing pool and the shouting and splashing and laughing were only just sufficient to bring them together again.

Simon was not in the bathing pool as they had expected. When the other two had trotted down the beach to look back at the mountain he had followed them for a few yards and then stopped. He had stood frowning down at a pile of sand on the beach where somebody had been trying to build a little house or hut. Then he turned his back on this and walked into the forest with an air of purpose. He was a small, skinny boy, his chin pointed, and his eyes so bright they had deceived Ralph into thinking him delightfully gay and wicked. The coarse mop of black hair was long and swung down, almost concealing a low, broad forehead. He wore the remains of shorts and his feet were bare like Jack's. Always darkish in color, Simon was burned by the sun to a deep tan that glistened with sweat.

He picked his way up the scar, passed the great rock where Ralph had climbed on the first morning, then turned off to his right among the trees. He walked with an accustomed tread through the acres of fruit trees, where the least energetic could find an easy if unsatisfying meal. Flower and fruit grew together on the same tree and everywhere was the scent of ripeness and the booming of a million bees at pasture. Here the littluns who had run after him caught up with him. They talked, cried out unintelligibly, lugged him toward the trees. Then, amid the roar of bees in the afternoon sunlight, Simon found for them the fruit they could not reach, pulled off the choicest from up in the foliage, passed them back down to the endless, outstretched hands. When he had satisfied them he paused and looked round. The littluns watched him inscrutably over double handfuls of ripe fruit.

Simon turned away from them and went where the just perceptible path led him. Soon high jungle closed in. Tall trunks bore unexpected pale flowers all the way up to the dark canopy where life went on clamorously. The air here was dark too, and the creepers dropped their ropes like the rigging of foundered ships. His feet left prints in the soft soil and the creepers shivered throughout their lengths when he bumped them.

He came at last to a place where more sunshine fell. Since they had not so far to go for light the creepers had woven a great mat that hung at the side of an open space in the jungle; for here a patch of rock came close to the surface and would not allow more than little plants and ferns to grow. The whole space was walled with dark aromatic bushes, and was a bowl of heat and light. A great tree, fallen across one corner, leaned against the trees that still stood and a rapid climber flaunted red and yellow sprays right to the top.

Simon paused. He looked over his shoulder as Jack had done at the close ways behind him and glanced swiftly round to confirm that he was utterly alone. For a moment his movements were almost furtive. Then he bent down and wormed his way into the center of the mat. The creepers and the bushes were so close that he left his sweat on them and they pulled together behind him. When he was secure in the middle he was in a little cabin screened off from the open space by a few leaves. He squatted down, parted the leaves and looked out into the clearing. Nothing moved but a pair of gaudy butterflies that danced round each other in the hot air. Holding his breath he cocked a critical ear at the sounds of the island. Evening was advancing toward the island; the sounds of the bright fantastic birds, the bee-sounds, even the crying of the gulls that were returning to their roosts among the square rocks, were fainter. The deep sea breaking miles away on the reef made an undertone less perceptible than the susurration of the blood.

Simon dropped the screen of leaves back into place. The slope of the bars of honey-colored sunlight decreased; they slid up the bushes, passed over the green candle-like buds, moved up toward the canopy, and darkness thickened under the trees. With the fading of the light the riotous colors died and the heat and urgency cooled away. The candle-buds stirred. Their green sepals drew back a little and the white tips of the flowers rose delicately to meet the open air.

Now the sunlight had lifted clear of the open space and withdrawn from the sky. Darkness poured out, submerging the ways between the trees till they were dim and strange as the bottom of the sea. The candle-buds opened their wide white flowers glimmering under the light that pricked down from the first stars. Their scent spilled out into the air and took possession of the island.

# CHAPTER FOUR

## *Painted Faces and Long Hair*

The first rhythm that they became used to was the slow swing from dawn to quick dusk. They accepted the pleasures of morning, the bright sun, the whelming sea and sweet air, as a time when play was good and life so full that hope was not necessary and therefore forgotten. Toward noon, as the floods of light fell more nearly to the perpendicular, the stark colors of the morning were smoothed in pearl and opalescence; and the heat—as though the impending sun's height gave it momentum—became a blow that they ducked, running to the shade and lying there, perhaps even sleeping.

Strange things happened at midday. The glittering sea rose up, moved apart in planes of blatant impossibility; the coral reef and the few stunted palms that clung to the more elevated parts would float up into the sky, would quiver, be plucked apart, run like raindrops on a wire or be repeated as in an odd succession of mirrors. Sometimes land loomed where there was no land and flicked out like a bubble as the children watched. Piggy discounted all this learnedly as a "mirage"; and since no boy could reach even the reef over the stretch of water where the snapping sharks waited, they grew accustomed to these mysteries and ignored them, just as they ignored the miraculous, throbbing stars. At midday the illusions merged into the sky and there the sun gazed down like an angry eye. Then, at the end of the afternoon, the mirage subsided and the horizon became level and blue and clipped as the sun declined. That was another time of comparative coolness but menaced by the coming of the dark. When the sun sank, darkness dropped on the island like an extinguisher and

53

soon the shelters were full of restlessness, under the remote stars.

Nevertheless, the northern European tradition of work, play, and food right through the day, made it impossible for them to adjust themselves wholly to this new rhythm. The littlun Percival had early crawled into a shelter and stayed there for two days, talking, singing, and crying, till they thought him batty and were faintly amused. Ever since then he had been peaked, red-eyed, and miserable; a littlun who played little and cried often.

The smaller boys were known now by the generic title of "littluns." The decrease in size, from Ralph down, was gradual; and though there was a dubious region inhabited by Simon and Robert and Maurice, nevertheless no one had any difficulty in recognizing biguns at one end and littluns at the other. The undoubted littluns, those aged about six, led a quite distinct, and at the same time intense, life of their own. They ate most of the day, picking fruit where they could reach it and not particular about ripeness and quality. They were used now to stomach-aches and a sort of chronic diarrhoea. They suffered untold terrors in the dark and huddled together for comfort. Apart from food and sleep, they found time for play, aimless and trivial, in the white sand by the bright water. They cried for their mothers much less often than might have been expected; they were very brown, and filthily dirty. They obeyed the summons of the conch, partly because Ralph blew it, and he was big enough to be a link with the adult world of authority; and partly because they enjoyed the entertainment of the assemblies. But otherwise they seldom bothered with the biguns and their passionately emotional and corporate life was their own.

They had built castles in the sand at the bar of the little river. These castles were about one foot high and were decorated with shells, withered flowers, and interesting stones. Round the castles was a complex of marks, tracks, walls, railway lines, that were of significance only if inspected with the eye at beach-level. The littluns played here, if not happily at least with absorbed attention; and often as many as three of them would play the same game together.

Three were playing here now. Henry was the biggest of them. He was also a distant relative of that other boy whose mulberry-marked face had not been seen since the evening of the great fire; but he was not old enough to understand this, and if he had been told that the other boy had gone home in an aircraft, he would have accepted the statement without fuss or disbelief.

Henry was a bit of a leader this afternoon, because the other two were Percival and Johnny, the smallest boys on the island. Percival was mouse-colored and had not been very attractive even to his mother; Johnny was well built, with fair hair and a natural belligerence. Just now he was being obedient because he was interested; and the three children, kneeling in the sand, were at peace.

Roger and Maurice came out of the forest. They were relieved from duty at the fire and had come down for a swim. Roger led the way straight through the castles, kicking them over, burying the flowers, scattering the chosen stones. Maurice followed, laughing, and added to the destruction. The three littluns paused in their game and looked up. As it happened, the particular marks in which they were interested had not been touched, so they made no protest. Only Percival began to whimper with an eyeful of sand and Maurice hurried away. In his other life Maurice had received chastisement for filling a younger eye with sand. Now, though there was no parent to let fall a heavy hand, Maurice still felt the unease of wrongdoing. At the back of his mind formed the uncertain outlines of an excuse. He muttered something about a swim and broke into a trot.

Roger remained, watching the littluns. He was not noticeably darker than when he had dropped in, but the shock of black hair, down his nape and low on his forehead, seemed to suit his gloomy face and made what had seemed at first an unsociable remoteness into something forbidding. Percival finished his whimper and went on playing, for the tears had washed the sand away. Johnny watched him with china-blue eyes; then began to fling up sand in a shower, and presently Percival was crying again.

When Henry tired of his play and wandered off along the beach, Roger followed him, keeping beneath the palms and drifting casually in the same direction. Henry walked at a distance from the palms and the shade because he was too young to keep himself out of the sun. He went down the beach and busied himself at the water's edge. The great Pacific tide was coming in and every few seconds the relatively still water of the lagoon heaved forwards an inch. There were creatures that lived in this last fling of the sea, tiny transparencies that came questing in with the water over the hot, dry sand. With impalpable organs of sense they examined this new field. Perhaps food had appeared where at the last incursion there had been none; bird droppings, insects perhaps, any of the strewn detritus of landward life. Like a myriad of tiny teeth in a saw, the transparencies came scavenging over the beach.

This was fascinating to Henry. He poked about with a bit of stick, that itself was wave-worn and whitened and a vagrant, and tried to control the motions of the scavengers. He made little runnels that the tide filled and tried to crowd them with creatures. He became absorbed beyond mere happiness as he felt himself exercising control over living things. He talked to them, urging them, ordering them. Driven back by the tide, his footprints became bays in which they were trapped and gave him the illusion of mastery. He squatted on his hams at the water's edge, bowed, with a shock of hair falling over his forehead and past his eyes, and the afternoon sun emptied down invisible arrows.

Roger waited too. At first he had hidden behind a great palm; but Henry's absorption with the transparencies was so obvious that at last he stood out in full view. He looked along the beach. Percival had gone off, crying, and Johnny was left in triumphant possession of the castles. He sat there, crooning to himself and throwing sand at an imaginary Percival. Beyond him, Roger could see the platform and the glints of spray where Ralph and Simon and Piggy and Maurice were diving in the pool. He listened carefully but could only just hear them.

A sudden breeze shook the fringe of palm trees, so that the fronds tossed and fluttered. Sixty feet above Roger, several nuts, fibrous lumps as big as rugby balls, were loosed from their stems. They fell about him with a series of hard thumps and he was not touched. Roger did not consider his escape, but looked from the nuts to Henry and back again.

The subsoil beneath the palm trees was a raised beach, and generations of palms had worked loose in this the stones that had lain on the sands of another shore. Roger stooped, picked up a stone, aimed, and threw it at Henry

—threw it to miss. The stone, that token of preposterous
time, bounced five yards to Henry's right and fell in the
water. Roger gathered a handful of stones and began to
throw them. Yet there was a space round Henry, perhaps
six yards in diameter, into which he dare not throw. Here,
invisible yet strong, was the taboo of the old life. Round
the squatting child was the protection of parents and school
and policemen and the law. Roger's arm was conditioned
by a civilization that knew nothing of him and was in ruins.

Henry was surprised by the plopping sounds in the
water. He abandoned the noiseless transparencies and
pointed at the center of the spreading rings like a setter.
This side and that the stones fell, and Henry turned obediently but always too late to see the stones in the air. At
last he saw one and laughed, looking for the friend who
was teasing him. But Roger had whipped behind the palm
again, was leaning against it breathing quickly, his eyelids
fluttering. Then Henry lost interest in stones and wandered
off.

"Roger."

Jack was standing under a tree about ten yards away.
When Roger opened his eyes and saw him, a darker
shadow crept beneath the swarthiness of his skin; but Jack
noticed nothing. He was eager, impatient, beckoning, so
that Roger went to him.

There was a small pool at the end of the river, dammed
back by sand and full of white water-lilies and needle-like
reeds. Here Sam and Eric were waiting, and Bill. Jack, concealed from the sun, knelt by the pool and opened the two
large leaves that he carried. One of them contained white
clay, and the other red. By them lay a stick of charcoal
brought down from the fire.

Jack explained to Roger as he worked.

"They don't smell me. They see me, I think. Something
pink, under the trees."

He smeared on the clay.

"If only I'd some green!"

He turned a half-concealed face up to Roger and answered the incomprehension of his gaze.

"For hunting. Like in the war. You know—dazzle paint.
Like things trying to look like something else—" He twisted
in the urgency of telling. "—Like moths on a tree trunk."

Roger understood and nodded gravely. The twins moved toward Jack and began to protest timidly about something. Jack waved them away.

"Shut up."

He rubbed the charcoal stick between the patches of red and white on his face.

"No. You two come with me."

He peered at his reflection and disliked it. He bent down, took up a double handful of lukewarm water and rubbed the mess from his face. Freckles and sandy eyebrows appeared.

Roger smiled, unwillingly.

"You don't half look a mess."

Jack planned his new face. He made one cheek and one eye-socket white, then he rubbed red over the other half of his face and slashed a black bar of charcoal across from right ear to left jaw. He looked in the pool for his reflection, but his breathing troubled the mirror.

"Samneric. Get me a coconut. An empty one."

He knelt, holding the shell of water. A rounded patch of sunlight fell on his face and a brightness appeared in the depths of the water. He looked in astonishment, no longer at himself but at an awesome stranger. He spilt the water and leapt to his feet, laughing excitedly. Beside the pool his sinewy body held up a mask that drew their eyes and appalled them. He began to dance and his laughter became a bloodthirsty snarling. He capered toward Bill, and the mask was a thing on its own, behind which Jack hid, liberated from shame and self-consciousness. The face of red and white and black swung through the air and jigged toward Bill. Bill started up laughing; then suddenly he fell silent and blundered away through the bushes.

Jack rushed toward the twins.

"The rest are making a line. Come on!"

"But—"

"—we—"

"Come on! I'll creep up and stab—"

The mask compelled them.

Ralph climbed out of the bathing pool and trotted up the beach and sat in the shade beneath the palms. His fair hair was plastered over his eyebrows and he pushed it back. Simon was floating in the water and kicking with his feet, and Maurice was practicing diving. Piggy was mooning about, aimlessly picking up things and discarding them. The rock-pools which so fascinated him were covered by the tide, so he was without an interest until the tide went back. Presently, seeing Ralph under the palms, he came and sat by him.

Piggy wore the remainders of a pair of shorts, his fat body was golden brown, and the glasses still flashed when he looked at anything. He was the only boy on the island whose hair never seemed to grow. The rest were shockheaded, but Piggy's hair still lay in wisps over his head as though baldness were his natural state and this imperfect covering would soon go, like the velvet on a young stag's antlers.

"I've been thinking," he said, "about a clock. We could make a sundial. We could put a stick in the sand, and then—"

The effort to express the mathematical processes involved was too great. He made a few passes instead.

"And an airplane, and a TV set," said Ralph sourly, "and a steam engine."

Piggy shook his head.

"You have to have a lot of metal things for that," he said, "and we haven't got no metal. But we got a stick."

Ralph turned and smiled involuntarily. Piggy was a bore; his fat, his ass-mar and his matter-of-fact ideas were dull, but there was always a little pleasure to be got out of pulling his leg, even if one did it by accident.

Piggy saw the smile and misinterpreted it as friendliness. There had grown up tacitly among the biguns the opinion that Piggy was an outsider, not only by accent, which did not matter, but by fat, and ass-mar, and specs, and a certain disinclination for manual labor. Now, finding that something he had said made Ralph smile, he rejoiced and pressed his advantage.

"We got a lot of sticks. We could have a sundial each. Then we should know what the time was."

"A fat lot of good that would be."

"You said you wanted things done. So as we could be rescued."

"Oh, shut up."

He leapt to his feet and trotted back to the pool, just as

Maurice did a rather poor dive. Ralph was glad of a chance to change the subject. He shouted as Maurice came to the surface.

"Belly flop! Belly flop!"

Maurice flashed a smile at Ralph who slid easily into the water. Of all the boys, he was the most at home there; but today, irked by the mention of rescue, the useless, footling mention of rescue, even the green depths of water and the shattered, golden sun held no balm. Instead of remaining and playing, he swam with steady strokes under Simon and crawled out of the other side of the pool to lie there, sleek and streaming like a seal. Piggy, always clumsy, stood up and came to stand by him, so that Ralph rolled on his stomach and pretended not to see. The mirages had died away and gloomily he ran his eye along the taut blue line of the horizon.

The next moment he was on his feet and shouting.

"Smoke! Smoke!"

Simon tried to sit up in the water and got a mouthful. Maurice, who had been standing ready to dive, swayed back on his heels, made a bolt for the platform, then swerved back to the grass under the palms. There he started to pull on his tattered shorts, to be ready for anything.

Ralph stood, one hand holding back his hair, the other clenched. Simon was climbing out of the water. Piggy was rubbing his glasses on his shorts and squinting at the sea. Maurice had got both legs through one leg of his shorts. Of all the boys, only Ralph was still.

"I can't see no smoke," said Piggy incredulously. "I can't see no smoke, Ralph—where is it?"

Ralph said nothing. Now both his hands were clenched over his forehead so that the fair hair was kept out of his eyes. He was leaning forward and already the salt was whitening his body.

"Ralph—where's the ship?"

Simon stood by, looking from Ralph to the horizon. Maurice's trousers gave way with a sigh and he abandoned them as a wreck, rushed toward the forest, and then came back again.

The smoke was a tight little knot on the horizon and was uncoiling slowly. Beneath the smoke was a dot that might be a funnel. Ralph's face was pale as he spoke to himself.

"They'll see our smoke."

Piggy was looking in the right direction now.

"It don't look much."

He turned round and peered up at the mountain. Ralph continued to watch the ship, ravenously. Color was coming back into his face. Simon stood by him, silent.

"I know I can't see very much," said Piggy, "but have we got any smoke?"

Ralph moved impatiently, still watching the ship.

"The smoke on the mountain."

Maurice came running, and stared out to sea. Both Simon and Piggy were looking up at the mountain. Piggy screwed up his face but Simon cried out as though he had hurt himself.

"Ralph! Ralph!"

The quality of his speech twisted Ralph on the sand.

"You tell me," said Piggy anxiously. "Is there a signal?"

Ralph looked back at the dispersing smoke on the horizon, then up at the mountain.

"Ralph—please! Is there a signal?"

Simon put out his hand, timidly, to touch Ralph; but Ralph started to run, splashing through the shallow end of the bathing pool, across the hot, white sand and under the palms. A moment later he was battling with the complex undergrowth that was already engulfing the scar. Simon ran after him, then Maurice. Piggy shouted.

"Ralph! Please—Ralph!"

Then he too started to run, stumbling over Maurice's discarded shorts before he was across the terrace. Behind the four boys, the smoke moved gently along the horizon; and on the beach, Henry and Johnny were throwing sand at Percival who was crying quietly again; and all three were in complete ignorance of the excitement.

By the time Ralph had reached the landward end of the scar he was using precious breath to swear. He did desperate violence to his naked body among the rasping creepers so that blood was sliding over him. Just where the steep ascent of the mountain began, he stopped. Maurice was only a few yards behind him.

"Piggy's specs!" shouted Ralph. "If the fire's all out, we'll need them—"

He stopped shouting and swayed on his feet. Piggy was only just visible, bumbling up from the beach. Ralph looked at the horizon, then up to the mountain. Was it better to fetch Piggy's glasses, or would the ship have gone? Or if they climbed on, supposing the fire was all out, and they had to watch Piggy crawling nearer and the ship sinking under the horizon? Balanced on a high peak of need, agonized by indecision, Ralph cried out:

"Oh God, oh God!"

Simon, struggling with bushes, caught his breath. His face was twisted. Ralph blundered on, savaging himself, as the wisp of smoke moved on.

The fire was dead. They saw that straight away; saw what they had really known down on the beach when the smoke of home had beckoned. The fire was out, smokeless and dead; the watchers were gone. A pile of unused fuel lay ready.

Ralph turned to the sea. The horizon stretched, impersonal once more, barren of all but the faintest trace of smoke. Ralph ran stumbling along the rocks, saved himself on the edge of the pink cliff, and screamed at the ship:

"Come back! Come back!"

He ran backwards and forwards along the cliff, his face always to the sea, and his voice rose insanely.

"Come back! Come back!"

Simon and Maurice arrived. Ralph looked at them with unwinking eyes. Simon turned away, smearing the water from his cheeks. Ralph reached inside himself for the worst word he knew.

"They let the bloody fire go out."

He looked down the unfriendly side of the mountain. Piggy arrived, out of breath and whimpering like a littlun. Ralph clenched his fist and went very red. The intentness of his gaze, the bitterness of his voice, pointed for him.

"There they are."

A procession had appeared, far down among the pink stones that lay near the water's edge. Some of the boys wore black caps but otherwise they were almost naked. They lifted sticks in the air together whenever they came to an easy patch. They were chanting, something to do with the bundle that the errant twins carried so carefully. Ralph picked out Jack easily, even at that distance, tall, red-haired, and inevitably leading the procession.

Simon looked now, from Ralph to Jack, as he had looked

from Ralph to the horizon, and what he saw seemed to make him afraid. Ralph said nothing more, but waited while the procession came nearer. The chant was audible but at that distance still wordless. Behind Jack walked the twins, carrying a great stake on their shoulders. The gutted carcass of a pig swung from the stake, swinging heavily as the twins toiled over the uneven ground. The pig's head hung down with gaping neck and seemed to search for something on the ground. At last the words of the chant floated up to them, across the bowl of blackened wood and ashes.

"*Kill the pig. Cut her throat. Spill her blood.*"

Yet as the words became audible, the procession reached the steepest part of the mountain, and in a minute or two the chant had died away. Piggy sniveled and Simon shushed him quickly as though he had spoken too loudly in church.

Jack, his face smeared with clays, reached the top first and hailed Ralph excitedly, with lifted spear.

"Look! We've killed a pig—we stole up on them—we got in a circle—"

Voices broke in from the hunters.

"We got in a circle—"

"We crept up—"

"The pig squealed—"

The twins stood with the pig swinging between them, dropping black gouts on the rock. They seemed to share one wide, ecstatic grin. Jack had too many things to tell Ralph at once. Instead, he danced a step or two, then remembered his dignity and stood still, grinning. He noticed blood on his hands and grimaced distastefully, looked for something on which to clean them, then wiped them on his shorts and laughed.

Ralph spoke.

"You let the fire go out."

Jack checked, vaguely irritated by this irrelevance but too happy to let it worry him.

"We can light the fire again. You should have been with us, Ralph. We had a smashing time. The twins got knocked over—"

"We hit the pig—"

"—I fell on top—"

"I cut the pig's throat," said Jack, proudly, and yet twitched as he said it. "Can I borrow yours, Ralph, to make a nick in the hilt?"

The boys chattered and danced. The twins continued to grin.

"There was lashings of blood," said Jack, laughing and shuddering, "you should have seen it!"

"We'll go hunting every day—"

Ralph spoke again, hoarsely. He had not moved.

"You let the fire go out."

This repetition made Jack uneasy. He looked at the twins and then back at Ralph.

"We had to have them in the hunt," he said, "or there wouldn't have been enough for a ring."

He flushed, conscious of a fault.

"The fire's only been out an hour or two. We can light up again—"

He noticed Ralph's scarred nakedness, and the sombre silence of all four of them. He sought, charitable in his happiness, to include them in the thing that had happened. His mind was crowded with memories; memories of the knowledge that had come to them when they closed in on the struggling pig, knowledge that they had outwitted a living thing, imposed their will upon it, taken away its life like a long satisfying drink.

He spread his arms wide.

"You should have seen the blood!"

The hunters were more silent now, but at this they buzzed again. Ralph flung back his hair. One arm pointed at the empty horizon. His voice was loud and savage, and struck them into silence.

"There was a ship."

Jack, faced at once with too many awful implications, ducked away from them. He laid a hand on the pig and drew his knife. Ralph brought his arm down, fist clenched, and his voice shook.

"There was a ship. Out there. You said you'd keep the fire going and you let it out!" He took a step toward Jack, who turned and faced him.

"They might have seen us. We might have gone home—"

This was too bitter for Piggy, who forgot his timidity

in the agony of his loss. He began to cry out, shrilly:

"You and your blood, Jack Merridew! You and your hunting! We might have gone home—"

Ralph pushed Piggy to one side.

"I was chief, and you were going to do what I said. You talk. But you can't even build huts—then you go off hunting and let out the fire—"

He turned away, silent for a moment. Then his voice came again on a peak of feeling.

"There was a ship—"

One of the smaller hunters began to wail. The dismal truth was filtering through to everybody. Jack went very red as he hacked and pulled at the pig.

"The job was too much. We needed everyone."

Ralph turned.

"You could have had everyone when the shelters were finished. But you had to hunt—"

"We needed meat."

Jack stood up as he said this, the bloodied knife in his hand. The two boys faced each other. There was the brilliant world of hunting, tactics, fierce exhilaration, skill; and there was the world of longing and baffled common-sense. Jack transferred the knife to his left hand and smudged blood over his forehead as he pushed down the plastered hair.

Piggy began again.

"You didn't ought to have let that fire out. You said you'd keep the smoke going—"

This from Piggy, and the wails of agreement from some of the hunters, drove Jack to violence. The bolting look came into his blue eyes. He took a step, and able at last to hit someone, stuck his fist into Piggy's stomach. Piggy sat down with a grunt. Jack stood over him. His voice was vicious with humiliation.

"You would, would you? Fatty!"

Ralph made a step forward and Jack smacked Piggy's head. Piggy's glasses flew off and tinkled on the rocks. Piggy cried out in terror:

"My specs!"

He went crouching and feeling over the rocks but Simon, who got there first, found them for him. Passions beat about Simon on the mountain-top with awful wings.

"One side's broken."

Piggy grabbed and put on the glasses. He looked malevolently at Jack.

"I got to have them specs. Now I only got one eye. Jus' you wait—"

Jack made a move toward Piggy who scrambled away till a great rock lay between them. He thrust his head over the top and glared at Jack through his one flashing glass.

"Now I only got one eye. Just you wait—"

Jack mimicked the whine and scramble.

"Jus' you wait—yah!"

Piggy and the parody were so funny that the hunters began to laugh. Jack felt encouraged. He went on scrambling and the laughter rose to a gale of hysteria. Unwillingly Ralph felt his lips twitch; he was angry with himself for giving way.

He muttered.

"That was a dirty trick."

Jack broke out of his gyration and stood facing Ralph. His words came in a shout.

"All right, all right!"

He looked at Piggy, at the hunters, at Ralph.

"I'm sorry. About the fire, I mean. There. I—"

He drew himself up.

"—I apologize."

The buzz from the hunters was one of admiration at this handsome behavior. Clearly they were of the opinion that Jack had done the decent thing, had put himself in the right by his generous apology and Ralph, obscurely, in the wrong. They waited for an appropriately decent answer.

Yet Ralph's throat refused to pass one. He resented, as an addition to Jack's misbehavior, this verbal trick. The fire was dead, the ship was gone. Could they not see? Anger instead of decency passed his throat.

"That was a dirty trick."

They were silent on the mountain-top while the opaque look appeared in Jack's eyes and passed away.

Ralph's final word was an ungracious mutter.

"All right. Light the fire."

With some positive action before them, a little of the tension died. Ralph said no more, did nothing, stood looking down at the ashes round his feet. Jack was loud and active. He gave orders, sang, whistled, threw remarks at the silent Ralph—remarks that did not need an answer, and therefore could not invite a snub; and still Ralph was silent. No one, not even Jack, would ask him to move and in the end they had to build the fire three yards away and in a place not really as convenient. So Ralph asserted his chieftainship and could not have chosen a better way if he had thought for days. Against this weapon, so indefinable and so effective, Jack was powerless and raged without knowing why. By the time the pile was built, they were on different sides of a high barrier.

When they had dealt with the fire another crisis arose. Jack had no means of lighting it. Then to his surprise, Ralph went to Piggy and took the glasses from him. Not even Ralph knew how a link between him and Jack had been snapped and fastened elsewhere.

"I'll bring 'em back."

"I'll come too."

Piggy stood behind him, islanded in a sea of meaningless color, while Ralph knelt and focused the glossy spot. Instantly the fire was alight Piggy held out his hands and grabbed the glasses back.

Before these fantastically attractive flowers of violet and red and yellow, unkindness melted away. They became a circle of boys round a camp fire and even Piggy and Ralph were half-drawn in. Soon some of the boys were rushing down the slope for more wood while Jack hacked the pig. They tried holding the whole carcass on a stake over the fire, but the stake burnt more quickly than the pig roasted. In the end they skewered bits of meat on branches and held them in the flames: and even then almost as much boy was roasted as meat

Ralph's mouth watered. He meant to refuse meat but his past diet of fruit and nuts, with an odd crab or fish, gave him too little resistance. He accepted a piece of half-raw meat and gnawed it like a wolf.

Piggy spoke, also dribbling.

"Aren't I having none?"

Jack had meant to leave him in doubt, as an assertion of power; but Piggy by advertising his omission made more cruelty necessary.

"You didn't hunt."

"No more did Ralph," said Piggy wetly, "nor Simon."

He amplified. "There isn't more than a ha'porth of meat in a crab."

Ralph stirred uneasily. Simon, sitting between the twins and Piggy, wiped his mouth and shoved his piece of meat over the rocks to Piggy, who grabbed it. The twins giggled and Simon lowered his face in shame.

Then Jack leapt to his feet, slashed off a great hunk of meat, and flung it down at Simon's feet.

"Eat! Damn you!"

He glared at Simon.

"Take it!"

He spun on his heel, center of a bewildered circle of boys.

"I got you meat!"

Numberless and inexpressible frustrations combined to make his rage elemental and awe-inspiring.

"I painted my face—I stole up. Now you eat—all of you —and I—"

Slowly the silence on the mountain-top deepened till the click of the fire and the soft hiss of roasting meat could be heard clearly. Jack looked round for understanding but found only respect. Ralph stood among the ashes of the signal fire, his hands full of meat, saying nothing.

Then at last Maurice broke the silence. He changed the subject to the only one that could bring the majority of them together.

"Where did you find the pig?"

Roger pointed down the unfriendly side. "They were there—by the sea."

Jack, recovering, could not bear to have his story told. He broke in quickly.

"We spread round. I crept, on hands and knees. The spears fell out because they hadn't barbs on. The pig ran away and made an awful noise—"

"It turned back and ran into the circle, bleeding—"

All the boys were talking at once, relieved and excited.

"We closed in—"

The first blow had paralyzed its hind quarters, so then the circle could close in and beat and beat—

"I cut the pig's throat—"

The twins, still sharing their identical grin, jumped up and ran round each other. Then the rest joined in, making pig-dying noises and shouting.

"One for his nob!"

"Give him a fourpenny one!"

Then Maurice pretended to be the pig and ran squealing into the center, and the hunters, circling still, pretended to beat him. As they danced, they sang.

"*Kill the pig. Cut her throat. Bash her in.*"

Ralph watched them, envious and resentful. Not till they flagged and the chant died away, did he speak.

"I'm calling an assembly."

One by one, they halted, and stood watching him.

"With the conch. I'm calling a meeting even if we have to go on into the dark. Down on the platform. When I blow it. Now."

He turned away and walked off, down the mountain.

# CHAPTER FIVE

## *Beast from Water*

The tide was coming in and there was only a narrow strip of firm beach between the water and the white, stumbling stuff near the palm terrace. Ralph chose the firm strip as a path because he needed to think, and only here could he allow his feet to move without having to watch them. Suddenly, pacing by the water, he was overcome with astonishment. He found himself understanding the wearisomeness of this life, where every path was an improvisation and a considerable part of one's waking life was spent watching one's feet. He stopped, facing the strip; and remembering that first enthusiastic exploration as though it were part of a brighter childhood, he smiled jeeringly. He turned then and walked back toward the platform with the sun in his face. The time had come for the assembly and as he walked into the concealing splendors of the sunlight he went carefully over the points of his speech. There must be no mistake about this assembly, no chasing imaginary. . . .

He lost himself in a maze of thoughts that were rendered vague by his lack of words to express them. Frowning, he tried again.

This meeting must not be fun, but business.

At that he walked faster, aware all at once of urgency and the declining sun and a little wind created by his speed that breathed about his face. This wind pressed his grey shirt against his chest so that he noticed—in this new mood of comprehension—how the folds were stiff like cardboard, and unpleasant; noticed too how the frayed edges of his shorts were making an uncomfortable, pink area on the front of his thighs. With a convulsion of the mind, Ralph discovered dirt and decay, understood how much he disliked perpetually flicking the tangled hair out of his eyes, and at last, when the sun was gone, rolling noisily to rest among dry leaves. At that he began to trot.

The beach near the bathing pool was dotted with groups of boys waiting for the assembly. They made way for him silently, conscious of his grim mood and the fault at the fire.

The place of assembly in which he stood was roughly a triangle; but irregular and sketchy, like everything they made. First there was the log on which he himself sat; a dead tree that must have been quite exceptionally big for the platform. Perhaps one of those legendary storms of the Pacific had shifted it here. This palm trunk lay parallel to the beach, so that when Ralph sat he faced the island but to the boys was a darkish figure against the shimmer of the lagoon. The two sides of the triangle of which the log was base were less evenly defined. On the right was a log polished by restless seats along the top, but not so large as the chief's and not so comfortable. On the left were four small logs, one of them—the farthest—lamentably springy. Assembly after assembly had broken up in laughter when someone had leaned too far back and the log had whipped and thrown half a dozen boys backwards into the grass. Yet now, he saw, no one had had the wit—not himself nor Jack, nor Piggy—to bring a stone and wedge the thing. So they would continue enduring the ill-balanced twister, because, because. . . . Again he lost himself in deep waters.

Grass was worn away in front of each trunk but grew tall and untrodden in the center of the triangle. Then, at the apex, the grass was thick again because no one sat there. All round the place of assembly the grey trunks rose, straight or leaning, and supported the low roof of leaves. On two sides was the beach; behind, the lagoon; in front, the darkness of the island.

Ralph turned to the chief's seat. They had never had an assembly as late before. That was why the place looked so different. Normally the underside of the green roof was lit by a tangle of golden reflections, and their faces were lit upside down—like, thought Ralph, when you hold an electric torch in your hands. But now the sun was slanting in at one side, so that the shadows were where they ought to be.

Again he fell into that strange mood of speculation that was so foreign to him. If faces were different when lit from above or below—what was a face? What was anything?

Ralph moved impatiently. The trouble was, if you were a chief you had to think, you had to be wise. And then the occasion slipped by so that you had to grab at a decision. This made you think; because thought was a valuable thing, that got results. . . .

Only, decided Ralph as he faced the chief's seat, I can't think. Not like Piggy.

Once more that evening Ralph had to adjust his values. Piggy could think. He could go step by step inside that fat head of his, only Piggy was no chief. But Piggy, for all his ludicrous body, had brains. Ralph was a specialist in thought now, and could recognize thought in another.

The sun in his eyes reminded him how time was passing, so he took the conch down from the tree and examined the surface. Exposure to the air had bleached the yellow and pink to near-white, and transparency. Ralph felt a kind of affectionate reverence for the conch, even though he had fished the thing out of the lagoon himself. He faced the place of assembly and put the conch to his lips.

The others were waiting for this and came straight away. Those who were aware that a ship had passed the island while the fire was out were subdued by the thought of Ralph's anger; while those, including the littluns who did not know, were impressed by the general air of solemnity. The place of assembly filled quickly; Jack, Simon, Maurice, most of the hunters, on Ralph's right; the rest on the left, under the sun. Piggy came and stood outside the triangle. This indicated that he wished to listen, but would not speak; and Piggy intended it as a gesture of disapproval.

"The thing is: we need an assembly."

No one said anything but the faces turned to Ralph were intent. He flourished the conch. He had learnt as a practical business that fundamental statements like this had to be said at least twice, before everyone understood them. One had to sit, attracting all eyes to the conch, and drop words like heavy round stones among the little groups that crouched or squatted. He was searching his mind for simple words so that even the littluns would understand what the assembly was about. Later perhaps, practiced debaters—Jack, Maurice, Piggy—would use their whole art to twist the meeting: but now at the beginning the subject of the debate must be laid out clearly.

"We need an assembly. Not for fun. Not for laughing and falling off the log"—the group of littluns on the twister giggled and looked at each other—"not for making jokes, or for"—he lifted the conch in an effort to find the compelling word—"for cleverness. Not for these things. But to put things straight."

He paused for a moment.

"I've been alone. By myself I went, thinking what's what. I know what we need. An assembly to put things straight. And first of all, I'm speaking."

He paused for a moment and automatically pushed back his hair. Piggy tiptoed to the triangle, his ineffectual protest made, and joined the others.

Ralph went on.

"We have lots of assemblies. Everybody enjoys speaking and being together. We decide things. But they don't get done. We were going to have water brought from the stream and left in those coconut shells under fresh leaves. So it was, for a few days. Now there's no water. The shells are dry. People drink from the river."

There was a murmur of assent.

"Not that there's anything wrong with drinking from the river. I mean I'd sooner have water from that place—you know, the pool where the waterfall is—than out of an old coconut shell. Only we said we'd have the water brought. And now not. There were only two full shells there this afternoon."

He licked his lips.

"Then there's huts. Shelters."

The murmur swelled again and died away.

"You mostly sleep in shelters. Tonight, except for Samneric up by the fire, you'll all sleep there. Who built the shelters?"

Clamor rose at once. Everyone had built the shelters. Ralph had to wave the conch once more.

"Wait a minute! I mean, who built all three? We all built the first one, four of us the second one, and me 'n

Simon built the last one over there. That's why it's so tottery. No. Don't laugh. That shelter might fall down if the rain comes back. We'll need those shelters then."

He paused and cleared his throat.

"There's another thing. We chose those rocks right along beyond the bathing pool as a lavatory. That was sensible too. The tide cleans the place up. You littluns know about that."

There were sniggers here and there and swift glances.

"Now people seem to use anywhere. Even near the shelters and the platform. You littluns, when you're getting fruit; if you're taken short—"

The assembly roared.

"I said if you're taken short you keep away from the fruit. That's dirty."

Laughter rose again.

"I said that's dirty!"

He plucked at his stiff, grey shirt.

"That's really dirty. If you're taken short you go right along the beach to the rocks. See?"

Piggy held out his hands for the conch but Ralph shook his head. This speech was planned, point by point.

"We've all got to use the rocks again. This place is getting dirty." He paused. The assembly, sensing a crisis, was tensely expectant. "And then: about the fire."

Ralph let out his spare breath with a little gasp that was echoed by his audience. Jack started to chip a piece of wood with his knife and whispered something to Robert, who looked away.

"The fire is the most important thing on the island. How can we ever be rescued except by luck, if we don't keep a fire going? Is a fire too much for us to make?"

He flung out an arm.

"Look at us! How many are we? And yet we can't keep a fire going to make smoke. Don't you understand? Can't you see we ought to—ought to die before we let the fire out?"

There was a self-conscious giggling among the hunters. Ralph turned on them passionately.

"You hunters! You can laugh! But I tell you the smoke is more important than the pig, ·however often you kill one. Do all of you see?" He spread his arms wide and turned to the whole triangle.

"We've got to make smoke up there—or die."

He paused, feeling for his next point.

"And another thing."

Someone called out.

"Too many things."

There came mutters of agreement. Ralph overrode them.

"And another thing. We nearly set the whole island on fire. And we waste time, rolling rocks, and making little cooking fires. Now I say this and make it a rule, because I'm chief. We won't have a fire anywhere but on the mountain. Ever."

There was a row immediately. Boys stood up and shouted and Ralph shouted back.

"Because if you want a fire to cook fish or crab, you can jolly well go up the mountain. That way we'll be certain."

Hands were reaching for the conch in the light of the setting sun. He held on and leapt on the trunk.

"All this I meant to say. Now I've said it. You voted me for chief. Now you do what I say."

They quieted, slowly, and at last were seated again. Ralph dropped down and spoke in his ordinary voice.

"So remember. The rocks for a lavatory. Keep the fire going and smoke showing as a signal. Don't take fire from the mountain. Take your food up there."

Jack stood up, scowling in the gloom, and held out his hands.

"I haven't finished yet."

"But you've talked and talked!"

"I've got the conch."

Jack sat down, grumbling.

"Then the last thing. This is what people can talk about." He waited till the platform was very still.

"Things are breaking up. I don't understand why. We began well; we were happy. And then—"

He moved the conch gently, looking beyond them at nothing, remembering the beastie, the snake, the fire, the talk of fear.

"Then people started getting frightened."

A murmur, almost a moan, rose and passed away. Jack had stopped whittling. Ralph went on, abruptly.

"But that's littluns' talk. We'll get that straight. So the last part, the bit we can all talk about, is kind of deciding on the fear."

The hair was creeping into his eyes again.

"We've got to talk about this fear and decide there's nothing in it. I'm frightened myself, sometimes; only that's nonsense! Like bogies. Then, when we've decided, we can start again and be careful about things like the fire." A picture of three boys walking along the bright beach flitted through his mind. "And be happy."

Ceremonially, Ralph laid the conch on the trunk beside him as a sign that the speech was over. What sunlight reached them was level.

Jack stood up and took the conch.

"So this is a meeting to find out what's what. I'll tell you what's what. You littluns started all this, with the fear talk. Beasts! Where from? Of course we're frightened sometimes but we put up with being frightened. Only Ralph says you scream in the night. What does that mean but nightmares? Anyway, you don't hunt or build or help—you're a lot of cry-babies and sissies. That's what. And as for the fear—you'll have to put up with that like the rest of us."

Ralph looked at Jack open-mouthed, but Jack took no notice.

"The thing is—fear can't hurt you any more than a dream. There aren't any beasts to be afraid of on this island." He looked along the row of whispering littluns. "Serve you right if something did get you, you useless lot of cry-babies! But there *is* no animal—"

Ralph interrupted him testily.

"What is all this? Who said anything about an animal?"

"You did, the other day. You said they dream and cry out. Now they talk—not only the littluns, but my hunters sometimes—talk of a thing, a dark thing, a beast, some sort of animal. I've heard. You thought not, didn't you? Now listen. You don't get big animals on small islands. Only pigs. You only get lions and tigers in big countries like Africa and India—"

"And the Zoo—"

"I've got the conch. I'm not talking about the fear. I'm talking about the beast. Be frightened if you like. But as for the beast—"

Jack paused, cradling the conch, and turned to his hunters with their dirty black caps.

"Am I a hunter or am I not?"

They nodded, simply. He was a hunter all right. No one doubted that.

"Well then—I've been all over this island. By myself. If there were a beast I'd have seen it. Be frightened because you're like that—but there is no beast in the forest."

Jack handed back the conch and sat down. The whole assembly applauded him with relief. Then Piggy held out his hand.

"I don't agree with all Jack said, but with some. 'Course there isn't a beast in the forest. How could there be? What would a beast eat?"

"Pig."

"We eat pig."

"Piggy!"

"I got the conch!" said Piggy indignantly. "Ralph—they ought to shut up, oughtn't they? You shut up, you littluns! What I mean is that I don't agree about this here fear. Of course there isn't nothing to be afraid of in the forest. Why—I been there myself! You'll be talking about ghosts and such things next. We know what goes on and if there's something wrong, there's someone to put it right."

He took off his glasses and blinked at them. The sun had gone as if the light had been turned off.

He proceeded to explain.

"If you get a pain in your stomach, whether it's a little one or a big one—"

"Yours is a big one."

"When you done laughing perhaps we can get on with the meeting. And if them littluns climb back on the twister again they'll only fall off in a sec. So they might as well sit on the ground and listen. No. You have doctors for everything, even the inside of your mind. You don't really mean that we got to be frightened all the time of nothing? Life," said Piggy expansively, "is scientific, that's what it is. In a year or two when the war's over they'll be traveling to Mars and back. I know there isn't no beast—not with claws and all that, I mean—but I know there isn't no fear, either."

Piggy paused.

"Unless—"

Ralph moved restlessly.

"Unless what?"

"Unless we get frightened of people."

A sound, half-laugh, half-jeer, rose among the seated boys. Piggy ducked his head and went on hastily.

"So let's hear from that littlun who talked about a beast and perhaps we can show him how silly he is."

The littluns began to jabber among themselves, then one stood forward.

"What's your name?"

"Phil."

For a littlun he was self-confident, holding out his hands, cradling the conch as Ralph did, looking round at them to collect their attention before he spoke.

"Last night I had a dream, a horrid dream, fighting with things. I was outside the shelter by myself, fighting with things, those twisty things in the trees."

He paused, and the other littluns laughed in horrified sympathy.

"Then I was frightened and I woke up. And I was outside the shelter by myself in the dark and the twisty things had gone away."

The vivid horror of this, so possible and so nakedly terrifying, held them all silent. The child's voice went piping on from behind the white conch.

"And I was frightened and started to call out for Ralph and then I saw something moving among the trees, something big and horrid."

He paused, half-frightened by the recollection yet proud of the sensation he was creating.

"That was a nightmare," said Ralph. "He was walking in his sleep."

The assembly murmured in subdued agreement.

The littlun shook his head stubbornly.

"I was asleep when the twisty things were fighting and when they went away I was awake, and I saw something big and horrid moving in the trees."

Ralph held out his hands for the conch and the littlun sat down.

"You were alseep. There wasn't anyone there. How could anyone be wandering about in the forest at night? Was anyone? Did anyone go out?"

There was a long pause while the assembly grinned at

the thought of anyone going out in the darkness. Then Simon stood up and Ralph looked at him in astonishment.

"You! What were you mucking about in the dark for?" Simon grabbed the conch convulsively.

"I wanted—to go to a place—a place I know."

"What place?"

"Just a place I know. A place in the jungle."

He hesitated.

Jack settled the question for them with that contempt in his voice that could sound so funny and so final.

"He was taken short."

With a feeling of humiliation on Simon's behalf, Ralph took back the conch, looking Simon sternly in the face as he did so.

"Well, don't do it again. Understand? Not at night. There's enough silly talk about beasts, without the littluns seeing you gliding about like a—"

The derisive laughter that rose had fear in it and condemnation. Simon opened his mouth to speak but Ralph had the conch, so he backed to his seat.

When the assembly was silent Ralph turned to Piggy.

"Well, Piggy?"

"There was another one. Him."

The littluns pushed Percival forward, then left him by himself. He stood knee-deep in the central grass, looking at his hidden feet, trying to pretend he was in a tent. Ralph remembered another small boy who had stood like this and he flinched away from the memory. He had pushed the thought down and out of sight, where only some positive reminder like this could bring it to the surface. There had been no further numberings of the littluns, partly because there was no means of insuring that all of them were accounted for and partly because Ralph knew the answer to at least one question Piggy had asked on the mountaintop. There were little boys, fair, dark, freckled, and all dirty, but their faces were all dreadfully free of major blemishes. No one had seen the mulberry-colored birthmark again. But that time Piggy had coaxed and bullied. Tacitly admitting that he remembered the unmentionable, Ralph nodded to Piggy.

"Go on. Ask him."

Piggy knelt, holding the conch.

"Now then. What's your name?"

The small boy twisted away into his tent. Piggy turned helplessly to Ralph, who spoke sharply.

"What's your name?"

Tormented by the silence and the refusal the assembly broke into a chant.

"What's your name? What's your name?"

"Quiet!"

Ralph peered at the child in the twilight.

"Now tell us. What's your name?"

"Percival Wemys Madison, The Vicarage, Harcourt St. Anthony, Hants, telephone, telephone, tele—"

As if this information was rooted far down in the springs of sorrow, the littlun wept. His face puckered, the tears leapt from his eyes, his mouth opened till they could see a square black hole. At first he was a silent effigy of sorrow; but then the lamentation rose out of him, loud and sustained as the conch.

"Shut up, you! Shut up!"

Percival Wemys Madison would not shut up. A spring had been tapped, far beyond the reach of authority or even physical intimidation. The crying went on, breath after breath, and seemed to sustain him upright as if he were nailed to it.

"Shut up! Shut up!"

For now the littluns were no longer silent. They were reminded of their personal sorrows; and perhaps felt themselves to share in a sorrow that was universal. They began to cry in sympathy, two of them almost as loud as Percival.

Maurice saved them. He cried out.

"Look at me!"

He pretended to fall over. He rubbed his rump and sat on the twister so that he fell in the grass. He clowned badly; but Percival and the others noticed and sniffed and laughed. Presently they were all laughing so absurdly that the biguns joined in.

Jack was the first to make himself heard. He had not got the conch and thus spoke against the rules; but nobody minded.

"And what about the beast?"

Something strange was happening to Percival. He yawned and staggered, so that Jack seized and shook him.

"Where does the beast live?"

Percival sagged in Jack's grip.

"That's a clever beast," said Piggy, jeering, "if it can hide on this island."

"Jack's been everywhere—"

"Where could a beast live?"

"Beast my foot!"

Percival muttered something and the assembly laughed again. Ralph leaned forward.

"What does he say?"

Jack listened to Percival's answer and then let go of him. Percival, released, surrounded by the comfortable presence of humans, fell in the long grass and went to sleep.

Jack cleared his throat, then reported casually.

"He says the beast comes out of the sea."

The last laugh died away. Ralph turned involuntarily, a black, humped figure against the lagoon. The assembly looked with him, considered the vast stretches of water, the high sea beyond, unknown indigo of infinite possibility, heard silently the sough and whisper from the reef.

Maurice spoke, so loudly that they jumped.

"Daddy said they haven't found all the animals in the sea yet."

Argument started again. Ralph held out the glimmering conch and Maurice took it obediently. The meeting subsided.

"I mean when Jack says you can be frightened because people are frightened anyway that's all right. But when he says there's only pigs on this island I expect he's right but he doesn't know, not really, not certainly I mean—" Maurice took a breath. "My daddy says there's things, what d'you call'em that make ink—squids—that are hundreds of yards long and eat whales whole." He paused again and laughed gaily. "I don't believe in the beast of course. As Piggy says, life's scientific, but we don't know, do we? Not certainly, I mean—"

Someone shouted.

"A squid couldn't come up out of the water!"

"Could!"

"Couldn't!"

In a moment the platform was full of arguing, gesticulating shadows. To Ralph, seated, this seemed the breaking up of sanity. Fear, beasts, no general agreement that the fire was all-important: and when one tried to get the thing straight the argument sheered off, bringing up fresh, unpleasant matter.

He could see a whiteness in the gloom near him so he grabbed it from Maurice and blew as loudly as he could. The assembly was shocked into silence. Simon was close to him, laying hands on the conch. Simon felt a perilous necessity to speak; but to speak in assembly was a terrible thing to him.

"Maybe," he said hesitantly, "maybe there is a beast."

The assembly cried out savagely and Ralph stood up in amazement.

"You, Simon? You believe in this?"

"I don't know," said Simon. His heartbeats were choking him. "But. . . ."

The storm broke.

"Sit down!"

"Shut up!"

"Take the conch!"

"Sod you!"

"Shut up!"

Ralph shouted.

"Hear him! He's got the conch!"

"What I mean is . . . maybe it's only us."

"Nuts!"

That was from Piggy, shocked out of decorum. Simon went on.

"We could be sort of. . . ."

Simon became inarticulate in his effort to express mankind's essential illness. Inspiration came to him.

"What's the dirtiest thing there is?"

As an answer Jack dropped into the uncomprehending silence that followed it the one crude expressive syllable. Release was immense. Those littluns who had climbed back on the twister fell off again and did not mind. The hunters were screaming with delight.

Simon's effort fell about him in ruins; the laughter beat him cruelly and he shrank away defenseless to his seat.

At last the assembly was silent again. Someone spoke out of turn.

"Maybe he means it's some sort of ghost."

Ralph lifted the conch and peered into the gloom. The lightest thing was the pale beach. Surely the littluns were nearer? Yes—there was no doubt about it, they were huddled into a tight knot of bodies in the central grass. A flurry of wind made the palms talk and the noise seemed very loud now that darkness and silence made it so noticeable. Two grey trunks rubbed each other with an evil squeaking that no one had noticed by day.

Piggy took the conch out of his hands. His voice was indignant.

"I don't believe in no ghosts—ever!"

Jack was up too, unaccountably angry.

"Who cares what you believe—Fatty!"

"I got the conch!"

There was the sound of a brief tussle and the conch moved to and fro.

"You gimme the conch back!"

Ralph pushed between them and got a thump on the chest. He wrested the conch from someone and sat down breathlessly.

"There's too much talk about ghosts. We ought to have left all this for daylight."

A hushed and anonymous voice broke in.

"Perhaps that's what the beast is—a ghost."

The assembly was shaken as by a wind.

"There's too much talking out of turn," Ralph said, "because we can't have proper assemblies if you don't stick to the rules."

He stopped again. The careful plan of this assembly had broken down.

"What d'you want me to say then? I was wrong to call this assembly so late. We'll have a vote on them; on ghosts I mean; and then go to the shelters because we're all tired. No—Jack is it?—wait a minute. I'll say here and now that I don't believe in ghosts. Or I don't think I do. But I don't like the thought of them. Not now that is, in the dark. But we were going to decide what's what."

He raised the conch for a moment.

"Very well then. I suppose what's what is whether there are ghosts or not—"

He thought for a moment, formulating the question.

"Who thinks there may be ghosts?"

For a long time there was silence and no apparent movement. Then Ralph peered into the gloom and made out the hands. He spoke flatly.

"I see."

The world, that understandable and lawful world, was slipping away. Once there was this and that; and now—and the ship had gone.

The conch was snatched from his hands and Piggy's voice shrilled.

"I didn't vote for no ghosts!"

He whirled round on the assembly.

"Remember that, all of you!"

They heard him stamp.

"What are we? Humans? Or animals? Or savages? What's grownups going to think? Going off—hunting pigs—letting fires out—and now!"

A shadow fronted him tempestuously.

"You shut up, you fat slug!"

There was a moment's struggle and the glimmering conch jigged up and down. Ralph leapt to his feet.

"Jack! Jack! You haven't got the conch! Let him speak."

Jack's face swam near him.

"And you shut up! Who are you, anyway? Sitting there telling people what to do. You can't hunt, you can't sing—"

"I'm chief. I was chosen."

"Why should choosing make any difference? Just giving orders that don't make any sense—"

"Piggy's got the conch."

"That's right—favor Piggy as you always do—"

"Jack!"

Jack's voice sounded in bitter mimicry.

"Jack! Jack!"

"The rules!" shouted Ralph. "You're breaking the rules!"

"Who cares?"

Ralph summoned his wits.

"Because the rules are the only thing we've got!"

But Jack was shouting against him.

"Bollocks to the rules! We're strong—we hunt! If there's a beast, we'll hunt it down! We'll close in and beat and beat and beat—!"

He gave a wild whoop and leapt down to the pale sand. At once the platform was full of noise and excitement, scramblings, screams and laughter. The assembly shredded away and became a discursive and random scatter from the palms to the water and away along the beach, beyond night-sight. Ralph found his cheek touching the conch and took it from Piggy.

"What's grownups going to say?" cried Piggy again. "Look at 'em!"

The sound of mock hunting, hysterical laughter and real terror came from the beach.

"Blow the conch, Ralph."

Piggy was so close that Ralph could see the glint of his one glass.

"There's the fire. Can't they see?"

"You got to be tough now. Make 'em do what you want."

Ralph answered in the cautious voice of one who rehearses a theorem.

"If I blow the conch and they don't come back; then we've had it. We shan't keep the fire going. We'll be like animals. We'll never be rescued."

"If you don't blow, we'll soon be animals anyway. I can't see what they're doing but I can hear."

The dispersed figures had come together on the sand and were a dense black mass that revolved. They were chanting something and littluns that had had enough were staggering away, howling. Ralph raised the conch to his lips and then lowered it.

"The trouble is: Are there ghosts, Piggy? Or beasts?"

"Course there aren't."

"Why not?"

" 'Cos things wouldn't make sense. Houses an' streets, an'—TV—they wouldn't work."

The dancing, chanting boys had worked themselves away till their sound was nothing but a wordless rhythm.

"But s'pose they don't make sense? Not here, on this island? Supposing things are watching us and waiting?"

Ralph shuddered violently and moved closer to Piggy, so that they bumped frighteningly.

"You stop talking like that! We got enough trouble, Ralph, an' I've had as much as I can stand. If there is ghosts—"

"I ought to give up being chief. Hear 'em."

"Oh lord! Oh no!"

Piggy gripped Ralph's arm.

"If Jack was chief he'd have all hunting and no fire. We'd be here till we died."

His voice ran up to a squeak.

"Who's that sitting there?"

"Me. Simon."

"Fat lot of good we are," said Ralph. "Three blind mice. I'll give up."

"If you give up," said Piggy, in an appalled whisper, "what 'ud happen to me?"

"Nothing."

"He hates me. I dunno why. If he could do what he wanted—you're all right, he respects you. Besides—you'd hit him."

"You were having a nice fight with him just now."

"I had the conch," said Piggy simply. "I had a right to speak."

Simon stirred in the dark.

"Go on being chief."

"You shut up, young Simon! Why couldn't you say there wasn't a beast?"

"I'm scared of him," said Piggy, "and that's why I know him. If you're scared of someone you hate him but you can't stop thinking about him. You kid yourself he's all right really, an' then when you see him again; it's like asthma an' you can't breathe. I tell you what. He hates you too, Ralph—"

"Me? Why me?"

"I dunno. You got him over the fire; an' you're chief an' he isn't."

"But he's, he's, Jack Merridew!"

"I been in bed so much I done some thinking. I know about people. I know about me. And him. He can't hurt you: but if you stand out of the way he'd hurt the next thing. And that's me."

"Piggy's right, Ralph. There's you and Jack. Go on being chief."

"We're all drifting and things are going rotten. At home there was always a grownup. Please, sir; please, miss; and then you got an answer. How I wish!"

"I wish my auntie was here."

"I wish my father . . . Oh, what's the use?"

"Keep the fire going."

The dance was over and the hunters were going back to the shelters.

"Grownups know things," said Piggy. "They ain't afraid

of the dark. They'd meet and have tea and discuss. Then things 'ud be all right—"

"They wouldn't set fire to the island. Or lose—"

"They'd build a ship—"

The three boys stood in the darkness, striving unsuccessfully to convey the majesty of adult life.

"They wouldn't quarrel—"

"Or break my specs—"

"Or talk about a beast—"

"If only they could get a message to us," cried Ralph desperately. "If only they could send us something grown-up . . . a sign or something."

A thin wail out of the darkness chilled them and set them grabbing for each other. Then the wail rose, remote and unearthly, and turned to an inarticulate gibbering. Percival Wemys Madison, of the Vicarage, Harcourt St. Anthony, lying in the long grass, was living through circumstances in which the incantation of his address was powerless to help him.

# CHAPTER SIX

## *Beast from Air*

There was no light left save that of the stars. When they had understood what made this ghostly noise and Percival was quiet again, Ralph and Simon picked him up unhandily and carried him to a shelter. Piggy hung about near for all his brave words, and the three bigger boys went together to the next shelter. They lay restlessly and noisily among the dry leaves, watching the patch of stars that was the opening toward the lagoon. Sometimes a littlun cried out from the other shelters and once a bigun spoke in the dark. Then they too fell asleep.

A sliver of moon rose over the horizon, hardly large enough to make a path of light even when it sat right down on the water; but there were other lights in the sky, that moved fast, winked, or went out, though not even a faint popping came down from the battle fought at ten miles' height. But a sign came down from the world of grownups, though at the time there was no child awake to read it. There was a sudden bright explosion and a corkscrew trail across the sky; then darkness again and stars. There was a speck above the island, a figure dropping swiftly beneath a parachute, a figure that hung with dangling limbs. The changing winds of various altitudes took the figure where they would. Then, three miles up, the wind steadied and bore it in a descending curve round the sky and swept it in a great slant across the reef and the lagoon toward the mountain. The figure fell and crumpled among the blue flowers of the mountain-side, but now there was a gentle breeze at this height too and the parachute flopped and banged and pulled. So the figure, with feet that dragged behind it, slid up the mountain. Yard by yard, puff by puff, the breeze hauled the figure through the blue flowers, over the boulders and red stones, till it lay huddled among the shattered rocks of the mountain-top. Here the breeze was fitful and allowed the strings of the parachute to tangle and festoon; and the figure sat, its helmeted head between its knees, held by a complication of lines. When the breeze blew, the lines would strain taut and some accident of this pull lifted the head and chest upright so that the figure seemed to peer across the brow of the mountain. Then, each time the wind dropped, the lines would slacken and the figure bow forward again, sinking its head between its knees. So as the stars moved across the sky, the figure sat on the mountain-top and bowed and sank and bowed again.

In the darkness of early morning there were noises by a rock a little way down the side of the mountain. Two boys rolled out of a pile of brushwood and dead leaves, two dim shadows talking sleepily to each other. They were the twins, on duty at the fire. In theory one should have been asleep and one on watch. But they could never manage to do things sensibly if that meant acting independently, and since staying awake all night was impossible, they had both gone to sleep. Now they approached the darker smudge that had been the signal fire, yawning, rubbing their eyes, treading with practiced feet. When they reached it they stopped yawning, and one ran quickly back for brushwood and leaves.

The other knelt down.

"I believe it's out."

He fiddled with the sticks that were pushed into his hands.

"No."

He lay down and put his lips close to the smudge and blew softly. His face appeared, lit redly. He stopped blowing for a moment.

"Sam—give us—"

"—tinder wood."

Eric bent down and blew softly again till the patch was bright. Sam poked the piece of tinder wood into the hot spot, then a branch. The glow increased and the branch took fire. Sam piled on more branches.

"Don't burn the lot," said Eric, "you're putting on too much."

"Let's warm up."

"We'll only have to fetch more wood."

"I'm cold."

"So'm I."

"Besides, it's—"

"—dark. All right, then."

Eric squatted back and watched Sam make up the fire. He built a little tent of dead wood and the fire was safely alight.

"That was near."

"He'd have been—"

"Waxy."

"Huh."

For a few moments the twins watched the fire in silence. Then Eric sniggered.

"Wasn't he waxy?"

"About the—"

"Fire and the pig."

"Lucky he went for Jack, 'stead of us."

"Huh. Remember old Waxy at school?"

" 'Boy—you-are-driving-me-slowly-insane!' "

The twins shared their identical laughter, then remembered the darkness and other things and glanced round uneasily. The flames, busy about the tent, drew their eyes back again. Eric watched the scurrying woodlice that were so frantically unable to avoid the flames, and thought of the first fire—just down there, on the steeper side of the mountain, where now was complete darkness. He did not like to remember it, and looked away at the mountain-top.

Warmth radiated now, and beat pleasantly on them. Sam amused himself by fitting branches into the fire as closely as possible. Eric spread out his hands, searching for the distance at which the heat was just bearable. Idly looking beyond the fire, he resettled the scattered rocks from their flat shadows into daylight contours. Just there was the big rock, and the three stones there, that split rock, and there beyond was a gap—just there—

"Sam."

"Huh?"

"Nothing."

The flames were mastering the branches, the bark was curling and falling away, the wood exploding. The tent fell inwards and flung a wide circle of light over the mountain-top.

"Sam—"

"Huh?"

"Sam! Sam!"

Sam looked at Eric irritably. The intensity of Eric's gaze made the direction in which he looked terrible, for Sam had his back to it. He scrambled round the fire, squatted by Eric, and looked to see. They became motionless, gripped in each other's arms, four unwinking eyes aimed and two mouths open.

Far beneath them, the trees of the forest sighed, then roared. The hair on their foreheads fluttered and flames blew out sideways from the fire. Fifteen yards away from them came the plopping noise of fabric blown open.

Neither of the boys screamed but the grip of their arms tightened and their mouths grew peaked. For perhaps ten seconds they crouched like that while the flailing fire sent smoke and sparks and waves of inconstant light over the top of the mountain.

Then as though they had but one terrified mind between them they scrambled away over the rocks and fled.

Ralph was dreaming. He had fallen asleep after what seemed hours of tossing and turning noisily among the dry leaves. Even the sounds of nightmare from the other shelters no longer reached him, for he was back to where he came from, feeding the ponies with sugar over the garden wall. Then someone was shaking his arm, telling him that it was time for tea.

"Ralph! Wake up!"

The leaves were roaring like the sea.

"Ralph, wake up!"

"What's the matter?"

"We saw—"

"—the beast—"

"—plain!"

"Who are you? The twins?"

"We saw the beast—"

"Quiet. Piggy!"

The leaves were roaring still. Piggy bumped into him and a twin grabbed him as he made for the oblong of paling stars.

"You can't go out—it's horrible!"

"Piggy—where are the spears?"

"I can hear the—"

"Quiet then. Lie still."

They lay there listening, at first with doubt but then with
terror to the description the twins breathed at them
between bouts of extreme silence. Soon the darkness was
full of claws, full of the awful unknown and menace. An
interminable dawn faded the stars out, and at last light,
sad and grey, filtered into the shelter. They began to stir
though still the world outside the shelter was impossibly
dangerous. The maze of the darkness sorted into near and
far, and at the high point of the sky the cloudlets
were warmed with color. A single sea bird flapped upwards
with a hoarse cry that was echoed presently, and something
squawked in the forest. Now streaks of cloud near the horizon began to glow rosily, and the feathery tops of
the palms were green.

Ralph knelt in the entrance to the shelter and peered
cautiously round him.

"Sam 'n Eric. Call them to an assembly. Quietly. Go on."

The twins, holding tremulously to each other, dared the
few yards to the next shelter and spread the dreadful news.
Ralph stood up and walked for the sake of dignity, though
with his back pricking, to the platform. Piggy and Simon
followed him and the other boys came sneaking after.

Ralph took the conch from where it lay on the polished
seat and held it to his lips; but then he hesitated and did
not blow. He held the shell up instead and showed it to
them and they understood.

The rays of the sun that were fanning upwards from below the horizon swung downwards to eye-level. Ralph
looked for a moment at the growing slice of gold that lit
them from the right hand and seemed to make speech possible. The circle of boys before him bristled with hunting
spears.

He handed the conch to Eric, the nearest of the twins.

"We've seen the beast with our own eyes. No—we
weren't asleep—"

Sam took up the story. By custom now one conch did
for both twins, for their substantial unity was recognized.

"It was furry. There was something moving behind its
head—wings. The beast moved too—"

"That was awful. It kind of sat up—"

"The fire was bright—"

"We'd just made it up—"

"—more sticks on—"

"There were eyes—"

"Teeth—"

"Claws—"

"We ran as fast as we could—"

"Bashed into things—"

"The beast followed us—"

"I saw it slinking behind the trees—"

"Nearly touched me—"

Ralph pointed fearfully at Eric's face, which was striped with scars where the bushes had torn him.

"How did you do that?"

Eric felt his face.

"I'm all rough. Am I bleeding?"

The circle of boys shrank away in horror. Johnny, yawning still, burst into noisy tears and was slapped by Bill till he choked on them. The bright morning was full of threats and the circle began to change. It faced out, rather than in, and the spears of sharpened wood were like a fence. Jack called them back to the center.

"This'll be a real hunt! Who'll come?"

Ralph moved impatiently.

"These spears are made of wood. Don't be silly."

Jack sneered at him.

"Frightened?"

" 'Course I'm frightened. Who wouldn't be?"

He turned to the twins, yearning but hopeless.

"I suppose you aren't pulling our legs?"

The reply was too emphatic for anyone to doubt them. Piggy took the conch.

"Couldn't we—kind of—stay here? Maybe the beast won't come near us."

But for the sense of something watching them, Ralph would have shouted at him.

"Stay here? And be cramped into this bit of the island, always on the lookout? How should we get our food? And what about the fire?"

"Let's be moving," said Jack restlessly, "we're wasting time."

"No we're not. What about the littluns?"

"Sucks to the littluns!"

"Someone's got to look after them."

"Nobody has so far."

"There was no need! Now there is. Piggy'll look after them."

"That's right. Keep Piggy out of danger."

"Have some sense. What can Piggy do with only one eye?"

The rest of the boys were looking from Jack to Ralph, curiously.

"And another thing. You can't have an ordinary hunt because the beast doesn't leave tracks. If it did you'd have seen them. For all we know, the beast may swing through the trees like what's its name."

They nodded.

"So we've got to think."

Piggy took off his damaged glasses and cleaned the remaining lens.

"How about us, Ralph?"

"You haven't got the conch. Here."

"I mean—how about us? Suppose the beast comes when you're all away. I can't see proper, and if I get scared—"

Jack broke in, contemptuously.

"You're always scared."

"I got the conch—"

"Conch! Conch!" shouted Jack. "We don't need the conch any more. We know who ought to say things. What good did Simon do speaking, or Bill, or Walter? It's time some people knew they've got to keep quiet and leave deciding things to the rest of us."

Ralph could no longer ignore his speech. The blood was hot in his cheeks.

"You haven't got the conch," he said. "Sit down."

Jack's face went so white that the freckles showed as clear, brown flecks. He licked his lips and remained standing.

"This is a hunter's job."

The rest of the boys watched intently. Piggy, finding himself uncomfortably embroiled, slid the conch to Ralph's knees and sat down. The silence grew oppressive and Piggy held his breath.

"This is more than a hunter's job," said Ralph at last, "because you can't track the beast. And don't you want to be rescued?"

He turned to the assembly.

"Don't you all want to be rescued?"

He looked back at Jack.

"I said before, the fire is the main thing. Now the fire must be out—"

The old exasperation saved him and gave him the energy to attack.

"Hasn't anyone got any sense? We've got to relight that fire. You never thought of that, Jack, did you? Or don't any of you want to be rescued?"

Yes, they wanted to be rescued, there was no doubt about that; and with a violent swing to Ralph's side, the crisis passed. Piggy let out his breath with a gasp, reached for it again and failed. He lay against a log, his mouth gaping, blue shadows creeping round his lips. Nobody minded him.

"Now think, Jack. Is there anywhere on the island you haven't been?"

Unwillingly Jack answered.

"There's only—but of course! You remember? The tail-end part, where the rocks are all piled up. I've been near there. The rock makes a sort of bridge. There's only one way up."

"And the thing might live there."

All the assembly talked at once.

"Quite! All right. That's where we'll look. If the beast isn't there we'll go up the mountain and look; and light the fire."

"Let's go."

"We'll eat first. Then go." Ralph paused. "We'd better take spears."

After they had eaten, Ralph and the biguns set out along the beach. They left Piggy propped up on the platform. This day promised, like the others, to be a sunbath under a blue dome. The beach stretched away before them in a gentle curve till perspective drew it into one with the forest; for the day was not advanced enough to be obscured by the shifting veils of mirage. Under Ralph's direction, they picked a careful way along the palm terrace, rather than dare the hot sand down by the water. He let Jack lead the way; and Jack trod with theatrical caution though they could have seen an enemy twenty yards away. Ralph walked in the rear, thankful to have escaped responsibility for a time.

Simon, walking in front of Ralph, felt a flicker of incredulity—a beast with claws that scratched, that sat on a mountain-top, that left no tracks and yet was not fast enough to catch Samneric. However Simon thought of the beast, there rose before his inward sight the picture of a human at once heroic and sick.

He sighed. Other people could stand up and speak to an assembly, apparently, without that dreadful feeling of the pressure of personality; could say what they would as though they were speaking to only one person. He stepped aside and looked back. Ralph was coming along, holding his spear over his shoulder. Diffidently, Simon allowed his pace to slacken until he was walking side by side with Ralph and looking up at him through the coarse black hair that now fell to his eyes. Ralph glanced sideways, smiled constrainedly as though he had forgotten that Simon had made a fool of himself, then looked away again at nothing. For a moment or two Simon was happy to be accepted and then he ceased to think about himself. When he bashed into a tree Ralph looked sideways impatiently and Robert sniggered. Simon reeled and a white spot on his forehead turned red and trickled. Ralph dismissed Simon and returned to his personal hell They would reach the castle some time; and the chief would have to go forward.

Jack came trotting back.

"We're in sight now."

"All right. We'll get as close as we can."

He followed Jack toward the castle where the ground rose slightly. On their left was an impenetrable tangle of creepers and trees.

"Why couldn't there be something in that?"

"Because you can see. Nothing goes in or out."

"What about the castle then?"

"Look."

Ralph parted the screen of grass and looked out. There were only a few more yards of stony ground and then the two sides of the island came almost together so that one expected a peak of headland. But instead of this a narrow ledge of rock, a few yards wide and perhaps fifteen long, continued the island out into the sea. There lay another of those pieces of pink squareness that underlay the structure of the island. This side of the castle, perhaps a hundred feet high, was the pink bastion they had seen from the mountain-top. The rock of the cliff was split and the top littered with great lumps that seemed to totter.

Behind Ralph the tall grass had filled with silent hunters. Ralph looked at Jack.

"You're a hunter."

Jack went red.

"I know. All right."

Something deep in Ralph spoke for him.

"I'm chief. I'll go. Don't argue."

He turned to the others.

"You. Hide here. Wait for me."

He found his voice tended either to disappear or to come out too loud. He looked at Jack.

"Do you—think?"

Jack muttered.

"I've been all over. It must be here."

"I see."

Simon mumbled confusedly: "I don't believe in the beast."

Ralph answered him politely, as if agreeing about the weather.

"No. I suppose not."

His mouth was tight and pale. He put back his hair very slowly.

"Well. So long."

He forced his feet to move until they had carried him out on to the neck of land.

He was surrounded on all sides by chasms of empty air. There was nowhere to hide, even if one did not have to go on. He paused on the narrow neck and looked down. Soon, in a matter of centuries, the sea would make an island of the castle. On the right hand was the lagoon, troubled by the open sea; and on the left—

Ralph shuddered. The lagoon had protected them from the Pacific: and for some reason only Jack had gone right down to the water on the other side. Now he saw the landsman's view of the swell and it seemed like the breathing of some stupendous creature. Slowly the waters sank among the rocks, revealing pink tables of granite, strange growths of coral, polyp, and weed. Down, down, the waters went, whispering like the wind among the heads of the forest. There was one flat rock there, spread like a table, and the waters sucking down on the four weedy sides made them seem like cliffs. Then the sleeping leviathan breathed out, the waters rose, the weed streamed, and the water boiled over the table rock with a roar. There was no sense of the passage of waves; only this minute-long fall and rise and fall.

Ralph turned away to the red cliff. They were waiting behind him in the long grass, waiting to see what he would do. He noticed that the sweat in his palm was cool now; realized with surprise that he did not really expect to meet any beast and didn't know what he would do about it if he did.

He saw that he could climb the cliff but this was not necessary. The squareness of the rock allowed a sort of plinth round it, so that to the right, over the lagoon, one could inch along a ledge and turn the corner out of sight. It was easy going, and soon he was peering round the rock.

Nothing but what you might expect: pink, tumbled boulders with guano layered on them like icing; and a steep slope up to the shattered rocks that crowned the bastion.

A sound behind him made him turn. Jack was edging along the ledge.

"Couldn't let you do it on your own."

Ralph said nothing. He led the way over the rocks, inspected a sort of half-cave that held nothing more terrible than a clutch of rotten eggs, and at last sat down, looking round him and tapping the rock with the butt of his spear.

Jack was excited.

"What a place for a fort!"

A column of spray wetted them.

"No fresh water."

"What's that then?"

There was indeed a long green smudge half-way up the rock. They climbed up and tasted the trickle of water.

"You could keep a coconut shell there, filling all the time."

"Not me. This is a rotten place."

Side by side they scaled the last height to where the diminishing pile was crowned by the last broken rock. Jack struck the near one with his fist and it grated slightly.

"Do you remember——?"

Consciousness of the bad times in between came to them both. Jack talked quickly.

"Shove a palm trunk under that and if an enemy came
—look!"

A hundred feet below them was the narrow causeway,
then the stony ground, then the grass dotted with heads,
and behind that the forest.

"One heave," cried Jack, exulting, "and—wheee—!"

He made a sweeping movement with his hand. Ralph
looked toward the mountain.

"What's the matter?"

Ralph turned.

"Why?"

"You were looking—I don't know why."

"There's no signal now. Nothing to show."

"You're nuts on the signal."

The taut blue horizon encircled them, broken only by the
mountain-top.

"That's all we've got."

He leaned his spear against the rocking stone and pushed
back two handfuls of hair.

"We'll have to go back and climb the mountain. That's
where they saw the beast."

"The beast won't be there."

"What else can we do?"

The others, waiting in the grass, saw Jack and Ralph un-
harmed and broke cover into the sunlight. They forgot the
beast in the excitement of exploration. They swarmed across
the bridge and soon were climbing and shouting. Ralph
stood now, one hand against an enormous red block, a block
large as a mill wheel that had been split off and hung, tot-
tering. Somberly he watched the mountain. He clenched
his fist and beat hammer-wise on the red wall at his right.
His lips were tightly compressed and his eyes yearned beneath the fringe of hair.

"Smoke."

He sucked his bruised fist.

"Jack! Come on."

But Jack was not there. A knot of boys, making a great
noise that he had not noticed, were heaving and pushing
at a rock. As he turned, the base cracked and the whole
mass toppled into the sea so that a thunderous plume of
spray leapt half-way up the cliff.

"Stop it! Stop it!"

His voice struck a silence among them.

"Smoke."

A strange thing happened in his head. Something flittered there in front of his mind like a bat's wing, obscuring his idea.

"Smoke."

At once the ideas were back, and the anger.

"We want smoke. And you go wasting your time. You roll rocks."

Roger shouted.

"We've got plenty of time!"

Ralph shook his head.

"We'll go to the mountain."

The clamor broke out. Some of the boys wanted to go back to the beach. Some wanted to roll more rocks. The sun was bright and danger had faded with the darkness.

"Jack. The beast might be on the other side. You can lead again. You've been."

"We could go by the shore. There's fruit."

Bill came up to Ralph.

"Why can't we stay here for a bit?"

"That's right."

"Let's have a fort."

"There's no food here," said Ralph, "and no shelter. Not much fresh water."

"This would make a wizard fort."

"We can roll rocks—"

"Right onto the bridge—"

"I say we'll go on!" shouted Ralph furiously. "We've got to make certain. We'll go now."

"Let's stay here—"

"Back to the shelter—"

"I'm tired—"

"No!"

Ralph struck the skin off his knuckles. They did not seem to hurt.

"I'm chief. We've got to make certain. Can't you see the mountain? There's no signal showing. There may be a ship out there. Are you all off your rockers?"

Mutinously, the boys fell silent or muttering.

Jack led the way down the rock and across the bridge.

# CHAPTER SEVEN

# Shadows and Tall Trees

The pig-run kept close to the jumble of rocks that lay down by the water on the other side and Ralph was content to follow Jack along it. If you could shut your ears to the slow suck down of the sea and boil of the return, if you could forget how dun and unvisited were the ferny coverts on either side, then there was a chance that you might put the beast out of mind and dream for a while. The sun had swung over the vertical and the afternoon heat was closing in on the island. Ralph passed a message forward to Jack and when they next came to fruit the whole party stopped and ate.

Sitting, Ralph was aware of the heat for the first time that day. He pulled distastefully at his grey shirt and wondered whether he might undertake the adventure of washing it. Sitting under what seemed an unusual heat, even for this island, Ralph planned his toilet. He would like to have a pair of scissors and cut this hair—he flung the mass back—cut this filthy hair right back to half an inch. He would like to have a bath, a proper wallow with soap. He passed his tongue experimentally over his teeth and decided that a toothbrush would come in handy too. Then there were his nails—

Ralph turned his hand over and examined them. They were bitten down to the quick though he could not remember when he had restarted this habit nor any time when he indulged it.

"Be sucking my thumb next—"

He looked round, furtively. Apparently no one had heard. The hunters sat, stuffing themselves with this easy meal, trying to convince themselves that they got sufficient kick out of bananas and that other olive-grey, jelly-like fruit.

With the memory of his sometime clean self as a standard, Ralph looked them over. They were dirty, not with the spectacular dirt of boys who have fallen into mud or been brought down hard on a rainy day. Not one of them was an obvious subject for a shower, and yet—hair, much too long, tangled here and there, knotted round a dead leaf or a twig; faces cleaned fairly well by the process of eating and sweating but marked in the less accessible angles with a kind of shadow; clothes, worn away, stiff like his own with sweat, put on, not for decorum or comfort but out of custom; the skin of the body, scurfy with brine—

He discovered with a little fall of the heart that these were the conditions he took as normal now and that he did not mind. He sighed and pushed away the stalk from which he had stripped the fruit. Already the hunters were stealing away to do their business in the woods or down by the rocks. He turned and looked out to sea.

Here, on the other side of the island, the view was utterly different. The filmy enchantments of mirage could not endure the cold ocean water and the horizon was hard, clipped blue. Ralph wandered down to the rocks. Down here, almost on a level with the sea, you could follow with your eye the ceaseless, bulging passage of the deep sea waves. They were miles wide, apparently not breakers or the banked ridges of shallow water. They traveled the length of the island with an air of disregarding it and being set on other business; they were less a progress than a momentous rise and fall of the whole ocean. Now the sea would suck down, making cascades and waterfalls of retreating water, would sink past the rocks and plaster down the seaweed like shining hair: then, pausing, gather and rise with a roar, irresistibly swelling over point and outcrop, climbing the little cliff, sending at last an arm of surf up a gully to end a yard or so from him in fingers of spray.

Wave after wave, Ralph followed the rise and fall until something of the remoteness of the sea numbed his brain. Then gradually the almost infinite size of this water forced itself on his attention. This was the divider, the barrier. On the other side of the island, swathed at midday with mirage, defended by the shield of the quiet lagoon, one might dream of rescue; but here, faced by the brute obtuseness of the ocean, the miles of division, one was clamped down, one was helpless, one was condemned, one was—

Simon was speaking almost in his ear. Ralph found that
he had rock painfully gripped in both hands, found his
body arched, the muscles of his neck stiff, his mouth
strained open.

"You'll get back to where you came from."

Simon nodded as he spoke. He was kneeling on one knee,
looking down from a higher rock which he held with both
hands; his other leg stretched down to Ralph's level.

Ralph was puzzled and searched Simon's face for a clue.

"It's so big, I mean—"

Simon nodded.

"All the same. You'll get back all right. I think so, anyway."

Some of the strain had gone from Ralph's body. He
glanced at the sea and then smiled bitterly at Simon.

"Got a ship in your pocket?"

Simon grinned and shook his head.

"How do you know, then?"

When Simon was still silent Ralph said curtly, "You're
batty."

Simon shook his head violently till the coarse black hair
flew backwards and forwards across his face.

"No, I'm not. I just *think you'll get back all right.*"

For a moment nothing more was said. And then they suddenly smiled at each other.

Roger called from the coverts.

"Come and see!"

The ground was turned over near the pig-run and there
were droppings that steamed. Jack bent down to them as
though he loved them.

"Ralph—we need meat even if we are hunting the other
thing."

"If you mean going the right way, we'll hunt."

They set off again, the hunters bunched a little by fear of
the mentioned beast, while Jack quested ahead. They went
more slowly than Ralph had bargained for; yet in a way
he was glad to loiter, cradling his spear. Jack came up
against some emergency of his craft and soon the procession stopped. Ralph leaned against a tree and at once the
daydreams came swarming up. Jack was in charge of the
hunt and there would be time to get to the mountain—

Once, following his father from Chatham to Devonport,

they had lived in a cottage on the edge of the moors. In the succession of houses that Ralph had known, this one stood out with particular clarity because after that house he had been sent away to school. Mummy had still been with them and Daddy had come home every day. Wild ponies came to the stone wall at the bottom of the garden, and it had snowed. Just behind the cottage there was a sort of shed and you could lie up there, watching the flakes swirl past. You could see the damp spot where each flake died, then you could mark the first flake that lay down without melting and watch the whole ground turn white. You could go indoors when you were cold and look out of the window, past that bright copper kettle and the plate with the little blue men.

When you went to bed there was a bowl of cornflakes with sugar and cream. And the books—they stood on the shelf by the bed, leaning together with always two or three laid flat on top because he had not bothered to put them back properly. They were dog-eared and scratched. There was the bright, shining one about Topsy and Mopsy that he never read because it was about two girls; there was the one about the magician which you read with a kind of tied-down terror, skipping page twenty-seven with the awful picture of the spider; there was a book about people who had dug things up, Egyptian things; there was *The Boy's Book of Trains, The Boy's Book of Ships*. Vividly they came before him; he could have reached up and touched them, could feel the weight and slow slide with which *The Mammoth Book for Boys* would come out and slither down. . . . Everything was all right; everything was good-humored and friendly.

The bushes crashed ahead of them. Boys flung themselves wildly from the pig track and scrabbled in the creepers, screaming. Ralph saw Jack nudged aside and fall. Then there was a creature bounding along the pig track toward him, with tusks gleaming and an intimidating grunt. Ralph found he was able to measure the distance coldly and take aim. With the boar only five yards away, he flung the foolish wooden stick that he carried, saw it hit the great snout and hang there for a moment. The boar's note changed to a squeal and it swerved aside into the covert. The pig-run filled with shouting boys again, Jack came running back, and poked about in the undergrowth.

"Through here—"

"But he'd do us!"

"Through here, I said—"

The boar was floundering away from them. They found another pig-run parallel to the first and Jack raced away. Ralph was full of fright and apprehension and pride.

"I hit him! The spear stuck in—"

Now they came, unexpectedly, to an open space by the sea. Jack cast about on the bare rock and looked anxious.

"He's gone."

"I hit him," said Ralph again, "and the spear stuck in a bit."

He felt the need of witnesses.

"Didn't you see me?"

Maurice nodded.

"I saw you. Right bang on his snout— Wheee!"

Ralph talked on, excitedly.

"I hit him all right. The spear stuck in. I wounded him!"

He sunned himself in their new respect and felt that hunting was good after all.

"I walloped him properly. That was the beast, I think!"

Jack came back.

"That wasn't the beast. That was a boar."

"I hit him."

"Why didn't you grab him? I tried—"

Ralph's voice ran up.

"But a boar!"

Jack flushed suddenly.

"You said he'd do us. What did you want to throw for? Why didn't you wait?"

He held out his arm.

"Look."

He turned his left forearm for them all to see. On the outside was a rip; not much, but bloody.

"He did that with his tusks. I couldn't get my spear down in time."

Attention focused on Jack.

"That's a wound," said Simon, "and you ought to suck it. Like Berengaria."

Jack sucked.

"I hit him," said Ralph indignantly. "I hit him with my spear, I wounded him."

He tried for their attention.

"He was coming along the path. I threw, like this—"

Robert snarled at him. Ralph entered into the play and everybody laughed. Presently they were all jabbing at Robert who made mock rushes.

Jack shouted.

"Make a ring!"

The circle moved in and round. Robert squealed in mock terror, then in real pain.

"Ow! Stop it! You're hurting!"

The butt end of a spear fell on his back as he blundered among them.

"Hold him!"

They got his arms and legs. Ralph, carried away by a sudden thick excitement, grabbed Eric's spear and jabbed at Robert with it.

"Kill him! Kill him!"

All at once, Robert was screaming and struggling with the strength of frenzy. Jack had him by the hair and was brandishing his knife. Behind him was Roger, fighting to get close. The chant rose ritually, as at the last moment of a dance or a hunt.

"*Kill the pig! Cut his throat! Kill the pig! Bash him in!*"

Ralph too was fighting to get near, to get a handful of that brown, vulnerable flesh. The desire to squeeze and hurt was over-mastering.

Jack's arm came down; the heaving circle cheered and made pig-dying noises. Then they lay quiet, panting, listening to Robert's frightened snivels. He wiped his face with a dirty arm, and made an effort to retrieve his status.

"Oh, my bum!"

He rubbed his rump ruefully. Jack rolled over.

"That was a good game."

"Just a game," said Ralph uneasily. "I got jolly badly hurt at rugger once."

"We ought to have a drum," said Maurice, "then we could do it properly."

Ralph looked at him.

"How properly?"

"I dunno. You want a fire, I think, and a drum, and you keep time to the drum."

"You want a pig," said Roger, "like in a real hunt."

"Or someone to pretend," said Jack. "You could, get

someone to dress up as a pig and then he could act—you know, pretend to knock me over and all that."

"You want a real pig," said Robert, still caressing his rump, "because you've got to kill him."

"Use a littlun," said Jack, and everybody laughed.

Ralph sat up.

"Well. We shan't find what we're looking for at this rate."

One by one they stood up, twitching rags into place.

Ralph looked at Jack.

"Now for the mountain."

"Shouldn't we go back to Piggy," said Maurice, "before dark?"

The twins nodded like one boy.

"Yes, that's right. Let's go up there in the morning."

Ralph looked out and saw the sea.

"We've got to start the fire again."

"You haven't got Piggy's specs," said Jack, "so you can't."

"Then we'll find out if the mountain's clear."

Maurice spoke, hesitating, not wanting to seem a funk.

"Supposing the beast's up there?"

Jack brandished his spear.

"We'll kill it."

The sun seemed a little cooler. He slashed with the spear.

"What are we waiting for?"

"I suppose," said Ralph, "if we keep on by the sea this way, we'll come out below the burnt bit and then we can climb the mountain."

Once more Jack led them along by the suck and heave of the blinding sea.

Once more Ralph dreamed, letting his skillful feet deal with the difficulties of the path. Yet here his feet seemed less skillful than before. For most of the way they were forced right down to the bare rock by the water and had to edge along between that and the dark luxuriance of the forest. There were little cliffs to be scaled, some to be used as paths, lengthy traverses where one used hands as well as feet. Here and there they could clamber over wave-wet rock, leaping across clear pools that the tide had left. They came to a gully that split the narrow foreshore like a defense. This seemed to have no bottom and they peered awe-stricken into the gloomy crack where water gurgled. Then the wave came back, the gully boiled before them and spray dashed up to the very creeper so that the boys were wet and shrieking. They tried the forest but it was thick and woven like a bird's nest. In the end they had to jump one by one, waiting till the water sank; and even so, some of them got a second drenching. After that the rocks seemed to be growing impassable so they sat for a time, letting their rags dry and watching the clipped outlines of the rollers that moved so slowly past the island. They found fruit in a haunt of bright little birds that hovered like insects. Then Ralph said they were going too slowly. He himself climbed a tree and parted the canopy, and saw the square head of the mountain seeming still a great way off. Then they tried to hurry along the rocks and Robert cut his knee quite badly and they had to recognize that this path must be taken slowly if they were to be safe. So they proceeded after that as if they were climbing a dangerous mountain, until the rocks became an uncompromising cliff, overhung with impossible jungle and falling sheer into the sea.

Ralph looked at the sun critically.

"Early evening. After tea-time, at any rate."

"I don't remember this cliff," said Jack, crestfallen, "so this must be the bit of the coast I missed."

Ralph nodded.

"Let me think."

By now, Ralph had no self-consciousness in public thinking but would treat the day's decisions as though he were playing chess. The only trouble was that he would never be a very good chess player. He thought of the littluns and Piggy. Vividly he imagined Piggy by himself, huddled in a shelter that was silent except for the sounds of nightmare.

"We can't leave the littluns alone with Piggy. Not all night."

The other boys said nothing but stood round, watching him.

"If we went back we should take hours."

Jack cleared his throat and spoke in a queer, tight voice.

"We mustn't let anything happen to Piggy, must we?"

Ralph tapped his teeth with the dirty point of Eric's spear.

"If we go across—"

He glanced round him.

"Someone's got to go across the island and tell Piggy we'll be back after dark."

Bill spoke, unbelieving.

"Through the forest by himself? Now?"

"We can't spare more than one."

Simon pushed his way to Ralph's elbow.

"I'll go if you like. I don't mind, honestly."

Before Ralph had time to reply, he smiled quickly, turned and climbed into the forest.

Ralph looked back at Jack, seeing him, infuriatingly, for the first time.

"Jack—that time you went the whole way to the castle rock."

Jack glowered.

"Yes?"

"You came along part of this shore—below the mountain, beyond there."

"Yes."

"And then?"

"I found a pig-run. It went for miles."

"So the pig-run must be somewhere in there."

Ralph nodded. He pointed at the forest.

Everybody agreed, sagely.

"All right then. We'll smash a way through till we find the pig-run."

He took a step and halted.

"Wait a minute though! Where does the pig-run go to?"

"The mountain," said Jack, "I told you." He sneered. "Don't you want to go to the mountain?"

Ralph sighed, sensing the rising antagonism, understanding that this was how Jack felt as soon as he ceased to lead.

"I was thinking of the light. We'll be stumbling about."

"We were going to look for the beast."

"There won't be enough light."

"I don't mind going," said Jack hotly. "I'll go when we get there. Won't you? Would you rather go back to the shelters and tell Piggy?"

Now it was Ralph's turn to flush but he spoke despairingly, out of the new understanding that Piggy had given him.

"Why do you hate me?"

The boys stirred uneasily, as though something indecent had been said. The silence lengthened.

Ralph, still hot and hurt, turned away first.

"Come on."

He led the way and set himself as by right to hack at the tangles. Jack brought up the rear, displaced and brooding.

The pig-track was a dark tunnel, for the sun was sliding quickly toward the edge of the world and in the forest shadows were never far to seek. The track was broad and beaten and they ran along at a swift trot. Then the roof of leaves broke up and they halted, breathing quickly, looking at the few stars that pricked round the head of the mountain.

"There you are."

The boys peered at each other doubtfully. Ralph made a decision.

"We'll go straight across to the platform and climb tomorrow."

They murmured agreement; but Jack was standing by his shoulder.

"If you're frightened of course—"

Ralph turned on him.

"Who went first on the castle rock?"

"I went too. And that was daylight."

"All right. Who wants to climb the mountain now?"

Silence was the only answer.

"Samneric? What about you?"

"We ought to go an' tell Piggy—"

"—yes, tell Piggy that—"

"But Simon went!"

"We ought to tell Piggy—in case—"

"Robert? Bill?"

They were going straight back to the platform now. Not, of course, that they were afraid—but tired.

Ralph turned back to Jack.

"You see?"

"I'm going up the mountain." The words came from Jack viciously, as though they were a curse. He looked at Ralph, his thin body tensed, his spear held as if he threatened him.

"I'm going up the mountain to look for the beast—now." Then the supreme sting, the casual, bitter word. "Coming?"

At that word the other boys forgot their urge to be gone and turned back to sample this fresh rub of two spirits in the dark. The word was too good, too bitter, too successfully daunting to be repeated. It took Ralph at low water when his nerve was relaxed for the return to the shelter and the still, friendly waters of the lagoon.

"I don't mind."

Astonished, he heard his voice come out, cool and casual, so that the bitterness of Jack's taunt fell powerless.

"If you don't mind, of course."

"Oh, not at all."

Jack took a step.

"Well then—"

Side by side, watched by silent boys, the two started up the mountain.

Ralph stopped.

"We're silly. Why should only two go? If we find anything, two won't be enough."

There came the sound of boys scuttling away. Astonishingly, a dark figure moved against the tide.

"Roger?"

"Yes."

"That's three, then."

Once more they set out to climb the slope of the mountain. The darkness seemed to flow round them like a tide. Jack, who had said nothing, began to choke and cough, and a gust of wind set all three spluttering. Ralph's eyes were blinded with tears.

"Ashes. We're on the edge of the burnt patch."

Their footsteps and the occasional breeze were stirring up small devils of dust. Now that they stopped again, Ralph had time while he coughed to remember how silly they were. If there was no beast—and almost certainly there was no beast—in that case, well and good; but if there was something waiting on top of the mountain—what was the use of three of them, handicapped by the darkness and carrying only sticks?

"We're being fools."

Out of the darkness came the answer.

"Windy?"

Irritably Ralph shook himself. This was all Jack's fault.

"'Course I am. But we're still being fools."

"If you don't want to go on," said the voice sarcastically, "I'll go up by myself."

Ralph heard the mockery and hated Jack. The sting of ashes in his eyes, tiredness, fear, enraged him.

"Go on then! We'll wait here."

There was silence.

"Why don't you go? Are you frightened?"

A stain in the darkness, a stain that was Jack, detached itself and began to draw away.

"All right. So long."

The stain vanished. Another took its place.

Ralph felt his knee against something hard and rocked a charred trunk that was edgy to the touch. He felt the sharp cinders that had been bark push against the back of his knee and knew that Roger had sat down. He felt with his hands and lowered himself beside Roger, while the trunk rocked among invisible ashes. Roger, uncommunicative by nature, said nothing. He offered no opinion on the beast nor told Ralph why he had chosen to come on this mad expedition. He simply sat and rocked the trunk gently. Ralph noticed a rapid and infuriating tapping noise and realized that Roger was banging his silly wooden stick against something.

So they sat, the rocking, tapping, impervious Roger and Ralph, fuming; round them the close sky was loaded with stars, save where the mountain punched up a hole of blackness.

There was a slithering noise high above them, the sound of someone taking giant and dangerous strides on rock or ash. Then Jack found them, and was shivering and croaking in a voice they could just recognize as his.

"I saw a thing on top."

They heard him blunder against the trunk which rocked violently. He lay silent for a moment, then muttered.

"Keep a good lookout. It may be following."

A shower of ash pattered round them. Jack sat up.

"I saw a thing bulge on the mountain."

"You only imagined it," said Ralph shakily, "because nothing would bulge. Not any sort of creature."

Roger spoke; they jumped, for they had forgotten him.

"A frog."

Jack giggled and shuddered.

"Some frog. There was a noise too. A kind of 'plop' noise. Then the thing bulged."

Ralph surprised himself, not so much by the quality of his voice, which was even, but by the bravado of its intention.

"We'll go and look."

For the first time since he had first known Jack, Ralph could feel him hesitate.

"Now—?"

His voice spoke for him.

"Of course."

He got off the trunk and led the way across the clinking cinders up into the dark, and the others followed.

Now that his physical voice was silent the inner voice of reason, and other voices too, made themselves heard. Piggy was calling him a kid. Another voice told him not to be a fool; and the darkness and desperate enterprise gave the night a kind of dentist's chair unreality.

As they came to the last slope, Jack and Roger drew near, changed from the ink-stains to distinguishable figures. By common consent they stopped and crouched together. Behind them, on the horizon, was a patch of lighter sky where in a moment the moon would rise. The wind roared once in the forest and pushed their rags against them.

Ralph stirred.

"Come on."

They crept forward, Roger lagging a little. Jack and Ralph turned the shoulder of the mountain together. The glittering lengths of the lagoon lay below them and beyond that a long white smudge that was the reef. Roger joined them.

Jack whispered.

"Let's creep forward on hands and knees. Maybe it's asleep."

Roger and Ralph moved on, this time leaving Jack in the rear, for all his brave words. They came to the flat top where the rock was hard to hands and knees.

A creature that bulged.

Ralph put his hand in the cold, soft ashes of the fire and smothered a cry. His hand and shoulder were twitching from the unlooked-for contact. Green lights of nausea appeared for a moment and ate into the darkness. Roger lay behind him and Jack's mouth was at his ear.

"Over there, where there used to be a gap in the rock.
A sort of hump—see?"

Ashes blew into Ralph's face from the dead fire. He could
not see the gap or anything else, because the green lights
were opening again and growing, and the top of the mountain was sliding sideways.

Once more, from a distance, he heard Jack's whisper.

"Scared?"

Not scared so much as paralyzed; hung up here immova-
ble on the top of a diminishing, moving mountain. Jack slid
away from him, Roger bumped, fumbled with a hiss of
breath, and passed onwards. He heard them whispering.

"Can you see anything?"

"There—"

In front of them, only three or four yards away, was a
rock-like hump where no rock should be. Ralph could hear
a tiny chattering noise coming from somewhere—perhaps
from his own mouth. He bound himself together with his
will, fused his fear and loathing into a hatred, and stood up.
He took two leaden steps forward.

Behind them the sliver of moon had drawn clear of the
horizon. Before them, something like a great ape was sitting asleep with its head between its knees. Then the wind
roared in the forest, there was confusion in the darkness
and the creature lifted its head, holding toward them the
ruin of a face.

Ralph found himself taking giant strides among the ashes,
heard other creatures crying out and leaping and dared
the impossible on the dark slope; presently the mountain
was deserted, save for the three abandoned sticks and the
thing that bowed.

# CHAPTER EIGHT

## *Gift for the Darkness*

Piggy looked up miserably from the dawn-pale beach to the dark mountain.

"Are you sure? Really sure, I mean?"

"I told you a dozen times now," said Ralph, "we saw it."

"D'you think we're safe down here?"

"How the hell should I know?"

Ralph jerked away from him and walked a few paces along the beach. Jack was kneeling and drawing a circular pattern in the sand with his forefinger. Piggy's voice came to them, hushed.

"Are you sure? Really?"

"Go up and see," said Jack contemptuously, "and good riddance."

"No fear."

"The beast had teeth," said Ralph, "and big black eyes."

He shuddered violently. Piggy took off his one round of glass and polished the surface.

"What we going to do?"

Ralph turned toward the platform. The conch glimmered among the trees, a white blob against the place where the sun would rise. He pushed back his mop.

"I don't know."

He remembered the panic flight down the mountainside.

"I don't think we'd ever fight a thing that size, honestly, you know. We'd talk but we wouldn't fight a tiger. We'd hide. Even Jack 'ud hide."

Jack still looked at the sand.

"What about my hunters?"

Simon came stealing out of the shadows by the shelters.

115

Ralph ignored Jack's question. He pointed to the touch of yellow above the sea.

"As long as there's light we're brave enough. But then? And now that thing squats by the fire as though it didn't want us to be rescued—"

He was twisting his hands now, unconsciously. His voice rose.

"So we can't have a signal fire. . . . We're beaten."

A point of gold appeared above the sea and at once all the sky lightened.

"What about my hunters?"

"Boys armed with sticks."

Jack got to his feet. His face was red as he marched away. Piggy put on his one glass and looked at Ralph.

"Now you done it. You been rude about his hunters."

"Oh shut up!"

The sound of the inexpertly blown conch interrupted them. As though he were serenading the rising sun, Jack went on blowing till the shelters were astir and the hunters crept to the platform and the littluns whimpered as now they so frequently did. Ralph rose obediently, and Piggy, and they went to the platform.

"Talk," said Ralph bitterly, "talk, talk, talk."

He took the conch from Jack.

"This meeting—"

Jack interrupted him.

"I called it."

"If you hadn't called it I should have. You just blew the conch."

"Well, isn't that calling it?"

"Oh, take it! Go on—talk!"

Ralph thrust the conch into Jack's arms and sat down on the trunk.

"I've called an assembly," said Jack, "because of a lot of things. First, you know now, we've seen the beast. We crawled up. We were only a few feet away. The beast sat up and looked at us. I don't know what it does. We don't even know what it is—"

"The beast comes out of the sea—"

"Out of the dark—"

"Trees—"

"Quiet!" shouted Jack. "You, listen. The beast is sitting up there, whatever it is—"

"Perhaps it's waiting—"

"Hunting—"

"Yes, hunting."

"Hunting," said Jack. He remembered his age-old tremors in the forest. "Yes. The beast is a hunter. Only— shut up! The next thing is that we couldn't kill it. And the next thing is that Ralph said my hunters are no good."

"I never said that!"

"I've got the conch. Ralph thinks you're cowards, running away from the boar and the beast. And that's not all."

There was a kind of sigh on the platform as if everyone knew what was coming. Jack's voice went on, tremulous yet determined, pushing against the unco-operative silence.

"He's like Piggy. He says things like Piggy. He isn't a proper chief."

Jack clutched the conch to him.

"He's a coward himself."

For a moment he paused and then went on.

"On top, when Roger and me went on—he stayed back."

"I went too!"

"After."

The two boys glared at each other through screens of hair.

"I went on too," said Ralph, "then I ran away. So did you."

"Call me a coward then."

Jack turned to the hunters.

"He's not a hunter. He'd never have got us meat. He isn't a prefect and we don't know anything about him. He just gives orders and expects people to obey for nothing. All this talk—"

"All this talk!" shouted Ralph. "Talk, talk! Who wanted it? Who called the meeting?"

Jack turned, red in the face, his chin sunk back. He glowered up under his eyebrows.

"All right then," he said in tones of deep meaning, and menace, "all right."

He held the conch against his chest with one hand and stabbed the air with his index finger.

"Who thinks Ralph oughtn't to be chief?"

He looked expectantly at the boys ranged round, who had frozen. Under the palms there was deadly silence.

"Hands up," said Jack strongly, "whoever wants Ralph not to be chief?"

The silence continued, breathless and heavy and full of shame. Slowly the red drained from Jack's cheeks, then came back with a painful rush. He licked his lips and turned his head at an angle, so that his gaze avoided the embarrassment of linking with another's eye.

"How many think—"

His voice tailed off. The hands that held the conch shook. He cleared his throat, and spoke loudly.

"All right then."

He laid the conch with great care in the grass at his feet. The humiliating tears were running from the corner of each eye.

"I'm not going to play any longer. Not with you."

Most of the boys were looking down now, at the grass or their feet. Jack cleared his throat again.

"I'm not going to be part of Ralph's lot—"

He looked along the right-hand logs, numbering the hunters that had been a choir.

"I'm going off by myself. He can catch his own pigs. Anyone who wants to hunt when I do can come too."

He blundered out of the triangle toward the drop to the white sand.

"Jack!"

Jack turned and looked back at Ralph. For a moment he paused and then cried out, high-pitched, enraged.

"—No!"

He leapt down from the platform and ran along the beach, paying no heed to the steady fall of his tears; and until he dived into the forest Ralph watched him.

Piggy was indignant.

"I been talking, Ralph, and you just stood there like—"

Softly, looking at Piggy and not seeing him, Ralph spoke to himself.

"He'll come back. When the sun goes down he'll come."

He looked at the conch in Piggy's hand.

"What?"

"Well there!"

Piggy gave up the attempt to rebuke Ralph. He polished his glass again and went back to his subject.

"We can do without Jack Merridew. There's others besides him on this island. But now we really got a beast, though I can't hardly believe it, we'll need to stay close to the platform; there'll be less need of him and his hunting. So now we can really decide on what's what."

"There's no help, Piggy. Nothing to be done."

For a while they sat in depressed silence. Then Simon stood up and took the conch from Piggy, who was so astonished that he remained on his feet. Ralph looked up at Simon.

"Simon? What is it this time?"

A half-sound of jeering ran round the circle and Simon shrank from it.

"I thought there might be something to do. Something we—"

Again the pressure of the assembly took his voice away. He sought for help and sympathy and chose Piggy. He turned half toward him, clutching the conch to his brown chest.

"I think we ought to climb the mountain."

The circle shivered with dread. Simon broke off and turned to Piggy who was looking at him with an expression of derisive incomprehension.

"What's the good of climbing up to this here beast when Ralph and the other two couldn't do nothing?"

Simon whispered his answer.

"What else is there to do?"

His speech made, he allowed Piggy to lift the conch out of his hands. Then he retired and sat as far away from the others as possible.

Piggy was speaking now with more assurance and with what, if the circumstances had not been so serious, the others would have recognized as pleasure.

"I said we could all do without a certain person. Now I say we got to decide on what can be done. And I think I could tell you what Ralph's going to say next. The most important thing on the island is the smoke and you can't have no smoke without a fire."

Ralph made a restless movement.

"No go, Piggy. We've got no fire. That thing sits up there—we'll have to stay here."

Piggy lifted the conch as though to add power to his next words.

"We got no fire on the mountain. But what's wrong with a fire down here? A fire could be built on them rocks. On the sand, even. We'd make smoke just the same."

"That's right!"

"Smoke!"

"By the bathing pool!"

The boys began to babble. Only Piggy could have the intellectual daring to suggest moving the fire from the mountain.

"So we'll have the fire down here," said Ralph. He looked about him. "We can build it just here between the bathing pool and the platform. Of course—"

He broke off, frowning, thinking the thing out, unconsciously tugging at the stub of a nail with his teeth.

"Of course the smoke won't show so much, not be seen so far away. But we needn't go near, near the—"

The others nodded in perfect comprehension. There would be no need to go near.

"We'll build the fire now."

The greatest ideas are the simplest. Now there was something to be done they worked with passion. Piggy was so full of delight and expanding liberty in Jack's departure, so full of pride in his contribution to the good of society, that he helped to fetch wood. The wood he fetched was close at hand, a fallen tree on the platform that they did not need for the assembly, yet to the others the sanctity of the platform had protected even what was useless there. Then the twins realized they would have a fire near them as a comfort in the night and this set a few littluns dancing and clapping hands.

The wood was not so dry as the fuel they had used on the mountain. Much of it was damply rotten and full of insects that scurried; logs had to be lifted from the soil with care or they crumbled into sodden powder. More than this, in order to avoid going deep into the forest the boys worked near at hand on any fallen wood no matter how tangled with new growth. The skirts of the forest and the scar were familiar, near the conch and the shelters and sufficiently friendly in daylight. What they might become in darkness nobody cared to think. They worked therefore with great energy and cheerfulness, though as time crept by there was a suggestion of panic in the energy and hysteria in the cheerfulness. They built a pyramid of leaves and twigs, branches and logs, on the bare sand by the platform. For the first time on the island, Piggy himself removed his one glass, knelt down and focused the sun on tinder. Soon there was a ceiling of smoke and a bush of yellow flame.

The littluns who had seen few fires since the first catastrophe became wildly excited. They danced and sang and there was a partyish air about the gathering.

At last Ralph stopped work and stood up, smudging the sweat from his face with a dirty forearm.

"We'll have to have a small fire. This one's too big to keep up."

Piggy sat down carefully on the sand and began to polish his glass.

"We could experiment. We could find out how to make a small hot fire and then put green branches on to make smoke. Some of them leaves must be better for that than the others."

As the fire died down so did the excitement. The littluns stopped singing and dancing and drifted away toward the sea or the fruit trees or the shelters.

Ralph flopped down in the sand.

"We'll have to make a new list of who's to look after the fire."

"If you can find 'em."

He looked round. Then for the first time he saw how few biguns there were and understood why the work had been so hard.

"Where's Maurice?"

Piggy wiped his glass again.

"I expect . . . no, he wouldn't go into the forest by himself, would he?"

Ralph jumped up, ran swiftly round the fire and stood by Piggy, holding up his hair.

"But we've got to have a list! There's you and me and Samneric and—"

He would not look at Piggy but spoke casually.

"Where's Bill and Roger?"

Piggy leaned forward and put a fragment of wood on the fire.

"I expect they've gone. I expect they won't play either."

Ralph sat down and began to poke little holes in the

sand. He was surprised to see that one had a drop of blood by it. He examined his bitten nail closely and watched the little globe of blood that gathered where the quick was gnawed away.

Piggy went on speaking.

"I seen them stealing off when we was gathering wood. They went that way. The same way as he went himself."

Ralph finished his inspection and looked up into the air. The sky, as if in sympathy with the great changes among them, was different today and so misty that in some places the hot air seemed white. The disc of the sun was dull silver as though it were nearer and not so hot, yet the air stifled.

"They always been making trouble, haven't they?"

The voice came near his shoulder and sounded anxious.

"We can do without 'em. We'll be happier now, won't we?"

Ralph sat. The twins came, dragging a great log and grinning in their triumph. They dumped the log among the embers so that sparks flew.

"We can do all right on our own, can't we?"

For a long time while the log dried, caught fire and turned red hot, Ralph sat in the sand and said nothing. He did not see Piggy go to the twins and whisper with them, nor how the three boys went together into the forest.

"Here you are."

He came to himself with a jolt. Piggy and the other two were by him. They were laden with fruit.

"I thought perhaps," said Piggy, "we ought to have a feast, kind of."

The three boys sat down. They had a great mass of the fruit with them and all of it properly ripe. They grinned at Ralph as he took some and began to eat.

"Thanks," he said. Then with an accent of pleased surprise—"Thanks!"

"Do all right on our own," said Piggy. "It's them that haven't no common sense that make trouble on this island. We'll make a little hot fire—"

Ralph remembered what had been worrying him.

"Where's Simon?"

"I don't know."

"You don't think he's climbing the mountain?"

Piggy broke into noisy laughter and took more fruit.

"He might be." He gulped his mouthful. "He's cracked."

Simon had passed through the area of fruit trees but today the littluns had been too busy with the fire on the beach and they had not pursued him there. He went on among the creepers until he reached the great mat that was woven by the open space and crawled inside. Beyond the screen of leaves the sunlight pelted down and the butterflies danced in the middle their unending dance. He knelt down and the arrow of the sun fell on him. That other time the air had seemed to vibrate with heat; but now it threatened. Soon the sweat was running from his long coarse hair. He shifted restlessly but there was no avoiding the sun. Presently he was thirsty, and then very thirsty.

He continued to sit.

Far off along the beach, Jack was standing before a small group of boys. He was looking brilliantly happy.

"Hunting," he said. He sized them up. Each of them wore the remains of a black cap and ages ago they had stood in two demure rows and their voices had been the song of angels.

"We'll hunt. I'm going to be chief."

They nodded, and the crisis passed easily.

"And then—about the beast."

They moved, looked at the forest.

"I say this. We aren't going to bother about the beast."

He nodded at them.

"We're going to forget the beast."

"That's right!"

"Yes!"

"Forget the beast!"

If Jack was astonished by their fervor he did not show it.

"And another thing. We shan't dream so much down here. This is near the end of the island."

They agreed passionately out of the depths of their tormented private lives.

"Now listen. We might go later to the castle rock. But now I'm going to get more of the biguns away from the conch and all that. We'll kill a pig and give a feast." He paused and went on more slowly. "And about the beast. When we kill we'll leave some of the kill for it. Then it won't bother us, maybe."

He stood up abruptly.

"We'll go into the forest now and hunt."

He turned and trotted away and after a moment they followed him obediently.

They spread out, nervously, in the forest. Almost at once Jack found the dung and scattered roots that told of pig and soon the track was fresh. Jack signaled the rest of the hunt to be quiet and went forward by himself. He was happy and wore the damp darkness of the forest like his old clothes. He crept down a slope to rocks and scattered trees by the sea.

The pigs lay, bloated bags of fat, sensuously enjoying the shadows under the trees. There was no wind and they were unsuspicious; and practice had made Jack silent as the shadows. He stole away again and instructed his hidden hunters. Presently they all began to inch forward sweating in the silence and heat. Under the trees an ear flapped idly. A little apart from the rest, sunk in deep maternal bliss, lay the largest sow of the lot. She was black and pink; and the great bladder of her belly was fringed with a row of piglets that slept or burrowed and squeaked.

Fifteen yards from the drove Jack stopped, and his arm, straightening, pointed at the sow. He looked round in inquiry to make sure that everyone understood and the other boys nodded at him. The row of right arms slid back.

"Now!"

The drove of pigs started up; and at a range of only ten yards the wooden spears with fire-hardened points flew toward the chosen pig. One piglet, with a demented shriek, rushed into the sea trailing Roger's spear behind it. The sow gave a gasping squeal and staggered up, with two spears sticking in her fat flank. The boys shouted and rushed forward, the piglets scattered and the sow burst the advancing line and went crashing away through the forest.

"After her!"

They raced along the pig-track, but the forest was too dark and tangled so that Jack, cursing, stopped them and cast among the trees. Then he said nothing for a time but breathed fiercely so that they were awed by him and looked at each other in uneasy admiration. Presently he stabbed down at the ground with his finger.

"There—"

Before the others could examine the drop of blood, Jack had swerved off, judging a trace, touching a bough that gave. So he followed, mysteriously right and assured, and the hunters trod behind him.

He stopped before a covert.

"In there."

They surrounded the covert but the sow got away with the sting of another spear in her flank. The trailing butts hindered her and the sharp, cross-cut points were a torment. She blundered into a tree, forcing a spear still deeper; and after that any of the hunters could follow her easily by the drops of vivid blood. The afternoon wore on, hazy and dreadful with damp heat; the sow staggered her way ahead of them, bleeding and mad, and the hunters followed, wedded to her in lust, excited by the long chase and the dropped blood. They could see her now, nearly got up with her, but she spurted with her last strength and held ahead of them again. They were just behind her when she staggered into an open space where bright flowers grew and butterflies danced round each other and the air was hot and still.

Here, struck down by the heat, the sow fell and the hunters hurled themselves at her. This dreadful eruption from an unknown world made her frantic; she squealed and bucked and the air was full of sweat and noise and blood and terror. Roger ran round the heap, prodding with his spear whenever pigflesh appeared. Jack was on top of the sow, stabbing downward with his knife. Roger found a lodgment for his point and began to push till he was leaning with his whole weight. The spear moved forward inch by inch and the terrified squealing became a high-pitched scream. Then Jack found the throat and the hot blood spouted over his hands. The sow collapsed under them and they were heavy and fulfilled upon her. The butterflies still danced, preoccupied in the center of the clearing.

At last the immediacy of the kill subsided. The boys drew back, and Jack stood up, holding out his hands.

"Look."

He giggled and flicked them while the boys laughed at his reeking palms. Then Jack grabbed Maurice and rubbed the stuff over his cheeks. Roger began to withdraw his spear and the boys noticed it for the first time. Robert stabilized the thing in a phrase which was received uproariously.

"Right up her ass!"

"Did you hear?"

"Did you hear what he said?"

"Right up her ass!"

This time Robert and Maurice acted the two parts; and Maurice's acting of the pig's efforts to avoid the advancing spear was so funny that the boys cried with laughter.

At length even this palled. Jack began to clean his bloody hands on the rock. Then he started work on the sow and paunched her, lugging out the hot bags of colored guts, pushing them into a pile on the rock while the others watched him. He talked as he worked.

"We'll take the meat along the beach. I'll go back to the platform and invite them to a feast. That should give us time."

Roger spoke.

"Chief—"

"Uh—?"

"How can we make a fire?"

Jack squatted back and frowned at the pig.

"We'll raid them and take fire. There must be four of you; Henry and you, Bill and Maurice. We'll put on paint and sneak up; Roger can snatch a branch while I say what I want. The rest of you can get this back to where we were. We'll build the fire there. And after that—"

He paused and stood up, looking at the shadows under the trees. His voice was lower when he spoke again.

"But we'll leave part of the kill for . . ."

He knelt down again and was busy with his knife. The boys crowded round him. He spoke over his shoulder to Roger.

"Sharpen a stick at both ends."

Presently he stood up, holding the dripping sow's head in his hands.

"Where's that stick?"

"Here."

"Ram one end in the earth. Oh—it's rock. Jam it in that crack. There."

Jack held up the head and jammed the soft throat down on the pointed end of the stick which pierced through into the mouth. He stood back and the head hung there, a little blood dribbling down the stick.

Instinctively the boys drew back too; and the forest was

very still. They listened, and the loudest noise was the buzzing of flies over the spilled guts.

Jack spoke in a whisper.

"Pick up the pig."

Maurice and Robert skewered the carcass, lifted the dead weight, and stood ready. In the silence, and standing over the dry blood, they looked suddenly furtive.

Jack spoke loudly.

"This head is for the beast. It's a gift."

The silence accepted the gift and awed them. The head remained there, dim-eyed, grinning faintly, blood blackening between the teeth. All at once they were running away, as fast as they could, through the forest toward the open beach.

Simon stayed where he was, a small brown image, concealed by the leaves. Even if he shut his eyes the sow's head still remained like an after-image. The half-shut eyes were dim with the infinite cynicism of adult life. They assured Simon that everything was a bad business.

"I know that."

Simon discovered that he had spoken aloud. He opened his eyes quickly and there was the head grinning amusedly in the strange daylight, ignoring the flies, the spilled guts, even ignoring the indignity of being spiked on a stick.

He looked away, licking his dry lips.

A gift for the beast. Might not the beast come for it? The head, he thought, appeared to agree with him. Run away, said the head silently, go back to the others. It was a joke really—why should you bother? You were just wrong, that's all. A little headache, something you ate, perhaps. Go back, child, said the head silently.

Simon looked up, feeling the weight of his wet hair, and gazed at the sky. Up there, for once, were clouds, great bulging towers that sprouted away over the island, grey and cream and copper-colored. The clouds were sitting on the land; they squeezed, produced moment by moment this close, tormenting heat. Even the butterflies deserted the open space where the obscene thing grinned and dripped. Simon lowered his head, carefully keeping his eyes shut, then sheltered them with his hand. There were no shadows under the trees but everywhere a pearly stillness, so that what was real seemed illusive and without definition. The pile of guts was a black blob of flies that buzzed like a saw. After a while these flies found Simon. Gorged, they alighted by his runnels of sweat and drank. They tickled under his nostrils and played leap-frog on his thighs. They were black and iridescent green and without number; and in front of Simon, the Lord of the Flies hung on his stick and grinned. At last Simon gave up and looked back; saw the white teeth and dim eyes, the blood—and his gaze was held by that ancient, inescapable recognition. In Simon's right temple, a pulse began to beat on the brain.

Ralph and Piggy lay in the sand, gazing at the fire and idly flicking pebbles into its smokeless heart.

"That branch is gone."

"Where's Samneric?"

"We ought to get some more wood. We're out of green branches."

Ralph sighed and stood up. There were no shadows under the palms on the platform; only this strange light that seemed to come from everywhere at once. High up among the bulging clouds thunder went off like a gun.

"We're going to get buckets of rain."

"What about the fire?"

Ralph trotted into the forest and returned with a wide spray of green which he dumped on the fire. The branch crackled, the leaves curled and the yellow smoke expanded.

Piggy made an aimless little pattern in the sand with his fingers.

"Trouble is, we haven't got enough people for a fire. You got to treat Samneric as one turn. They do everything together—"

"Of course."

"Well, that isn't fair. Don't you see? They ought to do two turns."

Ralph considered this and understood. He was vexed to find how little he thought like a grownup and sighed again. The island was getting worse and worse.

Piggy looked at the fire.

"You'll want another green branch soon."

Ralph rolled over.

"Piggy. What are we going to do?"

"Just have to get on without 'em."

"But—the fire."

He frowned at the black and white mess in which lay the unburnt ends of branches. He tried to formulate.

"I'm scared."

He saw Piggy look up; and blundered on.

"Not of the beast. I mean I'm scared of that too. But nobody else understands about the fire. If someone threw you a rope when you were drowning. If a doctor said take this because if you don't take it you'll die—you would, wouldn't you? I mean?"

" 'Course I would."

"Can't they see? Can't they understand? Without the smoke signal we'll die here? Look at that!"

A wave of heated air trembled above the ashes but without a trace of smoke.

"We can't keep one fire going. And they don't care. And what's more—" He looked intensely into Piggy's streaming face.

"What's more, I don't sometimes. Supposing I got like the others—not caring. What 'ud become of us?"

Piggy took off his glasses, deeply troubled.

"I dunno, Ralph. We just got to go on, that's all. That's what grownups would do."

Ralph, having begun the business of unburdening himself, continued.

"Piggy, what's wrong?"

Piggy looked at him in astonishment.

"Do you mean the—?"

"No, not it . . . I mean . . . what makes things break up like they do?"

Piggy rubbed his glasses slowly and thought. When he understood how far Ralph had gone toward accepting him he flushed pinkly with pride.

"I dunno, Ralph. I expect it's him."

"Jack?"

"Jack." A taboo was evolving round that word too.

Ralph nodded solemnly.

"Yes," he said, "I suppose it must be."

The forest near them burst into uproar. Demoniac figures with faces of white and red and green rushed out howling, so that the littluns fled screaming. Out of the corner of his eye, Ralph saw Piggy running. Two figures rushed at the fire and he prepared to defend himself but they grabbed half-burnt branches and raced away along the beach. The three others stood still, watching Ralph; and he saw that the tallest of them, stark naked save for paint and a belt, was Jack.

Ralph had his breath back and spoke.

"Well?"

Jack ignored him, lifted his spear and began to shout.

"Listen all of you. Me and my hunters, we're living along the beach by a flat rock. We hunt and feast and have fun. If you want to join my tribe come and see us. Perhaps I'll let you join. Perhaps not."

He paused and looked round. He was safe from shame or self-consciousness behind the mask of his paint and could look at each of them in turn. Ralph was kneeling by the remains of the fire like a sprinter at his mark and his face was half-hidden by hair and smut. Samneric peered together round a palm tree at the edge of the forest. A littlun howled, creased and crimson, by the bathing pool and Piggy stood on the platform, the white conch gripped in his hands.

"Tonight we're having a feast. We've killed a pig and we've got meat. You can come and eat with us if you like."

Up in the cloud canyons the thunder boomed again. Jack and the two anonymous savages with him swayed, looking up, and then recovered. The littlun went on howling. Jack was waiting for something. He whispered urgently to the others.

"Go on—now!"

The two savages murmured. Jack spoke sharply.

"Go on!"

The two savages looked at each other, raised their spears together and spoke in time.

"The Chief has spoken."

Then the three of them turned and trotted away.

Presently Ralph rose to his feet, looking at the place where the savages had vanished. Samneric came, talking in an awed whisper.

"I thought it was—"

"—and I was—"

"—scared."

Piggy stood above them on the platform, still holding the conch.

"That was Jack and Maurice and Robert," said Ralph. "Aren't they having fun?"

"I thought I was going to have asthma."

"Sucks to your ass-mar."

"When I saw Jack I was sure he'd go for the conch. Can't think why."

The group of boys looked at the white shell with affectionate respect. Piggy placed it in Ralph's hands and the littluns, seeing the familiar symbol, started to come back.

"Not here."

He turned toward the platform, feeling the need for ritual. First went Ralph, the white conch cradled, then Piggy very grave, then the twins, then the littluns and the others.

"Sit down all of you. They raided us for fire. They're having fun. But the—"

Ralph was puzzled by the shutter that flickered in his brain. There was something he wanted to say; then the shutter had come down.

"But the—"

They were regarding him gravely, not yet troubled by any doubts about his sufficiency. Ralph pushed the idiot hair out of his eyes and looked at Piggy.

"But the . . . oh . . . the fire! Of course, the fire!"

He started to laugh, then stopped and became fluent instead.

"The fire's the most important thing. Without the fire we can't be rescued. I'd like to put on war-paint and be a savage. But we must keep the fire burning. The fire's the most important thing on the island, because, because—"

He paused again and the silence became full of doubt and wonder.

Piggy whispered urgently. "Rescue."

"Oh yes. Without the fire we can't be rescued. So we must stay by the fire and make smoke."

When he stopped no one said anything. After the many brilliant speeches that had been made on this very spot Ralph's remarks seemed lame, even to the littluns.

At last Bill held out his hands for the conch.

"Now we can't have the fire up there—because we can't have the fire up there—we need more people to keep it going. Let's go to this feast and tell them the fire's hard on the rest of us. And the hunting and all that, being savages I mean—it must be jolly good fun."

Samneric took the conch.

"That must be fun like Bill says—and as he's invited us—"

"—to a feast—"

"—meat—"

"—crackling—"

"—I could do with some meat—"

Ralph held up his hand.

"Why shouldn't we get our own meat?"

The twins looked at each other. Bill answered.

"We don't want to go in the jungle."

Ralph grimaced.

"He—you know—goes."

"He's a hunter. They're all hunters. That's different."

No one spoke for a moment, then Piggy muttered to the sand.

"Meat—"

The littluns sat, solemnly thinking of meat, and dribbling. Overhead the cannon boomed again and the dry palm fronds clattered in a sudden gust of hot wind.

"You are a silly little boy," said the Lord of the Flies, "just an ignorant, silly little boy."

Simon moved his swollen tongue but said nothing.

"Don't you agree?" said the Lord of the Flies. "Aren't you just a silly little boy?"

Simon answered him in the same silent voice.

"Well then," said the Lord of the Flies, "you'd better run off and play with the others. They think you're batty. You don't want Ralph to think you're batty, do you? You like Ralph a lot, don't you? And Piggy, and Jack?"

Simon's head was tilted slightly up. His eyes could not break away and the Lord of the Flies hung in space before him.

"What are you doing out here all alone? Aren't you afraid of me?"

Simon shook.

"There isn't anyone to help you. Only me. And I'm the Beast."

Simon's mouth labored, brought forth audible words.

"Pig's head on a stick."

"Fancy thinking the Beast was something you could hunt and kill!" said the head. For a moment or two the forest and all the other dimly appreciated places echoed with the parody of laughter. "You knew, didn't you? I'm part of you? Close, close, close! I'm the reason why it's no go? Why things are what they are?"

The laughter shivered again.

"Come now," said the Lord of the Flies. "Get back to the others and we'll forget the whole thing."

Simon's head wobbled. His eyes were half closed as though he were imitating the obscene thing on the stick. He knew that one of his times was coming on. The Lord of the Flies was expanding like a balloon.

"This is ridiculous. You know perfectly well you'll only meet me down there—so don't try to escape!"

Simon's body was arched and stiff. The Lord of the Flies spoke in the voice of a schoolmaster.

"This has gone quite far enough. My poor, misguided child, do you think you know better than I do?"

There was a pause.

"I'm warning you. I'm going to get angry. D'you see? You're not wanted. Understand? We are going to have fun on this island. Understand? We are going to have fun on this island! So don't try it on, my poor misguided boy, or else—"

Simon found he was looking into a vast mouth. There was blackness within, a blackness that spread.

"—Or else," said the Lord of the Flies, "we shall do you. See? Jack and Roger and Maurice and Robert and Bill and Piggy and Ralph. Do you. See?"

Simon was inside the mouth. He fell down and lost consciousness.

# CHAPTER NINE

## *A View to a Death*

O ver the island the build-up of clouds continued. A
steady current of heated air rose all day from the
mountain and was thrust to ten thousand feet; re-
volving masses of gas piled up the static until the air was
ready to explode. By early evening the sun had gone and
a brassy glare had taken the place of clear daylight. Even
the air that pushed in from the sea was hot and held no re-
freshment. Colors drained from water and trees and pink
surfaces of rock, and the white and brown clouds brooded.
Nothing prospered but the flies who blackened their lord
and made the spilt guts look like a heap of glistening coal.
Even when the vessel broke in Simon's nose and the blood
gushed out they left him alone, preferring the pig's high
flavor.

With the running of the blood Simon's fit passed into the
weariness of sleep. He lay in the mat of creepers while the
evening advanced and the cannon continued to play. At
last he woke and saw dimly the dark earth close by his
cheek. Still he did not move but lay there, his face sideways on the earth, his eyes looking dully before him. Then
he turned over, drew his feet under him and laid hold of
the creepers to pull himself up. When the creepers shook
the flies exploded from the guts with a vicious note and
clamped back on again. Simon got to his feet. The light
was unearthly. The Lord of the Flies hung on his stick like
a black ball.

Simon spoke aloud to the clearing.

"What else is there to do?"

Nothing replied. Simon turned away from the open
space and crawled through the creepers till he was in the
dusk of the forest. He walked drearily between the trunks,

his face empty of expression, and the blood was dry round
his mouth and chin. Only sometimes as he lifted the ropes
of creeper aside and chose his direction from the trend of
the land, he mouthed words that did not reach the air.

Presently the creepers festooned the trees less frequently
and there was a scatter of pearly light from the sky down
through the trees. This was the backbone of the island, the
slightly higher land that lay beneath the mountain where
the forest was no longer deep jungle. Here there were wide
spaces interspersed with thickets and huge trees and the
trend of the ground led him up as the forest opened. He
pushed on, staggering sometimes with his weariness but
never stopping. The usual brightness was gone from his
eyes and he walked with a sort of glum determination like
an old man.

A buffet of wind made him stagger and he saw that he
was out in the open, on rock, under a brassy sky. He found
his legs were weak and his tongue gave him pain all the
time. When the wind reached the mountain-top he could
see something happen, a flicker of blue stuff against brown
clouds. He pushed himself forward and the wind came
again, stronger now, cuffing the forest heads till they
ducked and roared. Simon saw a humped thing suddenly
sit up on the top and look down at him. He hid his face,
and toiled on.

The flies had found the figure too. The life-like movement would scare them off for a moment so that they made
a dark cloud round the head. Then as the blue material of
the parachute collapsed the corpulent figure would bow
forward, sighing, and the flies settle once more.

Simon felt his knees smack the rock. He crawled forward
and soon he understood. The tangle of lines showed him
the mechanics of this parody; he examined the white nasal
bones, the teeth, the colors of corruption. He saw how piti-
lessly the layers of rubber and canvas held together the
poor body that should be rotting away. Then the wind blew
again and the figure lifted, bowed, and breathed foully at
him. Simon knelt on all fours and was sick till his stomach
was empty. Then he took the lines in his hands; he freed
them from the rocks and the figure from the wind's indignity.

At last he turned away and looked down at the beaches.
The fire by the platform appeared to be out, or at least

making no smoke. Further along the beach, beyond the little river and near a great slab of rock, a thin trickle of smoke was climbing into the sky. Simon, forgetful of the flies, shaded his eyes with both hands and peered at the smoke. Even at that distance it was possible to see that most of the boys—perhaps all the boys—were there. So they had shifted camp then, away from the beast. As Simon thought this, he turned to the poor broken thing that sat stinking by his side. The beast was harmless and horrible; and the news must reach the others as soon as possible. He started down the mountain and his legs gave beneath him. Even with great care the best he could do was a stagger.

"Bathing," said Ralph, "that's the only thing to do."

Piggy was inspecting the looming sky through his glass. "I don't like them clouds. Remember how it rained just after we landed?"

"Going to rain again."

Ralph dived into the pool. A couple of littluns were playing at the edge, trying to extract comfort from a wetness warmer than blood. Piggy took off his glasses, stepped primly into the water and then put them on again. Ralph came to the surface and squirted a jet of water at him.

"Mind my specs," said Piggy. "If I get water on the glass I got to get out and clean 'em."

Ralph squirted again and missed. He laughed at Piggy, expecting him to retire meekly as usual and in pained silence. Instead, Piggy beat the water with his hands.

"Stop it!" he shouted. "D'you hear?"

Furiously he drove the water into Ralph's face.

"All right, all right," said Ralph. "Keep your hair on."

Piggy stopped beating the water.

"I got a pain in my head. I wish the air was cooler."

"I wish the rain would come."

"I wish we could go home."

Piggy lay back against the sloping sand side of the pool. His stomach protruded and the water dried on it. Ralph squirted up at the sky. One could guess at the movement of the sun by the progress of a light patch among the clouds. He knelt in the water and looked round.

"Where's everybody?"

Piggy sat up.

"P'raps they're lying in the shelter."

"Where's Samneric?"

"And Bill?"

Piggy pointed beyond the platform.

"That's where they've gone. Jack's party."

"Let them go," said Ralph, uneasily, "I don't care."

"Just for some meat—"

"And for hunting," said Ralph, wisely, "and for pretending to be a tribe, and putting on war-paint."

Piggy stirred the sand under water and did not look at Ralph.

"P'raps we ought to go too."

Ralph looked at him quickly and Piggy blushed.

"I mean—to make sure nothing happens."

Ralph squirted water again.

Long before Ralph and Piggy came up with Jack's lot, they could hear the party. There was a stretch of grass in a place where the palms left a wide band of turf between the forest and the shore. Just one step down from the edge of the turf was the white, blown sand of above high water, warm, dry, trodden. Below that again was a rock that stretched away toward the lagoon. Beyond was a short stretch of sand and then the edge of the water. A fire burned on the rock and fat dripped from the roasting pig-meat into the invisible flames. All the boys of the island, except Piggy, Ralph, Simon, and the two tending the pig, were grouped on the turf. They were laughing, singing, lying, squatting, or standing on the grass, holding food in their hands. But to judge by the greasy faces, the meat eating was almost done; and some held coconut shells in their hands and were drinking from them. Before the party had started a great log had been dragged into the center of the lawn and Jack, painted and garlanded, sat there like an idol. There were piles of meat on green leaves near him, and fruit, and coconut shells full of drink.

Piggy and Ralph came to the edge of the grassy platform; and the boys, as they noticed them, fell silent one by one till only the boy next to Jack was talking. Then the silence intruded even there and Jack turned where he sat. For a time he looked at them and the crackle of the fire was the loudest noise over the droning of the reef. Ralph looked away; and Sam, thinking that Ralph had turned to him accusingly, put down his gnawed bone with a nervous giggle. Ralph took an uncertain step, poin₍ed to a palm tree, and whispered something inaudible to Piggy; and they both giggled like Sam. Lifting his feet high out of the sand, Ralph started to stroll past. Piggy tried to whistle.

At this moment the boys who were cooking at the fire suddenly hauled off a great chunk of meat and ran with it toward the grass. They bumped Piggy, who was burnt, and yelled and danced. Immediately, Ralph and the crowd of boys were united and relieved by a storm of laughter. Piggy once more was the center of social derision so that everyone felt cheerful and normal.

Jack stood up and waved his spear.

"Take them some meat."

The boys with the spit gave Ralph and Piggy each a succulent chunk. They took the gift, dribbling. So they stood and ate beneath a sky of thunderous brass that rang with the storm-coming.

Jack waved his spear again.

"Has everybody eaten as much as they want?"

There was still food left, sizzling on the wooden spits, heaped on the green platters. Betrayed by his stomach, Piggy threw a picked bone down on the beach and stooped for more.

Jack spoke again, impatiently.

"Has everybody eaten as much as they want?"

His tone conveyed a warning, given out of the pride of ownership, and the boys ate faster while there was still time. Seeing there was no immediate likelihood of a pause, Jack rose from the log that was his throne and sauntered to the edge of the grass. He looked down from behind his paint at Ralph and Piggy. They moved a little farther off over the sand and Ralph watched the fire as he ate. He noticed, without understanding, how the flames were visible now against the dull light. Evening was come, not with calm beauty but with the threat of violence.

Jack spoke.

"Give me a drink."

Henry brought him a shell and he drank, watching Piggy and Ralph over the jagged rim. Power lay in the brown swell of his forearms: authority sat on his shoulder and chattered in his ear like an ape.

"All sit down."

The boys ranged themselves in rows on the grass be-

fore him but Ralph and Piggy stayed a foot lower, standing on the soft sand. Jack ignored them for the moment,
turned his mask down to the seated boys and pointed at
them with the spear.

"Who is going to join my tribe?"

Ralph made a sudden movement that became a stum-
ble. Some of the boys turned toward him.

"I gave you food," said Jack, "and my hunters will
protect you from the beast. Who will join my tribe?"

"I'm chief," said Ralph, "because you chose me. And
we were going to keep the fire going. Now you run after
food—"

"You ran yourself!" shouted Jack. "Look at that bone in
your hands!"

Ralph went crimson.

"I said you were hunters. That was your job."

Jack ignored him again.

"Who'll join my tribe and have fun?"

"I'm chief," said Ralph tremulously. "And what about
the fire? And I've got the conch—"

"You haven't got it with you," said Jack, sneering. "You
left it behind. See, clever? And the conch doesn't count
at this end of the island—"

All at once the thunder struck. Instead of the dull boom
there was a point of impact in the explosion.

"The conch counts here too," said Ralph, "and all over
the island."

"What are you going to do about it then?"

Ralph examined the ranks of boys. There was no help
in them and he looked away, confused and sweating. Piggy
whispered.

"The fire—rescue."

"Who'll join my tribe?"

"I will."

"Me."

"I will."

"I'll blow the conch," said Ralph breathlessly, "and call
an assembly."

"We shan't hear it."

Piggy touched Ralph's wrist.

"Come away. There's going to be trouble. And we've
had our meat."

There was a blink of bright light beyond the forest and

the thunder exploded again so that a littlun started to whine. Big drops of rain fell among them making individual sounds when they struck.

"Going to be a storm," said Ralph, "and you'll have rain like when we dropped here. Who's clever now? Where are your shelters? What are you going to do about that?"

The hunters were looking uneasily at the sky, flinching from the stroke of the drops. A wave of restlessness set the boys swaying and moving aimlessly. The flickering light became brighter and the blows of the thunder were only just bearable. The littluns began to run about, screaming.

Jack leapt on to the sand.

"Do our dance! Come on! Dance!"

He ran stumbling through the thick sand to the open space of rock beyond the fire. Between the flashes of lightning the air was dark and terrible; and the boys followed him, clamorously. Roger became the pig, grunting and charging at Jack, who side-stepped. The hunters took their spears, the cooks took spits, and the rest clubs of firewood. A circling movement developed and a chant. While Roger mimed the terror of the pig, the littluns ran and jumped on the outside of the circle. Piggy and Ralph, under the threat of the sky, found themselves eager to take a place in this demented but partly secure society. They were glad to touch the brown backs of the fence that hemmed in the terror and made it governable.

"*Kill the beast! Cut his throat! Spill his blood!*"

The movement became regular while the chant lost its first superficial excitement and began to beat like a steady pulse. Roger ceased to be a pig and became a hunter, so that the center of the ring yawned emptily. Some of the littluns started a ring on their own; and the complementary circles went round and round as though repetition would achieve safety of itself. There was the throb and stamp of a single organism.

The dark sky was shattered by a blue-white scar. An instant later the noise was on them like the blow of a gigantic whip. The chant rose a tone in agony.

"*Kill the beast! Cut his throat! Spill his blood!*"

Now out of the terror rose another desire, thick, urgent, blind.

"*Kill the beast! Cut his throat! Spill his blood!*"

Again the blue-white scar jagged above them and the sulphurous explosion beat down. The littluns screamed and blundered about, fleeing from the edge of the forest, and one of them broke the ring of biguns in his terror.

"Him! Him!"

The circle became a horseshoe. A thing was crawling out of the forest. It came darkly, uncertainly. The shrill screaming that rose before the beast was like a pain. The beast stumbled into the horseshoe.

*"Kill the beast! Cut his throat! Spill his blood!"*

The blue-white scar was constant, the noise unendurable. Simon was crying out something about a dead man on a hill.

*"Kill the beast! Cut his throat! Spill his blood! Do°him in!"*

The sticks fell and the mouth of the new circle crunched and screamed. The beast was on its knees in the center, its arms folded over its face. It was crying out against the abominable noise something about a body on the hill. The beast struggled forward, broke the ring and fell over the steep edge of the rock to the sand by the water. At once the crowd surged after it, poured down the rock, leapt on to the beast, screamed, struck, bit, tore. There were no words, and no movements but the tearing of teeth and claws.

Then the clouds opened and let down the rain like a waterfall. The water bounded from the mountain-top, tore leaves and branches from the trees, poured like a cold shower over the struggling heap on the sand. Presently the heap broke up and figures staggered away. Only the beast lay still, a few yards from the sea. Even in the rain they could see how small a beast it was; and already its blood was staining the sand.

Now a great wind blew the rain sideways, cascading the water from the forest trees. On the mountain-top the parachute filled and moved; the figure slid, rose to its feet, spun, swayed down through a vastness of wet air and trod with ungainly feet the tops of the high trees; falling, still falling, it sank toward the beach and the boys rushed screaming into the darkness. The parachute took the figure forward, furrowing the lagoon, and bumped it over the reef and out to sea.

Toward midnight the rain ceased and the clouds drifted away, so that the sky was scattered once more with the incredible lamps of stars. Then the breeze died too and there was no noise save the drip and trickle of water that ran out of clefts and spilled down, leaf by leaf, to the brown earth of the island. The air was cool, moist, and clear; and presently even the sound of the water was still. The beast lay huddled on the pale beach and the stains spread, inch by inch.

The edge of the lagoon became a streak of phosphorescence which advanced minutely, as the great wave of the tide flowed. The clear water mirrored the clear sky and the angular bright constellations. The line of phosphorescence bulged about the sand grains and little pebbles; it held them each in a dimple of tension, then suddenly accepted them with an inaudible syllable and moved on.

Along the shoreward edge of the shallows the advancing clearness was full of strange, moonbeam-bodied creatures with fiery eyes. Here and there a larger pebble clung to its own air and was covered with a coat of pearls. The tide swelled in over the rain-pitted sand and smoothed everything with a layer of silver. Now it touched the first of the stains that seeped from the broken body and the creatures made a moving patch of light as they gathered at the edge. The water rose farther and dressed Simon's coarse hair with brightness. The line of his cheek silvered and the turn of his shoulder became sculptured marble. The strange attendant creatures, with their fiery eyes and trailing vapors, busied themselves round his head. The body lifted a fraction of an inch from the sand and a bubble of air escaped from the mouth with a wet plop. Then it turned gently in the water.

Somewhere over the darkened curve of the world the sun and moon were pulling, and the film of water on the earth planet was held, bulging slightly on one side while the solid core turned. The great wave of the tide moved farther along the island and the water lifted. Softly, surrounded by a fringe of inquisitive bright creatures, itself a silver shape beneath the steadfast constellations, Simon's dead body moved out toward the open sea.

# CHAPTER TEN

## *The Shell and the Glasses*

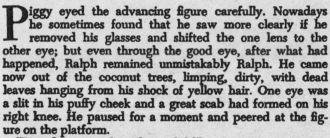

**P**iggy eyed the advancing figure carefully. Nowadays he sometimes found that he saw more clearly if he removed his glasses and shifted the one lens to the other eye; but even through the good eye, after what had happened, Ralph remained unmistakably Ralph. He came now out of the coconut trees, limping, dirty, with dead leaves hanging from his shock of yellow hair. One eye was a slit in his puffy cheek and a great scab had formed on his right knee. He paused for a moment and peered at the figure on the platform.

"Piggy? Are you the only one left?"

"There's some littluns."

"They don't count. No biguns?"

"Oh—Samneric. They're collecting wood."

"Nobody else?"

"Not that I know of."

Ralph climbed on to the platform carefully. The coarse grass was still worn away where the assembly used to sit; the fragile white conch still gleamed by the polished seat. Ralph sat down in the grass facing the chief's seat and the conch. Piggy knelt at his left, and for a long minute there was silence.

At last Ralph cleared his throat and whispered something.

Piggy whispered back.

"What you say?"

Ralph spoke up.

"Simon."

Piggy said nothing but nodded, solemnly. They continued to sit, gazing with impaired sight at the chief's seat and the glittering lagoon. The green light and the glossy patches of sunshine played over their befouled bodies.

At length Ralph got up and went to the conch. He took the shell caressingly with both hands and knelt, leaning against the trunk.

"Piggy."

"Uh?"

"What we going to do?"

Piggy nodded at the conch.

"You could—"

"Call an assembly?"

Ralph laughed sharply as he said the word and Piggy frowned.

"You're still chief."

Ralph laughed again.

"You are. Over us."

"I got the conch."

"Ralph! Stop laughing like that. Look, there ain't no need, Ralph! What's the others going to think?"

At last Ralph stopped. He was shivering.

"Piggy."

"Uh?"

"That was Simon."

"You said that before."

"Piggy."

"Uh?"

"That was murder."

"You stop it!" said Piggy, shrilly. "What good're you doing talking like that?"

He jumped to his feet and stood over Ralph.

"It was dark. There was that—that bloody dance. There was lightning and thunder and rain. We was scared!"

"I wasn't scared," said Ralph slowly, "I was—I don't know what I was."

"We was scared!" said Piggy excitedly. "Anything might have happened. It wasn't—what you said."

He was gesticulating, searching for a formula.

"Oh, Piggy!"

Ralph's voice, low and stricken, stopped Piggy's gestures. He bent down and waited. Ralph, cradling the conch, rocked himself to and fro.

"Don't you understand, Piggy? The things we did—"

"He may still be—"

"No."

"P'raps he was only pretending—"

Piggy's voice trailed off at the sight of Ralph's face.

"You were outside. Outside the circle. You never really came in. Didn't you see what we—what they did?"

There was loathing, and at the same time a kind of feverish excitement, in his voice.

"Didn't you see, Piggy?"

"Not all that well. I only got one eye now. You ought to know that, Ralph."

Ralph continued to rock to and fro.

"It was an accident," said Piggy suddenly, "that's what it was. An accident." His voice shrilled again. "Coming in the dark—he hadn't no business crawling like that out of the dark. He was batty. He asked for it." He gesticulated widely again. "It was an accident."

"You didn't see what they did—"

"Look, Ralph. We got to forget this. We can't do no good thinking about it, see?"

"I'm frightened. Of us. I want to go home. Oh God, I want to go home."

"It was an accident," said Piggy stubbornly, "and that's that."

He touched Ralph's bare shoulder and Ralph shuddered at the human contact.

"And look, Ralph"—Piggy glanced round quickly, then leaned close—"don't let on we was in that dance. Not to Samneric."

"But we were! All of us!"

Piggy shook his head.

"Not us till last. They never noticed in the dark. Anyway you said I was only on the outside."

"So was I," muttered Ralph, "I was on the outside too."

Piggy nodded eagerly.

"That's right. We was on the outside. We never done nothing, we never seen nothing."

Piggy paused, then went on.

"We'll live on our own, the four of us—"

"Four of us. We aren't enough to keep the fire burning."

"We'll try. See? I lit it."

Samneric came dragging a great log out of the forest. They dumped it by the fire and turned to the pool. Ralph jumped to his feet.

"Hi! You two!"

The twins checked a moment, then walked on.

"They're going to bathe, Ralph."

"Better get it over."

The twins were very surprised to see Ralph. They flushed and looked past him into the air.

"Hullo. Fancy meeting you, Ralph."

"We just been in the forest—"

"—to get wood for the fire—"

"—we got lost last night."

Ralph examined his toes.

"You got lost after the . . ."

Piggy cleaned his lens.

"After the feast," said Sam in a stifled voice. Eric nodded. "Yes, after the feast."

"We left early," said Piggy quickly, "because we were tired."

"So did we—"

"—very early—"

"—we were very tired."

Sam touched a scratch on his forehead and then hurriedly took his hand away. Eric fingered his split lip.

"Yes. We were very tired," repeated Sam, "so we left early. Was it a good—"

The air was heavy with unspoken knowledge. Sam twisted and the obscene word shot out of him. "—dance?"

Memory of the dance that none of them had attended shook all four boys convulsively.

"We left early."

When Roger came to the neck of land that joined the Castle Rock to the mainland he was not surprised to be challenged. He had reckoned, during the terrible night, on finding at least some of the tribe holding out against the horrors of the island in the safest place.

The voice rang out sharply from on high, where the diminishing crags were balanced one on another.

"Halt! Who goes there?"

"Roger."

"Advance, friend."

Roger advanced.

"The chief said we got to challenge everyone."

Roger peered up.

"You couldn't stop me coming if I wanted."

"Couldn't I? Climb up and see."

Roger clambered up the ladder-like cliff.

"Look at this."

A log had been jammed under the topmost rock and another lever under that. Robert leaned lightly on the lever and the rock groaned. A full effort would send the rock thundering down to the neck of land. Roger admired.

"He's a proper chief, isn't he?"

Robert nodded.

"He's going to take us hunting."

He jerked his head in the direction of the distant shelters where a thread of white smoke climbed up the sky. Roger, sitting on the very edge of the cliff, looked somberly back at the island as he worked with his fingers at a loose tooth. His gaze settled on the top of the distant mountain and Robert changed the unspoken subject.

"He's going to beat Wilfred."

"What for?"

Robert shook his head doubtfully.

"I don't know. He didn't say. He got angry and made us tie Wilfred up. He's been"—he giggled excitedly—"he's been tied for hours, waiting—"

"But didn't the chief say why?"

"I never heard him."

Sitting on the tremendous rocks in the torrid sun, Roger received this news as an illumination. He ceased to work at his tooth and sat still, assimilating the possibilities of irresponsible authority. Then, without another word, he climbed down the back of the rocks toward the cave and the rest of the tribe.

The chief was sitting there, naked to the waist, his face blocked out in white and red. The tribe lay in a semicircle before him. The newly beaten and untied Wilfred was sniffing noisily in the background. Roger squatted with the rest.

"Tomorrow," went on the chief, "we shall hunt again."

He pointed at this savage and that with his spear.

"Some of you will stay here to improve the cave and defend the gate. I shall take a few hunters with me and bring back meat. The defenders of the gate will see that the others don't sneak in."

A savage raised his hand and the chief turned a bleak, painted face toward him.

"Why should they try to sneak in, Chief?"

The chief was vague but earnest.

"They will. They'll try to spoil things we do. So the watchers at the gate must be careful. And then—"

The chief paused. They saw a triangle of startling pink dart out, pass along his lips and vanish again.

"—and then, the beast might try to come in. You remember how he crawled—"

The semicircle shuddered and muttered in agreement.

"He came—disguised. He may come again even though we gave him the head of our kill to eat. So watch; and be careful."

Stanley lifted his forearm off the rock and held up an interrogative finger.

"Well?"

"But didn't we, didn't we—?"

He squirmed and looked down.

"No!"

In the silence that followed, each savage flinched away from his individual memory.

"No! How could we—kill—it?"

Half-relieved, half-daunted by the implication of further terrors, the savages murmured again.

"So leave the mountain alone," said the chief, solemnly, "and give it the head if you go hunting."

Stanley flicked his finger again.

"I expect the beast disguised itself."

"Perhaps," said the chief. A theological speculation presented itself. "We'd better keep on the right side of him, anyhow. You can't tell what he might do."

The tribe considered this; and then were shaken, as if by a flaw of wind. The chief saw the effect of his words and stood abruptly.

"But tomorrow we'll hunt and when we've got meat we'll have a feast—"

Bill put up his hand.

"Chief."

"Yes?"

"What'll we use for lighting the fire?"

The chief's blush was hidden by the white and red clay. Into his uncertain silence the tribe spilled their murmur once more. Then the chief held up his hand.

"We shall take fire from the others. Listen. Tomorrow we'll hunt and get meat. Tonight I'll go along with two hunters—who'll come?"

Maurice and Roger put up their hands.

"Maurice—"

"Yes, Chief?"

"Where was their fire?"

"Back at the old place by the fire rock."

The chief nodded.

"The rest of you can go to sleep as soon as the sun sets. But us three, Maurice, Roger and me, we've got work to do. We'll leave just before sunset—"

Maurice put up his hand.

"But what happens if we meet—"

The chief waved his objection aside.

"We'll keep along by the sands. Then if he comes we'll do our, our dance again."

"Only the three of us?"

Again the murmur swelled and died away.

Piggy handed Ralph his glasses and waited to receive back his sight. The wood was damp; and this was the third time they had lighted it. Ralph stood back, speaking to himself.

"We don't want another night without fire."

He looked round guiltily at the three boys standing by. This was the first time he had admitted the double function of the fire. Certainly one was to send up a beckoning column of smoke; but the other was to be a hearth now and a comfort until they slept. Eric breathed on the wood till it glowed and sent out a little flame. A billow of white and yellow smoke reeked up. Piggy took back his glasses and looked at the smoke with pleasure.

"If only we could make a radio!"

"Or a plane—"

"—or a boat."

Ralph dredged in his fading knowledge of the world.

"We might get taken prisoner by the Reds."

Eric pushed back his hair.

"They'd be better than—"

He would not name people and Sam finished the sentence for him by nodding along the beach.

Ralph remembered the ungainly figure on a parachute.

"He said something about a dead man." He flushed painfully at this admission that he had been present at the dance. He made urging motions at the smoke with his body. "Don't stop—go on up!"

"Smoke's getting thinner."

"We need more wood already, even when it's wet."

"My asthma—"

The response was mechanical.

"Sucks to your ass-mar."

"If I pull logs about, I get my asthma bad. I wish I didn't, Ralph, but there it is."

The three boys went into the forest and fetched armfuls of rotten wood. Once more the smoke rose, yellow and thick.

"Let's get something to eat."

Together they went to the fruit trees, carrying their spears, saying little, cramming in haste. When they came out of the forest again the sun was setting and only embers glowed in the fire, and there was no smoke.

"I can't carry any more wood," said Eric. "I'm tired."

Ralph cleared his throat.

"We kept the fire going up there."

"Up there it was small. But this has got to be a big one."

Ralph carried a fragment to the fire and watched the smoke that drifted into the dusk.

"We've got to keep it going."

Eric flung himself down.

"I'm too tired. And what's the good?"

"Eric!" cried Ralph in a shocked voice. "Don't talk like that!"

Sam knelt by Eric.

"Well—what *is* the good?"

Ralph tried indignantly to remember. There was something good about a fire. Something overwhelmingly good.

"Ralph's told you often enough," said Piggy moodily. "How else are we going to be rescued?"

"Of course! If we don't make smoke—"

He squatted before them in the crowding dusk.

"Don't you understand? What's the good of wishing for radios and boats?"

He held out his hand and twisted the fingers into a fist.

"There's only one thing we can do to .get out of this mess. Anyone can play at hunting, anyone can get us meat—"

He looked from face to face. Then, at the moment of greatest passion and conviction, that curtain flapped in his head and he forgot what he had been driving at. He knelt there, his fist clenched, gazing solemnly from one to the other. Then the curtain whisked back.

"Oh, yes. So we've got to make smoke; and more smoke—"

"But we can't keep it going! Look at that!"

The fire was dying on them.

"Two to mind the fire," said Ralph, half to himself, "that's twelve hours a day."

"We can't get any more wood, Ralph—"

"—not in the dark—"

"—not at night—"

"We can light it every morning," said Piggy. "Nobody ain't going to see smoke in the dark."

Sam nodded vigorously.

"It was different when the fire was—"

"—up there."

Ralph stood up, feeling curiously defenseless with the darkness pressing in.

"Let the fire go then, for tonight."

He led the way to the first shelter, which still stood, though battered. The bed leaves lay within, dry and noisy to the touch. In the next shelter a littlun was talking in his sleep. The four biguns crept into the shelter and burrowed under the leaves. The twins lay together and Ralph and Piggy at the other end. For a while there was the continual creak and rustle of leaves as they tried for comfort.

"Piggy."

"Yeah?"

"All right?"

"S'pose so."

At length, save for an occasional rustle, the shelter was silent. An oblong of blackness relieved with brilliant spangles hung before them and there was the hollow sound of surf on the reef. Ralph settled himself for his nightly game of supposing. . . .

Supposing they could be transported home by jet, then

before morning they would land at that big airfield in Wiltshire. They would go by car; no, for things to be perfect they would go by train; all the way down to Devon and take that cottage again. Then at the foot of the garden the wild ponies would come and look over the wall. . . .

Ralph turned restlessly in the leaves. Dartmoor was wild and so were the ponies. But the attraction of wildness had gone.

His mind skated to a consideration of a tamed town where savagery could not set foot. What could be safer than the bus center with its lamps and wheels?

All at once, Ralph was dancing round a lamp standard. There was a bus crawling out of the bus station, a strange bus. . . .

"Ralph! Ralph!"

"What is it?"

"Don't make a noise like that—"

"Sorry."

From the darkness of the further end of the shelter came a dreadful moaning and they shattered the leaves in their fear. Sam and Eric, locked in an embrace, were fighting each other.

"Sam! Sam!"

"Hey—Eric!"

Presently all was quiet again.

Piggy spoke softly to Ralph.

"We got to get out of this."

"What d'you mean?"

"Get rescued."

For the first time that day, and despite the crowding blackness, Ralph sniggered.

"I mean it," whispered Piggy. "If we don't get home soon we'll be barmy."

"Round the bend."

"Bomb happy."

"Crackers."

Ralph pushed the damp tendrils of hair out of his eyes. "You write a letter to your auntie."

Piggy considered this solemnly.

"I don't know where she is now. And I haven't got an envelope and a stamp. An' there isn't a mailbox. Or a postman."

The success of his tiny joke overcame Ralph. His

sniggers became uncontrollable, his body jumped and twitched.

Piggy rebuked him with dignity.

"I haven't said anything all that funny."

Ralph continued to snigger though his chest hurt. His twitchings exhausted him till he lay, breathless and woebegone, waiting for the next spasm. During one of these pauses he was ambushed by sleep.

"Ralph! You been making a noise again. Do be quiet, Ralph—because."

Ralph heaved over among the leaves. He had reason to be thankful that his dream was broken, for the bus had been nearer and more distinct.

"Why—because?"

"Be quiet—and listen."

Ralph lay down carefully, to the accompaniment of a long sigh from the leaves. Eric moaned something and then lay still. The darkness, save for the useless oblong of stars, was blanket-thick.

"I can't hear anything."

"There's something moving outside."

Ralph's head prickled. The sound of his blood drowned all else and then subsided.

"I still can't hear anything."

"Listen. Listen for a long time."

Quite clearly and emphatically, and only a yard or so away from the back of the shelter, a stick cracked. The blood roared again in Ralph's ears, confused images chased each other through his mind. A composite of these things was prowling round the shelters. He could feel Piggy's head against his shoulder and the convulsive grip of a hand.

"Ralph! Ralph!"

"Shut up and listen."

Desperately, Ralph prayed that the beast would prefer littluns.

A voice whispered horribly outside.

"Piggy—Piggy—"

"It's come!" gasped Piggy. "It's real!"

He clung to Ralph and reached to get his breath.

"Piggy, come outside. I want you, Piggy."

Ralph's mouth was against Piggy's ear.

"Don't say anything."

"Piggy—where are you, Piggy?"

Something brushed against the back of the shelter. Piggy kept still for a moment, then he had his asthma. He arched his back and crashed among the leaves with his legs. Ralph rolled away from him.

Then there was a vicious snarling in the mouth of the shelter and the plunge and thump of living things. Someone tripped over Ralph and Piggy's corner became a complication of snarls and crashes and flying limbs. Ralph hit out; then he and what seemed like a dozen others were rolling over and over, hitting, biting, scratching. He was torn and jolted, found fingers in his mouth and bit them. A fist withdrew and came back like a piston, so that the whole shelter exploded into light. Ralph twisted sideways on top of a writhing body and felt hot breath on his cheek. He began to pound the mouth below him, using his clenched fist as a hammer; he hit with more and more passionate hysteria as the face became slippery. A knee jerked up between his legs and he fell sideways, busying himself with his pain, and the fight rolled over him. Then the shelter collapsed with smothering finality; and the anonymous shapes fought their way out and through. Dark figures drew themselves out of the wreckage and flitted away, till the screams of the littluns and Piggy's gasps were once more audible.

Ralph called out in a quavering voice.

"All you littluns, go to sleep. We've had a fight with the others. Now go to sleep."

Samneric came close and peered at Ralph.

"Are you two all right?"

"I think so—"

"—I got busted."

"So did I. How's Piggy?"

They hauled Piggy clear of the wreckage and leaned him against a tree. The night was cool and purged of immediate terror. Piggy's breathing was a little easier.

"Did you get hurt, Piggy?"

"Not much."

"That was Jack and his hunters," said Ralph bitterly. "Why can't they leave us alone?"

"We gave them something to think about," said Sam. Honestly compelled him to go on. "At least you did. I got mixed up with myself in a corner."

"I gave one of 'em what for," said Ralph, "I smashed him up all right. He won't want to come and fight us again in a hurry."

"So did I," said Eric. "When I woke up one was kicking me in the face. I got an awful bloody face, I think, Ralph. But I did him in the end."

"What did you do?"

"I got my knee up," said Eric with simple pride, "and I hit him with it in the pills. You should have heard him holler! He won't come back in a hurry either. So we didn't do too badly."

Ralph moved suddenly in the dark; but then he heard Eric working at his mouth.

"What's the matter?"

"Jus' a tooth loose."

Piggy drew up his legs.

"You all right, Piggy?"

"I thought they wanted the conch."

Ralph trotted down the pale beach and jumped on to the platform. The conch still glimmered by the chief's seat. He gazed for a moment or two, then went back to Piggy.

"They didn't take the conch."

"I know. They didn't come for the conch. They came for something else. Ralph—what am I going to do?"

Far off along the bowstave of beach, three figures trotted toward the Castle Rock. They kept away from the forest and down by the water. Occasionally they sang softly; occasionally they turned cartwheels down by the moving streak of phosphorescence. The chief led them, trotting steadily, exulting in his achievement. He was a chief now in truth; and he made stabbing motions with his spear. From his left hand dangled Piggy's broken glasses.

# CHAPTER ELEVEN

## *Castle Rock*

In the short chill of dawn the four boys gathered round the black smudge where the fire had been, while Ralph knelt and blew. Grey, feathery ashes scurried hither and thither at his breath but no spark shone among them. The twins watched anxiously and Piggy sat expressionless behind the luminous wall of his myopia. Ralph continued to blow till his ears were singing with the effort, but then the first breeze of dawn took the job off his hands and blinded him with ashes. He squatted back, swore, and rubbed water out of his eyes.

"No use."

Eric looked down at him through a mask of dried blood. Piggy peered in the general direction of Ralph.

"'Course it's no use, Ralph. Now we got no fire."

Ralph brought his face within a couple of feet of Piggy's.

"Can you see me?"

"A bit."

Ralph allowed the swollen flap of his cheek to close his eye again.

"They've got our fire."

Rage shrilled his voice.

"They stole it!"

"That's them," said Piggy. "They blinded me. See? That's Jack Merridew. You call an assembly, Ralph, we got to decide what to do."

"An assembly for only us?"

"It's all we got. Sam—let me hold on to you."

They went toward the platform.

"Blow the conch," said Piggy. "Blow as loud as you can."

The forest re-echoed; and birds lifted, crying out of the treetops, as on that first morning ages ago. Both ways the beach was deserted. Some littluns came from the shelters. Ralph sat down on the polished trunk and the three others stood before him. He nodded, and Samneric sat down on the right. Ralph pushed the conch into Piggy's hands. He held the shining thing carefully and blinked at Ralph.

"Go on, then."

"I just take the conch to say this. I can't see no more and I got to get my glasses back. Awful things has been done on this island. I voted for you for chief. He's the only one who ever got anything done. So now you speak, Ralph, and tell us what. Or else—"

Piggy broke off, sniveling. Ralph took back the conch as he sat down.

"Just an ordinary fire. You'd think we could do that, wouldn't you? Just a smoke signal so we can be rescued. Are we savages or what? Only now there's no signal going up. Ships may be passing. Do you remember how he went hunting and the fire went out and a ship passed by? And they all think he's best as chief. Then there was, there was . . . that's his fault, too. If it hadn't been for him it would never have happened. Now Piggy can't see, and they came, stealing—" Ralph's voice ran up "—at night, in darkness, and stole our fire. They stole it. We'd have given them fire if they'd asked. But they stole it and the signal's out and we can't ever be rescued. Don't you see what I mean? We'd have given them fire for themselves only they stole it. I—"

He paused lamely as the curtain flickered in his brain. Piggy held out his hands for the conch.

"What you goin' to do, Ralph? This is jus' talk without deciding. I want my glasses."

"I'm trying to think. Supposing we go, looking like we used to, washed and hair brushed—after all we aren't savages really and being rescued isn't a game—"

He opened the flap of his cheek and looked at the twins.

"We could smarten up a bit and then go—"

"We ought to take spears," said Sam. "Even Piggy."

"—because we may need them."

"You haven't got the conch!"

Piggy held up the shell.

"You can take spears if you want but I shan't. What's

the good? I'll have to be led like a dog, anyhow. Yes, laugh. Go on, laugh. There's them on this island as would laugh at anything. And what happened? What's grownups goin' to think? Young Simon was murdered. And there was that other kid what had a mark on his face. Who's seen him since we first come here?"

"Piggy! Stop a minute!"

"I got the conch. I'm going to that Jack Merridew an' tell him, I am."

"You'll get hurt."

"What can he do more than he has? I'll tell him what's what. You let me carry the conch, Ralph. I'll show him the one thing he hasn't got."

Piggy paused for a moment and peered round at the dim figures. The shape of the old assembly, trodden in the grass, listened to him.

"I'm going to him with this conch in my hands. I'm going to hold it out. Look, I'm goin' to say, you're stronger than I am and you haven't got asthma. You can see, I'm goin' to say, and with both eyes. But I don't ask for my glasses back, not as a favor. I don't ask you to be a sport, I'll say, not because you're strong, but because what's right's right. Give me my glasses, I'm going to say—you got to!"

Piggy ended, flushed and trembling. He pushed the conch quickly into Ralph's hands as though in a hurry to be rid of it and wiped the tears from his eyes. The green light was gentle about them and the conch lay at Ralph's feet, fragile and white. A single drop of water that had escaped Piggy's fingers now flashed on the delicate curve like a star.

At last Ralph sat up straight and drew back his hair.

"All right. I mean—you can try if you like. We'll go with you."

"He'll be painted," said Sam, timidly. "You know how he'll be—"

"—he won't think much of us—"

"—if he gets waxy we've had it—"

Ralph scowled at Sam. Dimly he remembered something that Simon had said to him once, by the rocks.

"Don't be silly," he said. And then he added quickly, "Let's go."

He held out the conch to Piggy who flushed, this time with pride.

"You must carry it."

"When we're ready I'll carry it—"

Piggy sought in his mind for words to convey his passionate willingness to carry the conch against all odds.

"I don't mind. I'll be glad, Ralph, only I'll have to be led."

Ralph put the conch back on the shining log.

"We better eat and then get ready."

They made their way to the devastated fruit trees. Piggy was helped to his food and found some by touch. While they ate, Ralph thought of the afternoon.

"We'll be like we were. We'll wash—"

Sam gulped down a mouthful and protested.

"But we bathe every day!"

Ralph looked at the filthy objects before him and sighed.

"We ought to comb our hair. Only it's too long."

"I've got both socks left in the shelter," said Eric, "so we could pull them over our heads like caps, sort of."

"We could find some stuff," said Piggy, "and tie your hair back."

"Like a girl!"

"No. 'Course not."

"Then we must go as we are," said Ralph, "and they won't be any better."

Eric made a detaining gesture.

"But they'll be painted! You know how it is."

The others nodded. They understood only too well the liberation into savagery that the concealing paint brought.

"Well, we won't be painted," said Ralph, "because we aren't savages."

Samneric looked at each other.

"All the same—"

Ralph shouted.

"No paint!"

He tried to remember.

"Smoke," he said, "we want smoke."

He turned on the twins fiercely.

"I said 'smoke'! We've got to have smoke."

There was silence, except for the multitudinous murmur of the bees. At last Piggy spoke, kindly.

" 'Course we have. 'Cos the smoke's a signal and we can't be rescued if we don't have smoke."

"I knew that!" shouted Ralph. He pulled his arm away from Piggy. "Are you suggesting—?"

"I'm jus' saying what you always say," said Piggy hastily. "I'd thought for a moment—"

"I hadn't," said Ralph loudly. "I knew it all the time. I hadn't forgotten."

Piggy nodded propitiatingly.

"You're chief, Ralph. You remember everything."

"I hadn't forgotten."

" 'Course not."

The twins were examining Ralph curiously, as though they were seeing him for the first time.

They set off along the beach in formation. Ralph went first, limping a little, his spear carried over one shoulder. He saw things partially, through the tremble of the heat haze over the flashing sands, and his own long hair and injuries. Behind him came the twins, worried now for a while but full of unquenchable vitality. They said little but trailed the butts of their wooden spears; for Piggy had found that, by looking down and shielding his tired sight from the sun, he could just see these moving along the sand. He walked between the trailing butts, therefore, the conch held carefully between his two hands. The boys made a compact little group that moved over the beach, four plate-like shadows dancing and mingling beneath them. There was no sign left of the storm, and the beach was swept clean like a blade that has been scoured. The sky and the mountain were at an immense distance, shimmering in the heat; and the reef was lifted by mirage, floating in a kind of silver pool halfway up the sky.

They passed the place where the tribe had danced. The charred sticks still lay on the rocks where the rain had quenched them but the sand by the water was smooth again. They passed this in silence. No one doubted that the tribe would be found at the Castle Rock and when they came in sight of it they stopped with one accord. The densest tangle on the island, a mass of twisted stems, black and green and impenetrable, lay on their left and tall grass swayed before them. Now Ralph went forward.

Here was the crushed grass where they had all lain when he had gone to prospect. There was the neck of land, the ledge skirting the rock, up there were the red pinnacles.

Sam touched his arm.

"Smoke."

There was a tiny smudge of smoke wavering into the air on the other side of the rock.

"Some fire—I don't think."

Ralph turned.

"What are we hiding for?"

He stepped through the screen of grass on to the little open space that led to the narrow neck.

"You two follow behind. I'll go first, then Piggy a pace behind me. Keep your spears ready."

Piggy peered anxiously into the luminous veil that hung between him and the world.

"Is it safe? Ain't there a cliff? I can hear the sea."

"You keep right close to me."

Ralph moved forward on to the neck. He kicked a stone and it bounded into the water. Then the sea sucked down, revealing a red, weedy square forty feet beneath Ralph's left arm.

"Am I safe?" quavered Piggy. "I feel awful—"

High above them from the pinnacles came a sudden shout and then an imitation war-cry that was answered by a dozen voices from behind the rock.

"Give me the conch and stay still."

"Halt! Who goes there?"

Ralph bent back his head and glimpsed Roger's dark face at the top.

"You can see who I am!" he shouted. "Stop being silly!"

He put the conch to his lips and began to blow. Savages appeared, painted out of recognition, edging round the ledge toward the neck. They carried spears and disposed themselves to defend the entrance. Ralph went on blowing and ignored Piggy's terrors.

Roger was shouting.

"You mind out—see?"

At length Ralph took his lips away and paused to get his breath back. His first words were a gasp, but audible.

"—calling an assembly."

The savages guarding the neck muttered among themselves but made no motion. Ralph walked forwards a couple of steps. A voice whispered urgently behind him.

"Don't leave me, Ralph."

"You kneel down," said Ralph sideways, "and wait till I come back."

He stood halfway along the neck and gazed at the savages intently. Freed by the paint, they had tied their hair back and were more comfortable than he was. Ralph made a resolution to tie his own back afterwards. Indeed he felt like telling them to wait and doing it there and then; but that was impossible. The savages sniggered a bit and one gestured at Ralph with his spear. High above, Roger took his hands off the lever and leaned out to see what was going on. The boys on the neck stood in a pool of their own shadow, diminished to shaggy heads. Piggy crouched, his back shapeless as a sack.

"I'm calling an assembly."

Silence.

Roger took up a small stone and flung it between the twins, aiming to miss. They started and Sam only just kept his footing. Some source of power began to pulse in Roger's body.

Ralph spoke again, loudly.

"I'm calling an assembly."

He ran his eye over them.

"Where's Jack?"

The group of boys stirred and consulted. A painted face spoke with the voice of Robert.

"He's hunting. And he said we weren't to let you in."

"I've come to see about the fire," said Ralph, "and about Piggy's specs."

The group in front of him shifted and laughter shivered outwards from among them, light, excited laughter that went echoing among the tall rocks.

A voice spoke from behind Ralph.

"What do you want?"

The twins made a bolt past Ralph and got between him and the entry. He turned quickly. Jack, identifiable by personality and red hair, was advancing from the forest. A hunter crouched on either side. All three were masked in black and green. Behind them on the grass the headless and paunched body of a sow lay where they had dropped it.

Piggy wailed.

"Ralph! Don't leave me!"

With ludicrous care he embraced the rock, pressing himself to it above the sucking sea. The sniggering of the savages became a loud derisive jeer.

Jack shouted above the noise.

"You go away, Ralph. You keep to your end. This is my end and my tribe. You leave me alone."

The jeering died away.

"You pinched Piggy's specs," said Ralph, breathlessly. "You've got to give them back."

"Got to? Who says?"

Ralph's temper blazed out.

"I say! You voted for me for chief. Didn't you hear the conch? You played a dirty trick—we'd have given you fire if you'd asked for it—"

The blood was flowing in his cheeks and the bunged-up eye throbbed.

"You could have had fire whenever you wanted. But you didn't. You came sneaking up like a thief and stole Piggy's glasses!"

"Say that again!"

"Thief! Thief!"

Piggy screamed.

"Ralph! Mind me!"

Jack made a rush and stabbed at Ralph's chest with his spear. Ralph sensed the position of the weapon from the glimpse he caught of Jack's arm and put the thrust aside with his own butt. Then he brought the end round and caught Jack a stinger across the ear. They were chest to chest, breathing fiercely, pushing and glaring.

"Who's a thief?"

"You are!"

Jack wrenched free and swung at Ralph with his spear. By common consent they were using the spears as sabers now, no longer daring the lethal points. The blow struck Ralph's spear and slid down, to fall agonizingly on his fingers. Then they were apart once more, their positions reversed, Jack toward the Castle Rock and Ralph on the outside toward the island.

Both boys were breathing very heavily.

"Come on then—"

"Come on—"

Truculently they squared up to each other but kept just out of fighting distance.

"You come on and see what you get!"

"You come on—"

Piggy clutching the ground was trying to attract Ralph's attention. Ralph moved, bent down, kept a wary eye on Jack.

"Ralph—remember what we came for. The fire My specs."

Ralph nodded. He relaxed his fighting muscles, stood easily and grounded the butt of his spear Jack watched him inscrutably through his paint. Ralph glanced up at the pinnacles, then toward the group of savages

"Listen. We've come to say this. First you've got to give back Piggy's specs. If he hasn't got them he can't see You aren't playing the game—"

The tribe of painted savages giggled and Ralph's mind faltered. He pushed his hair up and gazed at the green and black mask before him, trying to remember what Jack looked like.

Piggy whispered.

"And the fire."

"Oh yes. Then about the fire. I say this again. I've been saying it ever since we dropped in."

He held out his spear and pointed at the savages.

"Your only hope is keeping a signal fire going as long as there's light to see. Then maybe a ship'll notice the smoke and come and rescue us and take us home But without that smoke we've got to wait till some ship comes by accident. We might wait years; till we were old—"

The shivering, silvery, unreal laughter of the savages sprayed out and echoed away. A gust of rage shook Ralph His voice cracked.

"Don't you understand, you painted fools? Sam, Eric, Piggy and me—we aren't enough. We tried to keep the fire going, but we couldn't. And then you, playing at hunting. . . ."

He pointed past them to where the trickle of smoke dispersed in the pearly air.

"Look at that! Call that a signal fire? That's a cooking fire Now you'll eat and there'll be no smoke. Don't you under-stand? There may be a ship out there—"

He paused, defeated by the silence and the painted anonymity of the group guarding the entry. Jack opened a pink mouth and addressed Samneric, who were between him and his tribe.

"You two. Get back."

No one answered him. The twins, puzzled, looked at each other; while Piggy, reassured by the cessation of violence, stood up carefully. Jack glanced back at Ralph and then at the twins.

"Grab them!"

No one moved. Jack shouted angrily.

"I said 'grab them'!"

The painted group moved round Samneric nervously and unhandily. Once more the silvery laughter scattered.

Samneric protested out of the heart of civilization.

"Oh, I say!"

"—honestly!"

Their spears were taken from them.

"Tie them up!"

Ralph cried out hopelessly against the black and green mask.

"Jack!"

"Go on. Tie them."

Now the painted group felt the otherness of Samneric, felt the power in their own hands. They felled the twins clumsily and excitedly. Jack was inspired. He knew that Ralph would attempt a rescue. He struck in a humming circle behind him and Ralph only just parried the blow. Beyond them the tribe and the twins were a loud and writhing heap. Piggy crouched again. Then the twins lay, astonished, and the tribe stood round them. Jack turned to Ralph and spoke between his teeth.

"See? They do what I want."

There was silence again. The twins lay, inexpertly tied up, and the tribe watched Ralph to see what he would do. He numbered them through his fringe, glimpsed the ineffectual smoke.

His temper broke. He screamed at Jack.

"You're a beast and a swine and a bloody, bloody thief!"

He charged.

Jack, knowing this was the crisis, charged too. They met with a jolt and bounced apart. Jack swung with his fist at Ralph and caught him on the ear. Ralph hit Jack in the stomach and made him grunt. Then they were facing each other again, panting and furious, but unnerved by each other's ferocity. They became aware of the noise that was the background to this fight, the steady shrill cheering of the tribe behind them.

Piggy's voice penetrated to Ralph.

"Let me speak."

He was standing in the dust of the fight, and as the tribe saw his intention the shrill cheer changed to a steady booing.

Piggy held up the conch and the booing sagged a little, then came up again to strength.

"I got the conch!"

He shouted.

"I tell you, I got the conch!"

Surprisingly, there was silence now; the tribe were curious to hear what amusing thing he might have to say.

Silence and pause; but in the silence a curious air-noise, close by Ralph's head. He gave it half his attention—and there it was again; a faint "Zup!" Someone was throwing stones: Roger was dropping them, his one hand still on the lever. Below him, Ralph was a shock of hair and Piggy a bag of fat.

"I got this to say. You're acting like a crowd of kids."

The booing rose and died again as Piggy lifted the white, magic shell.

"Which is better—to be a pack of painted Indians like you are, or to be sensible like Ralph is?"

A great clamor rose among the savages. Piggy shouted again.

"Which is better—to have rules and agree, or to hunt and kill?"

Again the clamor and again—"Zup!"

Ralph shouted against the noise.

"Which is better, law and rescue, or hunting and breaking things up?"

Now Jack was yelling too and Ralph could no longer make himself heard. Jack had backed right against the tribe and they were a solid mass of menace that bristled with spears. The intention of a charge was forming among them; they were working up to it and the neck would be swept clear. Ralph stood facing them, a little to one side, his spear ready. By him stood Piggy still holding out the talisman, the fragile, shining beauty of the shell. The storm of sound beat at them, an incantation of hatred. High overhead, Roger, with a sense of delirious abandonment, leaned all his weight on the lever.

Ralph heard the great rock long before he saw it. He was aware of a jolt in the earth that came to him through the soles of his feet, and the breaking sound of stones at the top of the cliff. Then the monstrous red thing bounded across the neck and he flung himself flat while the tribe shrieked.

The rock struck Piggy a glancing blow from chin to knee; the conch exploded into a thousand white fragments and ceased to exist. Piggy, saying nothing, with no time for even a grunt, traveled through the air sideways from the rock, turning over as he went. The rock bounded twice and was lost in the forest. Piggy fell forty feet and landed on his back across that square red rock in the sea. His head opened and stuff came out and turned red. Piggy's arms and legs twitched a bit, like a pig's after it has been killed. Then the sea breathed again in a long, slow sigh, the water boiled white and pink over the rock; and when it went, sucking back again, the body of Piggy was gone.

This time the silence was complete. Ralph's lips formed a word but no sound came.

Suddenly Jack bounded out from the tribe and began screaming wildly.

"See? See? That's what you'll get! I meant that! There isn't a tribe for you any more! The conch is gone—"

He ran forward, stooping.

"I'm chief!"

Viciously, with full intention, he hurled his spear at Ralph. The point tore the skin and flesh over Ralph's ribs, then sheared off and fell in the water. Ralph stumbled, feeling not pain but panic, and the tribe, screaming now like the chief, began to advance. Another spear, a bent one that would not fly straight, went past his face and one fell from on high where Roger was. The twins lay hidden behind the tribe and the anonymous devils' faces swarmed across the neck. Ralph turned and ran. A great noise as of sea gulls rose behind him. He obeyed an instinct that he did not know he possessed and swerved over the open space so that the spears went wide. He saw the headless body of the sow and jumped in time. Then he was crashing through foliage and small boughs and was hidden by the forest.

The chief stopped by the pig, turned and held up his hands.

"Back! Back to the fort!"

Presently the tribe returned noisily to the neck where Roger joined them.

The chief spoke to him angrily.

"Why aren't you on watch?"

Roger looked at him gravely.

"I just came down—"

The hangman's horror clung round him. The chief said no more to him but looked down at Samneric.

"You got to join the tribe."

"You lemme go—"

"—and me."

The chief snatched one of the few spears that were left and poked Sam in the ribs.

"What d'you mean by it, eh?" said the chief fiercely. "What d'you mean by coming with spears? What d'you mean by not joining my tribe?"

The prodding became rhythmic. Sam yelled.

"That's not the way."

Roger edged past the chief, only just avoiding pushing him with his shoulder. The yelling ceased, and Samneric lay looking up in quiet terror. Roger advanced upon them as one wielding a nameless authority.

# CHAPTER TWELVE

## *Cry of the Hunters*

Ralph lay in a covert, wondering about his wounds. The bruised flesh was inches in diameter over his right ribs, with a swollen and bloody scar where the spear had hit him. His hair was full of dirt and tapped like the tendrils of a creeper. All over he was scratched and bruised from his flight through the forest. By the time his breathing was normal again, he had worked out that bathing these injuries would have to wait. How could you listen for naked feet if you were splashing in water? How could you be safe by the little stream or on the open beach?

Ralph listened. He was not really far from the Castle Rock, and during the first panic he had thought he heard sounds of pursuit. But the hunters had only sneaked into the fringes of the greenery, retrieving spears perhaps, and then had rushed back to the sunny rock as if terrified of the darkness under the leaves. He had even glimpsed one of them, striped brown, black, and red, and had judged that it was Bill. But really, thought Ralph, this was not Bill. This was a savage whose image refused to blend with that ancient picture of a boy in shorts and shirt.

The afternoon died away; the circular spots of sunlight moved steadily over green fronds and brown fiber but no sound came from behind the rock. At last Ralph wormed out of the ferns and sneaked forward to the edge of that impenetrable thicket that fronted the neck of land. He peered with elaborate caution between branches at the edge and could see Robert sitting on guard at the top of the cliff. He held a spear in his left hand and was tossing up a pebble and catching it again with the right. Behind him a column of smoke rose thickly, so that Ralph's nostrils flared and his mouth dribbled. He wiped his nose and

mouth with the back of his hand and for the first time since
the morning felt hungry. The tribe must be sitting round
the gutted pig, watching the fat ooze and burn among the
ashes. They would be intent.

Another figure, an unrecognizable one, appeared by
Robert and gave him something, then turned and went
back behind the rock. Robert laid his spear on the rock beside him and began to gnaw between his raised hands. So
the feast was beginning and the watchman had been given
his portion.

Ralph saw that for the time being he was safe. He limped
away through the fruit trees, drawn by the thought of the
poor food yet bitter when he remembered the feast. Feast
today, and then tomorrow. . . .

He argued unconvincingly that they would let him alone,
perhaps even make an outlaw of him. But then the fatal unreasoning knowledge came to him again. The breaking
of the conch and the deaths of Piggy and Simon lay over
the island like a vapor. These painted savages would go
further and further. Then there was that indefinable connection between himself and Jack; who therefore would
never let him alone; never.

He paused, sun-flecked, holding up a bough, prepared
to duck under it. A spasm of terror set him shaking and he
cried aloud.

"No. They're not as bad as that. It was an accident."

He ducked under the bough, ran clumsily, then stopped
and listened.

He came to the smashed acres of fruit and ate greedily.
He saw two littluns and, not having any idea of his own appearance, wondered why they screamed and ran.

When he had eaten he went toward the beach. The sunlight was slanting now into the palms by the wrecked shelter. There was the platform and the pool. The best thing
to do was to ignore this leaden feeling about the heart and
rely on their common sense, their daylight sanity. Now that
the tribe had eaten, the thing to do was to try again. And
anyway, he couldn't stay here all night in an empty shelter
by the deserted platform. His flesh crept and he shivered
in the evening sun. No fire; no smoke; no rescue. He turned
and limped away through the forest toward Jack's end of
the island.

The slanting sticks of sunlight were lost among the

branches. At length he came to a clearing in the forest where rock prevented vegetation from growing. Now it was a pool of shadows and Ralph nearly flung himself behind a tree when he saw something standing in the center; but then he saw that the white face was bone and that the pig's skull grinned at him from the top of a stick. He walked slowly into the middle of the clearing and looked steadily at the skull that gleamed as white as ever the conch had done and seemed to jeer at him cynically. An inquisitive ant was busy in one of the eye sockets but otherwise the thing was lifeless.

Or was it?

Little prickles of sensation ran up and down his back. He stood, the skull about on a level with his face, and held up his hair with two hands. The teeth grinned, the empty sockets seemed to hold his gaze masterfully and without effort.

What was it?

The skull regarded Ralph like one who knows all the answers and won't tell. A sick fear and rage swept him. Fiercely he hit out at the filthy thing in front of him that bobbed like a toy and came back, still grinning into his face, so that he lashed and cried out in loathing. Then he was licking his bruised knuckles and looking at the bare stick, while the skull lay in two pieces, its grin now six feet across. He wrenched the quivering stick from the crack and held it as a spear between him and the white pieces. Then he backed away, keeping his face to the skull that lay grinning at the sky.

When the green glow had gone from the horizon and night was fully accomplished, Ralph came again to the thicket in front of the Castle Rock. Peeping through, he could see that the height was still occupied, and whoever it was up there had a spear at the ready.

He knelt among the shadows and felt his isolation bitterly. They were savages it was true; but they were human, and the ambushing fears of the deep night were coming on.

Ralph moaned faintly. Tired though he was, he could not relax and fall into a well of sleep for fear of the tribe. Might it not be possible to walk boldly into the fort, say—"I've got pax," laugh lightly and sleep among the others? Pretend they were still boys, schoolboys who had said, "Sir, yes, Sir"—and worn caps? Daylight might have answered yes;

but darkness and the horrors of death said no. Lying there in the darkness, he knew he was an outcast.

" 'Cos I had some sense."

He rubbed his cheek along his forearm, smelling the acrid scent of salt and sweat and the staleness of dirt. Over to the left, the waves of ocean were breathing, sucking down, then boiling back over the rock.

There were sounds coming from behind the Castle Rock. Listening carefully, detaching his mind from the swing of the sea, Ralph could make out a familiar rhythm.

*"Kill the beast! Cut his throat! Spill his blood!"*

The tribe was dancing. Somewhere on the other side of this rocky wall there would be a dark circle, a glowing fire, and meat. They would be savoring food and the comfort of safety.

A noise nearer at hand made him quiver. Savages were clambering up the Castle Rock, right up to the top, and he could hear voices. He sneaked forward a few yards and saw the shape at the top of the rock change and enlarge. There were only two boys on the island who moved or talked like that.

Ralph put his head down on his forearms and accepted this new fact like a wound. Samneric were part of the tribe now. They were guarding the Castle Rock against him. There was no chance of rescuing them and building up an outlaw tribe at the other end of the island. Samneric were savages like the rest; Piggy was dead, and the conch smashed to powder.

At length the guard climbed down. The two that remained seemed nothing more than a dark extension of the rock. A star appeared behind them and was momentarily eclipsed by some movement.

Ralph edged forward, feeling his way over the uneven surface as though he were blind. There were miles of vague water at his right and the restless ocean lay under his left hand, as awful as the shaft of a pit. Every minute the water breathed round the death rock and flowered into a field of whiteness. Ralph crawled until he found the ledge of the entry in his grasp. The lookouts were immediately above him and he could see the end of a spear projecting over the rock.

He called very gently.

"Samneric—"

There was no reply. To carry he must speak louder; and this would rouse those striped and inimical creatures from their feasting by the fire. He set his teeth and started to climb, finding the holds by touch. The stick that had supported a skull hampered him but he would not be parted from his only weapon. He was nearly level with the twins before he spoke again.

"Samneric—"

He heard a cry and a flurry from the rock. The twins had grabbed each other and were gibbering.

"It's me. Ralph."

Terrified that they would run and give the alarm, he hauled himself up until his head and shoulders stuck over the top. Far below his armpit he saw the luminous flowering round the rock.

"It's only me. Ralph."

At length they bent forward and peered in his face.

"We thought it was—"

"—we didn't know what it was—"

"—we thought—"

Memory of their new and shameful loyalty came to them. Eric was silent but Sam tried to do his duty.

"You got to go, Ralph. You go away now—"

He wagged his spear and essayed fierceness.

"You shove off. See?"

Eric nodded agreement and jabbed his spear in the air. Ralph leaned on his arms and did not go.

"I came to see you two."

His voice was thick. His throat was hurting him now though it had received no wound.

"I came to see you two—"

Words could not express the dull pain of these things. He fell silent, while the vivid stars were spilt and danced all ways.

Sam shifted uneasily.

"Honest, Ralph, you'd better go."

Ralph looked up again.

"You two aren't painted. How can you—? If it were light—"

If it were light shame would burn them at admitting these things. But the night was dark. Eric took up; and then the twins started their antiphonal speech.

"You got to go because it's not safe—"

"—they made us. They hurt us—"

"Who? Jack?"

"Oh no—"

They bent to him and lowered their voices.

"Push off, Ralph—"

"—it's a tribe—"

"—they made us—"

"—we couldn't help it—"

When Ralph spoke again his voice was low, and seemed breathless.

"What have I done? I liked him—and I wanted us to be rescued—"

Again the stars spilled about the sky. Eric shook his head, earnestly.

"Listen, Ralph. Never mind what's sense. That's gone—"

"Never mind about the chief—"

"—you got to go for your own good."

"The chief and Roger—"

"—yes, Roger—"

"They hate you, Ralph. They're going to do you."

"They're going to hunt you tomorrow."

"But why?"

"I dunno. And Ralph, Jack, the chief, says it'll be dangerous—"

"—and we've got to be careful and throw our spears like at a pig."

"We're going to spread out in a line across the island—"

"—we're going forward from this end—"

"—until we find you."

"We've got to give signals like this."

Eric raised his head and achieved a faint ululation by beating on his open mouth. Then he glanced behind him nervously.

"Like that—"

"—only louder, of course."

"But I've done nothing," whispered Ralph, urgently. "I only wanted to keep up a fire!"

He paused for a moment, thinking miserably of the morrow. A matter of overwhelming importance occurred to him.

"What are you—?"

He could not bring himself to be specific at first; but then fear and loneliness goaded him.

"When they find me, what are they going to do?"

The twins were silent. Beneath him, the death rock flowered again.

"What are they—oh God! I'm hungry—"

The towering rock seemed to sway under him.

"Well—what—?"

The twins answered his question indirectly.

"You got to go now, Ralph."

"For your own good."

"Keep away. As far as you can."

"Won't you come with me? Three of us—we'd stand a chance."

After a moment's silence, Sam spoke in a strangled voice.

"You don't know Roger. He's a terror."

"And the chief—they're both—"

"—terrors—"

"—only Roger—"

Both boys froze. Someone was climbing toward them from the tribe.

"He's coming to see if we're keeping watch. Quick, Ralph!"

As he prepared to let himself down the cliff, Ralph snatched at the last possible advantage to be wrung out of this meeting.

"I'll lie up close; in that thicket down there," he whispered, "so keep them away from it. They'll never think to look so close—"

The footsteps were still some distance away.

"Sam—I'm going to be all right, aren't I?"

The twins were silent again.

"Here!" said Sam suddenly. "Take this—"

Ralph felt a chunk of meat pushed against him and grabbed it.

"But what are you going to do when you catch me?"

Silence above. He sounded silly to himself. He lowered himself down the rock.

"What are you going to do—?"

From the top of the towering rock came the incomprehensible reply.

"Roger sharpened a stick at both ends."

Roger sharpened a stick at both ends. Ralph tried to attach a meaning to this but could not. He used all the bad words he could think of in a fit of temper that passed into yawning. How long could you go without sleep? He yearned for a bed and sheets—but the only whiteness here was the slow spilt milk, luminous round the rock forty feet below, where Piggy had fallen. Piggy was everywhere, was on this neck, was become terrible in darkness and death. If Piggy were to come back now out of the water, with his empty head—Ralph whimpered and yawned like a littlun. The stick in his hand became a crutch on which he reeled.

Then he tensed again. There were voices raised on the top of the Castle Rock. Samneric were arguing with someone. But the ferns and the grass were near. That was the place to be in, hidden, and next to the thicket that would serve for tomorrow's hide-out. Here—and his hands touched grass—was a place to be in for the night, not far from the tribe, so that if the horrors of the supernatural emerged one could at least mix with humans for the time being, even if it meant . . .

What did it mean? A stick sharpened at both ends. What was there in that? They had thrown spears and missed; all but one. Perhaps they would miss next time, too.

He squatted down in the tall grass, remembered the meat that Sam had given him, and began to tear at it ravenously. While he was eating, he heard fresh noises—cries of pain from Samneric, cries of panic, angry voices. What did it mean? Someone besides himself was in trouble, for at least one of the twins was catching it. Then the voices passed away down the rock and he ceased to think of them. He felt with his hands and found cool, delicate fronds backed against the thicket. Here then was the night's lair. At first light he would creep into the thicket, squeeze between the twisted stems, ensconce himself so deep that only a crawler like himself could come through, and that crawler would be jabbed. There he would sit, and the search would pass him by, and the cordon waver on, ululating along the island, and he would be free.

He pulled himself between the ferns, tunneling in. He laid the stick beside him, and huddled himself down in the blackness. One must remember to wake at first light, in order to diddle the savages—and he did not know how quickly sleep came and hurled him down a dark interior slope.

He was awake before his eyes were open, listening to a noise that was near. He opened an eye, found the mold an inch or so from his face and his fingers gripped into it, light filtering between the fronds of fern. He had just time to realize that the age-long nightmares of falling and death were past and that the morning was come, when he heard the sound again. It was an ululation over by the seashore —and now the next savage answered and the next. The cry swept by him across the narrow end of the island from sea to lagoon, like the cry of a flying bird. He took no time to consider but grabbed his sharp stick and wriggled back among the ferns. Within seconds he was worming his way into the thicket; but not before he had glimpsed the legs of a savage coming toward him. The ferns were thumped and beaten and he heard legs moving in the long grass. The savage, whoever he was, ululated twice; and the cry was repeated in both directions, then died away. Ralph crouched still, tangled in the ferns, and for a time he heard nothing.

At last he examined the thicket itself. Certainly no one could attack him here—and moreover he had a stroke of luck. The great rock that had killed Piggy had bounded into this thicket and bounced there, right in the center, making a smashed space a few feet in extent each way. When Ralph had wriggled into this he felt secure, and clever. He sat down carefully among the smashed stems and waited for the hunt to pass. Looking up between the leaves he caught a glimpse of something red. That must be the top of the Castle Rock, distant and unmenacing. He composed himself triumphantly, to hear the sounds of the hunt dying away.

Yet no one made a sound; and as the minutes passed, in the green shade, his feeling of triumph faded.

At last he heard a voice—Jack's voice, but hushed.

"Are you certain?"

The savage addressed said nothing. Perhaps he made a gesture.

Roger spoke.

"If you're fooling us—"

Immediately after this, there came a gasp, and a squeal of pain. Ralph crouched instinctively. One of the twins was there, outside the thicket, with Jack and Roger.

"You're sure he meant in there?"

The twin moaned faintly and then squealed again.

"He meant he'd hide in there?"

"Yes—yes—oh—!"

Silvery laughter scattered among the trees.

So they knew.

Ralph picked up his stick and prepared for battle. But what could they do? It would take them a week to break a path through the thicket; and anyone who wormed his way in would be helpless. He felt the point of his spear with his thumb and grinned without amusement. Whoever tried that would be stuck, squealing like a pig.

They were going away, back to the tower rock. He could hear feet moving and then someone sniggered. There came again that high, bird-like cry that swept along the line. So some were still watching for him; but some—?

There was a long, breathless silence. Ralph found that he had bark in his mouth from the gnawed spear. He stood and peered upwards to the Castle Rock.

As he did so, he heard Jack's voice from the top.

"Heave! Heave! Heave!"

The red rock that he could see at the top of the cliff vanished like a curtain, and he could see figures and blue sky. A moment later the earth jolted, there was a rushing sound in the air, and the top of the thicket was cuffed as with a gigantic hand. The rock bounded on, thumping and smashing toward the beach, while a shower of broken twigs and leaves fell on him. Beyond the thicket, the tribe was cheering.

Silence again.

Ralph put his fingers in his mouth and bit them. There was only one other rock up there that they might conceivably move; but that was half as big as a cottage, big as a car, a tank. He visualized its probable progress with agonizing clearness—that one would start slowly, drop from ledge to ledge, trundle across the neck like an outsize steam roller.

"Heave! Heave! Heave!"

Ralph put down his spear, then picked it up again. He pushed his hair back irritably, took two hasty steps across the little space and then came back. He stood looking at the broken ends of branches.

Still silence.

He caught sight of the rise and fall of his diaphragm and was surprised to see how quickly he was breathing. Just left of center his heart-beats were visible. He put the spear down again.

"Heave! Heave! Heave!"

A shrill, prolonged cheer.

Something boomed up on the red rock, then the earth jumped and began to shake steadily, while the noise as steadily increased. Ralph was shot into the air, thrown down, dashed against branches. At his right hand, and only a few feet away, the whole thicket bent and the roots screamed as they came out of the earth together. He saw something red that turned over slowly as a mill wheel. Then the red thing was past and the elephantine progress diminished toward the sea.

Ralph knelt on the plowed-up soil, and waited for the earth to come back. Presently the white, broken stumps, the split sticks and the tangle of the thicket refocused. There was a kind of heavy feeling in his body where he had watched his own pulse.

Silence again.

Yet not entirely so. They were whispering out there; and suddenly the branches were shaken furiously at two places on his right. The pointed end of a stick appeared. In panic, Ralph thrust his own stick through the crack and struck with all his might.

"Aaa-ah!"

His spear twisted a little in his hands and then he withdrew it again.

"Ooh-ooh—"

Someone was moaning outside and a babble of voices rose. A fierce argument was going on and the wounded savage kept groaning. Then when there was silence, a single voice spoke and Ralph decided that it was not Jack's.

"See? I told you—he's dangerous."

The wounded savage moaned again.

What else? What next?

Ralph fastened his hands round the chewed spear and his hair fell. Someone was muttering, only a few yards away toward the Castle Rock. He heard a savage say "No!" in a shocked voice; and then there was suppressed laughter. He squatted back on his heels and showed his teeth at the wall of branches. He raised his spear, snarled a little, and waited.

Once more the invisible group sniggered. He heard a curious trickling sound and then a louder crepitation as if someone were unwrapping great sheets of cellophane. A stick snapped and he stifled a cough. Smoke was seeping through the branches in white and yellow wisps, the patch of blue sky overhead turned to the color of a storm cloud, and then the smoke billowed round him.

Someone laughed excitedly, and a voice shouted.

"Smoke!"

He wormed his way through the thicket toward the forest, keeping as far as possible beneath the smoke. Presently he saw open space, and the green leaves of the edge of the thicket. A smallish savage was standing between him and the rest of the forest, a savage striped red and white, and carrying a spear. He was coughing and smearing the paint about his eyes with the back of his hand as he tried to see through the increasing smoke. Ralph launched himself like a cat; stabbed, snarling, with the spear, and the savage doubled up. There was a shout from beyond the thicket and then Ralph was running with the swiftness of fear through the undergrowth. He came to a pig-run, followed it for perhaps a hundred yards, and then swerved off. Behind him the ululation swept across the island once more and a single voice shouted three times. He guessed that was the signal to advance and sped away again, till his chest was like fire. Then he flung himself down under a bush and waited for a moment till his breathing steadied. He passed his tongue tentatively over his teeth and lips and heard far off the ululation of the pursuers.

There were many things he could do. He could climb a tree; but that was putting all his eggs in one basket. If he were detected, they had nothing more difficult to do than wait.

If only one had time to think!

Another double cry at the same distance gave him a clue to their plan. Any savage balked in the forest would utter the double shout and hold up the line till he was free again. That way they might hope to keep the cordon unbroken right across the island. Ralph thought of the boar that had broken through them with such ease. If necessary, when the chase came too close, he could charge the cordon while it was still thin, burst through, and run back. But run back where? The cordon would turn and sweep again. Sooner or later he would have to sleep or eat—and then he would awaken with hands clawing at him; and the hunt would become a running down.

What was to be done, then? The tree? Burst the line like a boar? Either way the choice was terrible.

A single cry quickened his heart-beat and, leaping up, he dashed away toward the ocean side and the thick jungle till he was hung up among creepers; he stayed there for a moment with his calves quivering. If only one could have quiet, a long pause, a time to think!

And there again, shrill and inevitable, was the ululation sweeping across the island. At that sound he shied like a horse among the creepers and ran once more till he was panting. He flung himself down by some ferns. The tree, or the charge? He mastered his breathing for a moment, wiped his mouth, and told himself to be calm. Samneric were somewhere in that line, and hating it. Or were they? And supposing, instead of them, he met the chief, or Roger who carried death in his hands?

Ralph pushed back his tangled hair and wiped the sweat out of his best eye. He spoke aloud.

"Think."

What was the sensible thing to do?

There was no Piggy to talk sense. There was no solemn assembly for debate nor dignity of the conch.

"Think."

Most, he was beginning to dread the curtain that might waver in his brain, blacking out the sense of danger, making a simpleton of him.

A third idea would be to hide so well that the advancing line would pass without discovering him.

He jerked his head off the ground and listened. There was another noise to attend to now, a deep grumbling noise, as though the forest itself were angry with him, a somber noise across which the ululations were scribbled excruciatingly as on slate. He knew he had heard it before somewhere, but had no time to remember.

Break the line.

A tree.

Hide, and let them pass.

A nearer cry stood him on his feet and immediately he was away again, running fast among thorns and brambles. Suddenly he blundered into the open, found himself again in that open space—and there was the fathom-wide grin of the skull, no longer ridiculing a deep blue patch of sky but jeering up into a blanket of smoke. Then Ralph was running beneath trees, with the grumble of the forest explained. They had smoked him out and set the island on fire.

Hide was better than a tree because you had a chance of breaking the line if you were discovered.

Hide, then.

He wondered if a pig would agree, and grimaced at nothing. Find the deepest thicket, the darkest hole on the island, and creep in. Now, as he ran, he peered about him. Bars and splashes of sunlight flitted over him and sweat made glistening streaks on his dirty body. The cries were far now, and faint.

At last he found what seemed to him the right place, though the decision was desperate. Here, bushes and a wild tangle of creeper made a mat that kept out all the light of the sun. Beneath it was a space, perhaps a foot high, though it was pierced everywhere by parallel and rising stems. If you wormed into the middle of that you would be five yards from the edge, and hidden, unless the savage chose to lie down and look for you; and even then, you would be in darkness—and if the worst happened and he saw you, then you had a chance to burst out at him, fling the whole line out of step and double back.

Cautiously, his stick trailing behind him, Ralph wormed between the rising stems. When he reached the middle of the mat he lay and listened.

The fire was a big one and the drum-roll that he had thought was left so far behind was nearer. Couldn't a fire outrun a galloping horse? He could see the sun-splashed ground over an area of perhaps fifty yards from where he lay, and as he watched, the sunlight in every patch blinked at him. This was so like the curtain that flapped in his brain that for a moment he thought the blinking was inside him. But then the patches blinked more rapidly, dulled and went out, so that he saw that a great heaviness of smoke lay between the island and the sun.

If anyone peered under the bushes and chanced to

glimpse human flesh it might be Samneric who would pretend not to see and say nothing. He laid his cheek against the chocolate-colored earth, licked his dry lips and closed his eyes. Under the thicket, the earth was vibrating very slightly; or perhaps there was a sound beneath the obvious thunder of the fire and scribbled ululations that was too low to hear.

Someone cried out. Ralph jerked his cheek off the earth and looked into the dulled light. They must be near now, he thought, and his chest began to thump. Hide, break the line, climb a tree—which was the best after all? The trouble was you only had one chance.

Now the fire was nearer; those volleying shots were great limbs, trunks even, bursting. The fools! The fools! The fire must be almost at the fruit trees—what would they eat tomorrow?

Ralph stirred restlessly in his narrow bed. One chanced nothing! What could they do? Beat him? So what? Kill him? A stick sharpened at both ends.

The cries, suddenly nearer, jerked him up. He could see a striped savage moving hastily out of a green tangle, and coming toward the mat where he hid, a savage who carried a spear. Ralph gripped his fingers into the earth. Be ready now, in case.

Ralph fumbled to hold his spear so that it was point foremost; and now he saw that the stick was sharpened at both ends.

The savage stopped fifteen yards away and uttered his cry.

Perhaps he can hear my heart over the noises of the fire. Don't scream. Get ready.

The savage moved forward so that you could only see him from the waist down. That was the butt of his spear. Now you could see him from the knee down. Don't scream.

A herd of pigs came squealing out of the greenery behind the savage and rushed away into the forest. Birds were screaming, mice shrieking, and a little hopping thing came under the mat and cowered.

Five yards away the savage stopped, standing right by the thicket, and cried out. Ralph drew his feet up and crouched. The stake was in his hands, the stake sharpened at both ends, the stake that vibrated so wildly, that grew long, short, light, heavy, light again.

The ululation spread from shore to shore. The savage knelt down by the edge of the thicket, and there were lights flickering in the forest behind him. You could see a knee disturb the mold. Now the other. Two hands. A spear.

A face.

The savage peered into the obscurity beneath the thicket. You could tell that he saw light on this side and on that, but not in the middle—there. In the middle was a blob of dark and the savage wrinkled up his face, trying to decipher the darkness.

The seconds lengthened. Ralph was looking straight into the savage's eyes.

Don't scream.

You'll get back.

Now he's seen you. He's making sure. A stick sharpened.

Ralph screamed, a scream of fright and anger and desperation. His legs straightened, the screams became continuous and foaming. He shot forward, burst the thicket, was in the open, screaming, snarling, bloody. He swung the stake and the savage tumbled over; but there were others coming toward him, crying out. He swerved as a spear flew past and then was silent, running. All at once the lights flickering ahead of him merged together, the roar of the forest rose to thunder and a tall bush directly in his path burst into a great fan-shaped flame. He swung to the right, running desperately fast, with the heat beating on his left side and the fire racing forward like a tide. The ululation rose behind him and spread along, a series of short sharp cries, the sighting call. A brown figure showed up at his right and fell away. They were all running, all crying out madly. He could hear them crashing in the undergrowth and on the left was the hot, bright thunder of the fire. He forgot his wounds, his hunger and thirst, and became fear; hopeless fear on flying feet, rushing through the forest toward the open beach. Spots jumped before his eyes and turned into red circles that expanded quickly till they passed out of sight. Below him someone's legs were getting tired and the desperate ululation advanced like a jagged fringe of menace and was almost overhead.

He stumbled over a root and the cry that pursued him rose even higher. He saw a shelter burst into flames and the fire flapped at his right shoulder and there was the glitter of water. Then he was down, rolling over and over in the warm sand, crouching with arm up to ward off, trying to cry for mercy.

He staggered to his feet, tensed for more terrors, and looked up at a huge peaked cap. It was a white-topped cap, and above the green shade of the peak was a crown, an anchor, gold foliage. He saw white drill, epaulettes, a revolver, a row of gilt buttons down the front of a uniform.

A naval officer stood on the sand, looking down at Ralph in wary astonishment. On the beach behind him was a cutter, her bows hauled up and held by two ratings. In the stern-sheets another rating held a sub-machine gun.

The ululation faltered and died away.

The officer looked at Ralph doubtfully for a moment, then took his hand away from the butt of the revolver.

"Hullo."

Squirming a little, conscious of his filthy appearance, Ralph answered shyly.

"Hullo."

The officer nodded, as if a question had been answered. "Are there any adults—any grownups with you?"

Dumbly, Ralph shook his head. He turned a half-pace on the sand. A semicircle of little boys, their bodies streaked with colored clay, sharp sticks in their hands, were standing on the beach making no noise at all.

"Fun and games," said the officer.

The fire reached the coconut palms by the beach and swallowed them noisily. A flame, seemingly detached, swung like an acrobat and licked up the palm heads on the platform. The sky was black.

The officer grinned cheerfully at Ralph.

"We saw your smoke. What have you been doing? Having a war or something?"

Ralph nodded.

The officer inspected the little scarecrow in front of him. The kid needed a bath, a haircut, a nose-wipe and a good deal of ointment.

"Nobody killed, I hope? Any dead bodies?"

"Only two. And they've gone."

The officer leaned down and looked closely at Ralph. "Two? Killed?"

Ralph nodded again. Behind him, the whole island was

shuddering with flame. The officer knew, as a rule, when people were telling the truth. He whistled softly.

Other boys were appearing now, tiny tots some of them, brown, with the distended bellies of small savages. One of them came close to the officer and looked up.

"I'm, I'm—"

But there was no more to come. Percival Wemys Madison sought in his head for an incantation that had faded clean away.

The officer turned back to Ralph.

"We'll take you off. How many of you are there?"

Ralph shook his head. The officer looked past him to the group of painted boys.

"Who's boss here?"

"I am," said Ralph loudly.

A little boy who wore the remains of an extraordinary black cap on his red hair and who carried the remains of a pair of spectacles at his waist, started forward, then changed his mind and stood still.

"We saw your smoke. And you don't know how many of you there are?"

"No, sir."

"I should have thought," said the officer as he visualized the search before him, "I should have thought that a pack of British boys—you're all British, aren't you?—would have been able to put up a better show than that—I mean—"

"It was like that at first," said Ralph, "before things—" He stopped.

"We were together then—"

The officer nodded helpfully.

"I know. Jolly good show. Like the Coral Island."

Ralph looked at him dumbly. For a moment he had a fleeting picture of the strange glamour that had once invested the beaches. But the island was scorched up like dead wood—Simon was dead—and Jack had. . . . The tears began to flow and sobs shook him. He gave himself up to them now for the first time on the island; great, shuddering spasms of grief that seemed to wrench his whole body. His voice rose under the black smoke before the burning wreckage of the island; and infected by that emotion, the other little boys began to shake and sob too. And in the middle of them, with filthy body, matted hair, and unwiped nose, Ralph wept for the end of innocence, the darkness of man's heart, and the fall through the air of the true, wise friend called Piggy.

The officer, surrounded by these noises, was moved and a little embarrassed. He turned away to give them time to pull themselves together; and waited, allowing his eyes to rest on the trim cruiser in the distance.

# Interview with William Golding[1]

## JAMES KEATING

Purdue University; May 10, 1962

*Question:* It has often been said that wars are caused by the dictatorial few. Do you feel this to be so, or do you think anyone given the power is capable of such inhuman atrocity?

*Answer:* Well, I think wars are much more complicated than that. Some of them have been caused by a few. On the other hand if some of them are surely the bursting of some vicious growth, almost, in civilization, then who knows who applies the lancer to it? There's all the difference in the world between the wars of 1917—the Communist Revolution—on the one hand, and the wars of Genghis Khan on the other, isn't there?

*Q.:* Yes. Obviously, in *Lord of the Flies* society plays little part in determining the corruption and violence in man. You've said this is true in society, that it does play a minor role, but do you feel that there are societies that will enhance the possibility of man becoming good? And are we working toward this in democracy?

*A.:* By instinct and training, and by birth and by position on the face of the globe, I'm pretty well bound to subscribe to a democratic doctrine, am I not? This is so deeply woven into the way we live, or at least the way we live at home in England, that I don't suppose one really questions it much. I think I would say democracy is moving in the right direction, or the democratic way is the way in which to move; equally, it seems to me that a democracy has inherent weaknesses in it—built-in weaknesses. You can't give people freedom without weakening society as an implement of war, if you like, and so this is very much like a sheep among wolves. It's not a question with me as to whether democracy is the right way so much, as to whether democracy can survive and remain what it is. Every time democracy pulls itself together and says, "Well, now I'm being threatened by a totalitarian regime," the first thing it has to do is give up some of its own principles. In England during the Second World War we had to give up a tremendous number of principles in order to achieve the one pointed unity which could possibly withstand Hitler. It's possible to look at the question in this way and say, "Is the remedy not as bad as the disease?" I don't know.

Q.: Well, the innocence in man, for example, that you bring out among the boys in this novel, would you say it was an inherent kind of thing which materializes, or is it a thing from without which is taken on during a transitional process from innocence to non-innocence? Are the boys innocent of themselves or are they innocent of evil from without and evil of others?

A.: They're innocent of their own natures. They don't understand their own natures and therefore, when they get to this island, they can look forward to a bright future, because they don't understand the things that threaten it. This seems to me to be innocence; I suppose you could almost equate it with ignorance of men's basic attributes, and this is inevitable with anything which is born and begins to grow up. Obviously, it doesn't understand its own nature.

Q.: Then it's more a combination of innocence of their own and other's attributes?

A.: Yes. I think, quite simply, that they don't understand what beasts there are in the human psyche which have to be curbed. They're too young to look ahead and really put the curbs on their own nature and implement them, because giving way to these beasts is always a pleasure, in some ways, and so their society breaks down. Of course, on the other hand, in an adult society it is possible society will not break down. It may be that we can put sufficient curbs on our own natures to prevent it from breaking down. We may have the very common sense to say that if we have atom bombs and so on—H-bombs—well, we cannot possibly use these things.

Now that is, in a sense, the lowest possible bit of common sense—obviously we can't—but you know as well as I do that there is a large chance that those weapons will be used and we'll be done for. I think that democratic attitude of voluntary curbs put on one's own nature is the only possible way for humanity, but I wouldn't like to say that it's going to work out, or survive.

*Q.:* You recently stated your belief that humanity would either be saved, or save itself. Is that correct?

*A.:* Yes, but here again this is because I'm basically an optimist. Intellectually I can see man's balance is about fifty-fifty, and his chances of blowing himself up are about one to one. I can't see this any way but intellectually. I'm just emotionally unable to believe that he will do this. This means that I am by nature an optimist and by intellectual conviction a pessimist, I suppose.

*Q.:* The reason I posed that comment was because in your published notes in *Lord of the Flies* . . .

*A.:* They aren't my notes.

*Q.:* I'm sorry. I thought Mr. Epstein[2] quoted you.

*A.:* Did he?

*Q.:* In the summation . . .

*A.:* Oh, yes.

*Q.:* In the end the question is, who will rescue the adult and his cruiser? This seems to me a little fatalistic; it conveys the notion that there isn't really any hope.

*A.:* Yes, but there again you can take . . . there are two answers here; I think they are both valid answers. The first one is the one I made before, and that is that the quotation there is what I said is intellectual fatalism. It's making the thing a sort of series of Chinese boxes, one inside of the other. The other thing is to say that as the fabulist is always

---

[2] E. L. Epstein, "Notes on *Lord of the Flies*," reprinted below, p. 277.—Eds.

a moralist, he is always overstating his case, because he has
a point he wishes to drive home. I would perfer to say if
you don't curb yourself, then this is what will happen to
you.

*Q.:* Again, in *Lord of the Flies*, I noticed a very definite
relationship between Simon and his brutal death and Christ
and his crucifixion. Would you care to discuss this, or give
any omniscient judgment?

*A.:* Well, I can't give an omniscient judgment. I can only
say what I intended. First you've got to remember I haven't
read this book for ten years, so I may be a bit off. I intended
a Christ figure in the novel, because Christ figures occur in
humanity, really, but I couldn't have the full picture, or as
near as full a possible picture of human potentiality, unless
one was potentially a Christ figure. So Simon is the little
boy who goes off into the bushes to pray. He is the only
one to take any notice of the little 'uns—who actually hands
them food, gets food from places where they can't reach
it and hands it down to them. He is the one who is tempted
of the devil: he has this interview with the pig's head on the
stick, with Beelzebub, or Satan, the devil, whatever you'd
like to call it, and the devil says, "Clear off, you're not
wanted. Just go back to the others. We'll forget the whole
thing."

Well, this is, of course, the perennial temptation to the
saint, as I conceive it, to just go and be like ordinary men
and let the whole thing slide. Instead of that, Simon goes
up the hill and takes away from the island, removes, discovers what this dead hand of history is that's over them,
undoes the threads so that the wind can blow this dead
thing away from the island, and then when he tries to take
the good news back to ordinary human society, he's cruci-
fied for it. This is as far as I was able to find a Christ
parallel, you see.[3]

*Q.:* You mentioned that you couldn't give any omniscient
judgment, and you've earlier said that an author cannot
really say, after he has written a work, what he has given
from himself or created.[4] What do you feel the role of the

[3] For a further discussion of the role of Simon, see Donald
R. Spangler, "Simon," p. 211 in this volume.—Eds.

[4] Compare Golding's remarks here with his statements in the
interview with Frank Kermode, p. 199 in this volume.—Eds.

critic is here? Do you feel the critic has the right to bring these things out?

A.: Well, isn't this really a question without much meaning? Because whether a critic has rights or not he is going to do these things to a book which has got out of the author's control, and therefore you might just as well ask whether a man has a right to five fingers on each hand. This is a thing that happens. Are you really meaning do I think the critic has, by his nature or by his training, a better chance of saying what's in this book than the author has? Is that at all it?

Q.: Yes, that's mainly it. As an artist, do you feel the critics are justified?

A.: Some of them. As a practical matter some of them say things which I agree with and some say things which I don't agree with. I don't see there's much generalization that can be made here. The critic has as much right as any man to get what he can out of a book, and I would say that I think some critics that I've read have been extremely perceptive —or else I've been very lucky—in that they've seemed to put their fingers on certain things which I had deliberately intended and which I would have thought were rather subtle, and they have contrived to get hold of these. Equally, I would have to say that some critics seem to me to be miles off beam.

Q.: Well, perhaps Mr. Gindin[5] was a little off beam in his article which discusses your use of gimmicks. He mentions the saving of the boys as a gimmick that didn't quite fulfill the manifestations that were opened in the book . . . it didn't resolve them, I should think, as well as he would have liked. Do you feel this is justifiable criticism?

A.: I've been haunted by that word, "gimmick," ever since I used it in an interview explaining that I liked a sharp reversal at the end which would show the book in an entirely different light so that the reader would presumably be forced to rethink the book, which seems to me a useful thing to do. I don't know, in that event, whether the saving

⁵ James Gindin, " 'Gimmick' and Metaphor in the Novels of William Golding," *Modern Fiction Studies*, 6 (Summer, 1960), 145-152.—Eds.

of the boys at the end is a gimmick or not. The reason for that particular ending was twofold. First I originally conceived the book as the change from innocence—which is ignorance of self—to a tragic knowledge. If my boys hadn't been saved, I couldn't—at that time, at any rate—see any way of getting some one of them to the point where he would have this tragic knowledge. He would be dead. If I'd gone on to the death of Ralph, Ralph would never have had time to understand what had happened to him, so I deliberately saved him so that at this moment he could see —look back over what's happened—and weep for the end of innocence and the darkness of man's heart, which was what I was getting at. That's half the answer.

The other answer is that if, as in that quotation there, the book is supposed to show how the defects of society are directly traceable to the defects of the individual, then you rub that awful moral lesson in much more by having an ignorant, innocent adult come to the island and say, "Oh, you've been having fun, haven't you?" Then in the last sentence you let him turn away and look at the cruiser, and of course the cruiser, the adult thing, is doing exactly what the hunters do—that is, hunting down and destroying the enemy—so that you say, in effect, to your reader, "Look, you think you've been reading about little boys, but in fact you've been reading about the distresses and the wickednesses of humanity. If this is a gimmick, I still approve of it.

*Q.:* I think it fulfills what you said about the use of the gimmick at the end of a novel, making a reader go back and take another look at things.

Did the work by Richard Hughes, *High Wind in Jamaica*, have any influence on your writing *Lord of the Flies?*

*A.:* This is an interesting question. I can answer it simply: I've read this book and I liked it, but I read it after I'd written *Lord of the Flies*. And if you're going to come around to Conrad's *Heart of Darkness*, I might as well confess I've never read that.

*Q.:* Then if you hadn't read *High Wind in Jamaica* until you'd written *Lord of the Flies*, how do you feel about the thematic presentation, the parallel between the two works?

*A.:* There is a parallel, I think, but like so many literary parallels it's the plain fact that if people engage in writing about humanity, they're likely in certain circumstances to see something the same thing. They're both looking, after all, at the same object, so it would really be very surprising if there weren't literary parallels to be drawn between this book and that.

• • • • •

*Q.:* I have one more question about *Lord of the Flies*. Mr. Epstein talks about sex symbols in this work.[6] You have recently said that you purposely left man and woman off of the island to remove the . . .

*A.:* Remove the "red herring."

*Q.:* Yes. I wonder if you concur with Mr. Epstein's observations.

*A.:* You're probably thinking of the moment when they kill a pig . . .

*Q.:* Yes.

*A.:* And I'm assured that this is a sexual symbol and it has affinities of the Oedipadian wedding night. What am I to say to this? I suppose the only thing I can really say is there are in those circumstances, after all, precious few ways of killing a pig. The same thing's just as true of the Oedipadian wedding night.

---

[6] See below, p. 279.—Eds.

# The Meaning of It All[1]

Broadcast on the BBC Third Programme, August 28, 1959

KERMODE: I should like to begin, Golding, by talking about an article on your work which I know you liked which appeared in the *Kenyon Review*[2] about a year ago in which he says many admiring things about all your books but introduces a distinction between fable and fiction and puts you very much on the fable side, arguing, for example, that in *Lord of the Flies* you incline occasionally not to give a full-body presentation of people living and behaving, so much as an illustration of a particular theme; would you accept this as a fair comment on your work?

GOLDING: Well, what I would regard as a tremendous compliment to myself would be if someone would substitute the word "myth" for "fable" because I think a myth is a much profounder and more significant thing than a fable. I do feel fable as being an invented thing on the surface whereas myth is something which comes out from the roots of things in the ancient sense of being the key to existence, the whole meaning of life, and experience as a whole.

KERMODE: You're not primarily interested in giving the sort of body and pressure of lived life in a wide society; obviously not, because all your books have been concerned with either persons or societies, unnaturally isolated in some sense. It is legitimate to assume from that that you are

[1] The following interview was reprinted in this form in *Books and Bookmen*, 5 (October, 1959), 9-10, and is printed in part here by permission of Frank Kermode and William Golding.

[2] John Peter, "The Fables of William Golding," *Kenyon Review*, 19 (Autumn, 1957), 577-592. Reprinted below, pp. 229-234.—Eds.

concerned with people in this kind of extremity of solitariness.

GOLDING: Well, no, I don't think it is legitimate. My own feeling about it is that their isolation is a convenient one, rather than an unnatural one. Do you see what I mean?

KERMODE: Yes, I do see, but I'm not sure about the word "convenient" here. Convenient to *you* because you want to treat boys in the absence of grown-ups, is this what you mean?

GOLDING: Yes, I suppose so. You see it depends how far you regard intentions as being readable. Now, you know and I know about teaching people; we both do it as our daily bread. Well, you see, perhaps, people who are not quite as immature as those I see, but my own immature boys I watch carefully and there does come a point which is very legible in their society at which you can see all those things (as shown in *Lord of the Flies*) are within a second of being carried out—it's the master who gets the right boy by the scruff of the neck and hauls him back. He is God who stops a murder being committed.

KERMODE: Yes, this is why one of your boys, Piggy, often refers to the absence of grown-ups as the most important conditioning factor in the situation. The argument is, then, that out of a human group of this kind, the human invention of evil will proceed, provided that certain quite arbitrary checks are not present.

GOLDING: Yes, I think so; I think that the arbitrary checks that you talk about are nothing but the fruit of bitter experience of people who are adult enough to realise, "Well, I, I myself am vicious and would like to kill that man, and he is vicious and would like to kill me, and therefore, it is sensible that we should both have an arbitrary scheme of things in which three other people come in and separate us."

KERMODE: This makes it interesting, I think, to consider the place among your boys of the boy, Simon, in *Lord of the Flies*, who is different from the others and who understands something like the situation you're describing. He understands, for example, that the evil that the boys fear, the beast they fear, is substantially of their own invention, but when, in fact, he announces this, he himself is regarded as evil and killed accordingly. Are we allowed to infer from your myth that there will always be a person of that order in a group, or is this too much?

GOLDING: It is, I think, a bit unfair not so much because it isn't germane, but simply because it brings up too much. You see, I think on the one hand that it is true that there will always be people who will see something particularly clearly, and will not be listened to, and if they are a particularly outstanding example of their sort, will probably be killed for it. But, on the other hand, that in itself brings up such a vast kind of panorama. What so many intelligent people and particularly, if I may say so, so may literary people find, is that Simon is incomprehensible. But, he *is* comprehensible to the illiterate person. The illiterate person knows about saints and sanctity, and Simon is a saint.[8]

KERMODE: Yes, well he's a kind of scapegoat, I suppose.

GOLDING: No, I won't agree. You are really flapping a kind of *Golden Bough* over me, or waving it over my head, but I don't agree. You see, a saint isn't just a scapegoat, a saint is somebody who in the last analysis voluntarily embraces his fate, which is a pretty sticky one, and he is for the illiterate a proof of the existence of God because the illiterate person who is not brought up on logic and not brought up always to hope for the worst says, "Well, a person like this cannot exist without a good God." Therefore the illiterate person finds Simon extremely easy to understand, someone who voluntarily embraces this beast goes . . . and tries to get rid of him and goes to give the good news to the ordinary bestial man on the beach, and gets killed for it.

KERMODE: Yes, but may I introduce the famous Lawrence *caveat* here, "Never trust the teller, trust the tale"?

GOLDING: Oh, that's absolute nonsense. But *of course* the man who tells the tale if he has a tale worth telling will know exactly what he is about and this business of the artist as a sort of starry-eyed inspired creature, dancing along, with his feet two or three feet above the surface of the earth, not really knowing what sort of prints he's leaving behind him, is nothing like the truth.

---

[8] Compare the following remarks with Donald R. Spangler's essay "Simon" on pp. 211-215 in this volume.—Eds.

KERMODE: Well, I don't think it's necessary to state it quite so extremely. What I had in mind here was simply that Simon in fact is coming down from the top of the hill where he's seen the dead body of the parachutist, in order to tell the other people that all is well. He's not embracing his faith which is to be killed by the other people; he thinks he's going to put them right.

GOLDING: Ah, well, that's again a question of scale, isn't it? The point was that out of all the people on that island who would ascend the mountain, Simon was the one who saw it was the thing to do, and actually did it; nobody else dared. That is embracing your fate, you see.

KERMODE: Ah, yes, without really any sense that what will happen in the end is that he shall become the beast, which is what he does.

GOLDING: No, he *doesn't* become the beast, he becomes the beast *in other people's opinions*.

KERMODE: He becomes the beast in the text also: "The beast was on its knees in the centre, its arms folded over its face." Of course, you're here reporting what the boys in their orgiastic fury thought Simon was, but I should have said that that way of reporting allows a certain ambiguity of interpretation here, which you cannot, in fact, deny us.

GOLDING: I thought of it myself originally, I think, as a metaphor—the kind of metaphor of existence if you like, and the dead body on the mountain I thought of as being history, as the past. There's a point a couple of chapters before where these children on the island have got themselves into a hell of a mess, they're—it's the things that have crawled out of their own bones and their own veins, they don't know whether it's a beast from sky, air or where it's coming but there's something terrible about it as one of the conditions of existence.

At the moment when they're all most anguished they say, "If only grown-ups could get a sign to us, if only they could tell us what's what"—and what happens is that a dead man comes out of the sky. Now that is not God being dead, as some people have said, that is history. He's dead, but he won't lie down. All that we can give our children is to pass on to them this distressing business of a United

States of Europe, which won't work, because we all grin at each other across borders and so on and so forth. And if you turn round to your parents and say "Please help me," they are really part of the old structure, the old system, the old world, which ought to be good but at the moment is making the world and the air more and more radioactive.

KERMODE: I find it's extraordinarily interesting to think of that explanation in connection with the Ballantyne[4] treatment of the same theme. I don't know whether you would like to say just how far and how ironically we ought to treat this connection.

GOLDING: Well, I think, fairly deeply, but again, not ironically in the bad sense, but in almost a compassionate sense. You see, really, I'm getting at myself in this. What I'm saying to myself is, "Don't be such a fool, you remember when you were a boy, a small boy, how you lived on that island with Ralph and Jack and Peterkin"[5] (who is Simon, by the way, Simon called Peter, you see. It was worked out very carefully in every possible way, this novel). I said to myself finally, "Now you are grown up, you are adult; it's taken you a long time to become adult, but now you've got there you can see that people are not like that; they would not behave like that if they were God-fearing English gentlemen, and they went to an island like that." Their savagery would not be found in natives on an island. As like as not they would find savages who were kindly and uncomplicated and that the devil would rise out of the intellectual complications of the three white men on the island itself. It is really a pretty big connection [with Ballantyne].

KERMODE: In fact it's a kind of black mass version of Ballantyne, isn't it?

GOLDING: Well, I don't really think I ought to accept that. But I think I see what you mean. No, no, I disagree with it entirely, I think it is in fact a *realistic* view of the Ballantyne situation.

---

[4] R. M. Ballantyne's *The Coral Island* was published in 1857 in England. See Carl Niemeyer's "The Coral Island Revisited," *College English*, 22 (January, 1961), 241-245. Reprinted in this volume on pp. 217-223.—Eds.

[5] Characters in *The Coral Island*.—Eds.

# The Novels of William Golding[1]

## FRANK KERMODE

*Lord of the Flies* has "a pretty big connection" with Ballantyne.[2] In *The Coral Island* Ralph, Jack and Peterkin are cast
away on a desert island, where they live active, civilised,
and civilising lives. Practical difficulties are easily surmounted; they light fires with bowstrings and spy-glasses,
hunt pigs for food, and kill them with much ease and a
total absence of guilt—indeed of bloodshed. (They are all
Britons—a term they use to compliment each other—all
brave, obedient and honourable.) There is much useful information conveyed concerning tropical islands, including
field-workers' reporting of the conduct of cannibals: but
anthropology is something nasty that clears up on the
arrival of a missionary, and Jack himself prevents an act of
cannibalism by telling the flatnoses not to be such block-
heads and presenting them with six newly slaughtered pigs.
The parallel between the island and the Earthly Paradise
causes a trace of literary sophistication: "Meat and drink
on the same tree! My dear boys, we're set up for life; it must
be the ancient paradise—hurrah! . . . We afterwards
found, however, that these lovely islands were very unlike
Paradise in many things." But these "things" are non-Christian natives and, later, pirates; the boys themselves are

[1] This selection is taken from a longer essay that appeared in
the *International Literary Annual*, III (1961), 11-29, and is reprinted by permission of John Calder Limited.

[2] The relationship of R. M. Ballantyne's novel *The Coral Island*
to *Lord of the Flies* is taken up by Carl Niemeyer, "The Coral
Island Revisited," reprinted on pp. 217-223 in this volume. See
also the Foreword to this volume.—Eds.

cleanly (cold baths recommended) and godly—regenerate, empire-building boys, who know by instinct how to turn paradise into a British protectorate.

*The Coral Island* could be used as a document in the history of ideas; it belongs inseparably to the period when boys were sent out of Arnoldian schools certified free of Original Sin. Golding takes Ralph, Jack and Peterkin (altering this name to Simon "called Peter")[3] and studies them against an altered moral landscape. He is a schoolmaster, and knows boys well enough to make their collapse into savagery plausible, to see *them* as cannibals; the authority of the grown-ups is all there is to prevent savagery. If you dropped these boys into an Earthly Paradise "they would not behave like God-fearing English gentlemen" but "as like as not . . . find savages who were kindly and uncomplicated. . . . The devil would rise out of the intellectual complications of the three white men." Golding leaves the noble savages out of *Lord of the Flies*, but this remark is worth quoting because it states the intellectual position in its basic simplicity. It is the civilised who are corrupt, out of phase with natural rhythm. Their guilt is the price of evolutionary success; and our awareness of this fact can be understood by duplicating Ballantyne's situation, borrowing his island, and letting his theme develop in this new and more substantial context. Once more every prospect pleases; but the vileness proceeds, not from cannibals, but from the boys, though Man is not so much vile as "heroic and sick." Unlike Ballantyne's boys, these are dirty and inefficient; they have some notion of order, symbolised by the beautiful conch which heralds formal meetings; but when uncongenial effort is required to maintain it, order disappears. The shelters are inadequate, the signal fire goes out at the very moment when Jack first succeeds in killing a pig. Intelligence fades; irrational taboos and blood rituals make hopeless the task of the practical but partial intellect of Piggy; his glasses, the firemakers, are smashed and stolen, and in the end he himself is broken to pieces as he holds the conch. When civilised conditioning fades—how tedious Piggy's appeal to what adults might do or think!—the children are capable of neither savage nor civil gentleness. Always a

---

[3] It is interesting to ask why Golding changed the name. See the Foreword to this volume.—Eds.

little nearer to raw humanity than adults, they slip into a condition of animality depraved by mind, into the cruelty of hunters with their devil-liturgies and torture: they make an unnecessary, evil fortress, they steal, they abandon all operations aimed at restoring them to civility. Evil is the natural product of their consciousness. First, the smallest boys create a beastie, a snake—"as if it wasn't a good island." Then a beast is created in good earnest, and defined in a wonderful narrative sequence. The emblem of this evil society is the head of a dead pig, fixed, as a sacrifice, on the end of a stick and animated by flies and by the imagination of the *voyant*, Simon.

Simon is Golding's first "saint, and a most important figure." He is for the illiterate a proof of the existence of God because the illiterate (to whom we are tacitly but unmistakably expected to attribute a correct insight here) will say, "Well, a person like this cannot exist without a good God." For Simon "voluntarily embraces the beast . . . and tries to get rid of him." What he understands—and this is wisdom Golding treats with awe—is that evil is "only us." He climbs up to where the dead fire is dominated by the beast, a dead airman in a parachute, discovers what this terrible thing really is, and rushes off with the good news to the beach, where the maddened boys at their beast-slaying ritual mistake Simon himself for the beast and kill him. As Piggy, the dull practical intelligence, is reduced to blindness and futility, so Simon, the visionary, is murdered before he can communicate his comfortable knowledge.[4] Finally, the whole Paradise is destroyed under the puzzled eyes of an adult observer. Boys will be boys.

The difference of this world from Ballantyne's simpler construction from similar materials is not merely a matter of incomparability of the two talents at work; our minds have, in general, darker needs and obscurer comforts. It would be absurd to suppose that the change has impoverished us; but it has seemed to divide our world into "two cultures"—the followers of Jack and the admirers of Simon, those who build fortresses and those who want to name the beast.

---

[4] Cf. Donald R. Spangler's "Simon" on pp. 211-215 in this volume and also Golding's remarks on Simon in the interview with James Keating, p. 192.—Eds.

*Lord of the Flies* "was worked out carefully in every possible way," [5] and its author holds that the "programme" of the book *is* its meaning. He rejects Lawrence's doctrine, "Never trust the artist, trust the tale" and its consequence, "the proper function of the critic is to save the tale from the artist." He is wrong, I think; insofar as the book differs from its programme there is, as a matter of common sense, material over which the writer has no absolute authority. This means not only that there are possible readings which he cannot veto, but even that some of his own views on the book may be in a sense wrong. The interpretation of the dead parachutist is an example. This began in the "programme" as straight allegory; Golding says that this dead man "is" History.[6] "All that we can give our children" in their trouble is this monstrous dead adult, who's "dead, but won't lie down"; an ugly emblem of war and decay that broods over the paradise and provides the only objective equivalent for the beasts the boys imagine. Now this limited allegory (I may even have expanded it in the telling) seems to me not to have got out of the "programme" into the book; what does get in is more valuable because more like myth—capable, that is, of more various interpretation than the rigidity of Golding's scheme allows. And in writing of this kind all depends upon the author's mythopoeic power to transcend the "programme."

---

[5] Golding makes this statement in the interview with Frank Kermode, "The Meaning of It All." See above, p. 201.—Eds.

[6] In the interview "The Meaning of It All," p. 200.—Eds.

# Introduction[1]

## E. M. FORSTER

It is a pleasure and an honour to write an introduction to this remarkable book, but there is also a difficulty, for the reason that the book contains surprises, and its reader ought to encounter them for himself. If he knows too much he will lean back complacently. And complacency is not a quality that Mr. Golding values. The universe, in his view, secretes something that we do not expect and shall probably dislike, and he here presents the universe, under the guise of a school adventure story on a coral island.

How romantically it starts! Several bunches of boys are being evacuated during a war. Their plane is shot down, but the "tube" in which they are packed is released, falls on an island, and having peppered them over the jungle slides into the sea. None of them are hurt, and presently they collect and prepare to have a high old time. A most improbable start. But Mr. Golding's magic is already at work and he persuades us to accept it. And though the situation is improbable the boys are not. He understands them thoroughly, partly through innate sympathy, partly because he has spent much of his life teaching. He makes us feel at once that we are with real human beings, even if they are small ones, and thus lays a solid foundation for the horrors to come.

Meet three boys.

Ralph is aged a little over twelve. He is fair and well built, might grow into a boxer but never into a devil, for he

[1] Mr. Forster's Introduction appears in *Lord of the Flies*, New York: Coward-McCann, Inc., 1962. It is reprinted here by permission of the publisher.

is sunny and decent, sensible, considerate. He doesn't understand a lot, but has two things clear: firstly, they will soon be rescued—why, his daddy is in the Navy!—and secondly, until they are rescued they must hang together. It is he who finds the conch and arranges that when there is a meeting he who holds the conch shall speak. He is chosen as leader. He is democracy. And as long as the conch remains, there is some semblance of cooperation. But it gets smashed.

Meet Piggy.

Piggy is stout, asthmatic, shortsighted, underprivileged and wise. He is the brains of the party. It is the lenses of his spectacles that kindle fire. He also possesses the wisdom of the heart. He is loyal to Ralph, and tries to stop him from making mistakes, for he knows where mistakes may lead to in an unknown island. He knows that nothing is safe, nothing is neatly ticketed. He is the human spirit, aware that the universe has not been created for his convenience,[2] and doing the best he can. And as long as he survives there is some semblance of intelligence. But he too gets smashed. He hurtles through the air under a rock dislodged by savages. His skull cracks and his brains spill out.

Meet Jack.

Jack is head of a choir—a bizarre assignment considering his destiny. He marches them two and two up the sundrenched beach. He loves adventure, excitement, foraging in groups, orders when issued by himself, and though he does not yet know it and shrinks from it the first time, he loves shedding blood. Ralph he rather likes, and the liking is mutual. Piggy he despises and insults. He is dictatorship versus democracy. It is possible to read the book at a political level, and to see in its tragic trend the tragedy of our inter-war world. There is no doubt as to whose side the author is on here. He is on Ralph's. But if one shifts the

---

[2] While there is no question as to Piggy's intelligence, one must not overestimate the range of his awareness. His physical deficiencies suggest the weakness in his point of view. Piggy denies the existence of the beast and insists that "life is scientific"; even after the triumph of the hunters, he expects to enter Jack's fortress and reason with him for return of the bifocals. Like all of Golding's rationalists, Piggy has a one-dimensional view of human nature: he fails to perceive "the darkness of man's heart."—Eds.

vision to a still deeper level—the psychological—he is on the side of Piggy. Piggy knows that things mayn't go well because he knows what boys are, and he knows that the island, for all its apparent friendliness, is equivocal.

The hideous accidents that promote the reversion to savagery fill most of the book, and the reader must be left to endure them—and also to embrace them, for somehow or other they are entangled with beauty. The greatness of the vision transcends what is visible. At the close, when the boys are duly rescued by the trim British cruiser, we find ourselves on their side. We have shared their experience and resent the smug cheeriness of their rescuers. The naval officer is a bit disappointed with what he finds—everyone filthy dirty, swollen bellies, faces daubed with clay, two missing at least and the island afire. It ought to have been more like Coral Island, he suggests.

> Ralph looked at him dumbly. For a moment he had a fleeting picture of the strange glamour that had once invested the beaches. But the island was scorched up like dead wood—Simon was dead—and Jack had . . . The tears began to flow and sobs shook him. He gave himself up to them now for the first time on the island; great, shuddering spasms of grief that seemed to wrench his whole body. His voice rose under the black smoke before the burning wreckage of the island; and infected by that emotion, the other little boys began to shake and sob too. And in the middle of them, with filthy body, matted hair, and unwiped nose, Ralph wept for the end of innocence, the darkness of man's heart, and the fall through the air of the true, wise friend called Piggy.

This passage—so pathetic—is also revealing. Phrases like "the end of innocence" and "the darkness of man's heart" show us the author's attitude more clearly than has appeared hitherto. He believes in the Fall of Man and perhaps in Original Sin. Or if he does not exactly believe, he fears; the same fear infects his second novel, a difficult and profound work called *The Inheritors.* Here the innocent (the boys as it were) are Neanderthal Man, and the corrupters are Homo Sapiens, our own ancestors, who eat other animals, discover intoxicants, and destroy. Similar notions occur in his other novels.

Thus his attitude approaches the Christian: we are all born in sin, or will all lapse into it. But he does not complete the Christian attitude, for the reason that he never introduces the idea of a Redeemer. When a deity does appear, he is the Lord of the Flies, Beelzebub, and he sends a messenger to prepare his way before him.

The approach of doom is gradual. When the little boys land they are delighted to find that there are no grown-ups about. Ralph stands on his head with joy, and led by him they have a short period of happiness. Soon problems arise, work has to be assigned and executed, and Ralph now feels "we must make a good job of this, as grown-ups would, we mustn't let them down." Problems increase and become terrifying. In his desperation the child cries, "If only they could get a message to us, if only they could send us something grown-up . . . a sign or something." And they do. They send something grown-up. A dead parachutist floats down from the upper air, where they have been killing each other, is carried this way and that by the gentle winds, and hooks onto the top of the island.

This is not the end of the horrors. But it is the supreme irony. And it remains with us when the breezy rescuers arrive at the close and wonder why a better show wasn't put up.

*Lord of the Flies* is a very serious book which has to be introduced seriously. The danger of such an introduction is that it may suggest that the book is stodgy. It is not. It is written with taste and liveliness, the talk is natural, the descriptions of scenery enchanting. It is certainly not a comforting book. But it may help a few grown-ups to be less complacent and more compassionate, to support Ralph, respect Piggy, control Jack and lighten a little the darkness of man's heart. At the present moment (if I may speak personally) it is respect for Piggy that seems needed most. I do not find it in our leaders.

*King's College*
*Cambridge*
*May 14, 1962*

# Simon[1]

## DONALD R. SPANGLER

IN *Lord of the Flies* the character Simon has about him a
general aura of saintliness. Critics have suggested that
Simon is a Christ figure. And William Golding, on the
artist's part, has said that he intended to present a Christ
figure in the novel, intimating that Simon is the character he
meant so to present.[2] Accordingly, it might be of value to
examine what textual evidence there is to document the
function of Simon as a Christ or "saint" in *Lord of the Flies*.

Even before identified by name Simon is introduced as
the choir boy who had fainted, an oblique bit of characterization that, in retrospect, is seen to have impressed upon
the reader the hallucinatory, and hence, mystical-religious
proclivities of a boy who is subject to "spells." His name,
when we are given it, reveals in its etymology the distin-
guishing "attunedness" of the mystic—Simon, "the hearken-
ing." And the Mother Goose appellative, *simple*, hints of
the "holy idiot" folk-type.

Simon is skinny, a trait that, in a child, suggests the adult
correlative of ascetic self-abnegation. A "vivid little boy,"
his face "glows," radiant after the manner of nimbus and
halo. Jungle buds rejected by the others because inedible,
Simon's religious imagination sees as "candles." (The buds
open at night into aromatic white flowers, whose scent—
incense-prayer—and color—white-innocence—confirm the
value that he singularly had sensed them to have.)[3] And

---

[1] This article was written for this volume.

[2] James Keating, "Interview with William Golding," May 10,
1962. See p. 192 in this volume.

[3] The buds also appear in Ballantyne's *The Coral Island*, but
significant here is the rejection of them by everyone but Simon.

when the lethargic Piggy fails to help gather fire wood, Simon defends him to the others by observing that the fire had been started with Piggy's glasses, that Piggy had "helped that way," a ratiocination on Simon's part the casuistry of which is surely offset by its overriding compassion.

In the scene in which Simon "suffers the little children to come unto him," Golding's description unmistakably evokes the Biblical accounts of Christ amid the bread-hungry masses:

> Then, amid the roar of bees in the afternoon sunlight, Simon found for them the fruit they could not reach, pulled off the choicest from up in the foliage, passed them back down to the endless, outstretched hands. When he had satisfied them he paused and looked round.

In this passage and elsewhere Simon's abstinence from eating meat contributes to the impression of his saintliness, particularly since the novel implies that the hunt for meat as food disguises the blood-lust to kill for killing's sake, and further, that carnivorousness is linked with carnality (by the symbolic coitus of the sow killing).[4]

As a repeated object of ridicule, snickered over and laughed at, Simon's predicament recalls the New Testament details of the centurions' mocking of Jesus. And as Golding has pointed out, the Biblical temptation of Christ has its parallel in *Lord of the Flies,* in the confrontation between the boy and the "beast," between Simon and the sow's head, which tries to while him into complacency.

To Ralph, Simon prophesies that, " 'You'll get back where you came from,' " and by excluding himself from the predicted rescue, prophesies in that same breath his own fate, not to be rescued. Not to be rescued is not necessarily to die, but the attendant analogues being what they are, there seems to be a clear correspondence between Simon's foresight and that of Christ, as accounts hold Christ to have anticipated the imminence of his "hour."

Images of Gethsemane and Golgotha amass in the description of Simon's agony in his thicket sanctum, transfixed by the impaled head—the apparition of the beast in the

---

[4] Compare E. L. Epstein, "Notes on *Lord of the Flies*," p. 280 in this volume and, further, Golding's own remarks in the interview with James Keating, p. 195 in this volume.—Eds.

forest that induces in Simon his apprehension of the beast in man's heart, the boy-mystic's vision, to paraphrase Richard Wilbur, of how much we are the beast that prowls our woods. The incidents of Simon's kneeling and sweating accord directly with the story of Gethsemane; moreover, Golding's description reinforces those associations by half raising popular pictorial renderings of the person of Jesus and of the Agony in the Garden: Simon kneeling in an "arrow of sun," with "head tilted slightly up," sweat running from his "long, coarse hair." (The deft advantage to which Golding here puts calendar-art graphics is noteworthy.)

As the thicket is the setting for incidents that recall Gethsemane, it is the setting also for events that evoke images of Golgotha. Simon falls, in accord with gospel accounts of Jesus' ascent to the cross, and losing consciousness, regains it only after shedding blood, the nosebleed of the boy analogous to the lance-wounding of Jesus in the details of the crucifixion.

It is as sacrificial victim, however, that Simon most clearly emerges as a Christ figure. A lad whose feet "left prints in the soil" (the dirt-road treks of the teaching Master?), he is described as "burned by the sun," not tanned to gold like the other boys, but burnt, offering-like. When, after he has received the revelation that the "beast," the "thing" really to fear, is man's nature, it is with Christ-like resignation to inevitability ("What else is there to do?" /"Let Thy will be done.") that Simon sets out to discover what the "beast on the mountain" really is, since it is not a thing to fear. When he finds the body of the chutist and disentangles the lines, Simon is seen as ministering to the dead, committing the body to the earth so that the processes of decomposition can complete the return "to earth." However, because the wind takes hold of the chute and carries off the corpse, Simon becomes the exorcist from the island of the false menace, the mistakenly feared dead man. (Golding recollects in the Keating interview—after explaining that his momory of the novel might be blurred—that Simon releases the body "*so that* the wind *can* [italics mine] blow this dead thing away from the island," implying intention on Simon's part.) In any event, Simon's Christ-role is confirmed when, following his discovery that the "beast on the mountain" is only the dead airman, Simon comes down from the mountain—the "heights of truth"—to save the boys from their false fears and to turn their sights inward upon their own behavior, sharing the knowledge that, while the dead are not to be feared, the live are. (It might better be said that, while the dead are not to be feared, the killed are.)

The responsibility for the martyrdom of Simon, like the responsibility for that of Jesus, can be ascribed either to secular or sacred interests. At first the tribe maintains that it was not Simon they had killed, but the terrorizing "beast," and Simon is made a scapegoat, the capital-punishment of whom satisfies the established state (the tribe) by eliminating a supposed enemy. Later on the boys admit that it was not the "beast" that they had killed, but Simon, rationalizing that the human sacrifice will finally appease the "beast," which they have been placating with pigs' heads; and Simon is made a human offering, the immolation of whom assuages the established god (the "beast"), the priests of which the "celebrants" of the sacrificial feast become.

However, the analogue between Golding's Simon and Christianity's Saviour stops short of soteriology. Only Simon has hearkened. From his life and death no help accrues to that microcosm of humanity, on its island Earth in a space of sea, lost, and in need to be "saved." Upon Golding's Simon Peter no church is founded, no mechanism for salvation. In fact, the implication of the novel is, that the beast in man can never be recognized because it causes imagined "beasts" forever to be misidentified and slain before identified correctly, so that, unrecognized, the beast endures. The beast is man's inability to recognize his own responsibility for his own self-destruction.

Of course, what constitutes self-destruction the centuries have quarreled over. (What "good" is really evil, what "evil" really good? Does man destroy himself in being himself, or in trying not to be himself? What is his nature, for him to be guilty in response to, innocent in accord with, or guilty in accord with and innocent in response to? The physics and metaphysics of "self" produce the paradoxes of guilt: does man react to a basically innocent nature with misguided guilt, or react to a basically guilty nature with unrecognizing innocence?) Apollo and Dionysus still wrestle. Nevertheless, whatever in man is to blame, what is to blame is something in man. It is the shifting by man of responsibility onto "beasts" outside himself, his refusal to confront his own nature, that the sow's head symbolizes and Golding excoriates.

What finally happens to Simon the saviour the four paragraphs closing Chapter Nine relate, in detailing the disposition of Simon's body. These paragraphs emphasize the material assimilation of the corpse back into the material universe. It is true that the last glimpse Golding provides of the body is that of its drifting "out to sea," in the ancient symbolic act of the soul's "crossing over," but the absence of evidence that Simon is to have a conscious afterlife, that he will remain in any way intact as a person, makes the decorporealization seem very permanent. The body glows ironically, with the luminescence of scavengers, metamorphosing it into the subhuman world of ragged claws. Even as Simon's body is seen, at the close of Chapter Nine, to be a "silver form under the steadfast constellations" (the body to disintegrate, the stars to prevail), the intimations of immortality are quite evanescent. The romantic metaphor of its becoming a star obviates the urgent practicalities of the Christian's "getting into heaven." Simon's soul (breath-spirit) leaves him with a last gruesome "plop." At best the prospect seems to be the certainly non-Christian one of Simon's disembodied spirit's remaining forever disembodied. The drift of these paragraphs of *Lord of the Flies* seems to counter the Christian anticipation of an eventual hylozoic reunion of human body and soul. And though the reader's sympathies yearn that the beauty of Simon's spirit preclude its extinction, that beauty in the end only makes the oblivion Simon comes to more poignant.

# The Coral Island Revisited[1]

## CARL NIEMEYER

ONE interested in finding out about Golding for oneself should probably begin with *Lord of the Flies*, now available in a paperback. The story is simple. In a way not clearly explained, a group of children, all boys, presumably evacuees in a future war, are dropped from a plane just before it is destroyed, onto an uninhabited tropical island. The stage is thus set for a reworking of a favorite subject in children's literature: castaway children assuming adult responsibilities without adult supervision. Golding expects his readers to recall the classic example of such a book, R. M. Ballantyne's *The Coral Island* (1857),[2] where the boys rise to the occasion and behave as admirably as would adults. But in *Lord of the Flies* everything goes wrong from the beginning. A few boys representing sanity and common sense, led by Ralph and Piggy, see the necessity for maintaining a signal fire to attract a rescue. But they are thwarted by the hunters, led by red-haired Jack, whose lust for blood is finally not to be satisfied by killing merely wild pigs. Only the timely arrival of a British cruiser saves us from an ending almost literally too horrible to think about. Since Golding is using a naïve literary form to express sophisticated reflections on the nature of man and society, and since he refers obliquely

[1] This article appeared in *College English*, 22 (January, 1961), 241-45, and is reprinted here in slightly shortened form by permission of the National Council of the Teachers of English and the author.

[2] It is worthwhile to compare Frank Kermode's discussion of *The Coral Island* with Niemeyer's. See "The Novels of William Golding," reprinted in this volume on pp. 203-206. See also the Foreword to this volume.—Eds.

to Ballantyne many times throughout the book, a glance at *The Coral Island* is appropriate.

Ballantyne shipwrecks his three boys—Jack, eighteen; Ralph, the narrator, aged fifteen; and Peterkin Gay, a comic sort of boy, aged thirteen—somewhere in the South Seas on an uninhabited coral island. Jack is a natural leader, but both Ralph and Peterkin have abilities valuable for survival. Jack has the most common sense and foresight, but Peterkin turns out to be a skillful killer of pigs, and Ralph, when later in the book he is temporarily separated from his friends and alone on a schooner, coolly navigates it back to Coral Island by dead reckoning, a feat sufficiently impressive, if not quite equal to Captain Bligh's. The boys' life on the island is idyllic; and they are themselves without malice or wickedness, though there are a few curious episodes in which Ballantyne seems to hint at something he himself understands as little as do his characters. One is Peterkin's wanton killing of an old sow, useless as food, which the boy rationalizes by saying he needs leather for shoes. This and one or two other passages suggest that Ballantyne was aware of some darker aspects of boyish nature, but for the most part he emphasizes the paradisiacal life of the happy castaways. Like Golding's, however, Ballantyne's story raises the problem of evil, but whereas Golding finds evil in the boys' own natures, it comes to Ballantyne's boys not from within themselves but from the outside world. Tropical nature, to be sure, is kind, but the men of this non-Christian world are bad. For example, the island is visited by savage cannibals, one canoeful pursuing another, who fight a cruel and bloody battle, observed by the horrified boys, and then go away. A little later the island is again visited, this time by pirates (i.e., white men who have renounced or scorned their Christian heritage), who succeed in capturing Ralph. In due time the pirates are deservedly destroyed, and in the final episode of the book the natives undergo an unmotivated conversion to Christianity, which effects a total change in their nature just in time to rescue the boys from their clutches.

Thus Ballantyne's view of man is seen to be optimistic, like his view of English boys' pluck and resourcefulness, which subdues tropical islands as triumphantly as England imposes empire and religion on lawless breeds of men. Golding's naval officer, the *deus ex machina* of *Lord of the*

*Flies*, is only echoing Ballantyne when, perceiving dimly that all has not gone well on the island, he says (p. 186): "I should have thought that a pack of British boys—you're all British, aren't you?—would have been able to put up a better show than that—I mean—"

This is not the only echo of the older book. Golding boldly calls his two chief characters Jack and Ralph. He reproduces the comic Peterkin in the person of Piggy.[3] He has a wanton killing of a wild pig, accomplished, as E. L. Epstein points out, "in terms of sexual intercourse."[4] He uses a storm to avert a quarrel between Jack and Ralph, as Ballantyne used a hurricane to rescue his boys from death at the hands of cannibals. He emphasizes physical cruelty but integrates it into his story, and by making it a real if deplorable part of human, or at least boyish, nature improves on Ballantyne, whose descriptions of brutality—never of course performed by the boys—are usually introduced merely for their sensational effect. Finally, on the last page Golding's officer calls Ralph mildly to task for not having organized things better.

"It was like that at first," said Ralph, "before things—" He stopped.
"We were together then—"
The officer nodded helpfully.
"I know. Jolly good show. Like the Coral Island."

Golding invokes Ballantyne, so that the kind but uncomprehending adult, the instrument of salvation, may recall to the child who has just gone through hell the naïveté of the child's own early innocence, now forever lost; but he suggests at the same time the inadequacy of Ballantyne's picture of human nature in primitive surroundings.

Golding, then, regards Ballantyne's book as a badly falsified map of reality, yet the only map of this particular reality that many of us have. Ralph has it and, through harrowing experiences, replaces it with a more accurate one. The naval officer, though he should know better, since he is on

---

[3] Golding has declared that Peterkin of *The Coral Island* becomes Simon in *Lord of the Flies*. See Frank Kermode and William Golding, "The Meaning of It All," p. 201.—Eds.

[4] E. L. Epstein, "Notes on *Lord of the Flies*," p. 280 below.—Eds.

the scene and should not have to rely on memories of his boyhood reading, has it, and it seems unlikely that he is ever going to alter it, for his last recorded action is to turn away from the boys and look at his "trim" cruiser; in other words to turn away from a revelation of the untidy human heart to look at something manufactured, manageable, and solidly useful.

Golding, who being a grammar school teacher should know boys well, gives a corrective of Ballantyne's optimism. As he has explained, the book is "an attempt to trace the defects of society back to the defects of human nature." [5] These defects turn out, on close examination, to result from the evil of inadequacy and mistakenness. Evil is not the positive and readily identifiable force it appears to be when embodied in Ballantyne's savages and pirates. Golding's Ralph, for example, has real abilities, most conspicuous among them the gift of leadership and a sense of responsibility toward the "littluns." Yet both are incomplete. "By now," writes Golding, "Ralph had no self-consciousness in public thinking but would treat the day's decisions as though he were playing chess." Such detachment is obviously an important and valuable quality in a leader, but significantly the next sentence reads: "The only trouble was that he would never be a very good chess player" (p. 108). Piggy on the other hand no doubt would have been a good chess player, for with a sense of responsibility still more acute than Ralph's he combines brains and common sense. Physically, however, he is ludicrous—fat, asthmatic, and almost blind without his specs. He is forever being betrayed by his body. At his first appearance he is suffering from diarrhea; his last gesture is a literally brainless twitch of the limbs, "like a pig's after it has been killed" (p. 167). His further defect is that he is powerless, except as he works through Ralph. Though Piggy is the first to recognize the value of the conch and even shows Ralph how to blow it to summon the first assembly, he cannot sound it himself. And he lacks imagination. Scientifically minded as he is, he scorns what is intangible and he dismisses the possibility of ghosts or an imaginary beast. " 'Cos things wouldn't make sense. Houses an' streets, an'—TV— they wouldn't work" (p. 85). Of course he is quite right, save that he forgets he is now on an island where the artifacts of the civilization he has always known are meaningless.

It is another important character, Simon, who understands that there may indeed be a beast, even if not a palpable one—"maybe it's only us" (p. 82). The scientist Piggy has recognized it is possible to be frightened of people (p. 78), but he finds this remark of Simon's dangerous nonsense. Still Simon is right, as we see from his interview with the sow's head on a stake, which is the lord of the flies. He is right that the beast is in the boys themselves, and he alone discovers that what has caused their terror is in reality a dead parachutist ironically stifled in the elaborate clothing worn to guarantee survival. But Simon's failure is the inevitable failure of the mystic—what he knows is beyond words; he cannot impart his insights to others. Having an early glimpse of the truth, he cannot tell it.

> Simon became inarticulate in his effort to express mankind's essential illness. Inspiration came to him.
> "What's the dirtiest thing there is?"
> As an answer Jack dropped into the uncomprehending silence that followed it the one crude expressive syllable. Release was like an orgasm. Those littluns who had climbed back on the twister fell off again and did not mind. The hunters were screaming with delight.
> Simon's effort fell about him in ruins; the laughter beat him cruelly and he shrank away defenseless to his seat (p. 82).

Mockery also greets Simon later when he speaks to the lord of the flies, though this time it is sophisticated, adult mockery:

> "Fancy thinking the Beast was something you could hunt and kill!" said the head. For a moment or two the forest and all the other dimly appreciated places echoed with the parody of laughter (p. 133).

Tragically, when Simon at length achieves a vision so clear that it is readily communicable he is killed by the pig hunters in their insane belief that he is the very evil which he alone has not only understood but actually exorcised. Like the martyr, he is killed for being precisely what he is not.

The inadequacy of Jack is the most serious of all, and here perhaps if anywhere in the novel we have a personification of absolute evil. Though he is the most mature of the boys (he alone of all the characters is given a last name), and though as head of the choir he is the only one with any experience of leadership, he is arrogant and lacking in Ralph's charm and warmth. Obsessed with the idea of hunting, he organizes his choir members into a band of killers. Ostensibly they are to kill pigs, but pigs alone do not satisfy them, and pigs are in any event not needed for food. The blood lust once aroused demands nothing less than human blood. If Ralph represents purely civil authority, backed only by his own good will, Piggy's wisdom, and the crowd's easy willingness to be ruled, Jack stands for naked ruthless power, the police force or the military force acting without restraint and gradually absorbing the whole state into itself and annihilating what it cannot absorb. Yet even Jack is inadequate. He is only a little boy after all, as we are sharply reminded in a brilliant scene at the end of the book, when we suddenly see him through the eyes of the officer instead of through Ralph's (pp. 185-87), and he is, like all sheer power, anarchic. When Ralph identifies himself to the officer as "boss," Jack, who has just all but murdered him, makes a move in dispute, but overawed at last by superior power, the power of civilization and the British Navy, implicit in the officer's mere presence, he says nothing. He is a villain (Are his red hair and ugliness intended to suggest that he is a devil?), but in our world of inadequacies and imperfections even villainy does not fulfill itself completely. If not rescued, the hunters would have destroyed Ralph and made him, like the sow, an offering to the beast; but the inexorable logic of Ulysses makes us understand that they would have proceeded thence to self-destruction.

> Then everything includes itself in power,
> Power into will, will into appetite;
> And appetite, an universal wolf,
> So doubly seconded with will and power,
> Must make perforce an universal prey,
> And last eat up himself.

The distance we have traveled from Ballantyne's cheerful unrealities is both artistic and moral. Golding is admittedly symbolic; Ballantyne professed to be telling a true story. Yet it is the symbolic tale that, at least for our times, carries conviction. Golding's boys, who choose to remember nothing of their past before the plane accident; who, as soon as Jack commands the choir to take off the robes marked with the cross of Christianity, have no trace of religion; who demand to be ruled and are incapable of being ruled properly; who though many of them were once choir boys (Jack could sing C sharp) never sing a note on the island; in whose minds the great tradition of Western culture has left the titles of a few books for children, a knowledge of the use of matches (but no matches), and hazy memories of planes and TV sets—these boys are more plausible than Ballantyne's. His was a world of blacks and whites: bad hurricanes, good islands; good pigs obligingly allowing themselves to be taken for human food, bad sharks disobligingly taking human beings for shark food; good Christians, bad natives; bad pirates, good boys. Of the beast within, which demands blood sacrifice, first a sow's head, then a boy's, Ballantyne has some vague notion, but he cannot take it seriously. Not only does Golding see the beast; he sees that to keep it at bay we have civilization; but when by some magic or accident civilization is abolished and the human animal is left on his own, dependent upon his mere humanity, then being human is not enough. The beast appears, though not necessarily spontaneously or inevitably, for it never rages in Ralph or Piggy or Simon as it does in Roger or Jack; but it is latent in all of them, in the significantly named Piggy, in Ralph, who sometimes envies the abandon of the hunters (p. 69) and who shares the desire to "get a handful" of Robert's "brown, vulnerable flesh" (p. 106), and even in Simon burrowing into his private hiding place. After Simon's death Jack attracts all the boys but Ralph and the loyal Piggy into his army. Then when Piggy is killed and Ralph is alone, only civilization can save him. The timely arrival of the British Navy is less theatrical than logically necessary to make Golding's point. For civilization defeats the beast. It slinks back into the jungle as the boys creep out to be rescued; but the beast is real. It is there, and it may return.

# "A World of Violence
and Small Boys"[1]

## J. T. C. GOLDING

PROBABLY he will agree that his real education was picked
up, almost by the way, at home. In those days when the
radio was non-existent and the cost of gramophones pro-
hibitive the only local music was the town band. Bill was
lucky that Mom was good enough to accompany Dad
through Handel, Mozart and others. They were often joined
by an ex-bandmaster of the Coldstream Guards. The walls
of that small front room are probably vibrating still. Bill,
as a small boy, was terribly affected by Tosti's "Good-bye."
There was painting. Dad's own paintings of scenery in
Wiltshire and Cornwall hung on the walls and there were a
couple of books of cheap reprints of the great ones. There
were books. Chief among them was the *Children's Encyclo-
paedia* and of course Dad had access to the School Library.[2]
Bill was disappointed when he got to school to find he'd
read most of the library. It was a small one.

One book that was read and re-read was *Nat the Naturalist*, by George Manville Fenn. The scene was set somewhere
in the jungle in South East Asia. Bill could quote whole
pages by heart and it often accompanied him to the top of

---

[1] The following is an excerpt from a letter by J. T. C. Golding
(William Golding's brother) addressed to James R. Baker on
December 4, 1962. The letter appears here by permission of
J. T. C. Golding and James R. Baker.

[2] William Golding's father was Senior Master of Marlborough
Grammar School.—Eds.

the chestnut tree in the garden.[3] And all the time there was a father only too willing to give a logical answer to a small boy's questions.

Eventually he entered Marlborough Grammar School and emerged from a pretty sheltered life into a world of violence and small boys—and not-so-small boys. Here he met physical violence and the deliberate infliction of pain by boys. Also he noticed the tendency of small boys to gang up against the weak or those with a mannerism that put them out of step.[4] Not that it was a bad school for bullying— official policy was hot against it and in any case Bill was physically well-equipped enough to look after himself. Many others will have noticed all this but the effect, in this case, on an impressionable ten-year-old may have had important results. The conjunction of the boy in the jungle in *Nat the Naturalist* and the school playground may have lain dormant for years until some later experience pushed it to the surface as *Lord of the Flies*. On the other hand the explanation is so obvious and easy that it probably isn't true.

•   •   •

During these last years at school another writer, I think of considerable importance to him, entered his life. This was Mark Twain. Not Mark Twain of *Tom Sawyer* and *Huckleberry Finn* but of *Roughing It* and *Innocents Abroad*. He swallowed these almost as completely as he had done *Nat the Naturalist*. The humour of these books and their irreverence towards many accepted things encour-

---

[3] The symbolic significance of this tree is made clear in Golding's autobiographical essay, "The Ladder and the Tree," *The Listener*, 63 (March 24, 1960), 531-33). The essay is vital to an understanding of the basic dialectic which is dramatized in all the novels: the conflict between the rational and the irrational elements in man's nature and the effects of this conflict on both the individual and historical levels.—Eds.

[4] The "tendency" is obvious enough in *Lord of the Flies*: note Simon's position in Jack's chorus, Roger's attack on the "littluns," and the general abuse of Piggy. After fear drives most of the boys into the hunter tribe, they lose all capacity for dialectic and begin sadistic persecution of those who stand outside their powerful group. In *Free Fall* a similar pattern of behavior appears in the episodes which describe the rough-and-tumble boyhood adventures of Sammy Mountjoy.—Eds.

aged his own scepticism. It was an attitude he was already adopting toward the society of 4000 people around him. In addition he had a father who welcomed criticism of any institution under the sun, though any deviation in personal conduct produced a muted rumble of thunder.

# The Fables of William Golding[1]

## JOHN PETER

———— ◆ ————

A USEFUL critical distinction may be drawn between a fiction and a fable. Like most worthwhile distinctions it is often easy to detect, less easy to define. The difficulty arises because the clearest definition would be in terms of an author's intentions, his pre-verbal procedures, and these are largely inscrutable and wholly imprecise. For a definition that is objective and specific we are reduced to an "as if," which is at best clumsy and at worst perhaps delusive.

The distinction itself seems real enough. Fables are those narratives which leave the impression that their purpose was anterior, some initial thesis or contention which they are apparently concerned to embody and express in concrete terms. Fables always give the impression that they were preceded by the conclusion which it is their function to draw, though of course it is doubtful whether any author foresees his conclusions as fully as this, and unlikely that his work would be improved if he did. The effect of a fiction is very different. Here the author's aim, as it appears from what he has written, is evidently to present a more or less faithful reflection of the complexities, and often of the irrelevancies, of life as it is actually experienced. Such conclusions as he may draw—he is under much less compulsion to draw them than a writer of fables—do not appear to be anterior but on the contrary take their origin from the fiction itself, in which they are latent, and occasionally unrecognized. It is a matter of approach, so far as that can be

[1] This article first appeared in the *Kenyon Review*, 19 (Autumn, 1957), 577-592. It is reprinted in part here through the courtesy of the *Kenyon Review* and the author.

gauged. Fictions make only a limited attempt to generalize and explain the experience with which they deal, since their concern is normally with the uniqueness of this experience. Fables, starting from a skeletal abstract, must flesh out that abstract with the appearances of "real life" in order to render it interesting and cogent. *1984* is thus an obvious example of a fable, while *The Rainbow* is a fiction. Orwell and Lawrence, in these books, are really moving in opposite directions. If their movements could be geometrically projected to exaggerate and expose each other, Lawrence's would culminate in chaotic reportage, Orwell's in stark allegory.

. . . [The distinction] has a particular value for the critic whose concern is with novels, in that it assists him in locating and defining certain merits which are especially characteristic of novels and certain faults to which they are especially prone. Both types, the fiction and the fable, have their own particular dangers. The danger that threatens a fiction is simply that it will become confused, so richly faithful to the complexity of human existence as to lose all its shape and organization. . . . The danger that threatens a fable is utterly different, in fact the precise opposite. When a fable is poor—geometrically projected again—it is bare and diagrammatic, insufficiently clothed in its garment of actuality, and in turn its appeal is extra-aesthetic and narrow. Satires like *Animal Farm* are of this kind.

It will be said that any such distinction must be a neutral one, and that the best novels are fictions which have managed to retain their due share of the fable's coherence and order. No doubt this is true. But it also seems to be true that novels can go a good deal farther, without serious damage, in the direction of fiction than they can in the direction of fable, and this suggests that fiction is a much more congenial mode for the novelist than fable can ever be. The trouble with the mode of fable is that it is constricting. As soon as a novelist has a particular end in view the materials from which he may choose begin to shrink, and to dispose themselves toward that end. . . . The fact is that a novelist depends ultimately not only on the richness of his materials but on the richness of his interests too; and fable, by tying these to a specific end, tends to reduce both. Even the most chaotic fiction will have some sort of emergent meaning, provided it is a full and viable reflection of the life from which it derives, if only because the unconscious preoccupations of the novelist will help to impart such meaning to it, drawing it into certain lines like iron filing sprinkled in a magnetic field. Fables, however, can only be submerged in actuality with difficulty, and they are liable to bob up again like corks, in all their plain explicitness. It may even be true to say that they are best embodied in short stories, where economy is vital and "pointlessness" (except for its brevity) comparatively intolerable.

•     •     •

*Lord of the Flies,* which appeared in 1954, is set on an imaginary South Sea island, and until the last three pages the only characters in it are boys. They have apparently been evacuated from Britain, where an atomic war is raging, and are accidentally stranded on the island without an adult supervisor. The administrative duties of their society (which includes a number of "littluns," aged about six) devolve upon their elected leader, a boy of twelve named Ralph, who is assisted by a responsible, unattractive boy called Piggy, but as time passes an independent party grows up, the "hunters," led by an angular ex-choir leader named Jack Merridew. This party, soon habituated to the shedding of animal blood, recedes farther and farther from the standards of civilization which Ralph and Piggy are straining to preserve, and before very long it is transformed into a savage group of outlaws with a costume and a ritual of their own. In the course of one of their dance-feasts, drunk with tribal excitement, they are responsible for killing the one individual on the island who has a real insight into the problems of their lives, a frail boy called Simon, subject to fainting fits, and after this more or less intentional sacrifice they lose all sense of restraint and become a band of criminal marauders, a threat to everyone on the island outside their own tribe. Piggy is murdered by their self-constituted witch doctor and torturer, the secretive and sinister Roger, and Ralph is hunted by them across the island like the pigs they are accustomed to kill. Before they can kill and decapitate him a naval detachment arrives and takes charge of all the children who have survived.

It is obvious that this conclusion is not a concession to readers who require a happy ending—only an idiot will suppose that the book ends happily—but a deliberate device

by which to throw the story into focus. With the appearance
of the naval officer the bloodthirsty hunters are instantly
reduced to a group of painted urchins led by "a little boy
who wore the remains of an extraordinary black cap," yet
the reduction cannot expunge the knowledge of what they
have done and meant to do. The abrupt return to childhood,
to insignificance, underscores the argument of the narrative:
that Evil is inherent in the human mind itself, whatever
innocence may cloak it, ready to put forth its strength as
soon as the occasion is propitious. This is Golding's theme,
and it takes on a frightful force by being presented in
juvenile terms, in a setting that is twice deliberately likened
to the sunny Coral Island of R. M. Ballantyne.[2] The boys'
society represents, in embryo, the society of the adult world,
their impulses and convictions are those of adults incisively
abridged, and the whole narrative is a powerfully ironic
commentary on the nature of Man, an accusation levelled at
us all. There are no excuses for complacency in the fretful
conscientiousness of Ralph, the leader, nor in Piggy's anxious
commonsense, nor are the miscreants made to seem excep-
tional. When he first encounters a pig, Jack Merridew is
quite incapable of harming it, "because of the enormity of
the knife descending and cutting into living flesh," and even
the delinquent Roger is at first restrained by the taboos of
"parents and school and policemen and the law." Strip
these away and even Ralph might be a hunter: it is his
duties as a leader that save him, rather than any intrinsic
virtue in himself.[3] Like any orthodox moralist Golding insists that Man is a fallen creature, but he refuses to
hypostatize Evil or to locate it in a dimension of its own. On
the contrary Beelzebub, Lord of the Flies, is Roger and Jack
and you and I, ready to declare himself as soon as we per-
mit him to.

The intentness with which this thesis is developed leaves

---

[2] A discussion of the relationship between Ballantyne's novel
*The Coral Island,* published in 1857 in England, and *Lord of
the Flies* occurs in Carl Niemeyer's "The Coral Island Revisited,"
*College English,* 22 (January, 1961), 241-245. Reprinted in this
volume, pp. 217-223.—Eds.

[3] As an illustration of this argument, note Ralph's actions when
the boys attack Robert as the substitute pig. p. 106 and when
Simon is killed as the beast, p. 141.—Eds.

no doubt that the novel is a fable, a deliberate translation of a proposition into the dramatized terms of art, and as usual we have to ask ourselves how resourceful and complete the translation has been, how fully the thesis has been absorbed and rendered implicit in the tale as it is told. A writer of fables will heat his story at the fire of his convictions, but when he has finished, the story must glow apart, generating its own heat from within. Golding himself provides a criterion for judgment here, for he offers a striking example of how complete the translation of a statement into plastic terms can be. Soon after their arrival the children develop an irrational suspicion that there is a predatory beast at large on the island. This has of course no real existence, as Piggy for one points out, but to the littluns it is almost as tangible as their castles in the sand, and most of the older boys are afraid they may be right. One night when all are sleeping there is an air battle ten miles above the sea and a parachuted man, already dead, comes drifting down through the darkness, to settle among the rocks that crown the island's only mountain. There the corpse lies unnoticed, rising and falling with the gusts of the wind, its harness snagged on the bushes and its parachute distending and collapsing. When it is discovered and the frightened boys mistake it for the beast, the sequence is natural and convincing, yet the implicit statement is quite unmistakable too. The incomprehensible threat which has hung over them is, so to speak, identified and explained: a nameless figure who is Man himself, the boys' own natures, the something that all humans have in common.

This is finely done and needs no further comment, but unhappily the explicit comment has already been provided, in Simon's halting explanation of the beast's identity: "What I mean is . . . maybe it's only us." And a little later we are told that "However Simon thought of the beast, there rose before his inward sight the picture of a human at once heroic and sick." This over-explicitness is my main criticism of what is in many ways a work of real distinction, and for two reasons it appears to be a serious one. In the first place the fault is precisely that which any fable is likely to incur: the incomplete translation of its thesis into its story so that much remains external and extrinsic, the teller's assertion rather than the tale's enactment before our eyes. In the second place the fault is a persistent one, and cannot easily be discounted or ignored. It appears in expository annotations like this, when Ralph and Jack begin to quarrel:

> The two boys faced each other. There was the brilliant world of hunting, tactics, fierce exhilaration, skill; and there was the world of longing and baffled commonsense.

Less tolerably, it obtrudes itself in almost everything—thought, action, and hallucination—that concerns the clairvoyant Simon, the "batty" boy who understands "mankind's essential illness," who knows that Ralph will get back to where he came from, and who implausibly converses with the Lord of the Flies. Some warrant is provided for this clairvoyance in Simon's mysterious illness, but it is inadequate. The boy remains unconvincing in himself, and his presence constitutes a standing invitation to the author to avoid the trickiest problems of his method, by commenting too baldly on the issues he has raised. Any writer of fables must find it hard to ignore an invitation of this kind once it exists. Golding has not been able to ignore it, and the blemishes that result impose some serious, though not decisive, limitations on a fiery and disturbing story.

# Introduction[1]

## IAN GREGOR and MARK KINKEAD-WEEKES

THE urge to put things into categories seems to satisfy some
deep human need and in this matter at least, critics and
historians of literature are very human people indeed. A
brief glance at the English Literature section of any library
catalogue will show what I mean. There we find literature
divided up into various kinds of writings, and within the
kinds we have historical periods, and within the periods we
have groups or movements, and within the groups in-
dividuals who write various kinds. . . . Now up to a point
of course this sort of classification serves a very useful purpose. We need a map if we are going to do any exploring,
and the fact that it is the countryside we have come to
enjoy, not the map, doesn't make the map any less necessary. If we take out a map of The Novel we find, if it
is a general one, that it falls into three sections—the eight-
eenth-century novel, the Victorian novel, and the modern
novel. And these descriptions point not simply to three
centuries, but to decisive changes that have taken place
within the form of the novel. These changes are often due
to historical circumstances, and sometimes they can be described in terms of the ruling ideas of the age or the literary
expectations of the readers, but there are other changes and
shifts in fiction which seem to arise from the very nature of
the novel itself. A shift of this kind may be seen in a useful classification into "fables" and "fictions." It is a little

[1] This essay appears as the Introduction to the "School Edition"
of *Lord of the Flies* published by Faber and Faber, Ltd., London, 1962, pp. i-xii. It is reprinted here by permission of Faber
and Faber and the authors.

difficult to define this difference satisfactorily in the abstract, but it is fairly easy to see what is meant in practice. When, for instance, D. H. Lawrence wrote in one of his letters, "I am doing a novel which I have never grasped. Damn its eyes, here I am at page 145 and I've no notion what it's about . . . it's like a novel in a foreign language which I don't know very well," he was almost certainly occupied in writing a fiction and not a fable. In other words, a fiction is something which takes the form of an exploration for the novelist, even if it lacks the very extreme position which Lawrence describes; the concern is very much with trying to make clear the individuality of a situation, of a person; for these reasons it is extremely difficult to describe a fiction satisfactorily in abstract terms. With a fable, on the other hand, the case is very different. Here the writer begins with a general idea—"the world is not the reasonable place we are led to believe," "all power corrupts" —and seeks to translate it into fictional terms. In this kind of writing the interest of the particular detail lies in the way it points to the generalization behind it. It is generally very easy to say what a fable is "about," because the writer's whole purpose is to make the reader respond to it in precisely that way. Clear examples of fiction in the way I am using the word would be works like D. H. Lawrence's *Sons and Lovers* or Emily Brontë's *Wuthering Heights*; clear examples of fable, Swift's *Gulliver's Travels* or Orwell's *Animal Farm*. But these are extreme works and most novels have elements of both. *Oliver Twist*, for instance, is certainly a fiction in its portrayal of the intensely imagined criminal world; but it also moves towards fable when it describes the world of the poorhouse, and the people who finally rescue Oliver from that world, because here Dickens is moved to write primarily by abstract ideas, the educational hardships of children, the wisdom of benevolence. You will notice I said that *Oliver Twist* "moves towards" fiction, "moves towards" fable, and in this kind of alternation it is typical of many novels which lie between such extreme examples as I mentioned above. Now when we turn to Mr. Golding's *Lord of the Flies* we find that what is remarkable is that it is a fable and a fiction *simultaneously*. And I want to devote the remainder of this Introduction to developing that remark.

When we first begin to write and talk about Mr. Golding's novel, it is the aspect of fable which occupies our attention. And this is very natural because the book is a very satisfying one to talk about. Mr. Golding, our account might run, is examining what human nature is really like if we could consider it apart from the mass of social detail which gives a recognizable feature 'to our daily lives. That "really" is important and you may want to argue about it, but Mr. Golding's assumption here is one that most of us make at one time or another. "Of course," we say of some-one, "he's not *really* like that at all," and then we go on to construct an account which assumes that a distorting film of circumstance has come between us and the man's "real self." What Mr. Golding has done in *Lord of the Flies* is to create a situation which will reveal in an extremely direct way this "real self," and yet at the same time keep our sense of credibility, our sense of the day-to-day world, lively and sharp. It is rather like performing a delicate heart opera-tion, but feeling that the sense of human gravity comes not through the actual operation but through the external scene —the green-robed figures, the arc light which casts no shadow, the sound of a car in the street outside. And it was in Ballantyne's *Coral Island*, a book published in the middle of the last century, that Mr. Golding found the suggestion for his "external scene." This is not a question of turning Ballantyne inside out, so that where his boys are endlessly brave, resourceful and Christian, Mr. Golding's are fright-ened, anarchic and savage; rather Mr. Golding's adventure story is to point up in a forceful and economic way the terrifying gap between the appearance and the reality. We do not need to know *Coral Island* to appreciate *Lord of the Flies*, but if we do know it we will appreciate more vividly the power of Mr. Golding's book. If we take Ralph's remark about "the darkness of man's heart" as coming very close to the subject of the book, it is worth just remembering that this book, published in 1954, was written in a world very different from Ballantyne's, one which had seen within twenty years the systematic destruction of the Jewish race, a world war revealing unnumbered atrocities of what man had done to man, and in 1945 the mushroom cloud of the atomic bomb which has come to dominate all our political and moral thinking.

Turning from these general considerations of Mr. Gold-ing's fable to the way it is actually worked out, we find the novel divided into three sections. The first deals with the arrival of the boys on the island, the assembly, the early decisions about what to do; the emphasis falls on the paradisal landscape, the hope of rescue, and the pleasures of day-to-day events. Everything within this part of the book is contained within law and rule: the sense of the awe-ful and the forbidden is strong. Jack cannot at first bring himself to kill a pig because of "the enormity of the knife descending and cutting into living flesh; because of the unbearable blood." Roger throws stones at Henry, but he throws to miss because "round the squatting child was the protection of parents and school and policemen and the law." The world in this part of the book is the world of children's games. The difference comes when there is no parental summons to bring these games to an end. These games have to continue throughout the day, and through the day that follows. And it is worth noting that Mr. Golding creates his first sense of unease through something which is familiar to every child in however protected a society—the waning of the light. It is the dreams that usher in the beastie, the snake, the unidentifiable threat to security.

The second part of the book could be said to begin when that threat takes on physical reality, with the arrival of the dead airman. Immediately the fear is crystallized, all the boys are now affected, discussion has increasingly to give way to action. As the narrative increases in tempo, so its implications enlarge. Ralph has appealed to the adult world for help, "If only they could send us something grown-up . . . a sign or something," and the dead airman is shot down in flames over the island. Destruction is everywhere; the boy's world is only a miniature version of the adult's. By now the nature of the destroyer is becoming clearer; it is not a beastie or snake but man's own nature. "What I mean is . . . maybe it's only us," Simon's insight is confined to himself and he has to pay the price of his own life for trying to communicate it to others. Simon's death authenticates this truth, and now that the fact of evil has actually been created on the island, the airman is no longer necessary and his body vanishes in a high wind and is carried out to sea.

The third part of the book, and the most terrible, explores the meaning and consequence of this creation of evil. Complete moral anarchy is unleashed by Simon's murder. The world of the game, which embodied in however an elementary way, rule and order, is systematically destroyed, because hardly anyone can now remember when things were otherwise. When the destruction is complete, Mr. Golding suddenly restores "the external scene" to us, not the paradisal world of the marooned boys, but *our* world. The naval officer speaks, we realize with horror, our words, "the kid needed a bath, a hair-cut, a nose wipe and a good deal of ointment." He carries our emblems of power, the white drill, the epaulettes, the gilt-buttons, the revolver, the trim cruiser. Our everyday sight has been restored to us, but the experience of reading the book is to make us re-interpret what we see, and say with Macbeth "mine eyes are made the fools o' the other senses."

If we are to look at *Lord of the Flies* from the point of view of it being a fable this is the kind of account we might give. And, as far as it goes, it is a true account. The main weakness in discussing *Lord of the Flies* is that we are too often inclined to leave our description at this point. So we find a Christian being deeply moved by the book and arguing that its greatness is tied up with the way in which the author brings home to a modern reader the doctrine of Original Sin; or we find a humanist finding the novel repellent precisely because it endorses what he feels to be a dangerous myth; or again, on a different level, we find a Liberal asserting the importance of the book because of its unwavering exposure of the corruptions of power. Now whatever degree of truth we find in these views, it is important to be clear that the quality or otherwise of *Lord of the Flies* is not dependent upon any of them. Whether Mr. Golding has written a good novel or not is not because of "the views" which may be deduced from it, but because of his claim to be a novelist. And the function of the novelist as Joseph Conrad once said is "by the power of the written word to make you hear, to make you feel—it is, before all, to make you *see*." And it is recognition of this that must take us back from Mr. Golding's fable, however compelling, to his fiction. Earlier I suggested that these two aspects occur simultaneously, so that in moving from one to the other, we are not required to look at different parts of the novel, but at the same thing from a different point of view.

Let us begin by looking at the coral island. We have mentioned the careful literary reference to Ballantyne ("Like the Coral Island," the naval officer remarks), the theological overtones with the constant paradisal references, "flower and fruit grew together on the same tree," but all these things matter only because Mr. Golding has imaginatively put the island before us. The sun and the thunder come across to us as physical realities, not because they have a symbolic part to play in the book, but because of the novelist's superb resourcefulness of language. Consider how difficult it is to write about a tropical island and avoid any hint of the travel poster cliché or the latest documentary film about the South Seas. To see how the difficulty can be overcome look at the following paragraph:

Strange things happened at midday. The glittering sea rose up, moved apart in planes of blatant impossibility; the coral reef and the few, stunted palms that clung to the more elevated parts would float up into the sky, would quiver, be plucked apart, run like raindrops on a wire or be repeated as in an odd succession of mirrors. Sometimes land loomed where there was no land and flicked out like a bubble as the children watched. (p. 53.)

It is this kind of sensitivity to language, this effortless precision of statement that makes the novel worth the most patient attention. And what applies to the island applies to the characters also. As Jack gradually loses his name so that at the end of the novel he is simply the Chief we feel this terrible loss of identity coming over in his total inability to do anything that is not instinctively gratifying. He begins to talk always in the same way, to move with the same intent. But this is in final terrible stages of the novel. If we turn back to the beginning of the novel we find Mr. Golding catching perfectly a tone of voice, a particular rhythm of speech. Ralph is talking to Piggy shortly after they have met:

"I could swim when I was five. Daddy taught me. He's a commander in the Navy. When he gets leave he'll come and rescue us. What's your father?"

Piggy flushed suddenly.

"My dad's dead," he said quickly, "and my mum—"

He took off his glasses and looked vainly for something with which to clean them.

"I used to live with my auntie. She kept a candy store.
I used to get ever so many candies. As many as I liked.
When'll your dad rescue us?"
"Soon as he can." (p. 11.)

Notice how skilfully Mr. Golding has caught in that
snatch of dialogue, not only schoolboy speech rhythms,[2]
but also, quite unobtrusively, the social difference between
the two boys. "What's your father?", "When'll your dad
rescue us?" There are two continents of social experience
hinted at here. I draw attention to this passage simply to
show that in a trivial instance, in something that would
never be quoted in any account of "the importance" of the
book, it is the gifts which are peculiar to a novelist, "to
make you hear, to make you feel . . . to make you see,"
that are being displayed.

Perhaps, however, we feel these gifts most unmistakably
present not in the way the landscape is presented to us, nor
the characters, but rather in the extraordinary momentum
and power which drives the whole narrative forward, so
that one incident leads to another with an inevitability
which is awesome. A great deal of this power comes from
Mr. Golding's careful preparation for an incident: so that
the full significance of a scene is only gradually revealed.
Consider, for instance, one of these. Early in the book Ralph
discovers the nickname of his companion with delight:

"Piggy! Piggy!"
Ralph danced out into the hot air of the beach and
then returned as a fighter plane, with wings swept back,
and machine-gunned Piggy.

Time passes, games give way to hunting, but still the
hunting can only be talked about in terms of a game and
when Jack describes his first kill, it takes the form of a
game:

"I cut the pig's throat——"
The twins, still sharing their identical grin, jumped up
and ran round each other. Then the rest joined in, making
pig-dying noises and shouting.

---

[2] In their notes for this edition the authors define all of the
schoolboy slang terms that are likely to confuse adult readers.—
Eds.

"One for his nob!"
"Give him a fourpenny one!"
Then Maurice pretended to be the pig and ran squeal-
ing into the centre, and the hunters, circling still, pre-
tended to beat him. As they danced, they sang.
*"Kill the pig. Cut her throat. Bash her in."*
Ralph watched them, envious and resentful. Not till
they flagged and the chant died away, did he speak.
"I'm calling an assembly."

There is an exasperation in Ralph's statement which
places him outside the game, the fantasy fighter plane has
no place in this more hectic play; the line between pretense
and reality is becoming more difficult to see. The first incident emerged from an overflow of high spirits, the second
from the deeper need to communicate an experience. When
the game is next played, the exuberant mood has evaporated.
Maurice's place has been taken by Robert:

Jack shouted.
"Make a ring!"
The circle moved in and round. Robert squealed in
mock terror, then in real pain.
"Ow! Stop it! You're hurting!"
The butt end of a spear fell on his back as he blundered
among them.
"Hold him!"
They got his arms and legs. Ralph, carried away by a
sudden thick excitement, grabbed Eric's spear and jabbed
at Robert with it.
"Kill him! Kill him!"
All at once, Robert was screaming and struggling with
the strength of frenzy. Jack had him by the hair and was
brandishing his knife. Behind him was Roger, fighting to
get close. The chant rose ritually, as at the last moment
of a dance or a hunt.
*"Kill the pig! Cut his throat! Kill the pig! Bash him in!"*
Ralph too was fighting to get near, to get a handful of
that brown, vulnerable flesh. The desire to squeeze and
hurt was over-mastering.

The climax is reached when the game turns into the killing of Simon—the pig, first mentioned in Ralph's delighted
mockery of Piggy's name, made more real in the miming
of Maurice and then in the hurting of Robert, becomes in-
distinguishable from Simon who is trampled to death. This

series of incidents, unobtrusive in any ordinary reading, nevertheless helps to drive the book forward with its jet-like power and speed. Just before Simon's arrival at the feast, there is a sudden pause and silence, the game is suspended. "Roger ceased to be a pig and became a hunter, so that the centre of the ring *yawned emptily*." It is that final phrase which crystallizes the emotion, so that we feel we are suddenly on the brink of tragedy without being able to locate it. It is now, after the violence, that the way is clear for the spiritual climax of the novel. As Simon's body is carried out to sea we are made aware, in the writing, of the significance of Simon's whole function in the novel; the beauty of the natural world and its order hints at a harmony beyond the tortured world of man and to which now Simon has access. And Mr. Golding has made this real to us, not by asserting some abstract proposition with which we may or may not agree, but by "the power of the written word."

During the last part of this Introduction when I have been urging the importance of *Lord of the Flies* as a fiction, you may think that I am putting forward some claim for Mr. Golding as a stylist, a writer of fine prose, rather in the manner of Oscar Wilde saying that there is no such thing as good books and bad books, only well written and badly written books. This is dangerously misleading if we interpret this as meaning we can separate what is being said from how it is being said. If, on the other hand, we intend that the content of a novel only "lives" in direct relation to the writer's ability to communicate it imaginatively, then Wilde's remark is surely true. Ultimately, Mr. Golding's book is valuable to us, not because it *"tells us about"* the darkness of man's heart, but because it shows it, because it is a work of art which enables us to enter into the world it creates and live at the level of a deeply perceptive and intelligent man. His vision becomes ours, and such a translation should make us realize the truth of Shelley's remark that "the great instrument for the moral good is the imagination."

# *An Old Story Well Told*[1]

## WILLIAM R. MUELLER

## I

*Lord of the Flies* uncovers the fallen and unredeemed human heart; it sketches the enormities of which man, unrestrained by human law and resistant to divine grace, is capable. The varying degrees of goodness, as manifested by Simon, Piggy and Ralph, are simply no match for a murderous Jack or a head-hunting Roger. When we first meet the boys, recently dropped onto an island after escaping from their bomb-ravaged part of the world, they are still trailing faint clouds of glory. Even Roger, who shares with Jack the most diabolic potentialities of them all, early in the novel manifests a thin sheath of decency and restraint; in throwing stones at one of the smaller boys he is careful to miss, to leave untouched and inviolate a small circle surrounding his teased victim: "Here, invisible yet strong, was the taboo of the old life. Round the squatting child was the protection of parents and school and policemen and the law. Roger's arm was conditioned by a civilization that knew nothing of him and was in ruins." The novel delineates the gradual unconditioning of the arm and the unveiling of the heart of Roger and some of his companions.

*Lord of the Flies* is, of course, more than an expository disquisition on sin. Were it only that, it would have gone virtually unnoticed. The book is a carefully structured work of art whose organization—in terms of a series of hunts—serves to reveal with progressive clarity man's essential core. There are six stages, six hunts, constituting the dark-

[1] This article is reprinted in part by permission of *The Christian Century*, 80 (October 2, 1963), 1203-06. Copyright © 1963 by the Christian Century Foundation.

est of voyages as each successive one takes us closer to natural man. To trace the hunts—with pigs and boys as victims—is to feel Golding's full impact.

As Ralph, the builder of fires and shelters, is the main constructive force on the island, Jack, the hunter, is the primary destructive force. Hunting does of course provide food, but it also gratifies the lust for blood. In his first confrontation with a pig, Jack fails, unable to plunge his knife into living flesh, to bear the sight of flowing blood, and unable to do so because he is not yet far enough away from the "taboo of the old life." But under the questioning scrutiny of his companions he feels a bit ashamed of his fastidiousness, and, driving his knife into a tree trunk, he fiercely vows that the next time will be different.

And so it is. Returning from the second hunt he proclaims proudly that he has cut a pig's throat. Yet he has not reached the point of savage abandonment: we learn that he "twitched" as he spoke of his achievement—an involuntary gesture expressing his horror at the deed and disclosing the tension between the old taboo and the new freedom. His reflection upon the triumph, however, indicates that pangs of conscience must certainly fade before the glorious feeling of new and devastating power: "His mind was crowded with memories; memories of the knowledge that had come to them when they closed in on the struggling pig, knowledge that they had outwitted a living thing, imposed their will upon it, taken away its life like a long satisfying drink."

The third hunt is unsuccessful; the boar gets away. Nonetheless it plants the seed of an atrocity previously undreamed, and it is followed by an ominous make-believe, a mock hunt in which Robert, one of the younger boys, plays pig, the others encircling him and jabbing with their spears. The play becomes frenzied with cries of *"Kill the pig! Cut his throat! Kill the pig! Bash him in!"* An almost overwhelming dark desire possesses the boys. Only a fraction of the old taboo now remains; the terrified Robert emerges alive, but with a wounded rump. What is worse, the make-believe is but the prelude to an all too real drama.

## II

The fourth hunt is an electrifying success, a mayhem accomplished with no twitch of conscience, no element of pretense. The boys discover a sow "sunk in deep maternal bliss," "the great bladder of her belly , . . fringed with a row of piglets that slept or burrowed and squeaked." What a prize! Wounded, she flees, "bleeding and mad"; "the hunters followed, wedded to her in lust, excited by the long chase and the dropped blood." The sow finally falters and in a ghastly scene Jack and Roger ecstatically consummate their desires:

> Here, struck down by the heat, the sow fell and the hunters hurled themselves at her. This dreadful eruption from an unknown world made her frantic; she squealed and bucked and the air was full of sweat and noise and blood and terror. Roger ran round the heap, prodding with his spear whenever pigflesh appeared. Jack was on top of the sow, stabbing downward with his knife. Roger found a lodgment for his point and began to push till he was leaning with his whole weight. The spear moved forward inch by inch and the terrified squealing became a high-pitched scream. Then Jack found the throat and the hot blood spouted over his hands. The sow collapsed under them and they were heavy and fulfilled upon her. The butterflies still danced, preoccupied in the center of the clearing.

The fifth hunt, moving us even closer to the unbridled impulses of the human heart, is a fine amalgam of the third and fourth. This time Simon is at the center of the hideous circle, yet the pursuit is no more make-believe than it was with the heavy-teated sow. Simon is murdered not only without compunction but with orgiastic delight.

The final and climactic abhorrence is the hunt for Ralph. Its terror will not be celebrated here; suffice it to say that one refinement not present in the Simon episode is added —a stick Roger sharpens at both ends. It had indeed been used for the sow, with one point piercing the earth and the other supporting the severed head, but its human use had not yet been tested on that island paradise.

Such being Mr. Golding's art and conviction, it is little wonder that some readers have judged him offensive, revolting, depravedly sensational, utterly wicked. He has been impelled to say that many human beings, left unrestrainedly to their own devices, will find the most natural expression of their desires to lie in human head-hunting. Those who affirm that man is made in God's image will be given some pause, but upon reflection they will probably interpret the novel as a portrayal of the inevitable and ultimate condition of a world without grace. Those who affirm that man is basically and inherently good—and becoming better—may simply find the novel a monstrous perpetuation of falsehood.

Golding's main offense, I suppose, is that he profanes what many men hold most precious: belief that the human being is essentially good and the child essentially innocent. Yet his offense, as well as his genius, lies not in any original-ity of view or statement but in his startling ability to make his story real, so real that many readers can only draw back in terror. I would strongly affirm, however, that Gold-ing's intention is not simply to leave us in a negative state of horror. *Lord of the Flies* has a tough moral and religious flavor,[2] one which a study of its title helps make clear.

The term "lord of the flies" is a translation of the Hebrew word "Baalzebub" or "Beelzebub." The Baal were the local nature gods of the early Semitic peoples. In II Kings 1:2 Baalzebub is named as the god of Ekron. All three Synoptic Gospels refer to Beelzebub; in Luke 11:15 he is called "the chief of the devils." In English literature among those who refer to him are Christopher Marlowe and Robert Burton, though it is left to Milton to delineate his character at some length. Weltering by Satan's side he is described as "One next himself [Satan] in power, and next in crime,/Long after known in *Palestine*, and nam'd Beëlzebub." His subtle services to the great Adversary of mankind are well known. To disregard the historical background of Golding's title[3] or the place of the Lord of the Flies within the novel is to miss a good part of the author's intent; it is, indeed, to leave us with nothing but horror.

---

[2] Thomas M. Coskren, O. P., in "Is Golding Calvinistic?" *America*, 109 (July 6, 1963), 18-20, also speaks to this point at length. The essay is reprinted on pp. 253-260 in this volume.—Eds.

[3] Golding seems to attach no particular significance to the his-torical Beelzebub but to regard him as simply another mani-festation or creation of the human heart. (See James Keating and William Golding, "The Purdue Interview," p. 192 in this vol-ume.) It is difficult to see how the "historical background" for the title enhances understanding of Golding's basic fable, al-though it certainly figures as a clue to the theme.—Eds.

### III

At the conclusion of the fourth hunt, after the boys have hacked the multiparous sow, they place its head on a stick as a sacrificial offering for some reputedly mysterious and awesome beast—actually a dead parachutist who had plummeted to the ground, now unrecognizable as his body rises and falls each time the wind fills the parachute and then withdraws from it. Meanwhile Simon, whose love for his companions and desire to protect them instill a courage extraordinary, leaves them to search out the darksome creature. He finds himself confronted by the primitive offering, by "the head grinning amusedly in the strange daylight, ignoring the flies, the spilled guts, even ignoring the indignity of being spiked on a stick." As he is impelled to stare at the gruesome object, it undergoes a black, unholy transfiguration; he sees no longer just a pig's head on a stick; his gaze, we are told, is "held by that ancient, inescapable recognition." And that which is inescapably recognized by Simon is of primordial root. Its shrewdness and devastation have long been chronicled: it is on center stage in the third chapter of Genesis; it gained the rapt attention of Hosea and Amos and the prophets who followed them.

As Simon and the Lord of the Flies continue to face each other, the nature of the latter is clearly and explicitly set forth in an imaginary conversation which turns into a dramatic monologue. The head speaks:

"What are you doing out here all alone? Aren't you afraid of me?"

Simon shook.

"There isn't anyone to help you. Only me. And I'm the Beast."

Simon's mouth labored, brought forth audible words. "Pig's head on a stick."

"Fancy thinking the Beast was something you could hunt and kill!" said the head. . . . "You knew, didn't you? I'm part of you? Close, close, close! I'm the reason why it's no go? Why things are what they are?"

A moment later, the Beast goes on:

"I'm warning you. I'm going to get angry. D'you see? You're not wanted. Understand? We are going to have fun on this island. Understand? We are going to have fun on this island! So don't try it on, my poor misguided boy, or else—"

Simon found he was looking into a vast mouth. There was blackness within, a blackness that spread.

"—Or else," said the Lord of the Flies, "we shall do you. See? Jack and Roger and Maurice and Robert and Bill and Piggy and Ralph. Do you. See?"

Simon was inside the mouth. He fell down and lost consciousness.

The "ancient, inescapable recognition" is that the Lord of the Flies is a part of Simon, of all the boys on the island, of every man. And he is the reason "things are what they are." He is the demonic essence whose inordinate hunger, never assuaged, seeks to devour all men, to bend them to his will. He is, in Golding's novel, accurately identified only by Simon. And history has made clear, as the Lord of the Flies affirms, that the Simons are not wanted, that they do spoil what is quaintly called the "fun" of the world, and that antagonists will "do" them.

Simon does not heed the "or else" imperative, for he bears too important a message: that the beast is "harmless and horrible." The direct reference here is to the dead parachutist whose spectrally moving form had terrified the boys; the corpse is, obviously, both harmless and horrible. But it should also be remembered that the Lord of the Flies identified itself as the Beast and that it too might be termed "harmless and horrible." Simon alone has the key to its potential harmlessness. It will become harmless only when it becomes universally recognized, recognized not as a principle of fun but as the demonic impulse which is utterly destructive. Simon staggers on to his companions to bear the immediate good news that the beast (the rotting parachutist) is harmless. Yet he carries with him a deeper revelation; namely, that the Beast (the Lord of the Flies) is no overwhelming extrinsic force, but a potentially fatal inner itching, recognition of which is a first step toward its annihilation. Simon becomes, of course, the suffering victim of the boys on the island and, by extension, of the readers of the book.[4]

---

[4] Compare Donald R. Spangler, "Simon" on pp. 211-215 in this volume.—Eds.

## IV

To me *Lord of the Flies* is a profoundly true book. Its happy offense lies in its masterful, dramatic and powerful narration of the human condition, with which a peruser of the daily newspaper should already be familiar. The ultimate purpose of the novel is not to leave its readers in a state of paralytic horror. The intention is certainly to impress upon them man's, any man's, miraculous ingenuity in perpetrating evil; but it is also to impress upon them the gift of a saving recognition which, to Golding, is apparently the *only* saving recognition. An orthodox phrase for this recognition is the "conviction of sin," an expression which grates on many contemporary ears, and yet one which the author seemingly does not hold in derision.

Lecturing at Johns Hopkins University in the spring of 1962, Golding said that *Lord of the Flies* is a study of sin. And he is a person who uses words with precision. Sin is not to be confused with crime, which is a transgression of human law; it is instead a transgression of divine law. Nor does Golding believe that the Jacks and Rogers are going to be reconstructed through social legislation eventuating in some form of utopianism—he and Conrad's Mr. Kurtz are at one in their evaluation of societal laws which, they agree, exercise external restraint but have at best a slight effect on the human heart. Golding is explicit: "The theme [of *Lord of the Flies*]," he writes, "is an attempt to trace the defects of society back to the defects of human nature. The moral is that the shape of a society must depend on the ethical nature of the individual and not on any political system however apparently logical or respectable."

William Golding's story is as old as the written word. The figure of the Lord of the Flies, of Beelzebub, is one of the primary archetypes of the Western world. The novel is the parable of fallen man. But it does not close the door on that man; it entreats him to know himself and his Adversary, for he cannot do combat against an unrecognized force, especially when it lies within him.

# *Is Golding Calvinistic?*[1]

A more optimistic interpretation of the
symbolism found in *Lord of the Flies*

## THOMAS MARCELLUS COSKREN, O. P.

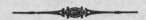

IN an issue of AMERICA last winter, two critics gave their
interpretations of William Golding's remarkably successful
*Lord of the Flies*.[2] While the approach of each of these
critics differed, Mr. Kearns being concerned with the socio-
political implications of the work and Fr. Egan with the
theological, both reached the same conclusion: *Lord of the
Flies* presents the Calvinist view of man as a creature essentially depraved. As one of the professors who has placed
the novel on his required reading list, I should like to raise
a dissenting voice.

While I am prepared to admit that *Lord of the Flies* is
hardly the most optimistic book that has appeared in recent
times, I find it difficult to accept the conclusion reached
by Fr. Egan and Mr. Kearns. Both, it seems to me, have
left too much of the novel unexplained; indeed, their view
of the work seems to render important sections inexplicable.
If Golding has presented man as essentially depraved, why
are three of his four major characters good people? Granted
that Ralph, Piggy and Simon possess a limited goodness,
the condition of all men, they are decidedly boys of high

[1] This article is reprinted with permission from *America*, the
National Catholic Weekly Review, 920 Broadway, New York
City. It appeared in the issue of July 6, 1963, Volume 109, pp.
18-20.

[2] Francis E. Kearns, "Salinger and Golding: Conflict on the
Campus," *America*, 108 (January 26, 1963), 136-39, and John
M. Egan, "Golding's View of Man," 140-41.—Eds.

purpose, who use good means to achieve their ends. Jack may strike many as the perfect symbol of essentially depraved man, but he is only one out of four. Three-to-one seems a rather impressive ratio favoring at least a limited goodness in the human community.

Moreover, if Golding hesitates "to view evil in a religious framework," as Mr. Kearns says, why is Simon, on the symbolic level, so cleverly identified with Christ? [3] In fact, this identification is so obvious that one is tempted to agree with Kearns' statement about *Lord of the Flies* being "too neatly symbolic, too patently artistic." Certainly, the very presence of a Christ-figure in the novel, a presence which pervades the work, implies some kind of religious framework.

Again, if man were not good or innocent at some time in the long history of the race, why should Ralph at the end of the novel weep "for the end of innocence, the darkness of man's heart, and the fall through the air of the true, wise friend called Piggy"? Ralph weeps for an innocence that man once possessed; he laments the *loss* of goodness, and this is not some vague goodness, but the palpable goodness in his "true, wise friend."

Thus far, the objections I have offered to the view presented by Mr. Kearns and Fr. Egan concern only the characters in *Lord of the Flies.* These objections are serious enough, but there are others which demand examination by the critic. If the world into which these characters have been placed is, as Fr. Egan states, a universe that is "a cruel and irrational chaos," why does Golding indicate, with almost obsessive attention to detail, the pattern, the order of the island world which the boys inhabit? Throughout the novel we find natural descriptions which use metaphors from the world of manufacturing.

In other words, the universe of *Lord of the Flies* is one that has been *made*, created. The novel is filled with phrases like the following: "a great *platform* of pink granite"; "a criss-cross *pattern* of trunks"; "the palms . . . made a green *roof*"; "the incredible *lamps* of stars." Further, Golding's adjectives indicate an ordered universe. This indication is especially apparent after the terrible storm accompanying Simon's death. In this section he uses such words as "angu-

---

[3] Cf. Donald R. Spangler's "Simon" on pp. 211-215 in this volume. See also Golding's remarks on Simon in the interview with James Keating, p. 192.—Eds.

lar" and "steadfast" to describe the constellations. If William Golding's universe is "a cruel and irrational chaos," he has certainly chosen most inappropriate words to describe it.

Basically, it seems to me, the real difficulty with the interpretation of *Lord of the Flies* offered by Fr. Egan and Mr. Kearns is its failure to treat the novel as a whole. William Golding's novel is not antihuman; it is anti-Rousseau. It does not portray human nature as such; it presents human nature as infected with the romantic chimera of inevitable human progress, a progress which will be achieved because of the innate nobility and innocence of the human species. In theological terms, which are perhaps the most accurate critical tools for explaining this novel, *Lord of the Flies* is not so much Manichean as it is anti-Pelagian. A more detailed analysis should help to show this anti-Pelagian character of the work.

*Lord of the Flies* begins with all the paraphernalia of the romantic, and sentimental, preconceptions that owe so much to Rousseau's social philosophy. In the first chapter we are presented with a group of children, the contemporary world's symbol of innocence. They are placed on a tropical island, an earthly paradise, Rousseau's habitat for the "noble savage." But these boys are not Adam-figures; they are not innocent. Each of them, in varying degrees, reflects the influence of the serpent—which, by the way, is introduced in the first chapter when Ralph unfastens "the snake-clasp of his belt." Here begins the terrible irony that runs through the whole novel. Romantic man thinks he can rid himself of evil merely by taking off his clothes, the symbol of civilization and its effects.

In this superficially idyllic community, made up of refugees from an atomic war, we discover Golding's four major characters: Ralph, Piggy, Jack and Simon. It is with these characters that Golding's symbolism becomes somewhat more complex than either Mr. Kearns or Fr. Egan suggests. *Lord of the Flies* is essentially a fable about contemporary man *and* contemporary ideas. Thus, Ralph is not only the symbol of the decent, sensible parliamentarian; he is also the figure of an idea: the abstract concept of democratic government. The same double role is filled by the other characters: Jack is at once the dictator and the concept of dictatorship; Piggy is the intellectual, with all his powers and deficiencies, and representative of the Enlightenment or scientific method. Finally, Simon is the mystic and poet, who is also a Christ-figure and thus the symbol of religious faith. The symbolism of *Lord of the Flies*, therefore, functions on a number of levels, and it seems to be an injustice to Golding's extraordinary dexterity in handling these multiple levels to reduce them to one level, that of universal human nature.

Golding suggests the complexity of these symbolic figures in their physical descriptions. Ralph is "the boy with fair hair [who has] a mildness about his mouth and eyes that proclaimed no devil." On the literal level we have the good boy, the "solid citizen." As such, Ralph engages our sympathies. And on the most obvious symbolic level he still has our sympathies, for he represents the decent, sensible parliamentarian, the political ideal of the Western world.

But on another, and deeper, level Golding has introduced an ironic twist. The symbolic value Ralph possesses as the abstract concept of the democratic process is presented as a challenge to the reader. If, as the Western world seems to believe, the democratic process of government is the best devised by man throughout his history, why doesn't it work always and everywhere? It is at this level that Golding suggests symbolically the inadequacy, not the depravity, of the solely human; it is at this level that he directs his devastatingly ironic commentary on the Rousseauvian myth of the general will and its unproved presupposition of the natural goodness of the human species.

In effect, Golding's modern fable puts Rousseau's social contract to the test: *Lord of the Flies* takes man back to the primitive condition of things, which the French social reformer had advocated as the one sure way of restoring man to his proper dignity. Then it shows that, far from being naturally good, man has some type of defect for which civilization is not responsible. Rousseau's social philosophy fails the test, and the essentially confused notion of nature which Rousseau bequeathed to the contemporary world is exposed for the fraud that it is.

Moreover, the irony implicit in Ralph's inadequacy is extended to the other characters, either as they participate in the same inadequacy or as they question symbolically the solution offered for human ills by Ralph's faith in Rousseauvian democracy. Piggy participates in the "grand design" of restoration. As a figure of the Enlightenment, he cannot accept the extremes of romanticism, and he votes for Ralph only "grudgingly"; but he will *use* the more popular romantic concept of government and will try to direct it. Yet, even with his discerning rational assessment of the problem of forming a government for the refugees, his inherent weaknesses are evident. Ultimately, he is destroyed, not because his intellectual gifts are depraved, but because he falls into the mistaken belief that they are sufficient unto themselves. Piggy is intelligent enough, for example, to question Ralph's blind faith in rescue by the military (a scathing commentary on the Western democracies' current worship at the shrine of Cape Canaveral), but he remains blind to the limitations of his own reason.

Jack and Simon, on the other hand, are not taken in by the Rousseauvian solution. Jack's approach to the human condition is much too twisted for even the remotest comparison with the idealism, fanciful though it is, implicit in Rousseau; Simon's view of humanity is so penetrated with realistic self-appraisal that he transcends the idealism of the French reformer. Jack descends to the subhuman; Simon soars to the superhuman. While Ralph and Piggy exemplify ironically the "noble savage," Jack and Simon provide the necessary counterpoint; Jack exploits the savagery, and Simon explores the nobility.

And it is probably through the figure of Jack that William Golding pronounces his severest condemnation of the romantic myth of human progress. For, in the last analysis, it is the dictator who has benefited most from Rousseau's social view. When man's efforts toward progress and eventual fulfillment, however altruistic his motivation, proceed from sloppy thinking, then brute force takes over to direct the course of progress and subverts even the good in human nature to its own destructive ends.

Yet, Golding is not interested merely in the altruism or the subversion; between these two forces in contemporary civilization he places the figure of Simon. He introduces him to the reader in somewhat melodramatic fashion: the boy faints. In this, the first of Simon's actions, we have a possible ironic twist on Swinburne's famous line: "Thou hast conquer'd, O pale Galilean; the world has grown gray from thy breath." It is obvious from Simon's subsequent history that he is a Christ-figure; and the romantic view of humanity proposed by Rousseau has so infiltrated every aspect of life in the contemporary world that even Christ is seen through the rose-colored glasses of sentimentality, which is the logical and real successor to romanticism.

Thus, the Christ of *Lord of the Flies* is the "pale Galilean"; yet it is this same weak Christ who, in the first act he performs, forces a concession from Jack, and the choir boys are allowed to rest. The irony is evident: even a weak Christ is more than a strong dictator.[4] Further, when Simon announces his name (and his name has the strongest biblical overtones), Jack says: "We've got to decide about being rescued." Immediately, Simon is linked, however vaguely, with the idea of salvation.

After the boys have elected Ralph as leader by "this toy of voting," Jack, Simon and Ralph begin exploring the mountain. This section of the novel is crucial, for it is here that Golding gives his abbreviated ironical summary of the romantic view of human progress. The passage needs analysis in depth (impossible in an article of this length), but it should be pointed out that Golding has chosen as explorers those who have dominated the history of man: the totalitarian, the parliamentarian and the mystic-poet. And, as is clear from the text, Simon is the realist of the triumvirate. When the boys examine the bushes on the mountain, Simon accepts them for what they are. Ralph and Jack are concerned only with how the buds can be used. That Golding's figure of religious faith accepts reality as it is provides an interesting comment on the limited approaches of the parliamentarian and the dictator.

As we follow Simon through the novel, we discover that he is the mystic who separates himself from the others to ponder the mysteries of existence. Simon is the carpenter who continues building the shelters after the other boys have abandoned the work; Simon feeds the "littluns"; Simon encounters the beast in all its loathsomeness and does not succumb to the beast's temptation to despair. This encounter is the boy's Gethsemane: he comes face to face with evil, recognizes it for what it is, and, despite the agony and horror of the meeting, he is neither defeated

---

[4] Simon's martyrdom, however, indicates that the saint or Christ-like personage (in spite of his spiritual strength) fails to rescue man from the nightmare of history.—Eds.

nor intimidated by it. Immediately after he recovers consciousness, he ascends the mountain to free the dead pilot, whose parachute lines have become entangled in the rocks. In other words, Simon climbs the mountain to free "fallen man."

He returns then to the boys to announce the good news; they need no longer fear the beast. But the group will not listen to him. Like the One in whose place he stands symbolically, Simon is murdered during a religious festival—the diabolical liturgy of the pig. His death occurs while the island world cowers under the lash of a gigantic storm. And it is only after Simon has actually died that the dead man in the parachute is finally *freed* and *washed* out to sea, the sea which is Golding's symbol of mystery, not ch☐ ☐s.

Finally, Simon has his symbolic hour of glorification: his body is surrounded by "moonbeam-bodied creatures with fiery eyes"; gleaming in this unearthly phosphorescence, he is carried gently out to sea. And it is difficult not to recognize the hint of a resurrection motif here, for the pattern is that of the hero carried through the waters to his apotheosis.

*Lord of the Flies,* as I have suggested, is not an optimistic novel, but at least it is pessimistic about the right things. It states quite clearly that the time has come for the Western world to abandon its fantastic belief in the Rousseauvian concept of the natural goodness of the human species, which goodness must lead inevitably to the total perfection of the race. It shows what happens to scientific man, when he trusts only in the activity of his unaided reason. It castigates the Western democracies for their blind acceptance of salvation through militarism. It pictures the tragic destruction of any society which nourishes and exalts the dictator. Ultimately, it presents the awesome spectacle of a world which, not satisfied with murdering Simon, continues to neglect the significance of his sacrifice.

But William Golding's world is not merely pessimistic. There is goodness in his characters; there is order in his universe.[5] However, like all authors who have tried their

---

[5] It might well be noted, however, that the goodness and the order are overcome in every instance. True, Ralph survives and he steps forward to announce himself to the "rescuer" as the leader, but the rescue is decidedly ironic; the boys are freed from primitive and childish militarism only by sophisticated adult militarism.—Eds.

hand at the intellectual exercise we call fable, he wants to teach man some hard truths about his own nature. In the complexity and ambiguity of a highly elaborated symbolism, he has reminded modern man of the fact of original sin. This is a reminder that we all need every so often. In a later novel, *The Inheritors*, Golding places the following ironic words in the mouth of one character: "People understand each other." *Lord of the Flies* answers: "Perhaps; but not well enough."

# "Men of a Smaller Growth": A Psychological Analysis of William Golding's Lord of the Flies[1]

## CLAIRE ROSENFIELD

WHEN an author consciously dramatizes Freudian theory—and dramatizes it successfully—only the imaginative re-creation of human behavior rather than the structure of ideas is apparent. In analyzing William Golding's *Lord of the Flies*, the critic should assume that Golding knows psychological literature,[2] and must then attempt to show how an author's knowledge of theory can vitalize his prose and characterization. The plot itself is uncomplicated; so simple, indeed, that one wonders how it so effortlessly absorbs the burden of meaning. During some unexplained man-made holocaust a plane, evacuating a group of children, crashes on the shore of a tropical island. All adults are conveniently killed. The narrative follows the children's gradual return to the amorality of childhood, a non-innocence which makes them small savages. Or we might make the analogy to the childhood of races and compare the child

---

[1] This essay appeared in *Literature and Psychology*, 11 (Autumn, 1961), 93-101, and is reprinted in a revised version here by permission of the author and the editor, Leonard F. Manheim.

[2] Note Golding's comment that he has read "absolutely no Freud" in "Lord of the Campus," *Time*, LXXIX (June 22, 1962), 64. Reprinted in this volume, p. 285.—Eds.

to the primitive. Denied the sustaining and repressing authority of parents, church, and state, the boys form a new culture, the development of which reflects that of the genuine primitive society, evolving its gods and demons, its rituals and taboos, its whole social structure. On the level of pure narrative, the action proceeds from the gradual struggle between Ralph and Jack, the two oldest boys, for precedence. Consistent clusters of imagery imply that one boy is godlike, the other satanic—thus making a symbolic level of meaning by transforming narrative events into an allegorical struggle between the forces of Good and those of Evil. Ralph is the natural leader by virtue of his superior height, his superior strength, his superior beauty. His mild expression proclaims him "no devil." He possesses the symbol of authority, the conch, or sea shell, which the children use to assemble their miniature councils. Golding writes, "The being that had blown . . . [the conch] had sat waiting for them on the platform with the delicate thing balanced on his knees, was set apart." Jack, on the other hand, is described in completely antithetical terms; he is distinguished by his ugliness and his red hair, a traditional demonic attribute. He first appears as the leader of a church choir, which "creature-like" marches in two columns behind him. All members of the choir wear black; "their bodies, from throat to ankle, were hidden by black cloaks." [3] Ralph initially blows the conch to discover how many children have escaped death in the plane crash. As Jack approaches with his choir from the "darkness of the forest," he cannot see Ralph, whose back is to the sun. The former is, symbolically, sun-blinded. These two are very obviously intended to recall God and the Devil, whose confrontation, in the history of Western religions, establishes the moral basis for all actions. But, as Freud reminds us, "metaphysics" becomes "metapsychology";[4] gods and devils are "nothing other than processes projected into the outer world." [5] If Ralph is a projection of man's good impulses from which we derive the authority figures—whether god, king, or father

---

[3] P. 16. All page references are to this edition of *Lord of the Flies* and will hereafter be noted in parentheses in the text.

[4] Sigmund Freud, *The Psychopathology of Everyday Life*, as quoted by Ernest Jones, *The Life and Work of Sigmund Freud* (New York: Basic Books, 1957), III, 53.

[5] *Ibid.*

—who establish the necessity for our valid ethical and social action, then Jack becomes an externalization of the evil instinctual forces of the unconscious; the allegorical has become the psychological.

The temptation is to regard the island on which the children are marooned as a kind of Eden, uncorrupted and Eveless. But the actions of the children negate any romantic assumptions about childhood innocence. Even though Golding himself momentarily becomes a victim of his Western culture and states at the end that Ralph wept for the "end of innocence," events have simply supported Freud's conclusion that no child is innocent. On a fourth level, Ralph is every man—or every child—and his body becomes the battleground where reason and instinct struggle, each to assert itself. For to regard Ralph and Jack as Good and Evil, as I do in the previous paragraph, is to ignore the role of the child Piggy, who in the child's world of make-believe is the outsider. Piggy's composite description not only manifests his difference from the other boys; it also reminds the reader of the stereotype image of the old man who has more-than-human wisdom: he is fat, inactive because asthmatic, and generally reveals a disinclination for physical labor. Because he is extremely near-sighted, he wears thick glasses— a further mark of his difference. As time passes, the hair of the other boys grows with abandon. "He was the only boy on the island whose hair never seemed to grow. The rest were shock-headed, but Piggy's hair still lay in wisps over his head as though baldness were his natural state, and this imperfect covering would soon go, like the velvet on a young stag's antlers" (59). In these images of age and authority we have a figure reminiscent of the children's past —the father. Moreover, like the father he counsels common sense; he alone leavens with a reasonable gravity the constant exuberance of the others for play or for play at hunting. When they scamper off at every vague whim, he scornfully comments, " 'Like a pack of kids.' " Ungrammatically but logically he tries to allay the "littluns" fear of a "beast." " 'Life is scientific, that's what it is. . . . I know there isn't no beast—not with claws and all that, I mean—but I know there isn't no fear, either' " (77). He has excessive regard for the forms of order: the conch must be held by a child before that child can speak at councils. When the others neglect responsibility, fail to build shelters, swim in the pools or play in the sand or hunt, allow the signal fire on the mountain to go out or get out of hand and burn up half the island, he seconds Ralph by admonishing the others vigorously and becomes more and more of a spoilsport who robs play of its illusions, like the adult who interrupts the game. Ralph alone recognizes Piggy's superior intelligence, but wavers between what he knows to be wise and the group acceptance his egocentricity demands. Finally, Piggy's role—as man's reasoning faculties and as a father—derives some of its complexity from the fact that the fire which the children foster and guard on the mountain in the hope of communicating with the adult world is lighted with his glasses. In classical mythology, after all, fire brought civilization—and, hence, repression—to man. As the hold of civilization weakens, the new community becomes more and more irrational, and its irrationality is marked by Piggy's progressive blindness. An accident following an argument between Ralph and Jack causes one of the lenses of Piggy's glasses to break. When the final breach between the two occurs and Piggy supports Ralph, his remaining lens is stolen in a night raid by Jack. This is a parody of the traditional fire theft, which was to provide light and warmth for mankind. After this event Piggy must be led by Ralph. When he is making his final plea for his glasses—reasoned as always—he is struck on the head by a rock and falls. "Piggy fell forty feet and landed on his back on that square, red rock in the sea. His head opened and stuff came out and turned red. Piggy's arms and legs twitched a bit, like a pig's after it has been killed" (167). What Golding emphasizes here is the complete animality to which Piggy is reduced. His mind is destroyed; his body is subject to motor responses alone; he is "like a pig after it has been killed."

The history of the child Piggy on the island dramatizes in terms of the individual the history of the entire group. When they first assemble to investigate their plight, they treat their island isolation as a temporary phenomenon. They are, after all, still children, wanting only to play games until they are interrupted by the action of parents, until the decisions of their elders take them from make-believe to the actuality of school or food or sleep; until they are rescued, as it were, from "play." This microcosm of the great world seems to them to be a fairy land.

A kind of glamour was spread over them and the scene and they were conscious of the glamour and made happy by it (22).

The coral was scribbled in the sea as though a giant had bent down to reproduce the shape of the island in a flowing, chalk line but tired before he had finished (25).

"This is real exploring," said Jack. "I'll bet nobody's been here before" (23).

Echoes and birds flew, white and pink dust floated, the forest further down shook as with the passage of an enraged monster: and then the island was still (24).

They compare this reality which as yet they do not accept as reality to their reading experiences: it is *Treasure Island* or *Coral Island* or like pictures from their travel books. This initial reaction reaffirms the pattern of play which Johan Huizinga establishes in *Homo Ludens*.[6] In its early stages their play has no cultural or moral function; it is simply a "stepping out of real life into a temporary sphere of activity."[7] Ironically, the child of *Lord of the Flies* who thinks he is "only pretending" or that this is "only for fun" does not realize that his play is the beginning of the formation of a new society which has regressed to a primitive state, with all its emphasis upon taboo and communal action. What begins by being like other games in having a distinct "locality and duration"[8] apart from ordinary life is—or becomes—reality. The spatial separation necessary for the make-believe of the game is represented first by the island. In this new world the playground is further narrowed: not only are their actions limited by the island, but also the gatherings of the children are described as a circle at several points, a circle from which Piggy is excluded:

For the moment the boys were a closed circuit of sympathy with Piggy outside (18).

They became a circle of boys round a camp fire and even Ralph and Piggy were half-drawn in (67).

Piggy approximates the spoilsport who "robs the play of its illusion,"[9] who reminds them of space and time outside the charmed circle, who demands responsibility.

[6] Johan Huizinga, *Homo Ludens* (Boston: Beacon Press, 1955).
[7] *Ibid.*, p. 8.
[8] *Ibid.*, p. 9.
[9] *Ibid.*, p. 7.

The games of the beginning of the novel have a double function: they, first of all, reflect the child's attitude toward play as a temporary cessation from the activities imposed by the adult world; but, like the games played before the formation of civilization, they anticipate the ritual which reveals a developing society. So the children move from voluntary play to ritual, from "only pretending" to reality, from representation or dramatization to identification. The older strictures imposed by parents are soon forgotten—but every now and then a momentary remembrance of past prohibitions causes restraint. One older child hides in order to throw stones at a younger one.

> Yet there was a space around Henry, perhaps six yards in diameter, into which he dare not throw. Here, invisible yet strong, was the taboo of the old life. Round the squatting child was the protection of parents and school and policemen and the law (57).

Jack hesitates when, searching for meat, he raises his knife to kill his first pig.

> The pause was only long enough for them to understand what an enormity the downward stroke would be. Then the piglet tore loose from the creepers and scurried into the undergrowth. . . .
> "Why didn't you—?"
> They knew very well why he hadn't: because of the enormity of the knife descending and cutting into living flesh; because of the unbearable blood (27).

The younger children first, then gradually the older ones, like primitives in the childhood of races, begin to people the darkness of night and forest with spirits and demons which had previously appeared only in their dreams or fairy tales. Now there are no comforting mothers to dispel the terrors of the unknown. They externalize these fears into the figure of a "beast." Once the word "beast" is mentioned, the menace of the irrational becomes overt; name and thing become one. Simply to mention the dreaded creature is to incur its wrath. At one critical council when the first communal feeling begins to disintegrate, Ralph cries, "If only they could send us something grown-up . . . a sign or something" (87). And a sign does come from the outside. That night, unknown to the children, a plane is shot down and its pilot parachutes dead to earth and is caught in the rocks on the mountain. It requires no more than the darkness of night together with the shadows of the forest vibrating in the signal fire to distort the tangled corpse with its expanding silk parachute into a demon that must be appeased. Ironically, the fire of communication does touch this object of the grown-up world, only to foster superstition. But the assurances of the civilized world provided by the nourishing and protective parents are no longer available. Security in this new situation can only be achieved by establishing new rules, new rituals to reassert the cohesiveness of the group.

·During the first days the children, led by Jack, play at hunting. But eventually the circle of the playground extends to the circle of the hunted and squealing pig seeking refuge which itself anticipates the circle of consecrated ground where the children perform the new rites of the kill.

The first hunt accomplishes its purpose: the blood of the animals is spilled; the meat used for food. But because Jack and his choir undertake this hunt, they desert the signal fire, the case of which is dictated by the common-sense desire for rescue; it goes out and a ship passes the island. Later the children re-enact the killing with one boy, Maurice, assuming the role of the pig running its frenzied circle. The others chant in unison: "Kill the pig. Cut her throat. Bash her in." At this dramatic representation each child is still aware that this is a display, a performance. He is never "so beside himself that he loses consciousness of ordinary reality." [10] Each time they re-enact the same event, however, their behavior becomes more frenzied, more cruel, less like dramatization or imitation than identification. The chant then becomes, "Kill the beast. Cut his throat. Spill his blood." It is as if the first event, the pig's actual death, is forgotten in the recesses of time; it is as if it happened so long ago that the children have lost track of their history on the island; facts are distorted, a new myth defines the primal act. Real pig becomes mythical beast to children for whom the forms of play have become the rituals of a social order.

Jack's ascendancy over the group begins when the children's fears distort the natural objects around them: twigs

---

[10] *Ibid.*, p. 14.

become creepers, shadows become demons. I have already discussed the visual imagery suggesting Jack's demonic function. He serves as a physical manifestation of irrational forces. After an indefinite passage of time, he appears almost dehumanized, his "nose only a few inches from the humid earth." He is "dog-like" and proceeds forward "on all fours" into the "semi-darkness of the undergrowth." His cloak and clothing have been shed. Indeed, except for a "pair of tattered shorts held up by his knife-belt, he was naked." His eyes seemed "bolting and nearly mad." He has lost his ability to communicate with Ralph as he had on the first day. "He tried to convey the compulsion to track down and kill that was swallowing him up" (46). "They walked along, two continents of experience and feeling, unable to communicate" (49). When Jack first explains to Ralph the necessity to disguise himself from the pigs he wants to hunt, he rubs his face with clay and charcoal. At this point he assumes a mask, begins to dance, is finally freed from all the repressions of his past. "He capered toward Bill, and the mask was a thing on its own, behind which Jack hid, liberated from shame and self-consciousness" (58). At the moment of the dance the mask and Jack are one. The first kill, as I have noted, follows the desertion of the signal fire and the conterminous passage of a possible rescue ship. Jack, however, is still revelling in the knowledge that they have "outwitted a living thing, imposed their will upon it, taken away its life like a long and satisfying drink" (64). Note that the pig is here described as a "living thing" not as an animal; only if there is equality between victor and victim can there be significance in the triumph of one over the other. Already he has begun to obliterate the distinction between animals and men, as do primitives; already he thinks in terms of the metaphor of a ritual drinking of blood, the efficacy of which depended on the drinker's assumption of his victim's strength and spirit. Ralph and Piggy confront him with his defection of duty, his failure to behave like a responsible member of Western society.

The two boys faced each other. There was the brilliant world of hunting, tactics, fierce exhilaration, skill; and there was the world of longing and baffled commonsense. Jack transferred the knife to his left hand and smudged blood over his forehead as he pushed down the plastered hair (65).

Jack's unconscious gesture is a parody of the ritual of initiation in which the hunter's face is smeared with the blood of his first kill. In the subsequent struggle one of the lenses of Piggy's spectacles is broken. The dominance of reason is over; the voice of the old world is stilled. The primary images are no longer those of fire and light but those of darkness and blood. The initial link between Ralph and Jack "had snapped and fastened elsewhere."

The rest of the group, however, shifts its allegiance to Jack because he has given them meat rather than something as useless as fire. Gradually, they begin to be described as "shadows" or "masks" or "savages" or "demoniac figures" and, like Jack, "hunt naked save for paint and a belt." Ralph now uses Jack's name with the recognition that "a taboo was evolving around that word too." Name and thing again become one; to use the word is to incite the bearer, who is not here a transcendent or supernatural creature but rather a small boy. But more significant, the taboo, according to Freud, is "a very primitive prohibition imposed from without (by an authority) and directed against the strongest desires of man." [11] In this new society it replaces the authority of the parents, whom the children symbolically kill when they slay the nursing sow. Now every kill becomes a sexual act, is a metaphor for childhood sexuality, an assertion of freedom from mores they had been taught to revere.

> The afternoon wore on, hazy and dreadful with damp heat; the sow staggered her way ahead of them, bleeding and mad, and the hunters followed, wedded to her in lust, excited by the long chase and the dropped blood. . . . The sow collapsed under them and they were heavy and fulfilled upon her (125).

Every subsequent ritual fulfills not only a desire for communication and for a security to substitute for that of civilization, but also a need to liberate themselves from both the repressions of the past and those imposed by Ralph. Indeed, the projection into a beast of those impulses that they cannot accept in themselves is the beginning of a new mythology. The earlier dreams and nightmares of individual children are now shared in this mutual creation.

---

[11] Sigmund Freud, *Totem and Taboo, The Basic Writings of Sigmund Freud*, trans. A. A. Brill (New York: Modern Library, 1938), p. 834.

When the imaginary demons become defined by the rotting corpse and floating parachute on the mountain which the boys' terror distorts into a beast, Jack wants to track the creature down. After the next kill, the head of the pig is placed upon a stake to placate the beast. Finally one of the children, Simon, after an epileptic fit, creeps out of the forest at twilight while the others are engaged in enthusiastic dancing following a hunt. Seized by the rapture of re-enactment or perhaps terrorized by fear and night into believing that this little creature is a beast, they circle Simon, pounce on him, bite and tear his body to death. He becomes not a substitute for beast but beast itself; representation becomes absolute identification, "the mystic repetition of the initial event." [12] At the moment of Simon's death, nature speaks as it did at Christ's crucifixion: a cloud bursts; rain and wind fill the parachute on the hill and the corpse of the pilot falls or is dragged among the screaming boys. Both Simon and the dead man, beast and beast, are washed into the sea and disappear. After this complete resurgence of savagery in accepted ritual, there is only a short interval before Piggy's remaining lens is stolen, he is intentionally killed as an enemy, and Ralph, the human being, becomes hunted like beast or pig.

Simon's mythic and psychological role has earlier been suggested in this essay. Undersized, subject to epileptic fits, bright-eyed, and introverted, he constantly creeps away from the others to meditate among the intricate vines of the forest. To him, as to the mystic, superior knowledge is intuitively given which he cannot communicate. When the first report of the beast-pilot reaches camp, Simon, we are told, can picture only "a human at once heroic and sick." He predicts that Ralph will " 'get back all right,' " only to be scorned as "batty" by the latter. In each case he sees the truth, but is overwhelmed with self-consciousness. During the day preceding his death, he walks away as if in a trance and stumbles upon a pig's head left in the sand in order to appease the demonic presence the children's terror has created. Shaman-like, he holds a silent and imaginary colloquy with it, a severed head covered with innumerable flies. It is itself the titled Lord of the Flies, a name applied to the Biblical demon Beelzebub and later used in Goethe's *Faust*,

*Part I,* to describe Mephistopheles.[13] From it he learns that it is the Beast, and the Beast cannot be hunted because it dwells within each child. Simon feels the advent of one of his fits. His visual as well as his auditory perception becomes distorted; the head of the pig seems to expand, an anticipation or intuition of the discovery of the pilot's corpse, whose expanding parachute causes the equally distorted perceptions of normal though frightened children. Suddenly Golding employs a startling image, "Simon was inside the mouth. He fell down and lost consciousness" (133). Literally, this image presents the hallucination of a sensitive child about to lose control of his rational faculties. Such illusions, or auras, frequently attend the onset of an epileptic seizure. Mythologically and symbolically, it recalls the quest in which the hero is swallowed by a serpent or dragon or beast whose belly represents the underworld, undergoes a ritual death in order to win the elixer to revitalize his stricken society, and returns with his knowledge to the timed world as a redeemer. So Christ, after his descent to the grave and to Hell, returns to redeem mankind from his fallen state. Psychologically, this figure of speech connoting the descent into the darkness of death represents the annihilation of the individual ego, an internal journey necessary for self-understanding, a return from the timelessness of the unconscious. When Simon wakes from his symbolic death, he suddenly realizes that he must confront the beast on the mountain because "what else is there to do?" Earlier he had been unable to express himself or give advice. Now he is relieved of "that dreadful feeling of the pressure of personality." When he discovers the corrupted corpse hanging from the rock, he first frees it in compassion though it is surrounded by flies, and then staggers unevenly down to report to the others. He attempts to assume a communal role from which his strangeness and nervous seizures formerly isolated him. Redeemer and scapegoat, he becomes the victim of the group he seeks to enlighten. In death—before he is pulled into the sea—the flies which have moved to his head from the bloodstained pig and from the decomposing body of the man are replaced by the phosphorescent creatures of the deep. Halo-like, these "moonbeam-bodied creatures" attend the seer who has been denied into the

---

[13] *Ibid.*

formlessness and freedom of the ocean. "Softly, surrounded by a fringe of inquisitive bright creatures, itself a silver shape beneath the steadfast constellations, Simon's dead body moved out toward the open sea" (142).[14]

Piggy's death, soon to follow Simon's, is foreshadowed when the former proclaims at council that there is no beast. "'What would a beast eat?'" "'Pig.'" "'We eat pig,'" he rationally answers. "'Piggy'" (77) is the emotional response, resulting in a juxtaposition of words which imply Piggy's role and Golding's meaning. At Piggy's death his body twitches "like a pig's after it has been killed." Not only has his head been smashed, but also the conch, symbol of order, is simultaneously broken. A complex group of metaphors unite to form a total metaphor involving Piggy and the pig, hunted and eaten by the children, and the pig's head which is at once left to appease the beast's hunger and is the beast itself. But the beast is within, and the children are defined by the very objects they seek to destroy.

In these associated images we have the whole idea of a communal and sacrificial feast and a symbolic cannibalism, all of which Freud discussed in *Totem and Taboo*. Here the psychology of the individual contributes the configurations for the development of religion. Indeed, the events of *Lord of the Flies* imaginatively parallel the patterns which Freud detects in primitive mental processes.

Having populated the outside world with demons and spirits which are projections of their instinctual nature, these children—and primitive men—must then unconsciously evolve new forms of worship and laws, which manifest themselves in taboos, the oldest form of social repression. With the exception of the first kill—in which the children still imagine they are *playing* at hunting—the subsequent deaths assume a ritual form; the pig is eaten communally by all and the head is left for the "beast," whose role consists in sharing the feast. This is much like the "public ceremony" [15] described by Freud in which the sacri-

---

[14] The reader will find it worthwhile to compare Donald R. Spangler's "Simon," reprinted on pp. 211-215 in this volume, with Professor Rosenfield's view of Simon.—Eds.

[15] There are further affinities to Sartre's *Les Mouches*.

fice of an animal provided food for the god and his worshipers. The complex relationships within the novel between the "beast," the pigs which are sacrificed, the children
whose asocial impulses are externalized in the beast—this
has already been discussed. So we see that, as Freud points
out, the "sacrificing community, its god [the 'beast'], and
the sacrificial animal are of the same blood," [16] members of
a clan. The pig, then, may be regarded as a totem animal,
an "ancestor, a tutelary spirit and protector";[17] it is, in any
case, a part of every child. The taboo or prohibition against
eating particular parts of the totem animal coincides with
the children's failure to eat the head of the pig. It is that
portion which is set aside for the "beast." Just as Freud
describes the primitive feast, so the children's festive meal
is accompanied by a frenzied ritual in which they temporarily release their forbidden impulses and represent the
kill. To consume the pig and to re-enact the event is not
only to assert a "common identity" [18] but also to share a
"common responsibility" for the deed. By this means the
children assuage the enormity of having killed a living thing.
None of the boys is excluded from the feast. The later ritual,
in which Simon, as a human substitute identified with the
totem, is killed, is in this novel not an unconscious attempt
to share the responsibility for the killing of a primal father
in prehistoric times, as Freud states; rather, it is here a social
act in which the participants celebrate their new society by
commemorating their severance from the authority of the
civilized state. Because of the juxtaposition of Piggy and
pig, the eating of pig at the communal feast might be regarded as the symbolic cannibalism by which the children
physically partake of the qualities of the slain and share
responsibility for their crime. (It must be remembered that,
although Piggy on a symbolic level represents the light of
reason and the authority of the father, as a human being he
shares that bestiality and irrationality which to Golding
dominate all men, even the most rational or civilized.)
    In the final action, Ralph is outlawed by the children and
hunted like an animal. One boy, Roger, sharpens a stick at

[16] *Totem and Taboo*, p. 878.
[17] *Ibid.*, p. 808.
[18] *Ibid.*, p. 914.

both ends so that it will be ready to receive the severed head of the boy as if he were a pig. Jack keeps his society together because it, like the brother horde of William Robertson Smith[19] and Freud, "is based on complicity in the common crimes."[20] All share the guilt of having killed Simon, of hunting Ralph down. In his flight Ralph, seeing the grinning skull of a pig, thinks of it as a toy and remembers the early days on the island when all were united in play. In the play world, the world of day, the world of the novel's opening, he has become a "spoilsport" like Piggy; in the world based upon primitive rites and taboos, the night world where fears become demons and sleep is like death, he is the heretic or outcast, the rejected god. This final hunt, after the conch is broken, is the pursuit of the figure representing civilized law and order; it is the law and order of a primitive culture. Finally, Jack, through misuse of the dead Piggy's glasses, accidentally sets the island on fire. A passing cruiser, seeing the fire, lands to find only a dirty group of sobbing little boys. "'Fun and games,' said the officer. . . . 'What have you been doing? Having a war or something?'" (185).

But are all the meanings of the novel as clear as they seem? To restrict it to an imaginative re-creation of Freud's theory that children are little savages, that no child is innocent whatever popular Christian theology would have us believe, is to limit its significance for the adult world. To say that the "beasts" we fear are within, that man is essentially irrational—or, to place a moral judgment on the irrational, that man is evil—that, again, is too easy. In this forced isolation of a group of children, Golding is making a statement about the world they have left—a world that we are told is "in ruins." According to Huizinga's theory of play, war is a game, a contest for prestige which, like the games of primitives or of classical athletes, may be fatal. It, too, has its rules, although the modern concept of total war tends to obscure both its ritualistic and its ennobling character. It, too, has its spatial and temporal limitations, as the rash of "limited" wars makes very clear. More than once the children's acts are compared to those of the outside

---

[19] William Robertson Smith, *Lectures on the Religion of the Semites*, 3rd ed., with an introduction by Stanley A. Cook (New York: Macmillan, 1927).

[20] *Totem and Taboo*, p. 916.

world. When Jack first blackens his face like a savage, he
gives his explanation: "'For hunting. Like in the war. You
know—dazzle paint. Like things trying to look like something else'" (57). Appalled by one of the ritual dances,
Piggy and Ralph discuss the authority and rationality of the
apparently secure world they have left:

> "Grownups know things," said Piggy. "They ain't
> afraid of the dark. They'd meet and have tea and discuss.
> Then things 'ud be all right—"
> "They wouldn't set fire to the island. Or lose—"
> "They'd build a ship—"
> The three boys stood in the darkness, striving unsuc-
> cessfully to convey the majesty of adult life.
> "They wouldn't quarrel—"
> "Or break my specs—"
> "Or talk about a beast—"
> "If only they could get a message to us," cried Ralph
> desperately. "If only they could send us something
> grown-up . . . a sign or something" (86-87).

The sign does come that night, unknown to them, in the
form of the parachute and its attached corpse. The pilot is
the analogue in the adult world to the ritual killing of the
child Simon on the island; he, like Simon, is the victim and
scapegoat of his society, which has unleashed its instincts
in war. Both he and Simon are associated by a cluster of
visual images. Both are identified with beasts by the children, who do see the truth—that all men are bestial—but
do not understand it. Both he and Simon attract the flies
from the Lord of the Flies, the pig's head symbolic of the
demonic; both he and Simon are washed away by a cleans-
ing but not reviving sea. His position on the mountain recalls the hanged or sacrificed god of Sir James Frazer's *The
Golden Bough*, in which an effigy of the corn god is buried
or thrown into the sea to insure fertility among many primitives; here, however, we have a parody of fertility. He is
dead proof that Piggy's exaggerated respect for adults is
itself irrational. When the officer at the rescue jokingly says,
"What have you been doing? Having a war or something?"
this representative of the grown-up world does not understand that the games of the children, which result in two
deaths, are a moral commentary upon the primitive nature
of his own culture. The ultimate irrationality is war. Para-

doxically, the children not only regress to a primitive and infantile morality, but they also degenerate into adults. They prove that, indeed, "children are but men of a smaller growth."

# *Notes on* Lord of the Flies[1]

## E. L. EPSTEIN

In answer to a publicity questionnaire from the American publishers of *Lord of the Flies*, William Golding (born Cornwall, 1911) declared that he was brought up to be a scientist, and revolted; after two years of Oxford he changed his educational emphasis from science to English literature, and became devoted to Anglo-Saxon. After publishing a volume of poetry he "wasted the next four years," and when World War II broke out he joined the Royal Navy. For the next five years he was involved in naval matters except for a few months in New York and six months with Lord Cherwell in a "research establishment." He finished his naval career as a lieutenant in command of a rocket ship; he had seen action against battleships, submarines and aircraft, and had participated in the Walcheren and D-Day operations. After the war he began teaching and writing. Today, his novels include *Lord of the Flies* (Coward-McCann), *The Inheritors* (which may loosely be described as a novel of prehistory but is, like all of Golding's work, much more), and *Pincher Martin* (published in this country by Harcourt Brace as *The Two Deaths of Christopher Martin*). He lists his Hobbies as thinking, classical Greek, sailing and archaeology, and his Literary Influences as Euripides and the anonymous Anglo-Saxon author of *The Battle of Maldon*.

The theme of *Lord of the Flies* is described by Golding as follows (in the same publicity questionnaire): "The theme is an attempt to trace the defects of society back

[1] This article appeared in the original Capricorn edition of *Lord of the Flies* (New York: Putnam's, 1959), 249-55.

to the defects of human nature. The moral is that the shape of a society must depend on the ethical nature of the individual and not on any political system however apparently logical or respectable. The whole book is symbolic in nature except the rescue in the end where adult life appears, dignified and capable, but in reality enmeshed in the same evil as the symbolic life of the children on the island. The officer, having interrupted a man-hunt, prepares to take the children off the island in a cruiser which will presently be hunting its enemy in the same implacable way. And who will rescue the adult and his cruiser?"

This is, of course, merely a casual summing-up on Mr. Golding's part of his extremely complex and beautifully woven symbolic web which becomes apparent as we follow through the book, but it does indicate that *Lord of the Flies* is not, to say the least, a simple adventure story of boys on a desert island. In fact, the implications of the story go far beyond the degeneration of a few children. What is unique about the work of Golding is the way he has combined and synthesized all of the characteristically twentieth-century methods of analysis of the human being and human society and used this unified knowledge to comment on a "test situation." In this book, as in few others at the present time, are findings of psychoanalysts of all schools, anthropologists, social psychologists and philosophical historians mobilized into an attack upon the central problem of modern thought: the nature of the human personality and the reflection of personality on society.[2]

---

[2] Epstein perhaps overstates here. The novel cannot be taken as a final synthesis of modern thought or as the ultimate comment on the "nature of the human personality." The boys are not completely free agents; they have been molded by British civilization for some years before being deposited on the island. They attempt to establish a government that imitates democracy, they retain confidence in adults, they, at least for a while, behave in accord with prior training, as when Roger throws the stones near but not at Henry, pp. 56-57. Some events that occur depend on circumstance rather than cause and effect. For example, when the boys ask for a sign from the adult world (p. 87), the sign conveniently appears (pp. 88-89). The fortuitous arrival of the cruiser at the climactic moment is also a result of obvious manipulation on the part of Golding. These maneuvers militate against the authenticity of the theme. They are not good "evidence."—Eds.

Another feature of Golding's work is the superb use of symbolism, a symbolism that "works." The central symbol itself, "the lord of the flies," is, like any true symbol, much more than the sum of its parts; but some elements of it may be isolated. "The lord of the flies" is, of course, a translation of the Hebrew *Ba'alzevuv* (*Beelzebub* in Greek) which means literally "lord of insects." It has been suggested that it was a mistranslation of a mistransliterated word which gave us this pungent and suggestive name for the Devil, a devil whose name suggests that he is devoted to decay, destruction, demoralization, hysteria and panic and who therefore fits in very well with Golding's theme. He does not, of course, suggest that the Devil is present in any traditional religious sense; Golding's Beelzebub is the modern equivalent, the anarchic, amoral, driving Id whose only function seems to be to insure the survival of the host in which it is embedded or embodied, which function it performs with tremendous and single-minded tenacity. Although it is possible to find other names for this force, the modern picture of the personality, whether drawn by theologians or psychoanalysts, inevitably includes this force or psychic structure as the fundamental principle of the Natural Man. The tenets of civilization, the moral and social codes, the Ego, the intelligence itself, form only a veneer over this white-hot power, this uncontrollable force, "the fury and the mire of human veins." Dostoievsky found salvation in this freedom, although he found damnation in it also. Yeats found in it the only source of creative genius ("Whatever flames upon the night,/ Man's own resinous heart has fed."). Conrad was appalled by this "heart of darkness," and existentialists find in the denial of this freedom the source of perversion of all human values. Indeed one could, if one were so minded, go through the entire canon of modern literature, philosophy and psychology and find this great basic drive defined as underlying the most fundamental conclusions of modern thought.

The emergence of this concealed, basic wildness is the theme of the book; the struggle between Ralph, the representative of civilization with his parliaments and his brain trust (Piggy, the intellectual whose shattering spectacles mark the progressive decay of rational influence as the story progresses), and Jack, in whom the spark of wildness burns hotter and closer to the surface than in Ralph and who is the leader of the forces of anarchy on the island, is also, of course, the struggle in modern society between those same forces translated onto a worldwide scale. The central incident of the book, and the turning point in the struggle between Ralph and Jack, is the killing of the sow on pp. 123-127). The sow is a mother: "sunk in deep maternal bliss lay the largest sow of the lot . . . the great bladder of her belly was fringed with a row of piglets that slept or burrowed and squeaked." The killing of the sow is accomplished in terms of sexual intercourse.

They were just behind her when she staggered into an open space where bright flowers grew and butterflies danced around each other and the air was hot and still. Here, struck down by the heat, the sow fell and the hunters hurled themselves at her. This dreadful eruption from an unknown world made her frantic; she squealed and bucked and the air was full of sweat and noise and blood and terror. Roger ran round the heap, prodding with his spear whenever pigflesh appeared. Jack was on top of the sow, stabbing downwards with his knife. Roger [a natural sadist, who becomes the "official" torturer and executioner for the tribe] found a lodgment for his point and began to push till he was leaning with his whole weight. The spear moved forward inch by inch, and the terrified squealing became a high-pitched scream. Then Jack found the throat and the hot blood spouted over his hands. The sow collapsed under them and they were heavy and fulfilled upon her. The butterflies still danced, preoccupied in the center of the clearing.

The entire incident is a horrid parody of an Oedipal wedding night and these emotions, the sensations aroused by murder and death, and the overpowering and unaccustomed emotions of sexual love experienced by the half-grown boys, release the forces of death and the devil on the island.[3]

The pig's head is cut off; a stick is sharpened at both ends and "jammed in a crack" in the earth. (The death planned for Ralph at the end of the book involves a stick sharpened at both ends.) The pig's head is impaled on the stick; ". . . the head hung there, a little blood dribbling down the stick. Instinctively the boys drew back too; and

---

[3] The reader will wish to compare Epstein's psychoanalytic interpretation with Claire Rosenfield's "Men of a Smaller Growth," reprinted on pp. 261-276.—Eds.

the forest was very still. They listened, and the loudest noise was the buzzing of flies over the spilled guts." Jack offers this grotesque trophy to "the Beast," the terrible animal that the littler children had been dreaming of, and which seems to be lurking on the island wherever they were not looking. After this occurs the most deeply symbolic incident in the book, the "interview" of Simon, an embryo mystic, with the head. The head seems to be saying, to Simon's heightened perceptions, that "Everything is a bad business. . . . The half-shut eyes were dim with the infinite cynicism of adult life." Simon fights with all his feeble power against the message of the head, against the "ancient, inescapable recognition." The recognition against which he struggles is the revelation to him of human capacities for evil and the superficial nature of human moral systems. It is the knowledge of the end of innocence, for which Ralph is to weep at the close of the book. The pig's head seems to threaten Simon with death and reveals that it is "the Beast." " 'Fancy thinking the Beast was something you could hunt and kill!' said the head. For a moment or two the forest and all the other dimly appreciated places echoed the parody of laughter. 'You knew, didn't you? I'm part of you? Close, close, close! I'm the reason why it's no go? Why things are what they are?' "

At the end of this fantastic scene Simon imagines he is looking into a vast mouth. "There was blackness within, blackness that spread . . . Simon was inside the mouth. He fell down and lost consciousness." This mouth,[4] the symbol of ravenous, unreasoning and eternally insatiable nature, appears again in *Pincher Martin*, in which the development of the theme of a Nature inimical to the conscious personality of man is developed in a stunning fashion. In *Lord of the Flies*, however, only the outline of a philosophy is sketched and the boys of the island are figures in a parable or fable which like all parables or fables contains an inherent tension between the innocent, time-passing, storytelling aspect of its surface and the great, "dimly appreciated" depths of its interior.

[4] Cf. Conrad's "Heart of Darkness": "I saw [the dying Kurtz] open his mouth wide—it gave him a weirdly voracious aspect, as though he wanted to swallow all the air, all the earth, all the men before him." Indeed Golding seems very close to Conrad, both in basic principles and in artistic method.

# Lord of the Campus[1]

BACK in England last week after a year in the U. S., British Author William Golding recalled his interrogation by American college students. "The question most asked was, 'Is there any hope for humanity?' I very dutifully said 'yes.'" Golding's credentials for being asked such a monumental query—and for answering it—rest on one accomplishment: his *Lord of the Flies*, a grim parable that holds out precious little hope for humanity, and is the most influential novel among U. S. undergraduates since Salinger's *Catcher in the Rye*.[2]

When *Lord of the Flies* was first published in the U. S. in 1955, it sold only 2,383 copies, and quickly went out of print. But British enthusiasm for it has been gradually exported to Ivy League English departments, and demand for the book is now high. The paperback edition, published in 1959, has already sold more than 65,000 copies. At the Columbia University bookstore, it outsells Salinger.

*Lord of the Flies* is required reading at a hundred U. S. colleges, is on the list of suggested summer reading for freshmen entering colleges from Occidental to Williams. At Harvard it is recommended for a social-relations course on "interpersonal behavior."

An M. I. T. minister uses it for a discussion group on original sin. At Yale and Princeton—where Salinger, like the three-button suit, has lost some of his mystique as he

---

[1] The following article is reprinted by permission from *Time* The Weekly Newsmagazine; copyright © Time Inc. 1962. See "Lord of the Campus," *Time*, LXXIX (June 22, 1962), 64.

[2] See Golding's remarks on Salinger's novel in the interview by Douglas M. Davis, "A Conversation with Golding," *New Republic*, 148 (May 4, 1963), 28-30.—Eds.

becomes adopted by the outlanders—the in-group popularity of Golding's book is creeping up. At Smith, where *Lord of the Flies* runs a close second in sales to Salinger's *Franny and Zooey*, 1,000 girls turned out for a lecture by Golding. The reception was the same at the thirty campuses Golding visited during his year as a rarely writer-in-residence at Virginia's Hollins College.[3]

CREATING THEIR OWN MISERY. The British schoolboys in *Lord of the Flies* are a few years younger than Salinger's Holden Caulfield—they are six to twelve—but are not self-pitying innocents in a world made miserable by adults. They create their own world, their own misery. Deposited unhurt on a deserted coral island by a plane during an atomic war, they form the responsible vacation-land democracy that their heritage calls for, and it gradually degenerates into anarchy, barbarism and murder. When adult rescue finally comes, they are a tribe of screaming painted savages hunting down their elected leader to tear him apart. The British naval officer who finds them says, "I should have thought that a pack of British boys would have been able to put up a better show than that." Then he goes back to his own war.

Says Golding: "The theme is an attempt to trace the defects of society back to the defects of human nature. Before the war, most Europeans believed that man could be perfected by perfecting society. We all saw a hell of a lot in the war that can't be accounted for except on the basis of original evil."

"PEOPLE I KNEW IN CAMP." What accounts for the appeal? Part of it is, of course, pure identification. A Harvard undergraduate says the book "rounds up all the people I knew in camp when I was a counselor." On another level, Golding believes students "seem to have it in for the whole world of organization. They're very cynical. And here was someone who was not making excuses for society. It was

---

[3] See Golding's series of four articles on his visit to the United States. "Touch of Insomnia," *Spectator*, 207 (October 27, 1961), 569-70; "Glass Door," *Spectator*, 207 (November 24, 1961), 732-33; "Body and Soul," *Spectator*, 208 (January 19, 1962), 65-66; "Gradus ad Parnassum," *Spectator*, 208 (September 7, 1962), 327-29.—Eds.

new to find someone who believes in original sin." The prickly belief in original sin is not Golding's only unfashionable stand. Under questioning by undergraduates, he cheerfully admitted he has read "absolutely no Freud"[4] (he prefers Greek plays in the original) and said there are no girls on the island because he does not believe that "sex has anything to do with humanity at this level."

At 51, bearded, scholarly William Golding claims to have been writing for 44 years—through childhood in Cornwall, Oxford, wartime duty as a naval officer, and 19 years as a schoolmaster. Golding claims to be an optimist—emotionally if not intellectually—and has a humor that belies the gloomy themes of his allegories. One critical appraisal of *Lord of the Flies* that impressed him came from an English s' 'ool-boy who went to an island near Puerto Rico last year to make a movie based on the book. Wrote the little boy from the idyllic island, surrounded by his happy peers and pampered by his producer: "I think *Lord of the Flies* stinks. I can't imagine what I'm doing on this filthy island, and it's all your fault." In Golding's view, a perfectly cast savage.

---

[4] An excellent "Freudian" analysis of *Lord of the Flies* appears in Claire Rosenfield's "Men of a Smaller Growth: A Psychological Analysis of William Golding's *Lord of the Flies,*" *Literature and Phychology*, XI (Autumn, 1961), 93-101. Reprinted, in a revised version, on pp. 261-276 in this volume.—Eds.

# A Checklist of Publications
## Relevant to *Lord of the Flies*

Allen, Walter, "New Novels." *New Statesman*, XLVIII (September 25, 1954), 370.

Amis, Kingsley, *New Maps of Hell*. New York: Ballantine Books, 1960, pp. 17 (note), 24, and 152.

Baker, James R., "Introduction." In *Lord of the Flies: Text, Notes and Criticism*, edited by James R. Baker and Arthur P. Ziegler, Jr. New York: Capricorn Books, 1964. An earlier version entitled "Why It's No Go" appeared in *Arizona Quarterly*, 19 (Winter, 1963), 293-305.

Bowen, John, "Bending Over Backwards." *Times Literary Supplement* (October 23, 1959), 608.

————, "One Man's Meat: The Idea of Individual Responsibility in Golding's Fiction." *Times Literary Supplement*, (August 7, 1959), 148.

Broes, Arthur T., "The Two Worlds of William Golding." *Carnegie Series in English*, No. 7 (1963), 1-7.

Colby, Vineta, "William Golding." *Wilson Library Bulletin*, XXXVII (February, 1963), 505.

Coskren, Thomas M., O. P., "Is Golding Calvinistic?" *America*, 109 (July 6, 1963), 18-20.

Cox, C. B., "*Lord of the Flies*." *Critical Quarterly*, 2 (Summer, 1960), 112-17.

Davis, Douglas M., "Golding, The Optimist, Belies His Somber Pictures and Fiction." *National Observer* (September 17, 1962), 17.

Drew, Philip, "Second Reading." *Cambridge Review*, 78 (1956), 78-84.

# Lord of the Flies

gan, John M., "Golding's View of Man." *America*, 108 (January 26, 1963), 140-41.

Epstein, E. L., "Notes on *Lord of the Flies*." In *Lord of the Flies*. New York: Capricorn Books, 1959, pp. 249-55.

Forster, E. M., "Introduction." In *Lord of the Flies*. New York: Coward-McCann, Inc., 1962, pp. ix-xii.

Freedman, Ralph, "The New Realism: The Fancy of William Golding." *Perspective*, 10 (Summer-Autumn, 1958), 118-28.

Fuller, Edmund, "Behind the Vogue: A Rigorous Understanding." New York *Herald Tribune* (November 4, 1962), 3.

Gindin, James, "'Gimmick' and Metaphor in the Novels of William Golding." *Modern Fiction Studies*, 6 (Summer, 1960), 145-52. Reprinted in Gindin's *Postwar British Fiction*. Berkeley: University of California Press, 1962, pp. 196-206.

Golding, J. T. C., "Letter to James R. Baker." In *Lord of the Flies: Text, Notes and Criticism*, edited by James R. Baker and Arthur P. Ziegler, Jr. New York: Capricorn Books, 1964.

Golding, William, "The Ladder and the Tree." *The Listener*, 63 (March 24, 1960), 531-33.

———, "Islands." *Spectator*, 204 (June 10, 1960), 844-46.

———, "Billy the Kid." *Spectator*, 205 (November 25, 1960), 808.

Grande, Luke M., "The Appeal of Golding." *Commonweal*, LXXVII (January 25, 1963), 457-59.

Green, Peter, "The World of William Golding." *A Review of English Literature*, 1 (April, 1960), 62-72.

Gregor, Ian, and Kinkead-Weekes, Mark, "Introduction." In *Lord of the Flies*. London: Faber and Faber School Editions, 1962, pp. i-xii.

———, "The Strange Case of Mr. Golding and His Critics." *The Twentieth Century*, CLXVII (February, 1960), 115-25.

Halle, Louis J., "*Lord of the Flies*." *Saturday Review*, 38 (October 15, 1955), 16.

Hannon, Leslie, "William Golding: Spokesman for Youth." *Cavalier,* 13 (December, 1963), 10-12, 92-93.

Hewitt, Douglas, "New Novels." *The Manchester Guardian,* LXXI (September 28, 1954), 4.

Hynes, Sam, "Novels of a Religious Man." *Commonweal,* 71 (March 18, 1960), 673-75.

Irwin, Joseph J., "The Serpent Coiled Within." *Motive,* 23 (May, 1963), 1-5.

Karl, Frederick R., "The Novel as Moral Allegory." In Karl's *The Contemporary English Novel.* New York: The Noonday Press, 1962, pp. 254-60.

Kearns, Francis E., "Salinger and Golding: Conflict on the Campus." *America,* 108 (January 26, 1963), 136-39.

Kearns, Francis E., and Grande, Luke M., "An Exchange of Views." *Commonweal,* LXXVII (February 22, 1963), 569-71.

Keating, James, and William Golding, "The Purdue Interview." Printed in part in *Lord of the Flies: Text, Notes and Criticism,* edited by James R. Baker and Arthur P. Ziegler, Jr. New York: Capricorn Books, 1964.

Kermode, Frank, "Coral Island." *The Spectator,* CCI (August 22, 1958), 257.

————, "The Novels of William Golding." *International Literary Annual,* No. 3 (1961), 11-29. Reprinted in Kermode's *Puzzles and Epiphanies.* New York: Chilmark Press, 1962, pp. 198-213.

Kermode, Frank, and William Golding, "The Meaning of It All." *Books and Bookmen,* 5 (October, 1959), 9-10.

Leed, Jacob R., "*Lord of the Flies.*" *Dimension,* Supplement to *Daily Northwestern* (January, 1963), 7-11.

"Lord of the Campus." *Time,* 79 (June 22, 1962), 64.

"*Lord of the Flies.*" *America,* 109 (October 5, 1963), 398.

Maclure, Millar, 'William Golding's Survival Stories." *Tamarack Review,* 4 (Summer, 1957), 60-67.

aclure, Millar, "Allegories of Innocence." *Dalhousie Review*, 40 (Summer, 1960), 144-56.

MacShane, Frank, "The Novels of William Golding." *Dalhousie Review*, 42 (Summer, 1962), 171-83.

Marcus, Steven, "The Novel Again." *Partisan Review*, 29 (Spring, 1962), 179-84.

Mueller, William R., "An Old Story Well Told." *Christian Century*, 80 (October 2, 1963), 1203-06.

Nelson, William, *William Golding's Lord of the Flies: A Source Book*. New York: Odyssey Press, 1963.

Niemeyer, Carl, "The Coral Island Revisited." *College English*, 22 (January, 1961), 241-45.

Nordell, Roderick, "Book Report." *Christian Science Monitor* (December 27, 1962), n. p.

Oldsey, Bern, and Weintraub, Stanley, "*Lord of the Flies*: Beelzebub Revisited." *College English*, 25 (November, 1963), 90-99.

Peter, John, "The Fables of William Golding." *Kenyon Review*, 19 (Autumn, 1957), 577-92.

Pritchett, V. S., "Secret Parables." *New Statesman* (August 2, 1958), 146-47.

Rosenfield, Claire, "Men of a Smaller Growth: A Psychological Analysis of William Golding's *Lord of the Flies*." *Literature and Psychology*, 11 (Autumn, 1961), 93-101.

Spangler, D. R., "Simon." In *Lord of the Flies: Text, Notes and Criticism*, edited by James R. Baker and Arthur P. Ziegler, Jr. New York: Capricorn Books, 1964.

Stern, James, "English Schoolboys in the Jungle." *New York Times Book Review* (October 23, 1955), 38.

Trilling, Lionel, "*Lord of the Flies*." *The Mid-Century*, Issue 45 (October, 1962), 10-12.

Wain, John, "Lord of the Agonies." *Aspect*, No. 3 (April, 1963), 56-57.

# A Checklist of Publications

Walters, Margaret, "Two Fabulists: Golding and Camus." *Melbourne Critical Review*, No. 4 (1961), 18-29.

Wasserstrom, William, and Rosenfield, Claire, "An Exchange of Opinion Concerning William Golding's *Lord of the Flies*." *Literature and Psychology*, 12 (Winter, 1962), 2-3, 11-12.

Young, Wayland, "Letter from London." *Kenyon Review*, 19 (Summer, 1957), 477-82.